LOYAL VOWS

KETLEY ALLISON

Editing by Jenny Sims

The cover uses stock photos from depositphotos and
is edited and designed through Photoshop 2024.

Visit Ketley Allison's official website at www.ketleyallison.com for the latest news, book details, and other information.

LOYAL VOWS PLAYLIST

Hide and Seek - Imogen Heap

Nothing Else Matters - Phoebe Bridgers

Gothicc - Deadicate

Lights Out - bludnymph

Bloody Mary - Lady Gaga

Stay [Feat. Patrick Wilson] - Ghost, Patrick Wilson

Freak Show - PI3RCE, Talia Stewart

Dream Girl Evil - Florence + the Machine

Cheerleader - Ashnikko

Antique Doll Shop - Derek Fletcher, Brandon Fiechter

Listen to the rest of the playlist on Spotify.

A NOT-SO-MYSTERIOUS WARNING

Well, hello, my delectable morsels of mayhem. Or should I say, my enticing little leaves caught in the winds of debauchery?

Welcome to our twisted lives. if you're a delicate flower or someone easily shocked by the, ahem, 'intricacies' of lust, perhaps you should take a detour to something more tepid.

This book isn't your typical boy-meets-girl, flowers-and-chocolates love story. No, we're talking about a much darker, spicier blend. Expect passion, tension, and yes, a fair share of things that might make you reach for the holy water, like crypt-fucking (you're welcome), MFM plus another M, group enjoyment, knife play, blood play, throat play, impact play, all the good plays.

If themes of violence, emotional trauma, and language offend you, then, my sweet, innocent, little leaf, you've wandered too close to Anderton Cottage.

If I haven't made you run away screaming yet, please enjoy. But don't assume I won't try again later.

Ready to sin? Oh, I mean read. Slip of the tongue.

Yours in impending chaos,

Morgan

CHAPTER 1
XAVIER

This is fucked.

Blinding pain bolts me awake, flashes of Clover's cries and a lump of rock morphing into a lump of flesh as I bash it, over and over again...

"Ah, he's awake," a male voice says.

Blearily, I try to raise my head, but it falls back down as if untethered from my neck. *Sleep seems nice...*

Something wriggles against my back, warm and frantic, jolting my eyes wide again.

"Xavier," someone whispers. "*Xavier.* Are you okay?"

It's Clover.

With a grunt, my spine goes rigid. I register the uncomfortable tightness of my arms, my hands wrenched behind my back.

Fingers that aren't mine tangle against my palms, cold, stiff, and panicked.

I'm bound. My wrists are tied with Clover's.

My shoes scrape across the floor as I curl my knees into my chest. We're seated on filthy ground, attached back-to-back.

Neither of us can see the other, and I have no idea where the *fuck* we are.

Clover's shoulders press against mine, offering reassurance when *I* should be the fully conscious one making sure she's all right.

I failed her.

I blink through the warm, sticky substance clogging my lashes and stinging my eyes.

"Are *you* all right?" I ask, my voice scratchy. "Have they done anything to you?"

She hesitates. "No. But, Xavier?"

"Yes?"

"I'm scared."

My head falls forward, and I thread my fingers through hers. "I know, darling. We must figure out where we are. Then we can escape."

But she's not listening.

Clover continues, "My best friend. Ardyn. She was taken when she was young. Kidnapped. I always felt terrible for her, what she went through, but now? I wasn't even close to understanding what she had to endure." Clover's breath hitches. "What are they going to do to us? Is this because of Sarah Anderton's jewels?"

"I honestly don't know."

Raising my head, I squint through the darkness, sifting through shadows and the meager moonlight coming from my left.

The dank air is tinged with mildew. Somewhere, water drips in an arrhythmic pattern.

"Xavier..."

"Focus on my voice, darling."

I press my back against her shaking form, offering the only

steadiness I can. "Tell me about yourself. I want to know everything."

"What? Xavier, this isn't the time—"

"Trust me, maiden." I'm still scanning frantically for a weapon—a sharp stick, a pebble, for God's sake—to help us out of here. "Have a chat with me."

Eventually, Clover speaks through her shuddering breaths.

"Well," she begins slowly. "I like old books—Dickens, the Brontës. Anything old and romantic. My favorite movie is the 1944 *Phantom of the Opera*."

I grin, chuckling lightly over my racing heart. "Of course it is. That fits you perfectly."

The moment she hears my laughter, her body eases into mine.

"What about you?" she asks.

"No one's ever asked me that before." A tinge of wonder coats my words despite our environment. "But let's see ... I love American Westerns. John Wayne, Clint Eastwood. And action movies too. *Die Hard*, that kind of thing... oh and, of course, *Bend it like Beckham*."

Clover's exhale hitches with a laugh. "I didn't take you for a romantic comedy type of guy."

"I'm full of pleasant surprises. We should have a movie night sometime. Watch our favorites together."

"I'd like that." Clover's voice thickens as her attention strays back to where we are, what's been done to us. "I would like it so much. Like, right now, actually..."

She trails off.

My vision clouds with shadows.

I stare down at my legs, visualizing the thick scar tissue across my right knee under my jeans. Maybe, if I were healthier, we wouldn't be in this position...

I knot my fingers tighter around hers.

"What is it?" she asks, sensing my internal struggle.

I keep my head down, saying, "I didn't have much choice, becoming part of the Vultures. I was on my way to stardom. Had a bright future ahead of me. Then I met a girl, who I later discovered was the daughter of an Irish mob boss. Her name was Meghan O'Malley. We had an adorable whirlwind romance. I even thought I loved her for a time."

I smile wryly.

"But I was young and stupid. I broke her heart and left her. Her father didn't take too kindly to that. Had his men corner me in the street and drag me into their car. They broke my kicking leg, ending my football career and any hope I had at a footballer's life."

I can hear the pain in my voice, both in my head and in the air. My heart aches for the man I could have been if not for that one mistake.

"After that, he sold me to Bianchi and betrothed Meg to him, too, for better American weapons access. I was in no shape to play football anymore, so Bianchi decided I could be of use to him in other ways. I was tortured again. *Uomo d'onore.* So Bianchi could have more made men. More scars on my body." I swallow hard. "But that can't account for the terrible things I've done since, maiden. Actions I'm not proud of. And I'm afraid if I don't obey, if I don't become the monster Bianchi wants me to be ... he'll make me suffer much more than I already have."

She whispers, "You're not a monster, Xavier."

"How can you know that?" My voice is ragged with pain and self-loathing. "You've sensed what we're capable of. Smelled the blood on our hands."

"I've also seen the good in you. The kindness, the compassion. You're more than the sum of your actions, and you always have a choice."

She curls her fingers inside my palms, willing me to believe her.

"You can be better than the Bianchis and the O'Malleys. You can rise above."

"If we ever fucking get out of here," I mutter too low for her to hear.

I feel the upward and downward motion of Clover's sigh when the same gravelly male voice that pulls me into old nightmares adds, "Best to direct that question to me, boy."

Boy.

My stomach turns to liquid. My chin shoots up.

I've heard this man before. Many times, in fact. And I especially remember him when he mutilated my chest and amputated my ring finger.

"What do you want?" I breathe out harshly.

"That's an interesting question."

A red circle of light appears in front of me, followed by the acrid smell of cigarette smoke.

A burly man in black clothing steps into the cone of light from a single lantern swinging above Clover and me that he turns on. He's easily over 115 kilos. I wouldn't be surprised if he was recruited by Bianchi directly out of pro wrestling school, as I do believe there's an old video of him deadlifting his teammates and turning them around in a small circle while holding them high into the air. He spoke of it often when I was coming back to consciousness during our "sessions."

He was certainly able to deadlift me into a wall.

Grimmer is his name. His neck is as big as his bald head, with black beetle eyes peeking out of it. During my more comedic hallucinations, I imagined him with a binky in his mouth, cooing *ma-ma*, his hairy, rounded belly hanging out of his pants.

"I'm on your side now," I say to him, drawing my head back to meet his void stare. "I told your *capo* I'd do whatever he wanted. Mr. Bianchi's the one who sent me here."

"And he's the one who sent me to *her*," Grimmer corrects, referring to Clover. "You are an unfortunate byproduct and highly disposable now that you've killed one of my men."

My lips curl away from my teeth. My second kill. And I didn't even register it.

I'm becoming as cold as them.

I answer with a brittle smirk. "He shouldn't have touched Clover the way he did."

Grimmer chuckles. "He made you angry, did he? Seems you've grown a temper since I've last seen you."

He walks a half-circle around me. I follow him with my eyes, glaring a slow death at him until he disappears from view.

After a few moments, Clover suddenly jerks against my back.

"Clover?" My back goes ramrod straight. "What's happening?"

"I'm touching her, Xavier. I think she likes it."

I'm yanked backward before I can react, Grimmer chuckling.

Clover's legs rake in panicked arcs against the filthy ground, her upper body arching on instinct, the back of her head smashing into mine.

"Don't you dare come near me, you motherfucker!" Clover cries.

"*Oh*, she has teeth, Xavvy. Did you know that? Little girl just tried to bite me."

"Get away from her. Get the *fuck* away from her." The words shred my throat.

"Not a big deal. I'll stroke where her pup fangs can't find me."

Clover yelps, smacking hard into my back.

"What's he doing?" I twist until tendons snap in my neck.

I'll happily decapitate myself if it means I can intercede.

"He's ... he's pulled my legs apart. He's kneeling between them."

Real fear laces Clover's voice.

"Not to worry, Xavvy, she's still clothed. Oh my, I can hold both her breasts in one hand. Have you ever tried? Have you gotten a taste of this delicious fruit?"

Oh, but I want to mutilate him. I want to take that gun from his holster, shoot him between the eyes, carve those eyes out, feed them to wild animals, then give them his dismembered cock for dessert. I want to bash his head, snap his ribs in two, and hold his heart in my hands and rip it to shreds. I want him to be unrecognizable.

I scream, ragged and raw, straining against the ties until Clover begs me to stop.

With our wrists bound together, I'm hurting her, too.

Stay calm.

Morgan is the king of mutilation, and did I ever see him lose control? Did he fall victim to bloodlust and fury? No. He keeps a level head even while his victims yowl.

"Well, this must be embarrassing for you," I say to Grimmer, my voice hollow and flat, my insides quaking.

Clover's quickened breaths slow. Hopefully that means he's taken his hands off her.

"Why the fuck would you say that, pretty boy?" Grimmer asks.

"Well, I'm here," I point out as if it were obvious. "And I clearly wasn't meant to be. And this pretty boy killed one of your big, scary men, so I'd say you'll have some explaining to do when your boss comes calling."

"I still managed to get the job done," he growls. "Kidnap the Callahan girl and get the location of the jewels from her cherry pie mouth. Bianchi didn't say I had to keep her in one piece while I did it."

"That's true," I respond without emotion, though molten fire blackens my organs. "But you should do it fast because ... *Tempest.*"

I can sense Grimmer's pause. There's a rustling as he shifts away from Clover, his knees cracking when he rises and strolls my way.

Good. Take your anger out on me, big man.

"Xavier," Clover whispers. "Don't do anything stupid. Please. I couldn't bear it if..."

"Same goes, maiden," I murmur in return.

Grimmer towers over me with a nasty grin. "I ain't afraid of that asshole brother of hers."

"I wasn't done. *Rio.*"

Grimmer grin stretches into that of a gruesome jack-o'-lantern. "Ain't afraid of that stalker skunk, either."

"*Morgan.*"

Grimmer loses his amusement. He stares over my head, demanding, "Tell me where the jewels are, princess, and I'll let you go. I'm not so sure about pretty boy."

"I don't know!" Clover replies.

"I bet you say that to all the guys who try to seduce you for the treasure, eh?" Grimmer laughs. "Is that what Morgan did to you, sweetheart? Flick his tongue between your legs until you sang like a canary?"

"Shut up," I say.

"Fuck you," Clover adds, twisting against our bonds.

She spits at his feet.

Grimmer storms toward her, his face reddened with fury. A loud *smack* rings out.

"Bastard!" I yell when both Clover and I topple sideways from the force of him hitting her. "Hit *me*! Then let's see what a big bad man you are instead of going after shackled girls."

"Why else would I be here?" Grimmer says to us both, ignoring my threat. "If I wasn't summoned by the *capo's* nephew? You're so close to giving Bianchi what he wants, Clover, sweetheart. Don't fail me now. As for which Bianchi requested my presence ... I'll let you be the judge of that."

"You're lying," Clover says. "Morgan wouldn't—"

"He would," I cut in. My shoulders slump away from my neck. "Clover, he would. Don't tell me you trusted him."

Clover trembles against me.

My heart breaks.

"Tell me what you've found," Grimmer repeats, "And I won't bring my other friends in to assist me in getting the answer."

"I'm not telling you a damn thing," Clover bites out.

"I was hoping you'd say that." Grimmer resumes his Halloween mask grin. "Because I'm looking forward to fucking it out of you."

I crane my neck. "You're so slow in the head you can't keep up with what she's telling you, can you?"

A beat passes. "What did you just say to me?"

"Clover's way ahead of an entire Mafia family in locating a mass of riches. Shite, that must *dig* at you, hey? I couldn't imagine being a full-grown, trained killer having to threaten a university freshman for information you should've gathered yourself—"

Grimmer storms to my side. He bends to his haunches, ensuring I can't miss his venomous beetle eyes. "You'll pay for that, you goddamn—"

Oh, and a perk of being a former pro football player?

I can head-butt like nobody's business.

My forehead smacks against his with such unexpected force. Grimmer's eyes pop wide, and he rolls on his heels, losing his balance and tipping over like a large tree trunk.

I waste no time. "Quick, Clover—Press against my back so we can lift and stand together."

Clover doesn't hesitate. She doesn't ask what just happened. She goes straight into action.

God, I think I love her.

As soon as I feel her pressure, I brace my legs, using equal force against Clover so we can rise.

We tip and dance, attempting to find equal footing.

When we do, I instruct, "Gun."

Clover spins with me to a bleary Grimmer who's collecting his marbles too quickly for my liking, though I can't be picky. A bulky man like this, his weight will allow me some time before he can sit and come to a stand and then probably kill me.

Clover and I have lean bodies—hers light and small, mine taut with refined muscle. I can pivot her around if I need to.

We sidestep to his rising form, and I bend at the waist, taking Clover with me and moving our hands until I can unclip and pull the handgun from its holster. My fingers find the clip, but they're so slippery with sweat that I miss it, cursing.

Trying again, I manage to flick it open. Grimmer realizes what we're doing and heaves his considerable bulk away from us, the gun slipping from my fingers.

"*Fuck.*"

I follow his roll.

Clover and I use our mutual pressure to tail him and lower to his belt. I spread my fingers, touching the cold, lethal metal, and hook the handle with my pointer finger and pull it out.

I say to Clover, "Help me angle it so I can get to the trigger—"

A loud *bang* rings in my ears. My knees buckle with shock.

"What the f—?" I have time to exclaim before Clover starts dragging us to the door.

"We have to go *now*," she heaves out, the gun tilted in her hands and her finger hot on the trigger. "If he has men outside, we need to move!"

"Jesus fuck, did you just shoot Grimmer?" I say, dancing with her to the exit.

"It was either you or me," she says. "And I got to the trigger first."

My face goes slack with admiration. "You're brilliant, maiden."

I doubt Clover has any more idea where we are than I do, but we both make our way to a dark gap in the room, or more like a gaping maw of black with tiny flickering lights along the sides.

Clover figures out our environment at the same time I do.

"We're in a cave."

We move sideways with the gun dangling between us. My wrists scream at the tightness, our hands becoming slick and wet with blood as the ties dig in with our struggles, but my maiden doesn't waver, and neither do I.

And true to our instincts, another man runs inside.

"Grim, what the fuck? Did you off one of them?"

Before he can understand his new situation, I assist Clover in angling the gun, and she shoots.

We have no true aim—just the barrel of this man's chest.

He goes down, but another one leaps from the shadows.

"Clover!" I yell in warning.

He gets off a shot before I bend forward at the waist. Lifting Clover onto my back like a fucking ladybug shell, I swing her until her legs make contact with the gun the man leveled at us.

His handgun clatters somewhere on the floor. If he shot me, I wouldn't know. I'm so full of adrenaline and the deep-seated urge to get Clover out of here that pain is just a numbed memory in my head.

I set Clover down, and she shoots again. He snaps back at the shoulder—not a lethal wound.

"Again!" I shout.

Clover pulls the trigger once as he drags himself toward us, clutching his shoulder.

Twice.

Three times, and he finally goes down, groaning.

"Run!" we shout in tandem.

Using the same strength as before, I bend until her upper body rests on my back and sprint with my long, athlete-trained legs. My bad knee screams as I head out of the mouth of the cave, plunging us into darkness.

There is no light because the tree cover is too dense. I can't do much but hope for the best when I dive into the brush, finding cover in case another henchman chases us.

The handgun digs into the small of my back as Clover maintains her deathly grip on it, her body sliding to and fro on my lower back.

My hands go numb, then start tingling painfully under her weight and the too-tight restraints.

I ask, breathless, “Where do you think we should—” I lose my footing on an unexpected hill, sending us plummeting in a tangle of limbs that set fire once the pain hits.

We smack against a tree—the one piece of nature that saves us from a deadly descent into a roaring river below.

Groaning, I shake myself, refusing to fall unconscious, though my injured knee feels like it’s not where surgery returned it to any longer.

“Clover? *Clover*. Are you all right?”

“The—the gun,” she says in a pained voice. “I lost the gun.”

“It’s all right. You did what you needed with it.”

“What if someone else comes?”

“Then we fight. We continue to fight. Tempest will come. I managed to get him a message before we were taken.”

Clover’s head falls against my shoulder.

“No, it won’t be my brother.” Her voice fades. “We’re in the forest. Rio. Rio will find... track us...”

“Clover? Clo? Are you hurt? Shot?”

“I ... don’t know.”

“Stay with me.”

“Yell for ... Rio,” she murmurs.

My heart dives into fresh agony as if receiving a second push down a wild, rocky hill in the middle of nowhere.

“Rio!” I scream hoarsely. “Clover, don’t go to sleep. Darling, do you hear me? You keep talking to me. Remind me how much I love hearing your voice.”

Silence.

“Clover?” My voice breaks. “Dark maiden, don’t you dare lose your moonlight on me.”

She doesn’t answer.

“*Rio*!” I yell savagely.

No one comes.

CHAPTER 2
ROSSI

Three Hours Earlier

I prefer reading by candlelight.

Call it the academic in me, but modern electricity doesn't give the same atmosphere of scholarly resonance when sitting in a mahogany office in the dead of night, going through a centuries-old tome penned by a murderess.

I may be a servant-assassin for most of my living hours, but I truly enjoy the cover of a professor. Reading calms even the blackest of souls, whether it be through the calculation of business decisions or educating myself on the gruesome history of this town.

Either way, I don't have to think of the Bianchis and how much of a hostile beast I've become under their thumb.

My reading glasses perch on my nose as I flip to another page containing Sarah Anderton's detailed recordings of her preferred alchemy ingredients. So far, I haven't encountered any clues related to the message Clover deciphered, then promptly (and accidentally) burned to ash.

Clover...

A Callahan I'm better off not knowing, yet her presence is so forceful and addicting, I can't brush her away.

I almost touched her—I almost held her soft, sensitive skin in my hands. I dreamed of circling her nipples, pinching them until they were hard enough to suck on.

With her head tipped back in pleasure, I nearly succumbed.

If it hadn't been for my mission, for the remembrance of what befell the last woman I cared for, I would have.

I rub the bridge of my nose with a sigh, forcing myself back to the problem at hand. What stone circled in summer? What flower? Sarah did not think to answer these questions in her grimoire, yet she gave me the full ingredient list for poisoning a man three times her size.

Indeed, it's an interesting concoction. I make a note to try it sometime.

My phone flashes on my desk, drawing my attention. Tempest's name scrolls across my screen. I open the line with a swipe of my thumb, then put it on speaker.

"Yes?"

"My insufferable sister found another clue."

I perk up. "Oh?"

Clover's involvement in our hunt is irritating, to say the least, but the girl gets it done. I'm convinced it's because she thinks in ways we can't. Our jaded natures don't allow us the baffling guilelessness she has to unearth important relics.

"She..." Tempest clears his throat. "She figured out the daughter's name."

My shoulders tense.

"Are you telling me Clover discovered the answer to a mystery that's eluded skilled historians for hundreds of years?"

"Yes." He draws out the word with reluctance. "If you heard

her ramble on about priest holes and fireplaces and invisible ink, you might get on her wavelength, but the rest of us are mystified. I've known Clo her entire life, and I can't begin to explain to you how her mind works."

My lips pull into a barely discernible smile. The girl I can't forget continues to give me reasons not to forget her. "What is the name?"

"Lillium. She scratched it on a wall that ended up being her tomb."

I push my brows together. "Come again?"

"The Anderton child was never executed as the records hint at. Sarah hid her in a priest hole—again, talk to Clover on how she came up with *that* realization—in the very cottage we've been living in where this kid lay undiscovered until now. Her skeleton's even intact."

"Why the hell would official transcripts allude to Lillium Anderton being tortured and killed?"

Tempest hesitates. "My goddamn sister came up with a good answer to that."

Again, with that grin tugging at my lips. "Which is?"

"Sarah had connections and also put the fear of God into the nobles who got away with their contract kills. She could've made a deal with a heavily connected person at the time to strike Lillium's name and location from the records. Sarah could've assumed or hoped her daughter could escape from the priest hole on her own when the time was right."

"And ended up trapped there instead." I pull my glasses off and lay them upside down on Sarah's grimoire, massaging my temples. "We're going to have to sit your sister down and see what else she knows."

"That ... may be a problem."

I close my eyes on a weary exhale. "Why is that?"

"I pissed her off to the point she won't want to give us answers anymore. I'm trying to keep her out of this, Rossi. It's important to me she stays safe."

"It's important to all of us."

Tempest goes silent. "Why does her safety mean so much to you?"

Shit. The Callahan instincts don't stop at Clover.

"She's your blood," I say as an excuse. "I've had enough experience to understand the unshakable desire to defend one's family."

Tempest pauses.

"That's the first time you've mentioned your past." Tempest's voice gentles as he dares to venture further into the forbidden topic. "In any form."

I shove away from my desk, my vision going dark. I don't talk about my former wife and child. To bring it up means remembering how much I loved them before I watched them die horribly.

Christ. Clover's weakening me even when she's not around —this *has* to stop.

"Lillium," I roughly redirect. "That's Latin for lily. It could be the flower Sarah mentioned in her hidden message."

"What are you talking about?"

"Right. I haven't explained that part to you." I rub at my tired eyes.

"If you tell me my sister's rifled around and revealed yet another missing piece of this fucking treasure map to the Vultures, I may have to dump her in our basement and never let her *out*."

"Then you'd best find a good lock."

Tempest growls a bone-chilling curse.

"Are there lilies growing in Titan Falls anywhere?" I ask. "Around a stone, perchance?"

"Rio would know."

"Good. Ask him." I close the grimoire and rise, tucking it under my arm. "I'm coming to you now."

"We'll be ready—hang on. A text just came in."

I round my desk, lifting my phone. "I doubt I need to be on the call while you read a text."

"The notification is two words from Xavier. It's—fuck. No. *No.*"

I halt in the middle of my office. "Speak."

"I asked Xavier to take Clover to the dorms after we fought. He said ... oh, fuck no ... he said: *Trouble. Come.*"

I click off the call and haul open my door.

It breaks at the hinges.

CHAPTER 3
RIO

What shred of soul I have left rips out of my body when Tempest explains that Clover and Xavier are in trouble.

I'm at the door before Tempest can so much as command, "Go," and fold into the night.

As I silently merge into the foliage, I hear Morgan say, "It's likely nothing. The boy's an idiot. They're fine. Sports Balls probably twisted an ankle on a tree branch."

My eye twitches at the unfamiliar panic lancing through his words.

That's not like him at all. Morgan fried off and cauterized his nerves years ago.

Tempest grunts at him, "You're joining in on the search whether you want to or not, you asshole."

"No orders necessary," Morgan says, his voice fading the deeper I sneak into the woods. "I'll gladly search for Clover. I don't want her hurt any more than you do."

My upper lip joins in on my curious eye twitch.

I don't have time to mull over Morgan's strange behavior

regarding Clover. Lucky is missing and in trouble. I'm the one man out of the Vultures who can track her through a forest I know better than my own bedroom.

It doesn't take long to find their tracks, though I keep well off the trail that they took leading to campus. Clover's and Xavier's shoe prints mix with others. I discern Tempest's soles and Morgan's, removing them from my study as I glide my flashlight over the imprints. Xavier's sneaker tread is obvious. He's heavy on the balls of his feet, as if always ready for an opportunity to pounce—or escape, with less pressure on his right foot, emphasizing his permanent injury. Clover's come next, her soft, light, unhindered pace walking beside Xavier's.

I pause when I notice the angle of their footprints change. They face each other, their prints indicating ... *hmm.*

I tilt my head at the story their marks tell.

My gut does a possessive flutter at the ghostly image my mind conjures of the two of them embracing or kissing. It's not jealousy so much as a sudden yank of defense that he'd better be treating Clover as well as me, if not better.

I blink away the image, and my focus snaps to the right at the broken branches and torn leaves barreling through the underbrush and heading straight toward their embrace.

This is where they were targeted.

When I come across Clover's bag, her items strewn in a haphazard, panicked circle, my spine snaps straight. I put two fingers to my mouth and emit a loud whistle to alert the Vultures.

Tempest responds with the same melody.

Unwilling to wait, I swipe her things into the tote, sling the bag over my shoulders, and creep forward.

I follow the struggle, my attention zipping between a retelling of Clover fighting against an attacker who drags her into a thicket and the rush of Xavier's desperation to catch up to her.

When I break into a clearing, I scour the ground, noting where the struggle ended.

Boot prints not matching Xavier or Clover move north, the indents much heavier despite the half-thawed ground. The person carries someone, and he's a heavyset man to begin with.

Clover.

Fury joins my determination to *find her*.

If anyone so much as flicks one of her eyelashes without her permission...

Yet destiny is on my side. Whoever took her isn't adept at covering his tracks. They should've considered a man like me would be steps behind her wherever she goes.

I live for this.

I live for *her.*

Thorns and the sharp ends of branches don't bother me as they scratch at my face and prickle against my hands. I trek deeper into the forest, following this abductor's ridiculous attempt to hide from me.

Every few minutes, I pause. Listening.

I can hear Tempest and Morgan coming from a distance. Their stealth, while skilled, is no match to mine. But I'm able to compartmentalize their journey and listen for other unique sounds, like Clover or Xavier.

My heart jolts at the thought of them being taken somewhere by vehicle, but we're much too centered within Mother Nature for even a top-of-the-line ATV to traverse this wilderness.

No, they would've had to take them to shelter. Somewhere

to do whatever they intended before daylight could help them get to a vehicle.

And that's when I hear it.

My name traveling on a light breeze, bringing with it a bone-chilling freeze.

My head whips toward the sound coming from the east.

Bending low, I follow the low, keening plea, recognizing Xavier's weakened voice.

Coming up against a sharp descent, I look down, frowning. Another round of my name comes from below.

Shit.

Carefully, I angle my body to slowly take the decline, noting the broken brush and drag marks of falling bodies. My flashlight moves back and forth, ensuring I don't miss any details.

Two lumps form in front of me at the base of a tree. One moves.

"Clover?" I say.

"It's me," Xavier responds. "Thank fuck. She's—I think she's hurt."

That spurs me on like nothing else can. I pull out my switchblade without thinking, ready to maim, skin, and kill whoever hurt my lucky clover.

My light lands on Xavier's face, bruised and bloody. One side of his hair is matted, and he can't open one eye.

"You look terrific," I assure him, swinging my light sideways.

It's then I land upon her, her face white—*too pale*—as her head lolls against Xavier's shoulder blade, and she faces the sky, blind and unconscious.

I fall to my knees in front of her, compartmentalizing

again. My mind tells me to release the binds at their wrists and do a visual search of her body.

I don't have to scan for long. Blood blooms like a flower at her hip.

My only tell of her consciousness is a hitch in her breath before I curl my arms around her broken body and lift, her head falling back and chin pointing at the stars.

As I carry her, I turn my head and croak to Xavier, "Behind me," hearing him shuffle to a stand and limp close to my back.

All without complaint.

He won't know it, but I give him points for that.

I don't talk to Xavier as we climb the hill. All I care about is getting Clover the help she needs. I move faster now that I'm not tracking, unworried about the men who took her cornering me.

Let them.

Taking pity on Xavier but holding Lucky tight against my chest, I break through the underbrush and walk the makeshift trail. There, we find Tempest and Morgan, and Tempest bursts forward the second he registers who's in my arms.

"Where?" he demands, placing one hand on Clover's knee and the other on her shoulder as he assesses her.

"Right hip," I reply. "Bullet wound."

For the first time in our entire brotherhood, Tempest wheezes in fear. "Rossi's coming. He can tend to her."

"Oh no," Morgan says with horror behind Tempest, his stare glued on Clover's unmoving form. "No, no, no ... this wasn't supposed to go this way. Oh, little leaf, what happened?"

Xavier palms my shoulder, leaning on me for balance, his chin jutting forward. "What the hell is that supposed to mean, Morgan?"

"I—" The whites of Morgan's shine through the break in the canopy above. "I told him where the tunnel under our cottage was. That's all. I didn't—I never gave the go-ahead to harm a hair on her head."

Tempest's expression morphs into a twisted, hell-bound creature when he wheels on Morgan. None of us see the punch coming until it lands on the side of Morgan's face with a *crunch,* and Morgan sprawls onto the frosted ground.

"What the *fuck* did you do?" Tempest looms over him, spittle flying from his mouth and raining down on Morgan.

To my surprise, Morgan stays down. He rubs at his jaw but raises his eyes until he meets Tempest's with flat acceptance. "I deserve what you have coming, Storm Cloud, but don't kill me until I'm sure she's all right."

Tempest shows his teeth. "I will take my time torturing you, Morgan. Damn the consequences."

"No time," I bite out even though I'm inclined to join Tempest in fast-tracking our trip to hell if it means getting Clover to safety. "She's lost a lot of blood."

"Morgan's also clued you into the culprits," Xavier says, his tone scratched with overuse. "Bianchi's behind this. He wants the jewels, too."

Tempest pales. "That can't be. We're supposed to be the ones who discover it. How did Bianchi know of its existence?"

Realization brings spots of color into Tempest's cheeks. "Morgan, you son of a *bitch*."

He stomps on Morgan's throat. Morgan thrashes, clutches his neck, and twists to retch on the ground.

I stop the fight by stepping over Morgan and continuing my determined pace to the Anderton Cottage, where Clover can get the help she needs.

Kicking the door open, I step over the threshold. Rossi rises from his preparation of the large coffee table in front of the fireplace, our ashy, charred footprints over the floorboards as we inspected the hidden priest hole contrasting with the pure white sheet Rossi has draped over the table.

Fuck, it seems like we unearthed Lillium Anderton's skeleton years ago, not hours.

"Tempest sent me a message," Rossi explains as he motions to the makeshift surgical table. He doesn't take his eyes off Clover. "I've come prepared."

I take in the array of medical supplies Rossi has spread over another white sheet on the couch.

There's no surprise in the fact that the Vultures have sustained many injuries. Our job description practically requires it. Rossi's tended to our wounds in the past, but with our expertise in the field, they're superficial. Dislocations and deep cuts at most. Maybe a bullet graze if we're distracted.

But this? These are professional instruments.

I stop short of laying Clover on the table.

Rossi's chest rises and falls as he waits for me to splay her out for his sick pleasure.

"Relax, Riordan," he says in his calming baritone. "In my life before, I was a surgeon."

My eyes jerk to his.

"I prefer not to remember it." The spaces between Rossi's words are thick with reluctance. "I'm perfectly capable of tending to her, and I swear to you I'll treat her as if—" Rossi loses his voice and has trouble regaining it. "As if she were my own on this operating table."

My vision tunnels in my attempt to assess this shrouded version of Miguel Rossi, my fearless, cold-hearted leader, with a white coat and patient files against his chest, strolling hospital corridors as he barks orders at residents.

Not a far cry, actually.

"Rio." Rossi's tone hardens as he brings me back to the present. He points at the table. "Trust me or not, but time is of the essence."

With great reluctance, I lower Clover's prone body and step away. I do not and will not remove my stare from her.

Heavy footsteps sound out behind me. Tempest storms in, dragging a trussed-up Morgan and tossing him onto the floor.

"Morgan is to remain hog-tied until I extract every traitorous detail from his reptilian tongue," Tempest says.

Rossi regards Morgan blandly. Neither of us argues.

Xavier's palms slam against the front door's frame next as he drags himself inside, his head hanging low.

He needs medical attention, too, but he doesn't request it when he limps to one of our wingback chairs and slumps into it, closing his eyes while his chest rattles.

Morgan groans, then laughs as Tempest drags him up by twisting his arms farther behind his shoulders. "You're focusing on the wrong enemy, my friends. I'm not going anywhere. Not when Clover's hurt."

"Shut the fuck up," Tempest snaps, then throws him on a wooden chair he's dragged from our dinner table, ensuring Morgan stays bound. "Anyone mind if I gag him?"

Resounding *no's* all around.

Morgan scowls but doesn't resist the duct tape Tempest gracelessly slaps over his mouth. His eyes have turned a cloudy green, but he stares at Clover like I do.

"Rio, grab some of your ketamine," Rossi directs.

My attention snaps to him. "For what? Clover?"

Rossi doesn't bother to confirm, his face expressing how obvious it should be. "We don't have any other anesthetic."

"I'm not sticking a needle into her neck."

To do that to her would be all too similar to my victims, and Clover is *not* my victim. I can't fathom forcing her to be vulnerable like that.

Rossi busies himself, cutting open Clover's shirt and exposing the bullet hole. He gently lifts her to inspect the other side. "It didn't go through. The bullet's still inside, so unless you want her to wake up in the middle of me carving into her, I suggest you find the fucking ketamine."

I swallow. Clover crying out in agony and begging when it doesn't relate to my tongue on her body is a worse nightmare than drugging her into a stupor.

My heels click together, and I stride up the stairs to my bedroom, pulling open a drawer and unzipping a medical bag containing syringes, alcohol swabs, and vials of ketamine.

Tempest meets me in the hall as I exit my room, grabbing the bag. "You're positive you know how much to give her?"

I nod. "Even if I'm off, I'm sure Dr. Rossi will correct me."

Tempest frowns at the unfamiliar title but doesn't comment as we head back to the main room.

Rossi lowers his gaze to Clover's neck, then back to me, a silent command to insert the needle through her delicate skin.

My stomach doesn't turn. It never has, yet as I prep the syringe and line it up to her throat, I hate every moment of breaking her trust.

Worse, it pains me to watch Rossi go through the motions, widening the bullet wound and using pliers I've employed to remove eyeballs to fish around for the bullet. It takes two hours, and whenever Clover tosses her head and mewls plaintively, my heart wrenches, but I give her more before Rossi can remind me.

Morgan starts making noises as Rossi finishes the surgery and begins stitching her up, all of us relieved she survived.

It gets to the point that Rossi pauses in his sewing and glares over his shoulder. "Someone keep him quiet."

Satisfied his sister is stable, Tempest spins and rips the duct tape off Morgan's mouth, ensuring bits of skin and blood drip from his face. "What is it?"

"We're sitting here like ducks." Morgan spits blood, then continues. "Allow me to text my uncle and assure him I have Clover and that his cronies are alive and well before he becomes concerned and sends more men."

"Like I'm about to give you a phone, dickless," Tempest says.

"Then I'll be sure to send flowers to your sister's funeral."

Tempest lashes out, lancing his switchblade across Morgan's thigh. Morgan clenches his teeth but otherwise smiles. "Do it to me the way I like, Storm Cloud."

"You're so fucking dead—"

"Wait." I step between them. "Morgan has a point. Radio silence from our end isn't good. We'll use his phone to text Bianchi."

"My uncle will expect a phone call," Morgan corrects.

I stare at him from the corner of my eye. "How much does he know about the Anderton jewels, and who gave him the information?"

"Truthfully? I don't know," Morgan says. "He's the one who told me of the fortune and sent me on this treasure hunt. I had an idea it existed through myth and legend, but I never thought it to be real until good ole Uncle treated it as fact. Then I was intrigued."

"Why does he want Clover?" Tempest clips out.

"Now that *is* my fault," Morgan confesses.

If I didn't know better, I'd say he actually sounds chagrined.

"She'd proven herself adept at sniffing out clues. I tried to follow her without alerting my uncle, but he has ways of knowing what I'm up to before I'm even aware I'm doing it. Her relation to Storm Cloud wasn't any help, either."

I continue side-eyeing him. "Why are you giving us this information so easily?"

"Because I love hearing your voice, and this topic makes you speak in full paragraphs." Morgan grins.

It falls as soon as his gaze slides to Clover.

"In truth, I never expected her to be in the crossfire. I told my uncle to excavate the tunnel below this house. I had no idea he'd figure out the source of that tunnel and want her for himself. The idea of him forcing her to give him answers..." Morgan trails off.

"He touched her, you know. Grimmer." Xavier's quiet voice comes from the chair he was falling in and out of consciousness in.

The three of us give Xavier our full attention.

"What did you just say?" Morgan asks hoarsely.

Xavier gives a slow nod. "Grimmer molested her. Threatened to rape her if she didn't give up the jewels' location."

"But she doesn't know!" Tempest explodes. "Clover got us as far as this *hole* in our house with an old skeleton. Why would he think she could go further?"

"Because she can."

Rossi doesn't look up from his stitching as he says it, though his tone is laced with impending doom on whoever violated her.

"That message, Tempest, the one I told you about involving lilies and a stone circled in summer," Rossi continues. "I'm certain Clover has almost led us to the conclusion. We'd be there already if it weren't for Morgan's meddling."

I purse my lips at this new development. Then debate the positives of killing Morgan on the spot. *We could've escaped had it not been for you.*

"Come now," Morgan says with what I'm sure he believes is a dashing smile while covered in blood and grime. "Don't be dramatic. I did not bring about the downfall of the Vultures. We have Clover. My uncle does not. If you'll allow me to keep it that way, more the better."

"Why help us?" I ask.

Morgan sighs, his chest concaving under his button-down with his exhale. "Because I care about her. Too much. I'm not loyal to the Vultures, I won't deny that, but I'm loyal to her. Slit my throat if you must, Storm Cloud." Morgan pauses to stare up at Tempest, who is truly at his boiling point. "But if you do me in, be so kind as to end the lives of Rio and Xavier, too, because they're just as smitten with her as I am."

Heavy, dangerous silence befalls the room.

Rossi stops his ministrations.

Neither of us dares to move a muscle.

"Excuse me?" Tempest's rasp of a question slithers through every ear.

"Go on, Rio," Morgan says, beaming up at me. "Deny it."

"I can't," I say simply. Witnessing Clover so close to death and holding her failing body in my arms forced me to face the truth—I can't deny my feelings for her anymore.

"Me neither," Xavier agrees.

Tempest blinks rapidly. He can't seem to focus on any one person in the room. Even his sleeping sister is granted a bewildered, slightly manic stare.

"The fuck is this?" Tempest's voice rises to the highest pitch. "What have I walked into? You *all* have feelings for her?"

"Even better," Morgan says. "I'm convinced we've all tasted her."

"Oh, you have a death wish," Xavier's tired voice says at the same moment Tempest unhinges his jaw with a roar and rears his fist back.

"You," he seethes to Morgan. "You will be the first to die."

"Good, because I wiggled out of my restraints forty-five minutes ago," Morgan quips, then pushes to his feet and dodges Tempest's merciless punch before throwing out one of his own.

Morgan sweeps his leg out into a roundhouse kick, nearly toppling Tempest. With a vengeful grunt, Tempest parries, and both men come to blows.

I dart away, uninterested in joining in.

Rossi shakes his head, but his stare shows utter impatience with his Vultures.

"Guys," Xavier says, lifting a hand in a form of defense when Morgan knocks against his chair. "Guys, listen."

"They're too far gone," I say as I sidle up to him. "Let Morgan get most of Tempest's energy because you and I are next."

"No, listen to me," Xavier says.

Frowning, I glance down at him. "What is it?"

He points in the direction of the table. "Clover's awake."

CHAPTER 4
CLOVER

D*id I eat too spicy food? Am I on a hot sauce high right now?*

I must've, because my stomach's on fire.

Ardyn must've provided a margarita pitcher to go along with it since my head is pounding so hard, it sounds like furniture being broken inside my skull.

Crashes ring against my ears, and I wince. Opening my eyes feels like peeling skin off my eyeballs.

Through a slit of vision, figures blur too fast for me to keep track. A voice shouts. Another swears. More banging and tearing of wood.

Wait.

This isn't all in my head.

I struggle to sit up until a gentle weight comes down on my chest, followed by a quiet, "Don't move quite yet, Miss Callahan."

The voice sounds eerily close to Rossi's.

Sluggishly, I slide my gaze in the direction of the sound.

Soft brown eyes hover over mine, framed by thick, gray-black tendrils of hair and olive skin. His tender survey sends pleasant fuzzies over the searing pain in my middle.

It *is* Rossi.

"What...?" I start to say until it all comes back.

Lillium Anderton's unintended grave. Kissing Xavier on the trail leading to campus. Harsh arms ripping me away from him.

The cave.

The gun...

My eyes pop wide.

"I shot people," I say.

"You *were* shot," Rossi replies. "Please, take it easy before you give me another heart attack."

A warm hand clasps mine. "My Lucky is a lucky shot, too."

"Rio," I whisper with a tiny smile as his shadow flickers on my other side.

"I'm here," he confirms. Then he asks over my head, "Can we put her somewhere more comfortable and away from the center of this death match?"

Rossi turns his head in the direction of the loud noises.

I crane my neck, looking over my torn-open shirt and the large square of white gauze on my right hip. My vision sharpens before going fuzzy, but it's enough to center myself in the middle of Anderton Cottage's living room.

I'd be concerned about the reasons for lying on the guys' coffee table if it weren't for Morgan flying across my horizon and smacking against the fireplace bricks.

My mouth drops open during his flight. He looks *awful*—his face bloody, his hair caked in dirt, and his shirt torn and hanging off his throbbing, tattooed body. But he laughs, long and hard.

Do *I* look that awful?

I do a quick recap of the past few hours in my head. Yes, I should look about how I feel.

Though my head pounds, I manage to speak through the pain. "You're hurting him. Stop."

Morgan stops his unsettling cackle and pushes off the brick-lined column, brushing the dust off his arms with crooked, limp fingers.

His bloodshot eyes land on mine. "Don't be concerned about me, little leaf. You're awake. I'm so glad."

"What happened to your fingers?" I ask in dismay.

"Oh, this?" He holds up his hand, his digits spearing out at odd angles. "I had to dislocate the joints so I could escape the bindings Tempest put me in when he tied me to that chair over there."

"I..." I scrunch my eyes shut, then open them. "What? Why?"

Tempest steps into my view, his chest rising and falling at a concerning rate. Fury leaches from his skin like toxic vapor as he approaches me.

"Morgan's a traitor. He gave you up to Bianchi," my brother says.

"*No.*" Morgan spears a broken finger at Tempest. "I did not. Like you, I tried to keep her out of this and protect her. Clover didn't get shot because of me. She's not struggling on our coffee table because of me. I did everything I could to meet my uncle's demands without involving her!"

Morgan's teeth drip with saliva as he shouts the words. To everyone else, he must look feral and unhinged. His face splotches with conviction, and his body trembles with it. But each time Morgan's gaze lands on mine, anguish fills those normally predatory green irises. He can't keep his focus on me for long before he has to tear it away.

I don't expect Tempest to see what I do, and he doesn't.

"You're a pathetic, nepotistic sperm," Tempest fumes. "You were a burden before this. Now you're a check mark off my list of kills."

"*I didn't want to hurt her!*" Morgan shouts, his voice cracking violently.

"Tempest," I say.

It takes effort, but Tempest turns his head to me.

I say to my brother, "I believe him."

Tempest's eyes slant incredulously. "Clo, you can't be serious."

"I am." I push to sit up, grimacing. Rossi tries to keep me down, but I wave him away, pleading with him to help me instead.

Rossi relents. Both he and Rio assist in propping me up.

My stomach hates me for the position, but I force the agony to the back of my mind. It doesn't compare to seeing the people I care about most fighting.

Over me.

"If I haven't proven myself before," I say to Tempest, "then I have now. I wouldn't be here without the help of Xavier, Rio, *and* Morgan, but I was the one who aimed the gun and fired at Bianchi's men. I was the one who endured rough hands on my body."

Tempest's expression tics with a barely controlled wince.

"It was *me* who found the essential clues to the Anderton treasure and drew Bianchi's attention. I believe Morgan when he says he tried to keep my name out of it, but that's kind of hard for him to do when I kept putting myself in the running. You, of all people, know how I work."

Tempest's lips curl with reluctant agreement.

"These men around me right now—including *you*, dear

brother—are a part of me because of my actions, my decisions, and my fucking consent. I am *done* being your doll on the highest shelf so nobody can touch and damage me. I want to be *here*. With them. With you. Well..." I struggle to correct myself. "Not *here* here, gravely wounded and on your coffee table, but you know what I mean. I know you love me; I love you, too. So much. But I don't want just your protection, Tempest. I deserve your respect."

My speech leaves me weak. I waver, and Rio sits on the edge of the table, holding my upper body against his chest. I lay back against him gratefully, closing my eyes in temporary bliss.

Tempest watches me melt into Rio with barely controlled disgust.

"Jesus," Tempest curses.

I crack an eye open to see him scrub his face in frustration.

"When did this *happen*? All of you—all fucking three of you —are involved with my sister?"

I scan the anxiety-ridden faces surrounding me. Xavier, barely conscious but fighting to keep an eye on me. Rossi (whom Tempest has no reason to know about yet. I doubt Rossi returns my feelings, anyway), keeping a protective hand on my arm as he regards my brother with silent reproach. Rio, assuring me with his solid presence. And Morgan, ready to fight for me and heedless of his injuries, both self-inflicted and not. Probably enjoying the pain of both.

I draw strength from each of them. I want to be with them.

Tempest's brows come down. He shakes his head, but it's an action that shows he's caving, not being stubborn.

"I can't deny the truth of your words," he says. "Because I have Ardyn, and I—I'm a hypocrite. If either of you were hurt ...

I can't think about it. I'd lock you both in a tower if I could. Clo, it's so hard for me to let you go."

I give him a tender smile. "You don't have to. Just let me take the lead on my life."

Morgan approaches, eyeing Tempest cautiously as he passes him. "I'm willing to stand by Clover in the face of my uncle. Tonight went too far. You want the jewels? I'll help you find them before he does."

Tempest sneers, "I'll never forgive you, never mind trust you for—"

"Tempest," Rossi says. He levels his second-in-command with a hard look too long to contain simple admonishment. "Enough. He could be an asset."

Tempest responds with a vibration familiar to me because he often uses that same stance when fighting the urge to let me have it.

I may be unbalanced and bleary, but I study their silent communication with interest. Why is Rossi coming to Morgan's defense instead of Tempest?

"A temporary alliance," Rio adds. "Until we find the jewels."

Rossi blinks. "Yes. Of course. That's what I meant."

The direction of their conversation rings a bell in my head.

"Lilium's name," I breathe out. "I found it."

"Yep." Tempest pops the *p*. "You're unstoppable, dear sister."

I grin at him. It's lopsided and drugged, but still an *I win*.

"It's Latin for lily," Rossi says to me. "Did you know that?"

"No." I straighten out of Rio's comforting hold, though it hurts. "That probably wasn't a common name back then. Wait. Sarah's message in her grimoire. 'My flower.' Do you think—"

Rossi's lips pull up. "That she meant her Lily? Yes."

"Fuck, you guys finish her sentences now?" Tempest stretches the skin on his cheeks has he drags his hands down. "I'm never getting used to this, Clo, I'll tell you now."

"All I ask is you don't solve your awkward feelings with death blows," I say. "Because that's what you do, right? Kill people. You're indentured to the Mafia, all of you."

Tempest stares at me with heavy eyes, then blinks. "I can't with you, Clo. Stop being such a fucking Nancy Drew." He regards everyone in the room. "We need to get Clover somewhere safe, and fast. To give us time to come up with a plan to find the jewels and take Bianchi down before he sends more men."

"I want you to explain everything to me when this is done," I say to him.

"Fuck no."

"Tempest," I add softly, "if you think I'm ashamed of you, I would never."

"You haven't heard exactly how we kill yet. And who," he says ominously, giving Morgan a long glare.

"Yes, yes, I'm trembling in fear." Morgan then glances down at his fingers. "But before we move Clover to a safe house, who wants to pop my joints back into their sockets?"

CHAPTER 5
CLOVER

Velvet drapes sway above my head as I blink my eyes open. My head throbs, a dull ache pulsing at the base of my skull.

Where am I?

The antique canopy bed I'm lying on is unfamiliar, the mattress cupping my body in delicate luxury beneath my weight. A certain scent is in the air, familiar but not, smoky and musky and masculine.

My breath catches as the events of the past few days rush back to me—finding Lillium Anderton, being dragged into a cave by Bianchi's men, and waking up strapped to a makeshift operating table as Professor Rossi, wearing kind brown eyes for the first time ever, stitched me back together.

The room around me is lavishly decorated in shades of crimson and gold. Heavy oak furniture crowds the space, ornate lamps casting flickering shadows over the walls. An antique clock on the mantel ticks away the seconds, its steady rhythm like a countdown to the apocolypse.

The floorboards outside the room creak, and I freeze,

clutching the velvet blankets around me like a shield. Another floorboard moans in the hallway, and I hear the distinct click of something hard tapping against the wood.

My breath catches in my throat as the gold doorknob turns, and Xavier peers around the edge of the doorframe, crystalline eyes meeting mine.

"You're awake," he says, lips curving into a smile. He hobbles into the room on crutches, settling on the edge of the bed beside me.

In the dim light of the room, I can see the bruises mottling his skin as well as heavy white bandages across his knee under his athletic shorts, a reminder of our shared trauma.

He holds out a glass of water and two white pills. "For the pain. And the fever." His gaze flicks to the bandage on my stomach, his eyes darkening with concern. "You should lie back and keep still."

I nod, hesitating before I take the pills and glass from his outstretched hand. Our fingers brush and a spark of electricity zips between us.

It happens every time he comes in and gives me medication. The hours are blurry, my shape a vulnerable form within these four walls, relying completely on these men to tend to me.

But I've only seen Xavier since my transfer here. I recall strong arms carrying me, the scent of wood smoke and evergreen—*Rio*—as well as Rossi's gruff instructions on my care. Tempest's growly agreement.

But otherwise, my memories are a patchwork quilt.

"Where am I?" I ask hoarsely before swallowing the pills. I have some time before sleep takes over again.

"One of the old manors outside of Titan Falls." He squeezes

my hand, the warmth of his palm seeping into my skin. "You're safe here, maiden."

His voice is soft and gentle.

A knot forms in my throat, and I blink back tears, overwhelmed by the kindness in his words. I was nearly raped and killed, but at this moment, with Xavier's hand enveloping mine, I want nothing more than to believe him.

"How are you feeling?" Xavier asks, his gaze searching my face. "It's been about three days since you were shot."

I consider lying and putting on a brave face. But something makes me answer honestly. "Everything hurts. My body, my mind ..." My voice breaks. "I thought my life was over."

Xavier's jaw tightens. "I know. And I'm sorry I didn't get us out sooner."

His apology surprises me. I study him, this reluctant Vulture who rescued me from hell. There's more to him than I realized. More depth, more heart than the charming mask he usually wears will ever give away.

"You have nothing to apologize for," I say. "You saved my life. I'm grateful."

"You saved your own life, dark maiden." Xavier smiles and looks down almost adoringly. But when he meets my eyes again, I glimpse through his mask to his own trauma, his own scars. "But I've been where you are. I know what it's like to feel ... broken. Used."

His candor stuns me. I never imagined someone like him—almost famous and stunningly handsome, amiable and cocky and sure—could understand my pain.

But the shadows in his eyes are all too familiar.

"Thank you," I say softly. "I'm not used to people being so ... open with me."

Xavier's expression blackens for a moment. "I won't let anyone else harm you again. You have my word."

His fierce protectiveness makes my heart skip a beat.

We sit in silence for a few minutes, taking comfort in each other's presence. The quiet is soothing, a respite from the chaos that has consumed my life lately.

Xavier stares at me for a long moment, eyes shining. Then he leans in and kisses me, soft and sweet.

I meet him all the way, our tongues stroking, the velvet of our moans mixing beautifully, the warmth of our bodies searching for the other.

The hard length of him spears between us. I cup it under his pants, squeezing, *needing.*

Xavier groans but places his palm on my hand, gently prying it off.

"You're in no condition, maiden, and neither am I. Not for what I wish I could do to you right now."

When he reluctantly pulls away, his pastel eyes display a flicker of regret.

He clears his throat, his dick still straining as he winces and rubs it.

As much as I'd love to assist in his release, Xavier's right. We'd put ourselves in emergency triage if we tried to have sex. But *oh,* would I love to have him inside me, filling the black depths that replaced the bullet in my side.

"Tell me more about yourself," Xavier begs, taking the sexual weight off the direction of our conversation. "That seems to have become our thing in tense moments. You've heard my tragic backstory. What's yours?"

I take a deep breath, wondering how much of the truth I should share. But Xavier opened up to me when I was close to losing my mind in the cave, trusting me with his sweetest vulnerabilities and fears to bring me out of it. I owe him the same honesty.

"My childhood was lonely," I begin slowly. "My parents were very wealthy but also very distant. My father was a gambling addict, and my mother lived in her own world. I didn't have many friends. Books were my escape." I pause, the familiar ache of loneliness and neglect flaring to life for a moment before fading again. "I suppose, in some ways, being with the Vultures has been less lonely than my actual life."

I give a mirthless laugh.

Xavier squeezes my hand.

"I'm sorry you went through that," he says softly. "You deserved so much better."

I shrug. "It is what it is. But escaping with you in the cave, fighting alongside you to survive, *shooting* ... made me realize I'm stronger than I ever knew. And for the first time, I don't feel alone."

Xavier strokes his thumb over my knuckles, his touch soothing the rawness of my confession.

"You'll never be alone again," he promises. "Not as long as I'm with you. Now, sleep, love. I'll be right here."

The instinct to fight to stay awake is long gone. The drugs fizz in my blood, making me float into the air, and I float into dreamless clouds.

I WAKE SLOWLY, drifting up through layers of sleep like a diver coming up for air. The velvet drapes are drawn, shadows lurking in the corners of the room, but a golden beam of sunlight streams across the bed.

Xavier is gone, the spot where he lay empty and cold.

Disappointment flares, quickly followed by alarm—but then I notice a single red rose on the nightstand, its petals still damp with dew.

A smile tugs at my lips as I pick it up, inhaling its sweet scent.

Rio.

He found this to lay it by my head, a simple gesture that makes my chest ache with tenderness.

He hasn't forgotten about me.

I trace the velvet softness of the rose petal, wondering what Rio's doing right now or where Xavier has gone and when he'll return. There's still so much uncertainty with these men. I feel like a princess trapped in a tower. I know I need to heal, but I'm starting to get twitchy with the need to *do* something else other than lie in repose in a Victorian primary bedroom.

A sharp knock sounds at the thick wooden door, and I jolt. "Xavier? You don't have to knock."

I brave sliding out of the covers and shuffle to the bay window overlooking the expansive, snow-coated acreage of the manor. With the rose still clutched in my hand, I use my other to press against the frosted window, imagining Rio somewhere on the other side, his—

Hand meeting mine on the other side of the glass.

Gasping, I pull my hand away and peer closer, finding Rio's silhouette through my soft, snowflaked reflection on the glass. He's perched on a thick branch, his legs dangling boyishly while the rest of him is poised to pounce.

He was watching me sleep, I'm sure of it. Always keeping me safe.

At this point in our relationship, I'm not shocked by his habitual stalking. I'm flattered.

Rio gestures for me to open the window, the breaking dawn coating him in a bluish-gold glow.

I push one pane open, the icy air biting my warmed cheeks.

"Come with me," he says before swinging off the branch and landing in the snow with the graceful stealth of a jaguar leaping from its watchful perch.

Except there's no pitiful mouse to pounce on down below. I'm all he wants.

Smiling, I shut the window and dress carefully but smartly, taking extra care around my stomach and holding my arm against it as I slouch out of my room and to the grand staircase.

Rio meets me at the top, crooking his arm and inclining his head.

He could carry me like a damsel down the stairs—all it would take is a plea and I'd be swept up into his arms and pressing safely against his chest. A large part of me wants that, wants to feel him and hear his heartbeat at the same time, but another part of me, the new, tentative part growing branches and sprouting leaves despite its cold environment, wants to be brave for him.

I wrap my arm through the space between his solid torso and steady arm, allowing him to guide me down the stairs and through the foyer until we're outside in the chill.

Our boots leave a trail of twin prints across the pristine white lawn. Rio walks with purpose, his strides long and graceful and taking most of my weight as he holds me by the waist, ensuring he avoids my injuries as he helps me along.

Neither of us speaks, the hush of the winter morning wrapping around us like my luxurious sheets in the bedroom.

Sensing my need for rest through the short puffs of my breaths, Rio comes to a halt by a frozen pond and gently sets me down on an iron bench nearby.

We both stare ahead, the pond's icy surface so smooth that it could be a mirror reflecting the winter sky. He turns to me, his eyes finding mine through the light snowfall.

"You're still wearing my necklace."

I finger the shape of the heart pendant through my coat, self-consciously trailing my fingers up until they rub against the exposed length of gold chain at the nape of my neck. "I never take it off."

Not since he hung it over my dorm room's doorknob as one of his strange, secret gifts. His one way of expressing devotion when he didn't have the words.

A ghost of a smile crosses over his full mouth. "I'm glad."

"I'm sorry about the doll," I say, my lips twisting at the thought of Minnie smashing the Victorian doll against my floorboards, porcelain shards cutting into my ankles.

"You deserve so much more than forgotten toys and unappreciated jewels," Rio responds.

Then, after moments of heavy winter cloaking our breaths, he adds, "I'm so closed off, so resistant to share, whereas the others are able to give you all of themselves despite our circumstances."

His voice is so low, I have to strain to hear.

Once I do, my breath stalls in my lungs. Rio is never one to share, not since his stay at Briarcliff with my brother, and it's because of that I assumed he never would.

"I accept you for who you are, Rio," I say. "It doesn't matter to me how much of yourself you want to give."

Rio lifts his head to the cloudless sky. "I admit, I was getting comfortable with your acceptance of only pieces of me when you deserve far more."

"I decide—"

"—what you deserve. I agree. But almost losing you,

carrying you out of the woods and bearing your weight as your soul looked upward ... all I wanted was for my soul to rise with yours, as tattered as it is."

"Oh, Rio."

Rio pauses for so long, his bare hands shoved in his coat pockets, that I'm convinced he's finished. This is already more than I expected.

But right when I start to push to my feet, he stops me with a gentle pressure to my shoulder. "You've given all of yourself to us, the Vultures. Therefore, you deserve more of me."

I cover his chilled hand on my shoulder with my gloved one. "Only if you're comfortable. I mean it when I say I accept you, Rio. Always."

The muscles of his cheeks tic with an almost-smile. "I used to be loud, obnoxious even, a bully to the core."

I snort, remembering a twelve-year-old Rio pounding on the stairs of our estate and chasing me out of corners, crowing, "Got the little sneak, Tempest! What do you want to do with her?"

To which Tempest would reply, "Ignore her. She's annoying but harmless."

He was so different then, such a mischievous asshole who I secretly crushed on because he was mean to me, but hot.

"Tempest, James, Chase, and me were a solid crew, as you know. Fuck, I was so different at sixteen—boisterous, domineering. I had a voice that I used recklessly, without a care for the damage it might inflict."

"I remember," I supply, cautiously prompting him to continue. I'm desperate not to spook him. "You would spend all summer at our estate. I'd sneak around, trying to catch glimpses of you. Now that I've realized what happened to my brother at Briarcliff, I know you went through the same thing. You shouldn't have to feel guilt over what happened ..."

"I owe you an answer on why I'm now so silent, so contained."

"I have to admit," I confess softly, "I've been curious."

Rio clenches his fists, as if gathering the strength to dig through scar tissue and rip open old wounds. "I also had love during that time. I don't speak of it, I blame myself for the loss, so I will only say it once. Her name was Ivy. When I was with her, my words were gentler, kinder. She was the one person who could tame the reckless energy inside me. But she didn't survive Briarcliff and losing her shattered me."

As Rio shares his past, his scars laid bare, my heart aches for the young boy who lost so much.

"Catching you sneaking around was another lifetime, Lucky. But I loved you then. I loved Tempest. After Briarcliff fell, I thought I could save Tempest. Save him from a fate that was even worse than the hellhole we had just escaped. I'd already lost Ivy; I couldn't lose him too. My best friend, sold by his own father to pay off gambling debts to the Mafia. I couldn't let him face that alone. No brother would. So I followed him—learning how to be quiet, unseen, every step of the way. From the moment he was taken by your father onto a private plane until he landed on Bianchi's property. It was there that I got caught."

I stop breathing, gathering the emotional stamina to hear what he'll say next.

"I became silent not by choice but by force, the result of countless hours of unimaginable torture and cruelty. My voice was taken from me long before I chose to give it up."

My heart aches for him, every word Rio utters adding a layer of complexity to the man standing before me. It's hard to reconcile the young, wounded, prideful Rio with the stoic figure he is now.

"But you know what surprised me?" Rio continues, "Bianchi's men, they tried to break me. The suffering, the torment—it was nothing like I had ever experienced. But I never made a sound. Not one. It was like Ivy and the love we had protected me, even in her absence. But in my silent endurance, Bianchi saw something—someone who could serve him, a villain hiding behind a boy's eyes."

He bends to my level in front of me, his eyes never leaving mine, his pupils black holes that demons have made their home. "He didn't kill me. Bianchi reforged me. I was molded into a weapon. Now I use words sparingly, having learned the acute power of action. But sometimes..." He trails off, looking inward at those clawed, hungry demons. "Sometimes I miss the part of myself that Ivy loved. But I'm glimpsing it again with you."

I reach out, wiping away a solitary tear that has escaped his eye. Probably the only one he's shed in years.

"Rio, you may have been remade, but we all carry blisters, scabs, *craters* where peace once filled, that have made us who we are. And I'm ready to hear your voice, see that part of you that Ivy loved and I love too, whenever you choose to use it again."

Rio's eyes glisten as if on the verge of spilling over. And then, without another word, he allows winter to freeze them dry and kisses me.

But this is no ordinary kiss; it's filled with years of pent-up emotions, of silent screams and unspoken confessions, a cascade of everything he's held back.

We break apart to breathe, the chill in the air frosting my lips, so freshly seared by Rio's.

But Rio doesn't completely let me go. He holds my face in his hands, his voice husky with our kiss when he says, "Ivy may have been my past, a beautiful chapter in a life that needed it. But you, Clover, you are the story I was always meant to complete. You are the epic tale I never knew I'd have the privilege to live."

Now it's my turn for my eyes to well, my hands to wrap around his forearms, my lips to say—

"Why, hello, lovebirds."

Rio and I jolt apart at the wry voice. I glance over to find Morgan, a towel slung low around his hips, quickly freezing water droplets glistening on his inked-over skin and turning into frozen tears.

This insane man is even barefoot.

My brows scrunch at the same time I say, "Morgan, what the hell are you doing?"

He ignores my concern, as I knew he would. "We're all waiting for you two in the drawing room. Time to break up your lovefest, little leaf. You ready for your first Vulture groupthink?"

I hear what he says, the opportunity I've been given to be included, but delectable heat flashes through me for an entirely different reason as I drink in the sight of him. So lean and toned and covered neck to toe in elaborate tattoos ranging from gothic skeletons, ancient runes, and climbing, poisonous vines. The depravity he's branded on his skin achingly contrasts with his angelic features: sandy blonde hair, angular cheekbones, and bright, summer grass eyes.

I clear my throat, glancing away before the tingle down below turns into a full-on bonfire of desire that Rio helped ignite. "We'll be right behind you. And please ... get dressed before you freeze to death."

Morgan's lips curve. "If this is hell frozen over and you're with me, I'll be just dandy."

Morgan swivels back to the manor. Rio and I exchange amused, intimate glances before following.

As we trail Morgan's barefooted path, Rio grabs my hand and pulls me back, turning me toward him for a brief moment. "I meant every word I said. And I also know that a lot of changes are coming, and fast. Just remember, no matter what happens in this manor, you're where you're supposed to be."

His lips meet mine in a brief, but profound kiss. We begin walking again, and that's when I see him.

Through the manor's frosted window, Rossi watches us. The look on his face isn't one I can decipher easily, but it injects a new layer of complexity to the feeling bubbling over my bones.

Rio's grip tightens around my hand, noticing, too.

BUT HIS WORDS wrap around me like an unsaid vow as we near the manor's imposing

doors.

And then we step inside, the door shutting with a finality that echoes in the marrow of my spine, leaving the bitter cold behind, replaced only by the frenzied wildness that comes when Vultures prepare to feast.

CHAPTER 6
ROSSI

I stand near the fireplace in the sitting room of our unlisted and, therefore, untraceable Victorian manor. The warmth heats my back but does little to ease the chill that's settled within.

As leader of the Vultures, I've earned a reputation for being tough and brutal. My intimidating presence is only matched by my intelligence, yet there's an uncertainty I can't shake. Uncertainty for the misshapen family I've created with the Vultures versus my desire for revenge against Bianchi.

"Sir." My right-hand man, Tempest, enters the room, his gruff voice breaking the silence as the door creaks shut behind him. "We're all waiting in the drawing room."

"Let them wait," I reply, my voice laced with quiet impatience as I stare out into the dead gardens, watching Rio take Clover's hand and guiding her back to us.

My men grow so close to her—are affectionate toward her. Affection leaves an opening for your enemy. It is a weakness that will get you killed.

I notice Tempest's gaze narrowing at me in my periphery.

Tempest is the only one who knows about my struggle with my remaining humanity and the beast gnawing within. He's the only one who knows my darkest secret, my greatest betrayal to the Vultures.

"You're spiraling again."

Tempest emerges from the edges of the room and comes into the circle of light from the fire, his gaze piercing.

"I'm fine," I say, clenching my jaw.

"You're not."

He comes to stand beside me, our shoulders brushing as we watch Clover, Rio, and a ridiculously clad Morgan, traipse into the house. "You can't keep punishing yourself for what happened, Rossi. It won't bring them back."

I laugh harshly. "You think for one second I don't wish I could turn back time?"

"Rossi—"

"Don't."

Tempest speaks up anyway, his voice low and cautious. "You don't have to carry this burden alone."

I sigh, my gaze flicking to a boy made into a fiend. One I've come to dangerously care for. It's because of that *fucking* affection I don't slice his throat where he stands, proving my own goddamn point.

And so, I switch to a topic that will both appease and prevent him from chewing further into my mental vault rather than bringing up my family while I stare at Clover.

I glance at Morgan instead, ensuring Tempest tracks where my attention goes. "You're the only one who knows about Nico Bianchi. It has to stay that way."

"All right," Tempest agrees to the not-so-subtle segue solemnly. "But remember, I'm here for you like you've always been for me."

I nod briefly. Our relationship is unique, built on trust, loyalty, and a bond almost like father and son. The depth of our connection is something I never expected to conjure, especially considering the degeneracy that surrounds us both.

"Your family didn't deserve what happened to them," Tempest persists, a rare hint of emotion seeping into his voice. "And neither did you. Killing Nico Bianchi was justified, Rossi."

"Maybe," I mutter, the fire playing across my vision. "But it doesn't change the fact that I took the life of a father, even if it was to avenge my own family's deaths. I've kept it hidden from everyone, especially Morgan. He doesn't need to know his father is dead by my hand."

"Likely because Morgan would go batshit and destroy everyone if he ever found out."

But Tempest grows serious. "We've taken the lives of many fathers, sons, brothers, sisters, mothers. And I'd do it again. Sometimes we have to embrace the hellspawn within us to protect the ones we love."

I grimace, torn between the creature I helped create beside me and the man I used to be.

Before.

The weight of my past decisions is etched across Tempest's features, a constant reminder of the line he walked when he helped me corner Bianchi's brother, Morgan's father, at a secret auction house in New York City and executed Nico Bianchi.

"Promise me, Tempest," I say now. "Promise that you'll keep my secret, no matter what."

Tempest answers without hesitation. "I won't let you down."

My knuckles ache with the memory of impact, the sharp crack of bone giving way under them. Nico's face, twisted in rage and shock, flashes behind my eyes before I aim my silencer at his stunned, crumpled form and shoot him dead center in the forehead.

I should've tortured him first. Dragged out his death. Because it was much too quick, and I have no closure to show for it. My ragged suffering continues.

I drag a hand over my mouth. The rough scrape of it under my palm anchors me in the present.

Tempest heads to the drinks cart beside the hearth. He pours two healthy crystal glasses of bourbon. "You did everything you could. If you hadn't agreed to work with Bianchi, he still would have killed your wife and daughter. Just to hurt you."

"I don't need you to make me feel better," I rasp, my voice eroding from the venom.

I was a top cardiothoracic surgeon at New York Presbyterian, newly married with a six-year-old daughter we'd had in medical school and made a flower girl for our wedding. Even now, I can't breathe their names out loud, can't *think* them.

Marco Bianchi found me through his brother, a man wounded in the chest by a bullet from a rival mob in front of his favorite Halal cart in Manhattan. I was the surgeon tasked to save his life.

My biggest mistake was that I did. I resurrected what should've been a guaranteed death certificate and made the Bianchis notice my tendency to perform miracles.

What they, and I, never expected was that I also had an innate talent to kill as much as save.

A rock forms in my throat at Tempest's words. He knows forgiveness over what we do isn't possible.

As I accept the drink Tempest offers, I'm convinced there is only one path to absolution—and it ends with Bianchi's empire in ruins at my feet.

THE WIND HOWLS OUTSIDE, rattling the windows and rain splattering against the panes as Tempest and I stride across the foyer and into the dimly lit drawing room.

The flickering light from the massive fireplace in this room versus the one I've holed myself in casts eerie shadows on the worn, antique furniture that fills the space. Heavy velvet curtains, an ornate chandelier dangling overhead, and dark, brooding portraits of long-dead aristocrats adorn the walls.

Clover reclines in a maroon upholstered settee across from a hearth taller than she is, her pale face painted orange from the fire's glow. My charred heart wrenches at the sight of her, still so weak and vulnerable as she cradles her stomach.

Xavier sits in an armchair to the right, his knee I was barely able to save a second time propped on an ottoman, its legs creaking every time Xavier shifts to get more comfortable.

It secretly amazes me that the boy has gone up and down the grand staircase multiple times a day to be with Clover. Respect blooms in my damn soul for the kid, even if it continues to erode my careful work on his leg.

Morgan sits in a chair on the opposite side of Clover, his hair damp from no doubt what was a luxurious shower after his impulsive cryotherapy outside in one of the many guest rooms upstairs.

I may have kept the neglected atmosphere of the manor intact, but I sure as hell demanded updated plumbing in my search for long-forgotten, abandoned homes in the mountains.

My gaze flicks to him only momentarily. Tempest's and my

conversation flares much too close to my conscious for me to regard Morgan longer than that.

Besides, there's still the issue of his continued open line to Marco Bianchi, as evidenced by Clover's and Xavier's recent abduction and escape.

Stupid boy. These damn Vultures. My goddamn joke of an afterlife.

"Where's Rio?" I demand.

Morgan shrugs. "Off doing forest-folk things, I'd guess. He dropped Clover off from their jaunty winter walk and departed again."

"He'll be here shortly," Tempest cuts in, eyeing Morgan in warning. His attention darts to Morgan's taped and splinted fingers to enunciate his point.

"No repeat performances," I warn them both before coming to a stand in front of them. I set my empty glass on the mantel.

"Rossi," Clover calls out to me, her voice barely above a whisper.

I turn to her, my vision naturally softening around the edges at the sight of her.

She is a vision, whether injured or in a flawless state. My mind flashes back to the archives below Titan Falls library, where I instructed Rio to taste her fully and lick her clean while I watched. Her breasts glistened in the candlelight, her plump, rose-colored lips slack and open to the ceiling in benediction.

My name on her lips.

Throat muscles constrict against the sudden thickness in my neck.

"How can we be sure Bianchi won't find us here?" she asks me, remnants of fear evident in her gaze.

"You must trust me, Clover." I keep my tone calm but firm.

"The Vultures are resourceful. We've managed to evade him all week, and we'll continue to do so."

"He's aware of our interceding on Clover's behalf," Morgan adds. "Of that, I have no doubt. Grimmer survived. He chirped like the oversized parrot that he is."

A shiver runs down my spine, not just from the cold draft that sweeps through the room despite the fire but from the immense weight of responsibility.

My desire to protect us all, especially Clover, is palpable, and I can't help but feel penitence for dragging her into this mess.

"Let him come," I growl, my voice low and menacing. "We'll be ready for him. We'll protect—"

An urgent knock on the door interrupts our conversation. The sound echoes through the room like a gunshot.

"Who could that be?" Morgan wonders aloud, his brow furrowing in believable suspicion.

After a long, assessing stare at Morgan, Tempest replies, "Only one way to find out," as he moves out of the drawing room and into the main foyer.

I follow closely behind.

When Tempest swings the front door open, a gust of wind rushes inside, carrying with it an ominous sense of foreboding. Standing on the doorstep, with shoulders and hair covered in snow and clutching a tattered piece of paper, is Rio, his expression a rare mixture of anger and stress.

"Sir," he pants, his breath ragged from running through the growing snowstorm, "we've got a problem."

CHAPTER 7
CLOVER

I tense at Rio's words.

I'm learning there's always a problem, always a threat looming over us. I have to stay calm and keep a clear head to survive, the same way the Vultures do.

"What does it say?" Rossi asks.

There's a rustle. I can't see the exchange because of my recent fusion with this couch while they're talking in the foyer, but I crane my neck to peek through the open double doors in time to see Rio hand over the note, which Rossi studies closely.

"First, we figure out where he's keeping them," Rio says, his jaw set.

"Who is 'they'?" Tempest asks, peering over Rossi's shoulder.

"Girls," Rio answers. That single syllable contains ripe anger. "Bianchi will capture one on campus, abducting them every time he sees fit, until we hand over Clover, the treasure, or both."

There's a crumpling sound. The note balls up in Rossi's clenched fist.

"Read it out loud before you destroy it, for God's sake," Morgan calls from his perch beside me.

He hasn't moved an inch since coming to sit in the drawing room, and most notably when Rio burst in.

I'm not given a choice in the matter, as any effort I put into movement results in an agonizing wail from my stomach after my impromptu exercise, and I don't want to be on pain medication anymore. My head throbs, my vision sharpening and receding at concerning intervals, but I'm determined to remain on this couch and not be ushered upstairs again.

Morgan has no such excuse.

He meets my eye and winks. "They'll include us in their gabfest, little leaf, don't you worry."

"Not if they don't trust you anymore," I retort. "Which you've done nothing to try to regain."

"She's all too right," Xavier adds. "If it weren't for you, Clover and I wouldn't be irritable invalids and could provide more help."

"I've done nothing wrong." True sorrow glazes over his eyes as Morgan speaks to me. "But I'm incredibly contrite over what you endured."

Morgan's words should be coated with sarcasm since that's the way he operates. But I sense the culpability in his tone.

I give a quick nod of acknowledgment, softening against my twisted professor. I can never ignore him for long. He brushes up against the itch inside me, satisfying my darker desires without hesitation or judgment. There is no one like him, and I never want him to change.

Well, maybe he could take dire situations seriously now and again.

Rossi and Rio prowl into our room, redirecting my attention, their faces grim.

Rossi comes to the edge of my couch, his dark chocolate, smoky cigar scent floating from his tweed jacket like seductive tendrils. I tip my chin up, inhaling the vapor and nestling it close inside my chest. His strong, massive presence provides comfort despite his severe expression and the horrible note in his hands.

He flips around a Polaroid nestled with the note, showing me a pale, terrified face surrounded by fine-brown hair and a bright-red slap mark on her cheek.

"Oh no," I say. "That's Lauren."

Rio's expression behind Rossi goes from grim to inscrutable. I furrow my brows at the shift but can't stray from the photo for long.

"Lauren Amos?" Morgan leans forward. "Perhaps the world is better off."

"Don't say that." My tone rises in panic. "Minnie and Kirsty —her friends—they called me a curse and bullied me relentlessly on campus, true, but they don't deserve—"

"I don't believe that's the c-word they used," Xavier mutters.

"They hurt you," Morgan says simply. "Therefore, I don't give a flying fuck what happens to them." He motions to the photo. "Or, currently, her."

Rio makes a low sound of agreement.

"I wanted them to suffer with with potions and hallucinations, not be abducted and go through torture, or rape, or—" I swivel around, searching blindly for Tempest. "Where's my brother? He needs to find Ardyn, bring her here, before they—"

"He left as soon as he read the note," Rossi assures. "Ardyn's coming."

My shoulders fall. "Thank God."

Rossi makes a quick assessment of my face with that eerie

talent of his. "Perhaps this was too much for you, too soon. You should go back to your room. Rest."

"I can't think of a worse idea," I say. "I want to be here. Do what needs to be done. Be a part of this."

Rossi meets every one of my points with a slow shake of his head. "I will not be raising your blood pressure and hindering your recovery any longer, Miss Callahan. I agreed to your short participation without considering Rio might barge in with upsetting news."

"Upsetting?" I repeat, dumbfounded. "Abducting innocent women isn't just *upsetting*, Professor Rossi. God, what is with you? With all of you? Why can't you be more concerned about this?"

Rossi darts his apathetic gaze toward Rio. With a curt nod, Rio rounds the couch and collects me into his arms.

"Put me down." My shoves against Rio's practically bullet-proof chest are feeble and useless. The muscles in his face don't even react with the impact. "I don't want to leave, dammit!"

"You're our priority, darling," Xavier says. He shifts his hips in the antique armchair with a wince. "We'll get to Lauren, but right now, we need you to be all right."

"Don't doubt our abilities, little leaf."

Morgan pushes to his feet, his brows shadowing the color in his eyes as he follows Rio while I bristle in Rio's stronghold.

"Put me back into my bed at your own peril," I hiss into Rio's ear.

His brow quirks. "Don't make such bold promises, Lucky."

Rio takes the grand staircase two steps at a time, Morgan following closely, his expression cunning, voracious, and all too interested in our trek to the bedroom.

Rio carries me across the threshold of my room, the familiar scent of roses, musk, and smoke enveloping me. I cling to his broad shoulders, my fingers digging into his leather jacket as another wave of dizziness washes over me.

"Easy now," he murmurs, his breath warm against my ear.

Morgan appears at his side, scowling. "I hate to admit it, but Rossi is right. It was too soon to move you. The wound could reopen." His pale eyes flick over my bandages peeking out from my oversized T-shirt, and a crease forms between his brows. "Your outdoor tête-à-tête with Rio didn't help matters."

"All I *do* is rest. My stomach's healing perfectly, but my brain's turning to sludge." The words come out as a rasp. I clear my throat. "Put me down."

Rio chuckles, the sound reverberating through his chest. "So stubborn."

He sets me on the edge of the bed with care, his hands remaining at my waist a beat too long. I stare at his throat, acutely aware of his warmth and the hard lines of his body. My pulse thrums as he pulls away, already mourning the loss of contact.

Morgan crouches before me, clasping my hands in his bandaged ones. "We'll find Lauren, despite her horrid personality and crooked teeth. I swear it."

His grip is almost painful as if he's afraid I'll pull away, and it's the first time I've ever seen him uncertain.

I meet his gaze, noticing the savage possessiveness in his eyes. Savageness I put there.

"I know you will." My voice catches. "Thank you. For realizing the mistake you made with your uncle and saving me instead."

"You don't get to thank us." Morgan's lips curl into a snarl with fury etched into his angelic features. "Not when you were shot and almost died."

"Hey." Rio rests a hand on Morgan's shoulder. "Enough."

Morgan pulls away and rises with a scowl, raking a hand through his hair.

I swallow against the lump in my throat. "I didn't mean to worry either of you. I just—"

"You just had to get in the middle of it." Morgan whirls on me, eyes blazing. "I had it under control. I did. All you needed to do, little leaf, was tell me the clues you'd found to the jewels, and I could've been the one they targeted, not you. But instead, you refused my advice and—"

"Morgan." Rio's tone is sharp. Warning.

Morgan inhales a ragged breath, visibly reining in his anger. He closes his eyes for a long moment.

I reach for his wrist, squeezing gently. He stills, opening his eyes and softening as he looks down.

"You rescued me," I say, glancing back and forth between them. "Both of you. And I'm going to be fine. You know how I know that? Because I'm *itching* to move and get out of here. I'm so uncomfortable and insatiable at the same time. Food isn't working. Short walks to the balcony for fresh air aren't working. It's like I'm combusting in my own body."

Morgan's tendons tighten under my grip while Rio takes my other hand and presses a soft kiss to my knuckles.

"The only pleasure I take in locking you up is that I'm here with you," he says.

With the way his heated chestnut eyes meet mine, he melts away any last argument on my tongue.

A shiver of desire runs through me at their touch, the memory of sex with Rio in the archives while Rossi watched, of Morgan licking between my legs in his classroom.

Did all of that happen a mere two weeks ago?

Heat pools low in my belly, and I bite my lip to stifle a gasp as my body thrills with need as much as pain.

Morgan's gaze darkens, pupils dilating as he tracks the movement.

"Does it still hurt?" His voice drops an octave, rough with barely restrained hunger.

I swallow hard, torn between the ache in my stomach and the growing ache between my legs. "Not too much."

Rio's hand slides up my arm, leaving a trail of fire in its wake. "I tired you out too much. We should leave you."

"No. The opposite. Please."

Both their foreheads crease in confusion and concern.

My breath hitches, heat suffusing my cheeks. "I need you. Both of you. Please. Don't make me beg."

"That may not be wise." Rio stares at my lips while the denial leaves his.

But Morgan's lips curl into a wicked smile as he pulls me up to him.

CHAPTER 8
CLOVER

With a groan of defeat, Rio follows suit, both men crowding me between their hard bodies.

I gasp, trembling in delicious anticipation, hands grasping at their shirts.

"What do you want, Lucky?" Rio purrs, nuzzling my neck. His breath washes over my skin, and I shiver, arousal pooling hot and thick inside me.

"You," I breathe. "Both of you."

Morgan growls, fisting a hand in my hair to tilt my head back.

"I can be gentle with your wound but not with your mouth, little leaf."

His mouth crashes down on mine, tongue plunging past my lips to duel with my own.

I moan into the kiss, hands sliding down his back to grip his ass, pulling him flush against me.

He breaks away with a snarl, eyes wild as he pulls my shirt over my head. I do the same to him, fumbling with the buttons of his shirt in my haste.

Rio chuckles, nipping at the curve of my shoulder. "Easy, Lucky. Or you'll prove Morgan right and break your stitches."

"True. Nobody likes a Morgan who flaunts his intelligence," Morgan agrees with a cheeky grin.

Rio's hands slide over my hips and under my sports bra, callused palms skimming up my sides. I gasp as he brushes the bandage on my stomach, but the brief flare of pain is soon forgotten under the onslaught of pleasure.

My chest is exposed as Morgan divests me of my bra, ducking his head to capture a nipple in his mouth. I cry out, back arching, and Rio takes advantage, sliding a thigh between my legs. I rock against him with a desperate moan, slick heat coating my inner thighs.

"Please," I rasp, fingers digging into Morgan's shoulders.

I'm burning up, consumed by the all-encompassing need for them. For this.

"Shh." Rio nuzzles my neck, hands drifting down to pull off my sweatpants. "We've got you."

As cotton pools at my feet, I believe him.

I'm drowning in sensation, anchored only by Rio's and Morgan's hands on my body. Rio cups my cheek and claims my mouth in a searing kiss as Morgan kneels behind me, fingers tracing the curve of my spine.

Heat pools low in my belly, intensifying with each stroke of their hands. I rock back against Morgan, seeking more, and he chuckles. "Eager, aren't we?"

His hands drift lower, gripping my ass, and I gasp into Rio's mouth.

Rio breaks the kiss, eyes glinting.

A jolt of electricity shoots through me at Morgan's words and Rio's stare, arousal spiking sharply.

To be wanted so intensely by both of them is intoxicating. Addictive.

Morgan's broken fingers trail over the bandage on my stomach, a featherlight caress, and my breath hitches.

"Are we hurting you?" His voice is rough with concern and a barely leashed appetite.

I shake my head, my pulse racing. "Don't stop."

"I wouldn't be able to," Morgan admits. "I like hurting you while in the throes of desire."

Rio claims my lips again, tongue tangling with mine, and I moan. His hands slide down to grip my thighs, lifting me easily, and I wrap my legs around his waist. Our bodies align in a burst of pleasure so sharp it steals my breath, and I break away from the kiss with a gasp.

Morgan is there to capture it, mouth slanting over mine, and I surrender to the twin sensations of them pressed so intimately against me.

It's too much and not enough, pleasure and pain warring within me, but I chase it eagerly. I want to drown in them at this moment.

Tonight, I am theirs.

My senses fix on the feel of their hands on my skin, their mouths claiming mine again and again. The ache in my wound is a distant thing, insignificant in the face of this blistering need.

Rio carries me to the bed, laying me on the cool sheets, and warmth blooms in my chest at the tender care. Morgan stretches out beside me, hand trailing down my side in a featherlight caress that leaves goose bumps in its wake.

I reach for him blindly, tangling my fingers in his hair to drag his mouth back to mine. He groans into the kiss, the sound vibrating through me, and then Rio is there too, a line of heat against my back.

"You're exquisite," Rio murmurs, lips brushing the curve of my neck.

Morgan growls his agreement, fingers trailing lower, teasing along the edge of my panties. "And all ours."

The words send a spear of heat through me, and I arch into his touch with a gasp. "Yes, yours, please—"

My panties are gone instantly. My only remaining adornment is a necklace gifted from Rio that I never take off, a diamond heart pendant nestled between my breast and sparkling, warming with heat.

Rio's clever fingers replace my underwear, stroking and teasing until I'm writhing against the sheets. I'm aware of their clothing disappearing too, Morgan's ink and Rio's scars, the feel of bare skin against mine, and then Morgan slides into me in one smooth thrust.

Pleasure whites out my vision, a broken cry escaping me, and Rio swallows it with his tongue. His hands are everywhere, stroking and teasing, as Morgan begins to move.

Rio's fingers dance to my apex. I'm so stretched around Morgan's tattooed dick, but that doesn't stop Rio from finding my clit and pinching, squeezing to the point that the rapture almost transforms into purgatory.

It's too much, sensation crashing over me in waves, but I chase it eagerly, rocking to meet each flick and thrust.

Rio trails his lips down my neck. He sucks the sensitive skin over my pulse point, sure to leave a mark. "Come for us, Lucky."

The velvet timbre of his voice, coupled with Morgan's hard strokes, his thighs audibly slapping against mine, sends me tumbling over the edge. Pleasure washes over me in waves as I come undone between them.

Through my climax, they continue their sensual assault on my body. My release triggers Morgan's own, a low growl tearing from his throat.

Rio lifts his head, eyes glowing with possessiveness—and something more.

I stare up at Rio, heart pounding.

Did I imagine it? No, there's no mistaking the tenderness in his gaze.

Morgan withdraws, and I whimper at the loss. He fists his still-hard dick, stroking once before raising that hand and licking it from palm to the tip of his middle finger, tasting my essence, his blood from his previous wounds, with a groan.

A flush creeps up my cheeks as I watch him, arousal stirring again despite my recent release.

Morgan grins when he catches me, eyes crinkling at the corners. "This is only the beginning, little leaf. We have so much more to show you now that I'm aware Rio doesn't mind company."

A delicious shiver runs down my spine at the promise in his tone. I have no doubt they can deliver, and I plan on enjoying every moment.

I reach for Rio lying beside me, running my hands over his chest. His heart pounds under my palm as I slide lower, fingertips grazing the defined muscles of his abdomen and the thin, white scars that decorate him.

He sucks in a sharp breath when I wrap my hand around his length, giving it an experimental stroke. A groan rumbles in his chest as his head falls back, eyes sliding closed.

I smile, pleased with his reaction, and turn my attention to Morgan. He watches us with hooded eyes, one hand lazily stroking himself. I beckon him closer with a crook of my finger.

"Don't start again without me," I chide playfully, shocked at my bluntness but also loving it, too.

Morgan stalks forward, eyes glowing. His hand tangles in my hair to angle my head. I moan into his mouth, another round of heat pooling between my legs.

He bends forward and latches onto one breast, sucking the nipple into his mouth. Rio lavishes attention on the other, pinching and rolling the sensitive bud.

Pleasure spikes through me, and I whimper, sagging against the mattress.

"So responsive," Rio praises, eyes glowing with lust and something more. Possession.

Rio moves from my nipple to my neck—his favorite spot—with a hint of teeth that makes me shudder and remember how he marked me before. "And ours."

I moan in agreement, beyond caring how wanton I seem.

They ignite a hunger in me that only they can satisfy. And by the looks on their faces, they plan on satiating me as much as I want.

My inner muscles clench in anticipation.

I trail my fingers down Rio's chest, relishing the feel of hard muscle under warm skin. He catches my hand, bringing it to his lips. His gaze holds mine as he sucks two fingers into his mouth, tongue swirling around the digits.

Heat blooms in my core, and I squirm, rubbing my thighs together. Morgan chuckles on the other side of me, sliding a hand between my legs. I gasp as he strokes through my folds, gathering the slick evidence of my arousal.

"So wet with my cum and your sweet dessert," he

murmurs, nipping at the shell of my ear. "You love watching him, don't you?"

I nod, unable to form words. Rio releases my fingers with a pop, a satisfied smirk on his face.

"On your hands and knees, Lucky." Rio's gaze smolders.

He's past asking me if I'm hurting or exercising caution with my injury. But the instant I cry out with anything but pleasure, he'll retreat. I know this to my bones. Morgan may not be able to stop on his own, but Rio would be here to curb him.

They may not like each other, and I may be the only thing keeping these two men together, but Rio and Morgan complement each other, especially when it comes to me.

Arousal and nerves war inside me, but I position myself as directed. Morgan strokes down my spine in approval, and I shiver.

The mattress dips as Rio settles in place. Large, calloused hands grip my hips, angling them higher. I bury my face in the blankets, my heart pounding.

A single thick finger traces my back entrance before pressing in deep. I cry out, inner walls clenching around the welcome intrusion. Rio works the digit in and out, crooking to stroke that sensitive spot.

"So tight," he murmurs. "A perfect fit."

Morgan slips under me, drawing one of my nipples into his mouth. I keen at the dual sensations, rocking back onto Rio's finger. He chuckles and adds another, stretching me deliciously.

"That's it, little leaf," Morgan croons. "Let him stretch you out so you can take what we give you."

Rio's hand releases my hips, sliding around my belly. His

thumb presses against my clit, sending sparks of pleasure through me. I gasp, writhing against them both.

He adds a third finger in my ass, spitting on me for lubrication, and I'm ready to come undone. I'm on fire.

Rio withdraws his fingers and prods my ass with his saliva-slickened dick, then fills me with a slow, careful thrust. I gasp, my abdomen muscles clenching and angering my injury, but I set the warning aside, too immersed in these men.

Morgan slides into me from below, and I'm filled by both of them.

Together, they move in and out. Morgan raises his head, pressing his forehead to mine. "Come for us again, little leaf."

His words ignite something inside me, a spark that quickly becomes a raging inferno. I scream in pleasure, my body shaking with the intensity of my orgasm while Morgan and Rio are still inside me, filling parts of me I never knew were so empty before.

The two men hold me close as I ride out the waves, and they release their own inferno. When I finally come back down to earth, I'm sated and content.

Rio pulls me back against his chest and wraps his arms around me, stroking my bandages gently.

His fingers pause with what he finds. "You're bleeding, Lucky."

"Worth it," I mumble through half-closed lids, my head lolling against his collarbone.

Rio stirs, and I tilt my face up to his chin, eyes blinking open.

For a moment, his face is unreadable, but then he smiles. It's a slow, wicked curve of his lips that sends heat pooling low in my belly. "No regrets?"

"None," I assure him, reaching up to trace the line of his

jaw. He turns his head to press a kiss to my palm, the rasp of stubble against my skin maddeningly erotic. "You?"

"Never." His gaze is intent, searching. "You are a gift, Clover. One I intend to keep."

Morgan grunts his agreement as he lays back on my pillows, tightening his arm around my thigh in emphasis and showcasing his body in flawless, fully inked relief.

Possessive, protective—and entirely irresistible. I can feel the truth of Rio's words in my bones and know with sudden certainty that I am theirs, now and always.

The thought should terrify me. But cradled between them in the sanctuary of their embrace, I have never felt safer.

I WAKE WITH A GASP, clutching at my stomach. For a moment, panic overwhelms me, the memory of searing agony and blood-slicked hands vivid in my mind.

Then I notice the softness of the mattress beneath me, the silken sheets tangled around my legs. I'm not in that dank cave anymore. I'm safe.

Rubbing the sleep from my eyes, I glance around the room. Shadows pool in the corners, broken only by the pale moonlight filtering through sheer curtains billowing softly from my cracked window. Everything is silent, still.

Too still.

My bed is cool where my body doesn't touch it. Rio and Morgan disappeared after I fell asleep but left behind a pleasurable ache between my legs. I'm still naked, the chilled outside air goose-pimpling my skin as I raise my arms for a stretch.

I strain to hear the sounds of the old manor settling for the night—the creak of floorboards, the groan of pipes, the rustle of branches outside my window.

But there is nothing.

An eerie chill crawls down my spine.

Something isn't right.

I throw off the covers, slipping from the bed with a wince. My wound may be healing, but it's not quite ready for sudden movements. The ache left behind by Morgan and Rio adds to my stiffness.

Gritting my teeth against the discomfort, I creep toward the door and press my ear against the wood.

No voices. No footsteps. These men work at night. Usually, I can hear their low voices coming up the stairs or the clink of cutlery as they eat.

Where is everyone? Rio promised he would be close by, but I don't sense his presence. Not at the door or through the windows. The house feels empty, abandoned.

Panic claws at my throat as I think of being alone, becoming a target, fending for myself when I can't take the stairs without losing my breath.

I yank open the door. "Rio? Morgan?"

No response.

Dread pools in my stomach, cold and heavy. Lauren's terrified face in the photo echoes in my memory—

A floorboard creaks behind me. I whip around, heart leaping into my throat at the sight of a figure emerging from a darkened corner of my bedroom.

Familiar brown eyes reflect the pale moonlight, staring at me with a strange, empty intensity that makes my breath catch.

"Professor Rossi." His name comes out on a shuddering breath. "You scared me."

He prowls toward me, movements fluid and predatory and completely at odds with his deadened expression. “Did I?”

I take an involuntary step back. Something is off in his tone, in the way he looks at me. A dangerous edge I’ve never seen before.

My pulse thrums wildly as I’m backed into a corner.

Turns out, I may have been mistaken.

This isn’t Rossi at all.

CHAPTER 9
CLOVER

Rossi's golden skin is paler, his eyes unlived in.

It's as if he's not fully there.

And then, in an instant, he lunges at me.

I stumble back, tripping over my own feet. My hands flail out, searching for anything to grab onto. But there's nothing.

He's on top of me now, his cold fingers wrapping around my throat.

Panic sets in.

I can't breathe.

I can't move.

"Rossi—it's me. Clover. You know me," I gasp out, struggling to break free.

Rossi leans closer, his face inches away from mine.

"I am the darkness that haunts your dreams," he whispers, his breath so hot against my cheek, it turns to dew on my skin.

Fear grips me like a vise as I struggle against the foreign strength of him.

This isn't the man I know—the Miguel Rossi who shows

tremendous restraint and constantly wears a pained expression for his efforts.

He abruptly pulls back from his encroachment, snagging my upper arm and dragging me onto the bed until I'm splayed before him. I don't have time to yelp before his large, heavy body presses on top of my naked one, the mattress dipping with his solid weight and swallowing me in blankets.

I twist under him in both anguish and fear. "Rossi—*please—*"

Rossi cuffs me under the jaw, squeezing hard enough to cut off my air supply. My hands grasp at his wrist, trying to pry him away, but his grip only tightens.

"You're not supposed to be here," he growls into my face. "You killed them. I've been waiting the entirety of my prison sentence to maim you. Torture you. *Haunt you.*"

Dread sets in as I struggle for breath.

It finally registers that I'm going to die here, in an unfamiliar, desolate bedroom, at the hands of a man I trusted. A weaponized man. A killer. A monstrosity.

You have to stop seeing the good in everyone, my brother's past voice echoes inside my mind. *We're predators, all of us. Even you, dear sister, would do anything to survive.*

As my brother's lecture swirls, my own subconscious sings, *I can't die. I've escaped too much to just* DIE *this way.*

I will do anything to survive.

A sudden surge of adrenaline kicks in, and I lash out with a knee to his groin.

Rossi lifts off the bed, doubling over in pain and releasing his hold on me just long enough for me to gasp in a lungful of air.

I don't waste a moment. I roll and grab the nearest object, a lamp from my bedside table, and swing it with all my might. It connects with a sickening thud against the side of Rossi's head. To my shock, he crumples to the ground after a single blow, moaning and clutching his head.

I blink out of my startle and jump off the bed, the lamp still in my hand, ready to strike again if I need to. My heart pounds. I'm shaking.

I can't fully process the scene in front of me, even when I reply it back in my head. Rossi, the man I thought I knew so well, has shown who he truly is—what he fights against.

And he *hates* me.

With agonizing clarity, I start to take a step toward him, but then stop myself.

Rossi isn't just a random college dude who broke into my dorm and drunkenly felt me up before I whacked him upside the head. He's so much more lethal than I gave him credit for. I'm like a mouse approaching a sleeping lion.

As I'm weighing the pros and cons of stepping over his prone form and getting the hell out of this room, the door to my room bangs open.

"Clover?" Xavier's voice rings out as he hobbles through the doorway. "What—oh, fuck me."

His attention first goes to the lamp I'm holding frozen mid-arc, then falls on Rossi's groaning form on the ground.

With a hand on the side of his head, Rossi rises into a sit between us. "Whoever hit me, consider my brief interlude of recovery your version of heaven before I send you to the ghouls."

I back away with wide eyes, still holding the lamp tightly in my hand.

Xavier shuffles closer to me, one hand on the wall to maintain stability while he stretches out the other to beckon me closer.

"Clover, darling, put the lamp down," he says softly.

I hesitate for a moment, but then slowly lower the lamp onto the bed.

Rossi watches me carefully, his one open eye never leaving my face as his clouded expression shifts from one of violence to sheet-white mortification.

"Clover?" he asks roughly, pushing to his feet. "What the hell is going on?"

"That's what I'd like to know," Xavier says, moving until he's in front of me and facing Rossi. "Why are you in Clover's room? You've never visited before, and now you've suddenly decided to in the dead of night? I'd fucking crack your head open, too."

"I..." Rossi's hand falls from his face, and he blinks, taking in my shaking form behind Xavier. "Good God, I..."

"Did he rip your clothes off?" Xavier's tone takes on a dangerous edge as he glances over his shoulder at me. "Say the word, and I'll kill him where he stands. I don't care who he is."

Right. I'm ass-crack naked and have only now concluded that I just fought for my life with a lethal assassin in my birthday suit.

"No, I was like this ... before." I struggle to come up with what to say without admitting it was Rio and Morgan who ripped off my clothes, actually. "I, um, sleep naked. It helps not to have anything rub up against my bandages."

The skin under Xavier's eye crinkles with suspicion, but he says nothing as he returns his attention to Rossi.

"The *hell*?"

Tempest's palm slams against the doorframe as he comes to a sudden stop in the hallway. In less than a second, his eyes widen with rage as he assesses the situation and barrels toward—

"Tempest, no!" I swoop in front of Xavier, the long sheets tangling at my ankles.

I know my brother and his temper all too well. He sees who's closest to me and decides that's the one to kill first.

But my defense is all in vain. As soon as Tempest gets within feet of Xavier, Rossi growls, "You were supposed to be watching my door, Tempest."

Tempest's eyes slit. He sees me lay my hand on Xavier's arm, his cheek twitching, but turns to Rossi.

"I locked you in. See?" Tempest pulls out an ornate gold key to show Rossi.

I incline my head, observing the open keyhole in my bedroom door behind him. It occurs to me that I could've been imprisoned in this room at any time, yet my overprotective brother chose not to do it.

It's baby steps, but it's something.

"Rewind," Xavier demands of Tempest, making a circular motion with his fingers. "You locked Rossi in a room? And he allowed it? And now he's here, in Clover's room, doing...? What was he doing?" Xavier addresses me. "We haven't covered that."

Instinctually, I hold a hand to my neck, trying to find the words to describe Rossi's massive body overtaking mine, desperate to squeeze the life out of me.

Rossi doesn't need elaboration. His face blanches further as he stares at my neck. "Christ. I hurt you?"

With a lethal sneer, he says to Tempest, "You were meant to stand watch outside my room while we're all in the same house together. *I ordered you*!"

I jolt at the unexpected roar. The room is thrown into silence as the two men glare at each other.

Xavier is the first to break it. "Becaaaause .... you're a werewolf who must be locked down and chained during full moons? What the *fuck* is going on? Somebody explain this to me!"

"I said I locked you in and took the key." Tempest brandishes the key again for effect. "I don't know how you got out. Apparently, you're a crafty motherfucker even while sleepwalking. And, as a reminder, we've received threats to our women's lives, and I wanted to help mine go to sleep because, not to shock you, she's having trouble doing that at the moment."

Rossi's lips thin.

"Right, then. Tempest was fucking Ardyn and left Rossi's door unguarded." Xavier nods as if he figured out the answer to a difficult puzzle. Tempest levels a brittle glare his way.

I grimace at the image conjured but move on, asking Rossi quietly, "You were sleepwalking?"

"It's why I live alone," Rossi bites out. "Away from Anderton Cottage and the campus. I can't trust myself." The barest sliver of agony crosses his face as he meets my eye. "Clearly."

"I thought you lived in Teacher's Row at TFU," Xavier wonders out loud.

I clutch my sheet tighter around my body, just as confused.

Xavier continues, "If you're not there, then where...?"

My mouth parts in shock. "This is your home, isn't it? This dilapidated manor is yours."

Rossi confirms with a tight nod.

"This is his bedroom," Tempest adds tiredly, dragging a hand through his hair. "And probably why he traveled here while asleep. Not that it's an excuse. If you corner my sister again, *I* will be the one unable to trust myself."

Rossi rasps a hand across his mouth. "Miss Callahan, I am

truly sorry. I don't expect you to forgive me. It's not safe to leave you all here and find somewhere else, but I will do everything I can to not do this to you again."

"I won't leave my post," Tempest assures. "Ever."

I shake my head, questions riddling my brain where so many have already nested. "You said I killed them."

Rossi visibly stiffens. Tempest's expression turns stone cold, and Xavier sighs while eyeing me like I won't enjoy the answer I might bring forth.

"My wife and child. Ten years ago." Rossi's face twists like the very words hurt him. "I've struggled with their murders ever since. Soon after their deaths, the nightmares started, then the sleepwalking."

My eyes heat with desolate emotion. "I'm so sorry."

"Don't be." Rossi's stare grows hard. "I broke into your room and frightened you, tried to harm you."

Tempest studies his leader. "Sleeping pills would work, but not while we're under threat."

Rossi's mouth turns grim. "Not while I'm still breathing. My family didn't get to choose dreamless sleep, so neither do I."

"If it involves my sister and Ardyn, I want you to consider it," Tempest says.

"No."

Xavier's cheeks expand as he blows out a long exhale. "Perhaps we can address this in the morning? Clover probably wants to put on pajamas, at the very least, without the three of us crowding her."

Tempest dips his chin in acknowledgment but says, "Then we have to solve our Bianchi problem soon because I'm not about to put Ardyn and Clover in more danger than they're already in."

Tempest regards me, shaking his head with such tired resignation that I almost want to reach out for his hand and apologize.

For *what,* I'm not sure. For existing? For being someone who isn't smart enough to want to be safe but plucky enough to figure out who the Vultures are and make myself comfortable in their nest?

I notch my chin under his study. I can't be sorry for who I am. I won't be.

"We'll leave you be, Clover." Rossi's voice sounds like gravel. "And..."

I shake my head at his impending apology. "Don't. I'll be okay."

After all, I joined this world with open arms.

Fell for these high-risk men.

Tempest's gaze lingers on me for a disquieting moment before he follows Rossi out of the room.

I'm left alone with Xavier, who also watches me with a level of scrutiny that makes my skin prickle.

"You're not afraid of Rossi," he observes, breaking the silence.

I tilt my head, considering him. "The man who attacked me tonight, that wasn't him. Not truly."

Xavier doesn't answer right away, instead studying me with a quiet intensity. "Most people would be terrified of Rossi after what he did. And petrified at the mere idea of the Vultures. Yet here you are, back from the brink of death again. Without the blink of an eye."

"I'm not most people."

"No, you're not." He rests his hands on my arms. "You're more different from anyone I've ever met."

My cheeks flush at the compliment, but I push it aside,

trying for a joke to lighten the somber mood. "Different how? Like a special snowflake?"

"You're fearless in a way that's both admirable and dangerous." His cat-green eyes hold mine. "You're playing a dangerous game, maiden. Tempest might be able to prevent Rossi from coming for you again, but the others won't be so understanding if they find out. Morgan's out searching the TFU campus for tips about Lauren, and Rio's taken that search to the woods. When they return, they'll want to see you. And with that honest face of yours, they'll know immediately."

Xavier is right, but I file that warning in the same mental folder as the others.

"Good night, Xavier."

Xavier regards me sadly, maybe hoping for a different answer, his mouth pulling to the side. "Sweet dreams, dark maiden."

I take a deep breath when he limps out, trying to calm my racing heart. The events of the past few weeks have been overwhelming, and I'm not sure how much longer I can keep up this facade of strength.

But then, I think of Ardyn, these men, and my brother, and my resolve hardens. I won't let anything happen to them.

They want to protect me, but I'll do whatever it takes to keep them safe, too.

As I change into my pajamas, I catch a glimpse of myself in the mirror. Dark circles ring my eyes, and my skin is pale and drawn. But there's a fire in my gaze that wasn't there before.

A will to survive.

trying for a joke to lighten the somber mood. "Different how? Like a special snowflake?"

"You're fearless in a way that's both admirable and dangerous." His cat-green eyes hold mine. "You're playing a dangerous game, maiden. Tempest might be able to prevent Roast from coming for you again, but the others won't be so understanding if they find out. Morgan's out searching the TFU campus for tips about Lauren and Rio's taken that search to the woods. When they return, they'll want to see you. And with that famous face of yours, they'll know immediately."

Xavier is right, but I file that warning in the same mental folder as the others.

"Goodnight, Xavier."

Xavier regards me sadly, maybe hoping for a different answer, his mouth pulling to the side. "Sweet dreams, dark maiden."

I take a deep breath when he limps out, trying to calm my racing heart. The events of the past few weeks have been overwhelming, and I'm not sure how much longer I can keep up this facade of strength.

But then, I think of Ardyn, those men, and my brothers, and my resolve hardens. I won't let anything happen to them.

They want to protect me, but I'll do whatever it takes to keep them safe too.

As I change into my pajamas, I catch a glimpse of myself in the mirror. Dark circles ring my eyes, and my skin is pale and drawn. But there's a fire in my gaze that wasn't there before.

A will to survive.

CHAPTER 10
CLOVER

Rossi isn't the only one who can't sleep.

I throw off my covers with a frustrated motion, deciding to tiptoe downstairs. I could use the exercise, and a glass of water sounds amazing right now. My throat throbs hotly, and my saliva hasn't returned since Rossi almost choked me to death.

The hallway's ancient sconces light my way, and after careful consideration, I confirm that the shadows in the darkness are caused by cobwebs moving with the manor's constant draftiness, not Rossi's Goliath hulk.

I descend the staircase by clutching the banister and being careful not to trip. Once on the ground floor and on the way to the kitchen, I notice Tempest in the aviary, staring into the rusty cages that once held exotic birds, now empty and gathering dust.

A neglected garden rims the circular, glass-encased room, weeds overtaking the rugged plants determined not to die in here, but most greenery has faded to papery brown.

Tempest's shoulders are tense, hands curled into fists at his sides. I know that stance. It's the coiled energy of a starving hunter desperate to strike.

Tempest senses me without turning around. "This isn't a game, Clo. Go to bed."

His voice is gravel and shade, the tone he uses when all pretenses have been stripped away.

"It wasn't your fault," I say softly.

Tempest's jaw clenches as he turns his head sideways. "I should have known better than to bring you here. Rossi's sleepwalking is getting worse the more stress he's under, and he almost killed you tonight."

I step inside the glass enclosure and through the swaying iron cages, walking to him and placing a gentle hand on his arm. "But he didn't. I'm fine."

Tempest shrugs me off, turning away. "You can't stay with us, Clover. It's too dangerous. This life ... you have no idea what you've stumbled into. Bianchi won't hesitate to sell or kill you if he gets his hands on you again. I'll end anyone who dares to threaten you, but tonight proves I can't always be there to watch your back."

Frustration wells up inside me. I stare at a cage above our heads. "I can take care of myself. I want to help the Vultures, not hide away in some gilded prison."

"Absolutely not." Tempest's voice drops low and hoarse. "I won't let you get dragged further into this evil."

"Why does Ardyn get to know your secrets, then?" I demand. "She's been a part of this from the beginning while you've kept me ignorant."

Tempest drags a hand through his hair. "It's complicated. I'm trying to protect you the same way I tried to protect her."

"I don't need your protection!" My voice echoes shrilly off the broken glass and rusted cages.

Outside, the wind whips through the trees as if underscoring the tension crackling between us.

Tempest turns away, shoulders tense as he walks between the iron enclosures.

"Please, Clover," he says quietly. "Just trust me on this. You don't understand the things we've done ... the blood on our hands."

I grip the cold iron bars separating us. "Then help me understand. Stop trying to shield me from the truth."

"You deserve better than this world of violence and sin. Stay where it's safe. Don't make the same mistakes I did."

"I want to help you and Rossi find Sarah's fortune and take down Bianchi. Let me prove myself."

Tempest's jaw tightens, resolve hardening his eyes. "No."

His denial stings with finality. The aviary falls silent, the gulf between us widening with all that remains unsaid.

He seeks to protect me, but all I feel is betrayal.

"Tell me about the Vultures," I say, my voice low but firm. "I want to know the truth, not some sugarcoated version."

Tempest hesitates, searching my face. After a long moment, he sighs and leans back against the aviary bars.

"It's an ugly, violent world," he says quietly. "Most of us were forced into it from a young age, other than Rossi."

His eyes take on a faraway look.

"You form bonds closer than blood. But there's always a brother looking to stick a knife in your back and take what's yours."

He focuses on me again, virescent eyes intense.

I suppress a shiver at the bleak picture he paints. But I lift my chin. "You've survived it. So can I."

Tempest shakes his head, mouth set in a grim line. "You have no idea what you'd be facing. What you'd have to become." His voice drops to a pained whisper. "I don't want that for you, Clo."

My defiance melts at the anguish in his eyes.

I walk around the cage separating us until I'm in front of him and take his hand.

"I'm not asking you to like it," I say gently. "Just give me the chance to decide for myself."

Tempest closes his eyes, leaning his forehead against the cool metal.

When he looks at me again, his expression is one of grave resignation. "You won't let this go, will you?"

I give a small smile. "Not a chance."

Tempest stares at me for a long moment, his jaw clenched and the cords in his neck standing out in sharp relief.

I stare back, willing him to understand. To see that the girl he once had to protect has grown into a woman capable of defending herself and those she cares about.

One side of his mouth quirks up despite himself. After a long moment, he sighs and runs a hand through his hair.

"You always were too stubborn for your own good," he mutters. But there's a hint of grudging pride in his tone.

I smile. Morgan marveled at that same trait of mine before he helped bring me to bed with Rio. "One of my more endearing qualities, or so I've been told."

I nestle into Tempest's side, squeezing him gently.

His chest rumbles with an annoyed chuckle. "You're impossible. I'll talk to Rossi and see if we can find a way to use your skills without putting you at risk." His eyes bore into mine, deadly serious as he looks down at me. "But you do exactly as I say. No running off on your own. Promise me."

Joy and apprehension war within me. But I meet his gaze steadily.

"I promise."

The aviary falls into warm gold and pinks as the sun rises. Its rays through the cold, fogged-over glass feel good. But the chance to prove my worth feels wonderful.

I say, "You're a Vulture, and the Vultures are my family now. No, more than that. You're my coven."

Tempest shakes his head, the tension easing from his shoulders. "If anything happens to you..." He scowls. "Come on. You should try to catch some sleep."

I fall into step beside him as we head back through the overgrown garden, back to the manor that has become both shelter and stronghold.

Back to the family that has become so much more than blood.

CHAPTER 11
MORGAN

After another two weeks cooped up in this musty manor, Clover finally ventures out of her room more often to explore.

The Vultures have kept me busy searching campus for any witnesses to Lauren's abduction and locating my uncle, who, it turns out, also likes to play hide-and-seek. He and his new wife have disappeared from their city estate, likely choosing one of his multiple unlisted houses somewhere in the world while his men stay back as Uncle figures out how best to smite us.

It's not looking too good for Lauren.

I applaud Rio, Tempest, and Rossi for their attempts to locate and save such a vapid girl. But when I was young, vulnerable, and unused to cruelty, I could barely survive an afternoon in Uncle's world.

Hard to believe, I know, considering how much I *love* cruelty now.

Poor girl's close to worm food at this point.

But, to keep up appearances, I give Clover a genuine,

smitten grin and set down my coffee on the settee next to my armchair.

My gaze tracks her lithe figure as she descends the grand staircase in a simple black lace knee-length dress, copper eyes glowing with curiosity. Her canvas tote is slung over her shoulder like she's ready to greet the world after so long.

Correction: to greet the world as far as she's allowed, which would be to the property gates.

"Morning," her musical voice greets, much stronger than before. "Can I ask you a question? Do you think secret rooms and passageways exist in a mansion like this?"

I rise to meet her at the base of the staircase, my fingertips gliding along the oak banister.

"There are hidden tunnels everywhere," I say. "A safe room, tower room, a hidden level with a bar built during the Prohibition—even a crypt."

Crypt. The word sends a thrill through me.

I wink at her. "You're not the only one who enjoys exploring while bored."

She bites her lip, pale cheeks flushing. I can almost taste her hesitation, ripe with fear and longing. "Could you show me?"

My mouth moves with a slow, sly grin. "Feeling better, are we?"

Considering she was able to take Rio and me at the same time when she was unwell, my impure mind cannot *wait* to see what she'll want to do with us when feeling 100 percent.

"Much better," Clover replies. "Ardyn's still asleep, and the rest of the house is trying to find Lauren. I want to do something, too. Refresh my mind. Tempest and Rossi have approved information gathering so long as it doesn't affect my recovery."

Clover rolls her eyes after she says it.

"Very well." I shrug. It's no skin off my bones to lead her into a crypt and satisfy her hungry curiosity over old bones. "I have some time before heading out myself. Follow me."

I lead her down a narrow passage behind the stairs into musty darkness. The air grows chilled, heavy with the scent of decay.

The stale air is thick, clinging to my skin, and the walls damp, moss creeping into the crevices of stone as we descend deeper and deeper into the bowels of the manor.

Shadows dance across the stone as I light each sconce, and Clover descends the spiral staircase, her boots tapping against the cobblestone steps.

The corridor narrows until we reach an unassuming wooden door, its paint peeling and tarnished brass handle discolored with age.

Finally, the staircase levels out into a vast, shadow-filled crypt. Stone sarcophagi line the walls, some broken and emptied, all carved with grotesque visages twisted in eternal anguish or ecstasy—I can't tell. An altar stands in the center, cluttered with ancient tomes, skull-shaped candles, and vials of indecipherable substances.

"It's freezing down here," she says, wrapping her arms around herself as I light the candles at the altar.

Her gaze slides over the cobwebs clinging to the corners before settling on the rows of sarcophagi. "Who's buried here?"

"Former occupants of Blackwood Manor."

I lean against the wall, watching her as she crosses in front of me and explores.

I'll admit, I was growing bored being the only spider crawling along these walls in search of something more. It's nice to have company.

"The crypt was built in the early 1800s," I add.

"Hmm. I didn't know this house had a name."

"Indeed. All old houses bear a family name."

Clover brushes away strands of cobweb stretched between two tombs and kneels to get a closer look at the engravings. "Do you know anything about them?"

"Some." I shrug. "The usual. Wealthy aristocrats who valued tradition and propriety."

"It's sad, isn't it?" She glances over her shoulder at me, a frown tugging at her lips. "That this is all that's left of them. Just bones and dust in a dark, forgotten place."

I arch a brow. "You're waxing philosophical today."

"I can't help it. Death has been on my mind a lot lately."

She turns back to the tombs with a sigh and begins unpacking various items from her bag—white candles, a worn leather-bound book, and a bundle of dried herbs.

My lips quirk up at the sight. I should have known she would insist on attempting a séance down here.

"I'm afraid you won't find any ghosts in the Blackwood crypt, little leaf. It's been unoccupied for at least a hundred years."

"We'll see about that."

She arranges the candles in a circle and lights them with a match, closing her eyes as the flickering light casts shadows over her face.

"It's been a while since I've tried to contact Sarah. Too long."

When she begins chanting under her breath, I can't hold back a snort. She pries one eye open and shoots me an annoyed look, a line forming between her brows.

"Do you mind? I'm trying to concentrate."

I raise my hands in surrender, unable to keep the amusement from my tone. "My apologies. Please, continue with your ghost summoning."

Clover huffs and turns away, but I catch the hint of a smile tugging at her lips before she hides it. My own smile widens as I watch her, a surge of warmth flooding my chest at this private moment we share.

It makes total sense I'd find a kindred spirit in this place.

In the candlelight, her pale skin seems to glow, and I'm struck by the urge to run my fingers along the curve of her neck to feel her pulse fluttering under my palm.

I clench my hands at my sides, tamping down the impulse. Now is not the time.

Not yet.

Clover's chanting grows louder, her voice taking on an eerie quality that sends a delighted shiver down my spine. When she opens her eyes, they seem almost luminous in the candlelight, gazing into the black places as if seeing something I can't.

"Do you feel that?" she whispers. "There's a presence here with us."

"Is there?"

I keep my tone light, not wanting to discourage her enthusiasm.

She nods, eyes bright with excitement. "Sarah is here. I can sense her."

"How intriguing."

I step closer until I stand behind her, hands resting on her shoulders. She doesn't flinch at my touch, too focused on her ritual.

"What is she telling you?"

"It's a feeling she's giving me, not words." Clover scrunches her eyes shut, her movements rapid under the lids. "My heart's racing."

I brush a strand of hair from her face, pulse quickening at her nearness. "Your heart is mine now. She's telling you to get into the open tomb over there and spread your legs for me."

Clover's lips part on a soft gasp, and I swoop down to capture them in a bruising kiss, unable to resist any longer.

She responds with equal fervor, winding her arms around my neck to pull me closer. Her ritual candles sputter and go out.

Lifting her, I back Clover against the edges of the open tomb, hands roaming under her skirt to explore soft skin and lace. A throaty moan escapes her when I palm her breasts, rolling her nipples between my fingers.

I dip a finger inside her and murmur against her mouth, "What is she telling you to do now?"

Clover's breath comes in short pants as she clings to me. "To surrender to you."

I release her nipples, a ragged chuckle escaping me. I thrust my hips forward to rub against her with a groan, finding the hem of her dress and yanking it over her head.

Her pale skin glimmers with the wall sconces' flames. Clover is braless and soon to be panty-less when I pull at her G-string's straps and snap them in half.

"Get into the tomb on all fours," I command.

Clover's black hair falls down her shoulders like a cloak of shadows, the tendrils caressing her taut nipples as she turns and does as I ask.

She waits for me while I undress, my naked, toned, inked body climbing in behind hers as soon as the stale air wafts against my painful erection.

My hand slides down Clover's spine, tracing over each

vertebra until I reach her ass. I grab a cheek in either hand and squeeze, my cock twitching against the smoothness of her back.

With a smirk, I whisper in her ear. "Now, what is Sarah telling you?"

Clover's voice is low and husky. "To let go of control and allow you to have me in whatever way you crave."

My stomach muscles clench, and my smile falls. "Don't make promises that are all but guaranteed to make you bleed, little leaf."

"I want it," she breathes out, pressing her ass against my thighs, the final tattooed ring on my cock reaching her middle back, begging me with her body. "I want you to take me, Hunter. To make me yours."

I momentarily freeze at her unbridled use of my first name. No one calls me that, yet it sounds like destiny coming from her mouth. I practically ejaculate at the tone she uses with it.

"Stick your fingers in yourself," I say, my voice a rasp of its former sound. "As many as you can fit. And I'll do the same to your ass."

"It won't be enough," she whimpers.

"I'm aware, little leaf. After I've had you, I want no one *but* you. I'm as celibate as you've been these past weeks."

Clover purrs in approval.

I smirk. "You like that I've saved myself for you?"

"I love it," she admits. "I don't want you with anyone else."

Before I can respond to what has strangely chipped away a piece of the charcoal coating my heart, Clover does as I ask, slipping first one, then two, then three fingers in herself. I follow in sync, spitting first on her hole, then slipping one, two, three, four fingers inside.

Clover clenches with surprise, but I massage her gently, crooning at her to relax and allow me in.

As soon as I feel her silky, gracious stretch against my multiple fingers, I raise my other arm and bite hard into the inner flesh of my wrist.

My eyes roll back into my head at the pleasure/pain swirl that clouds my mind.

Clover turns to look over her shoulder at my groans, the whites of her eyes glaringly obvious as she realizes what I've done.

My blood drips down my arm, splattering against the top of her ass and lower back like raindrops from hell.

"Hunter?" she croaks, her voice tight with alarm.

I lick the blood off my bottom lip, making sure she's watching. "I promised you blood, little leaf. Mine mixing with yours. My oath to you."

Without breaking our stare, I use my blood-soaked hand to stroke myself, making the six black rings on my cock shine under the flames surrounding us.

I hear her palms scrape against the grit-filled tomb we've climbed in, but Clover stays on all fours. She doesn't run. Doesn't scream for mercy.

Clover gulps, her throat bobbing up and down like a fish out of water. "Oh."

She watches me as I continue to stroke my length, her eyes widening at the sight of my arousal, her breathing increasing.

I give one last anticipatory pump and place my bloody hand on her lower back, leaving a ruby-red imprint.

"Ready?" I ask.

Her fingers curl against the stone bottom of the tomb, her answer evident in her body language.

Still connected by our gaze, I thrust forward, pushing my full length inside her ass.

The sensation is electric, our energies mixing to create something beautiful. Heat ignites between us, our arteries and veins intertwining, our hearts beating as one.

Clover cries out, her voice echoing off the walls around us.

I grip her hips firmly, pushing deeper and deeper inside her until I can't go any farther.

We stay like that for a moment, our bodies fused before I start to move.

I pull out slowly, only to thrust back in quickly, the sensation making us moan with pleasure.

While I'm buried inside her and grimacing from how close I am to coming—not yet, not yet, *not yet*—I use the last of my blood on my fingers to draw a rune on her back, appearing like an *M* with long sides.

Ehwaz, a Viking bind rune representing an unbreakable connection between two people, runs so deep that it's considered more ancient and powerful than soulmates.

"My blood is your blood," I say, my voice rubbed raw. "My body yours. My pleasure yours. No one else. Only you."

My thrusts become more powerful, and I reach my climax faster than I ever have before as the walls of her tight ass quiver around me.

I let out a satisfied grunt as I collapse against her, my breath coming in short, sharp gasps.

The tomb is musty and cold, the stone sapping what little warmth lingers in my skin.

Clover's breath hitches as she traces the jagged scar underneath a tattoo of skulls and writhing black snakes bisecting my chest, a relic from my first kill. Her fingers curl into my hair, nails scraping my scalp. I groan, dragging her closer.

She tastes of sin and salvation, damnation and deliverance.

She smells of centuries-old air, blood, sweat, and *her*. Primal and sweet.

When she breaks away, cheeks flushed and lips swollen, I chase her mouth for another taste.

"I want you to wear my blood for the rest of the day. I want to know that whenever I approach you, you smell and taste like I've had you. You belong to me now, Clover. There's no going back."

She dips her chin to nudge me into looking at her, where I'm gifted with a wicked curve of her lips. "Likewise, Morgan."

I chuckle. "Mm, back to Morgan now, are we—"

A loud *boom* and a cloud of dust interrupt our afterglow. I rear up, alert to enemies and prepared to do violence.

A soft hand cups my bicep. "It's okay. It was just the lid of the tomb. Our ... movements ... must have loosened it from resting against the coffin."

I blink, literally feeling my pupils contract back to normal. I find my grin again as my stone heart releases its grip on inhumane hungers.

"Which we've fully desecrated," I add.

Clover huffs an uncomfortable laugh, her gaze searching the chamber we've made a bedroom in. "It *is* empty, right? We didn't..."

I shrug. "Whatever, whoever was here, eroded to dust a long time ago and had anything precious to them raided, considering the lid was angled open."

"Oh my God." Clover's grip spasms on my arm. "Oh my *God.*"

"What?"

My detestable heart starts up again at the rising pitch of her voice.

"A tomb! A body! I found Lillium Anderton before I was shot!"

"Yeeess," I drag out the word, peering at her cautiously. "And why is that relevant at this moment?"

"No, I mean, yes. I mean, I found something *else* lying with her bones. With everything that happened after, being taken, then hidden, and all this recovery, it hasn't occurred to me until now what I have. What I hid from Tempest, mostly, because he rudely kicked me out of the cottage after I discovered Lillium in your fireplace. I dropped my bag on the trail when I tried to fight them off. Rio found it and put it somewhere in my room upstairs."

My breath stills. Could it be?

"My, oh my, what do you have, little leaf?"

CHAPTER 12
MORGAN

Clover scrambles out of the coffin, pulling on her dress. "There are clues in Lily's diary, Morgan. We have to find them."

Clover has always been intelligent, but at this moment, watching her get her zeal back and piece together a mystery that has remained unsolved for centuries, she is radiant. I can deny her nothing.

"And you trust me with this knowledge?" I ask, clambering out after her, pulling on my briefs and leaving it at that. I'll revisit this place later to collect my clothes so I can sniff them in private and jack off into the very tomb I bloodied Clover in.

A decent end to the rite of binding to her to me.

Clover pauses with her shoes dangling from her fingers.

"Morgan, I let you paint me in your blood. Put it *inside* me. I heard you speak an oath to me as we came together. After all that, would you still betray me?"

"*Never*," I repeat with raw emotion.

Her lips soften. "Then, yes, I trust you with this information, so long as we include the rest of the Vultures."

My lips pull back with a sneer.

"Oh, stop," Clover admonishes. "We need them. *I* need them."

I mumble a reluctant, "*Fine,*" following Clover out of the crypt and up to her room. I watch with interest as she bends down and yanks open the oak chest at the foot of her bed, rifling through the contents.

Still under the effects of sex, sweat, and blood, I make myself comfortable on her bed. I lean back against the headboard with my hands behind my head, intrigued by her frantic energy.

When she pulls out a leather-bound book, time seems to slow. This journal has been lost for generations, a relic of a world long forgotten. Better yet, it's an artifact unknown to my uncle and has the potential to give us the win. I've long stopped giving him what he wants.

Hunger heats the backs of my eyes. I have to resist leaping for the journal and scurrying away with it.

She crawls onto the bed and into my lap, straddling me as she flips through the journal, her eyes scanning the pages.

"Here," she says, flipping it around and pointing at an entry.

Lillium Anderton's spidery handwriting fills the yellowed pages. Most of it is the fanciful scribblings of a young girl. But the last entry—

Dearest Mother,

If you are reading this, I have expired. I am running out of light and have lost all sense of time as I wait for you to return to me. You created this space for me to hide in if we were ever discovered, and here I sit. My last true vision, other than stone walls, was your worried face as you slid the lid in place. You constructed it so it cannot be opened by a person without the knowledge that it exists.

Did you mean for me to die in here, Mother? Was all your practice on me a poison?

There is no food left. I have no water. I am sitting in my own filth, waiting for you.

If this is my grave, I am trying my hardest not to believe you put me in it knowingly.

I love you. So dearly. But I cannot hang on any longer.

Your daughter,

Lily

I HUM IN THOUGHT. "Looks like dear, sweet Lil offed herself in the priest hole."

Clover glances at me sharply over the leather-bound journal.

A war of emotion emerges in my chest at her look, a foreign sickness battling with my usual *laissez-faire* attitude when it comes to facing terrible things.

An apology is almost on my lips before I bite it back in hopes my stomach acid will dissolve it entirely.

I cock a brow at Clover instead, inviting her to contradict me. "It would've been the better way to go if she were stuck in there. Thirst and starvation would surely give her a slow, painful demise."

The line between Clover's brow disappears as she realizes my point.

Good. I've appeased her. *Because apparently, that matters to me now.*

Clover goes back to the journal.

"In the pages before her last entry, she writes poetry as well as her thoughts."

"Lovely," I murmur, not in the mood for more witchy riddles. "We should consider unlocking the '*we are at war, my flower, may ye find spiritual peace where our stone is circled by summer*' nugget that Mother Anderton provided us first."

"You're right, but ... here. Look. This isn't her handwriting. It's Sarah's." Clover pushes a page closer to my nose. "What is she saying, do you think? It *has* to be related to the hidden fortune."

Summer's stone,
Five points astray,
An eastward path,
To light the way.

The musty, neglected smell combined with the words sends a nostalgic signal to my brain. My knowledge of Latin, Old English, and history could be helpful deciphering any clues. Puzzles and codes have always come easily to me, a way to sharpen my mind between the violent abuse.

But all I want right now is more Clover.

I snatch the journal from her hands, placing it face down on the bed and gripping her waist, pulling her against me. "Lillium Anderton can wait."

Clover laughs. "Not a chance. There are jewels to be found, a Mafia king to defeat..."

What Clover doesn't realize is that the jewels are fast becoming secondary to unlocking these secrets with my little leaf by my side.

It's a frightening thought, *wanting* a woman like this not simply for my sadistic entertainment, but for company, too. Multiple orgasms, yes, but her voice, the feel of her, the way she looks at me like I'm a man, not a waste of humanity.

You are worse than a monster, my uncle's low, scratched voice says in my head. *You're a mistake of nature. You live to kill, wake up to feed, and torture for pleasure. You are my perfect heir if you would just get your head into it. Or should I keep forcing you to bow to me?*

"Morgan?" Clover prompts, concern creasing her forehead in her attempt to read my closed-off expression.

Her fingers curl through my hair. My body hums at her touch, heat pooling low in my gut.

She kisses the corner of my mouth and my lips part with a quiet sigh.

"You're all I care about." I capture her mouth in a bruising kiss, and she moans, melting against me. The heady scent of her arousal clouds my senses, dulling the sharp edges of my conflicting emotions.

She breaks the kiss with a gasp.

"We should finish getting dressed and go to the rest of the Vultures to help us with this."

Her breath ghosts over my lips, and I chase it with my own, nipping at her mouth.

"Other than mind-blowing sex, I'm having trouble sharing you. Your mind, your soul." I grip her hips, grinding her down onto my hardening cock. A broken whimper escapes her lips, and triumph surges through me.

"Morgan, please."

Clover's fingers curl into my shoulders, her nails biting into my skin. I hiss in ecstasy at the sting, nudging her skirt aside with my hard cock, then thrusting up into her heat.

She clenches around me, and I see stars, a strangled groan tearing from my throat.

"Say you're mine." I drive into her again, relentless, chasing the edge of oblivion. "Say it."

Clover shakes her head, her eyes glassy with tears and lust. "So much of me is yours, but the others have pieces of me, too."

I growl, fisting a hand in her hair to yank her head back. She cries out, trembling against me, her inner walls fluttering around my cock.

"Say it," I snarl, "or I'll stop as soon as you're on the edge. And I'll keep edging you until you beg me to send you into my nirvana and keep you there." My upper lip curls with a sneer. "That's a dungeon, by the way. I'll lock you up and never let you out. Test me. *Test me,* little leaf, and see what I'll do."

A broken sob escapes her as she surrenders. "I'm yours."

Triumph surges through my veins like fire. I come with a shout, filling her, claiming her, owning her.

Clover collapses against my chest, and I cradle her close, stroking her hair.

My little leaf has no idea what she's unleashed, making me care for her.

Because I'm just as unenlightened as to what I'm becoming, too.

THE POEM LOOPS through my mind as Clover sleeps beside me, her breaths soft and even.

SUMMER'S STONE,

Five points astray,

An eastward path,

To light the way.

THE PROSE TWISTS on my tongue as I translate the lines with a quiet murmur while I stare at the canopy above Clover's bed.

Well, Rossi's bed, originally, but I've certainly claimed my territory on it.

Summer's stone ... a sundial, perhaps.

Five points astray ... the gnomon's shadow indicating the five cardinal points of a compass, gone awry.

An eastward path ... to the east.

To light the way. Illuminate the path.

"The clues lead east, toward the rising sun. Toward a sundial with a misaligned gnomon."

Clover stirs beside me, her eyes blinking open. I smooth a hand down her spine. She arches into my touch with a sleepy purr.

"We'll need the others to help us locate a sundial," she says, her voice husky with slumber, propping herself on an elbow.

Her gaze locks with mine, russet eyes gleaming. "So you're saying the riddle leads east? We should start planning an expedition as soon as we can."

I frown, tracing the curve of her hip. "I don't mean to rain on your spooky adventure parade, but it's unlikely your brother or Rossi will let you out of here anytime soon."

Clover's expression transforms as if her blood boils underneath.

My relaxed smile sharpens into a smug smile. "I love it when you get angry, little leaf. Go on, take it out on me. Preferably physically."

Her nose wrinkles with frustration. "Bianchi and his men have Lauren. They've threatened to take another innocent girl until you either hand me over or give him the jewels. We have to do something to stop him, and finding the treasure before he does is it. I can stop this."

I cup her flushed cheek. "I never said I was against setting you loose, so long as I'm by your side."

"I'm not being 'set loose,'" Clover says, resolve lacing her voice as she slides out of bed and slips on her sweatpants. I get a lovely glimpse of my dried blood on her back before she does, though.

While pulling the sweatshirt over her head, she says, "I will break out of here to find that damn sundial if I have to step over my brother's unconscious body to do it."

I grin, slow and satisfied, like a python strangling the moronic human who traipsed into his jungle. "Well, this is going to be fun."

CHAPTER 13
CLOVER

Night cloaks the sky, the New Moon leaving no trace of itself behind the clouds as the clock ticks into the early hours.

We emerge from my room to find the rest of the Vultures sprawled in the formal dining room downstairs, Rio at the long table with a map spread out before him. He glances up at our entrance, gaze flicking between Morgan and me.

Seeing Rio after so many days without him reawakens my need. I want to sit on his lap, breathe in his forest scent from his neck, and be chilled from his outdoor skin before he warms me under his hands.

Morgan bares his teeth in a mockery of a smile. Rio's jaw tightens, but he says nothing, simply tapping the map with a finger.

Rio and Rossi exchange a look but make no comment. I can't fully make Rossi out as he keeps to the corner of the room, draped in shadow and away from scrutiny. I make a mental note to talk to him about his sleepwalking, that he shouldn't be afraid. I'll have one of the Vultures in my room every night—or more than one. I won't put Rossi in that position again.

Xavier simply watches us, arms folded over his chest as he reclines in the head chair.

"Feeling better?" Xavier asks, his eyes hooded as he glances between us, likely noticing our messy hair and flushed cheeks.

I notice the crutches are nowhere to be found.

"Same as you, it looks like," I say. "You don't need crutches anymore?"

Xavier's eyes stay on mine, softening as he takes me in. "I'm happy to hear it. And no, a simple cane sometimes will do."

"I feel well enough to get out of here," I start to say. "Do you?"

Tempest comes in behind us with a scowl, releasing a caustic "Nope" before taking a seat next to Rio at the dark mahogany table.

Ardyn isn't far behind, immediately coming to my side and squeezing. "I've tried reasoning with him," Ardyn says under her breath, "but he's more unreasonable than usual."

She releases me and takes the next available chair.

I blurt out, "I found something."

All heads turn to me.

Wandering beside Rio, I ask him, "Is that a map of Titan Falls in the 1700s? The one that was hanging in the cottage?"

My attention drifts to the small flower drawn in the corner, easily overlooked if you're not searching for it, the symbol a large reason for how I found Lillium Anderton's body hidden under the fireplace. *Sarah's symbol.*

The tendons in his neck stiffen at my proximity, his nostrils twitching at my scent. But Rio acknowledges me with a slight tilt to his head.

God, what I must smell like. A true Crypt Keeper, for sure.

Morgan refused to let me wash off his blood. To keep him sane, leashed, and less likely to commit atrocities in the manor, I did as he asked, but his mark is as stiff as dried paint on my lower back. Even my butt cheeks stick together when I walk.

What Morgan does to me cannot be measured or understood by anyone, including me, and for that, I love it.

I see enough of Rio's eye to notice his pupils dilate. His upper lip twitches with feral recognition, catching my wild, animalistic scent, and the crotch of his pants tent.

"Easy," I murmur, massaging the back of his neck.

His shoulders lower slightly at my touch.

"We haven't discovered any other symbols. But." Rio shifts the map to reveal the modern topographical map of Titan Falls underneath. "We're comparing the two."

Nodding, I ask, "Will it be helpful to finding out where Lauren might be?"

"No."

Oh. Okay. Rio is nothing if not succinct.

He shifts with an arched brow, including Morgan, when he adds, "Locating any Bianchi safeholds in Titan Falls was Morgan's job."

I whirl on Morgan. "What? You should've left me and gone to find her."

"Do I even want to know why you didn't go?" Tempest cuts in with mild viciousness.

Morgan responds with a disingenuous smile, slinking into the last available seat at the head of the table and singsonging,

"*Summer's stone,*

Five points astray,

An eastward path,

To light the way..."

Xavier reacts by allowing his head to fall back with an exasperated sigh. "I simply cannot with this man."

I open my mouth to explain Morgan's sudden karaoke, but Rossi beats me to it, drifting out of the darkness. "You found another clue."

Nodding, I point at Morgan. "With his help."

Rossi's coal eyes shine in the golden dining room light. "Continue."

"I found Lillium's journal in the tomb with her, took it with me, and had it in my bag when I was kidnapped."

I get it over with as fast as I can, not looking at my brother.

"Hang on." Tempest palms the table and rises. Ardyn puts a soothing hand on his arm to stop him.

In that second, I'm struck by how similar Ardyn and I have become in taming our monsters. All during the time when I thought we were drifting apart and becoming complete opposites of each other, we were moving in the same direction.

Not to tame them, but love them.

I send her a thankful smile for curbing my brother, which she returns with soft, understanding eyes.

Tempest stops halfway, relenting to Ardyn, but seethes at me, "You had a crucial piece to solving the *very* problem we're dealing with, save for the bonus round of a girl being abducted, and you're only telling us now?"

Xavier pipes in, "In her defense, Clover's been dealing with the realization that her brother's a lethal assassin, her two professors are enslaved to the Mafia, and the former pro-football star she had some nice flirtation going on with"—Xavier points at himself—"is the most recent member of the Vultures." Xavier raises a single finger into the air. "Oh, and a bullet wound."

Morgan blows out his cheeks. "That about sums it up."

"Just—everybody shut the fuck up for a second." Tempest rubs his temples with aggravated yet fatigued strokes. "Sir, do you have any input on this mess?"

"We've yet to hear what Clover's discovered," Rossi replies quietly, "due to the unnecessary bickering between you men, like a flock of pecking birds."

The room quiets, properly chastened.

I want to squeeze Rossi's large, calloused hand. Tell him it's all right. I want to end the swirls of torture within the black depths of his eyes.

Rossi meets my gaze with unrelenting power, barely contained within the clear, thin walls of his corneas.

If he's begging, warning, or if he despises me with that look, I can't tell.

I struggle to answer within his inescapable hold. "I may not be able to assist with Lauren's location, but that's not what I excel at. Old mysteries, ancient witches—that's where I can help."

Morgan gives an approving nod, pride filling his expression as he regards me.

I square my shoulders under his strong, silent support. "I found an entry before Lillium's final note to her mother, asking her not to kill her."

My voice breaks as I say it. Lillium may have died over 200 years ago, but her pleading words sound in my ears as if she were right next to me. Nausea churns in my gut, and I'd like to think it's from Sarah and all her regret when it came to her daughter's lonely death.

I continue, "Morgan's figured out each line of the poem. The first line refers to a sundial, the second line, a—gnomon?"

"Gnomon's shadow," Morgan says for clarification. "Laymen's terms: it's the part of a sundial that casts a shadow."

Rio's head tilts with intrigue. He returns to his maps with fresh eyes.

It's enough information to make Tempest sit down again. Rossi crosses his arms in thought.

Morgan crosses his legs at the ankle with a toothy grin, relishing one-upping these men.

I let him. If it weren't for Morgan's fiendish mind, we'd be in the exact position we were in yesterday: stuck and panicked.

"And last, a path to the east that needs to be illuminated," I finish.

"A sundial." Rossi's tone is low with contemplation. "There aren't any on campus, to my knowledge. Or in the surrounding areas. Rio?"

"I haven't stumbled across any. There are a circle of manmade large stones in the northern woods that hikers love climbing to, half formed now and broken, but that can't be a sundial." Rio drags his finger, his nail encrusted with dirt, eastward along the old map until he stops at—

"The fountain," I exclaim. "The one at the center of the TFU quad. Look at the old map versus our modern one—it used to be a sundial before the fountain was built over it in 1902."

Rossi circles the table to get a better look, peering at the map. Xavier pushes to his feet to join him, and the rest of us lean forward.

"That makes sense," Morgan says. "The electric clock was invented in 1895. Watches and clocks weren't common in colonial America. Most relied on the sun to tell time. *Why* didn't I think of one in existence during Sarah's lifetime?"

No longer feeling the win, Morgan frowns and re-takes his seat, glowering at the map as if it wronged him somehow.

"It was in the center of town back then," Tempest observes. He glances sidelong at Morgan. "Which also makes sense."

Unexpected fear grips me at the sight of the inked sundial resting in such an obvious place beneath the fountain.

"Do you really think we'll find anything out there?" My voice is a hushed whisper. "Or are we just chasing down more chaos?"

"We have a solid lead," Rossi reminds.

He's come so close to me, yet I didn't notice how much his body eclipsed mine until just now. Restrained emotions emit from his form like invisible rays. My skin tingles under his proximity.

Rossi notches my chin up. "Your clue led us to this path. Have confidence in it."

I worry my lower lip between my teeth, tingles from his touch dancing across my face. "I know, it's just—what if we've interpreted everything wrong? What if there's nothing to actually find?"

Xavier reaches out, tucking a stray lock of ebony hair behind my ear, his knuckles brushing the soft skin of her cheek.

"Have faith, maiden," he says. "We're going to find Sarah's treasure and Lauren, I promise you that."

"Careful, buddy," Morgan says, eyeing me carefully. "Broken promises lead to broken beauties."

"This is so fucking gross," Tempest mutters within earshot, though it's directed at Ardyn. "Everybody, get your hands off my sister—Sir," he corrects at Rossi's authoritarian glare. "would you *please* stop touching Clover in front of me."

Rossi drops his hand, but not before rendering me with a searing look and retreating.

My heart hammers under my ribs. *Holy hell. What am I going to do with that man?*

Xavier gives one last stroke before finding a respectful distance, too.

Disappointed, I pull a face at my brother.

He's too disciplined to pull one back, but the skin above his upper lip contracts with his older-brother attitude.

"Regardless, there's nothing to be done now," Rossi says. "Miss Callahan, you're better off getting some sleep, and we can resume in the morning."

"What about you?" I can't help but ask him.

Rossi gives a single shake of his head. "I'll patrol the manor and ensure your continued safety before heading to campus in the morning. Bianchi won't try anything in broad daylight, and while the university has accepted all of our sabbaticals, including Miss Kaine and Miss Callahan's deferred semester, I'd like to patrol the campus. It'll come as no surprise if Bianchi planted men there posing as students or visiting professors." Rossi eyes Morgan drolly after saying that. "Tempest, Rio, I'd like you two to continue patrolling campus as, ensure no other girls are taken under our noses while we locate Lauren. It might be beneficial to talk to anyone that knew her, discover what they know."

I brighten. "Ardyn and I could talk to students. We're *way* less intimidating and they might open up to us—"

"Nope," Tempest bites out again. "You and Ardyn are staying here."

"You can't keep me cooped up," I argue, fisting my hands at my sides. "This is ridiculous, Tempest, and I'm truly about to break windows and pull every fucking fire alarm in this house to get out from under your dickish, ridiculous helicopter parenting." I pull one of Morgan's lines, "*Test* me, Tempest. I dare you."

"Oh, goodie." Morgan tents his fingers in anticipation of the spectacle.

But it's the voice I expect the least who speaks first.

"Hey, Clover, it's all right." Ardyn rises, rounding the table and taking my vibrating arm. "Sleep with me tonight, okay? We can talk."

I pry my lips open to argue—loudly—that we've had so, *so* many talks and chats and boardgames all these weeks, but the weight of her stare makes me second-guess that decision.

I forget sometimes that Ardyn is just as crafty as me.

So as not to draw suspicion, I sputter and act like the last thing I want is to be dragged away by Ardyn.

Tempest eyes us warily as if I'm about to pull something sneaky on him.

Which, given the chance, I absolutely will.

But he lets us go, probably well up to his eyeballs in drama and picking his battles. He's comfortable with the fact that Rossi is on patrol and Rio is a night owl. Combined with Morgan's obsession with me, our chances of doing anything under their watch are dim.

Ardyn, on the other hand, gives me a coy smile as soon as we're out of ear and eyeshot.

"You're not the only one exploring the manor out of pure monotony," she explains as we climb the grand staircase. "What do you say we get the hell out of here?"

CHAPTER 14
CLOVER

My heart leaps at Ardyn's suggestion.

A chance for freedom, however brief?

I can't refuse.

Ardyn grins, pressing a finger to her lips. We creep up the stairs and down the hall, avoiding the usual creaks and groans.

We pause at every other step to listen for sounds of life but all is quiet on the second floor.

She stops inside her room, grabbing two coats, scarves, and beanies that we pull on.

"Oh hey, Hermy!" I whisper, bending low to stroke Ardyn's old, crotchety white cat as she slinks around me. "I'm so glad you brought her. I was wondering."

"I wouldn't dare leave her in our dorm room," Ardyn says. "She'd poop on our beds, pee on our comforters, tear apart our curtains, and for good measure, get into the fridge and steal all our food."

I laugh when Hermione swipes and hisses to let me know

she's done with the petting before resuming her spot on Tempest's side of the bed. "Missed you, too, Herms."

Ready, Ardyn catches my hand as I push to my feet and squeezes, her palm clammy. Despite her cheeky dare, she's nervous, too.

Nobody, including us, enjoys crossing the Vultures, but with so many days of twiddling my thumbs while in recovery, I'm desperate for adventure.

"Keep our secret, Hermione," Ardyn whispers as she opens the door.

Hermione offers us a bland stare, then licks her paw.

We shut the door behind us and scurry to the end of the hallway, where Ardyn pulls up a section of the worn runner to reveal wooden floorboards. She then lifts a section of flooring to reveal a trapdoor.

"After you," she whispers.

"How did you find this?" I exclaim in a hushed voice.

"It's right outside my room. I'd walk into the hallway and notice that one part of the floor sounded hollower than others. So I investigated."

"You're taking after me," I say with a smile. "Maybe too much. How has Tempest not figured this out?"

Ardyn's mouth quirks. "These guys power-walk everywhere and rarely stop on the way to their destination. So far, he's missed it."

"Yeah, so far," I point out. "And I'm all for getting out of here before he figures it out."

Ardyn descends first. I wait until her white-blond hair turns black before I climb down the rickety ladder into darkness.

The air is musty and stale. I test along the walls. Rough-hewn, cool, damp stone rubs against my hand.

Pausing, I tap my phone's flashlight. We keep climbing the ladder down—I count at least fifty rungs until we hit gritty, flattened ground.

I spin, arcing the light around to gauge my surroundings. We're in a narrow tunnel and have to crouch so we don't bang our heads on the ceiling.

"This way."

Ardyn's voice echoes softly. She points to the right.

We creep through the tunnel, cobwebs brushing our faces, rats skittering away from the beam of our flashlights. Ardyn hisses and does a little jump every time a squeak sounds in front of us, but I don't mind nocturnal animals, especially the smart ones.

"Remember when I had a pet rat in fourth grade?" I ask Ardyn in a whisper.

"Ugh. Don't remind me."

"I named her Caramel."

"That didn't make it cuter."

The corridor opens up into an archway. Ardyn and I step into a rectangular room with an old, dilapidated wooden shelf on the wall opposite us containing cloudy, dusty bottles, both clear and brown. A row of lopsided tables and broken chairs line the other side.

"I know what this is," I say, bouncing on my heels. "Morgan mentioned a hidden level that was a speakeasy during the Prohibition era."

Ardyn's eyes gleam under my scope. "That means we're on a shorter clock than I thought."

"He didn't say he knew *where* it was."

I don't believe my own words. It's only a matter of time before someone checks in on us and finds us gone, so we don't waste any more time and scamper past the long-abandoned tavern and the ghosts still waiting for their next drink.

Ardyn leads me to the left, pushing open a heavy door and gesturing for me to accompany her. Cobwebs break and dangle under her pressure, their tickle against my face making me sneeze.

"We should talk Rossi into reopening this. It'd be an excellent meeting point for them," I muse.

"Better than the hidden dungeon at the cottage, that's for sure."

Ardyn shudders at the thought, and I don't blame her. So much blood coats that basement, centuries-old and in the present.

We're in another hallway, this one mostly dirt and grime. The floor slopes upward, taking us closer to the surface.

After a few minutes of walking, we emerge inside the dilapidated stables built separately from the manor. I peek through a knothole in the wood and spot Rossi in the gardens, smoking a cigar as he scans the foliage surrounding his massive backyard.

Ardyn tugs my sleeve. "This way."

We slip out the back of the stables, his one blind spot, and into the night. The air is crisp and fresh after the mustiness of the tunnel and the confines of my room. My heart pounds with exhilaration and panic.

We've done it. We've escaped.

Now, to find that sundial before anyone notices we're gone.

Using our phones on their dimmest setting as a guide, we creep through the woods, keeping to the trails and saying little to each other so we don't give ourselves away, heading for the TFU campus.

The university can't be too far with the way the men come and go. It'd be just their style to have their hideaway right under Bianchi's nose, where he wouldn't think to find it.

Within thirty minutes, the moonlight glints off the Gothic stone buildings of TFU, its twisting spires silhouetting over the inky sky.

We shut off our phones and keep vigilant, checking for any sign of either the Vultures, Bianchi's men, or TFU security, but we don't run into anyone. It's three o'clock in the morning on a Wednesday, and the campus is dead.

After climbing over locked, wrought-iron gates (and carefully avoiding the sharp arrowhead designs on top) and weaving between cold, gray buildings, we reach the quad. In the center sits an old stone fountain, water trickling from the mouths of carved half-human, half-demon gargoyles.

My sudden presence on campus gives me instant nostalgia after being sequestered away for a month.

I loved it here for a time. Even when I didn't belong with the people, the library accepted me. The books loved me.

I remember seeing Xavier here for the first time, contrasting his beauty with the ghastly creatures behind him, the stonemasons using talons, feathers, and fangs to elevate the human form.

Out of all the girls surrounding Xavier that day, out of everyone on campus wanting to meet him and his clear chance at growing popularity, he'd sacrificed it all, noticed me, and smiled.

"What should we be looking for?" Ardyn asks, bringing me out of my reverie.

I pull my lips to the side in thought. "I don't know. It's not like we can dig through stone and reveal the sundial."

"Yeah, I think an excavator would be noticed."

I shine my flashlight across the cracked basin. When that's not enough, I climb in, the fountain dry during winter, and bend down, investigating the stonework. Ardyn keeps to the outside, studying the fountain's circumference.

Muttering the poem, I glide my spotlight across the inner sides of the basin. *"Summer's stone ... five points astray ..."*

Finding nothing, I plop onto the bottom of the basin and cross my legs, glancing up at the underside of the gargoyles, through the spaces between their incredibly muscled thighs and the stone loincloths and strips along the women's chests until I reach their chins.

My heart leaps.

"Look," I breathe, "there are five gargoyles. And see how that one right above me is facing a different direction, away from the others?"

"You're right." Ardyn's tone tightens with anticipation.

"The poem has to be referring to the five gargoyles. Only one looks east."

I stand to get a closer look at the east-facing gargoyle. I have to climb onto his bent knee and cling to the fountain he's draped across, but I need to see *exactly* what he's looking at.

"Keep a lookout," I say to Ardyn. "I'm not sure how I'd explain scaling the fountain at three o'clock to anyone asking."

"Just say you're drunk. Being drunk and adorable will get us out of anything."

"Besides Vulture prison, that is," I quip, but I'm distracted by a mark on the inside of the gargoyle.

There, behind its stone head, is a small hole. It's big enough to wriggle two fingers in.

Dare I do it?

The thought of coming up against a spider doesn't bother me. But a booby trap where I lose a digit? That makes me hesitate.

"Clo? What's going on?"

"I found a hole at the back of this guy's head." I level my phone to try to see inside. A dull gleam reflects back at me. "There's something inside."

"Is it sharp? Could it hurt you?"

"I'm a little nervous to become Indiana Jones right now," I say to her, closing one eye to peer closer into the hole. "But ... I don't think so."

Then I just do it. There needs to be *something* that comes out of us sneaking out of Blackwood Manor while under the supervision of an exiled Mafia group. This may just exonerate us if we're caught.

My fingers close around something inside.

I pull it out fast, unwilling to waggle my digits in there too long.

An old iron key takes shape under the moonlight, cobwebbed with age.

My chest tightens with equal parts apprehension and excitement. I turn the key over in my hands, feeling the weight of it, studying its ornate loops and whirls, searching for a message.

Ardyn hops on her feet and hugs her body in an attempt to keep warm. "Well? What is it?"

I shake my head. "An iron key. Clearly important, but I have no idea what it unlocks."

"The mystery deepens." Ardyn billows out a tired, cloudy breath. "Love that for us."

I climb down the demon man and land with both feet in

the basin. "We should get back soon."

"Agreed."

I pocket the key, and we hurry across the quad, sticking to the shadows, retracing our steps into the woods and back to the manor.

Our walk is hurried and determined, both of us conscious of Vultures circling nearby.

Then, a flicker of movement behind an ancient evergreen tree catches my eye.

I freeze, my heart pounding. "Did you see that?"

Ardyn straightens. "See what? One of the guys?"

A dark shape darts behind a scraggly, half-dead bush, too quick for me to make out clearly.

I grab Ardyn's arm, pulse racing.

"We're not alone," I say.

Silence fills the winter forest as we stand motionless, waiting. Watching.

My heart thunders in my chest, breaths coming quick and sharp until a pair of glowing eyes reflect the light from my flashlight, and my breaths stop.

"Ardyn, I ... I don't think it's one of the guys."

A low, menacing growl fills the air.

A creature emerges from the shadows, lips curled back to reveal sharp teeth, glaring balefully at us.

I take a step back, clutching Ardyn. "We should go. Run."

"Now," she agrees, eyes fixed on the snarling beast.

We back into a thicket as the creature stalks forward, blocking our path to the manor, teeth bared in a vicious snarl.

My heart vacates my body as it lunges straight for us.

CHAPTER 15
RIO

I pace the dimly lit courtyard in front of Blackwood Manor, my boots crunching on dead leaves.

Where the hell did they go?

The iron gates are shut, the stone walls intact. No one has broken in.

Yet Clover and Ardyn have vanished.

My jaw clenches as I scan the shadows, looking for any trace of movement.

How did they slip past me? It's impossible to believe, but after everything I've done to keep Clover safe, she still finds new ways to test my limits.

I vow that when I *do* find her, she'll wish she never left my sight.

Her absence is tangible, her defiance carving a wound in my chest where others lay. I can feel it as soon as she leaves my side, like the twist of a knife the second they snuck out of the manor.

With a gruff, annoyed sound in my throat, I slink out of the courtyard and follow a curious trail leading from the stables, intrigued enough to follow the girls rather than stop them.

She knows I can track her. Anywhere she goes, I'll follow.

When I realize they're headed to campus, I take a wide arc around their growing trail until I'm in the lead, ensuring no threats await them. Covering my tracks is second nature. There's no way Ardyn or Clover will realize they're being watched.

Unless I want them to.

I glance at my smartwatch. Tempest's curt *Get them* text is enough notification that I'll be ensnaring them soon.

Crouched under the cover of an exterior buttress from one of the pointed stone archways of the university, I watch with interest as the girls climb the dry fountain in the quad, their voices reaching my ears easily due to their position in the center of the buildings protecting them from the elements.

Clover pops out of the basin, holding a small item. It's too dark to make it out, but it makes them excited enough to leave.

I follow with the soundless steps of a panther.

The girls bump shoulders on their way back, clearly excited about their find—a find they should have waited for us to assist them with.

Why they couldn't wait, why Clover feels the need to find the clues first, is beyond me.

Besides the brewing anger at the thought of harm coming to her if I'm sent on a mission and unable to watch her, it blows my mind that the girl continues to show such stubborn bravery despite facing murderers and assassins, risking death, and loving us still.

Because she's one of us.

That sudden realization brings me to a halt, my body

becoming uncomfortably still as I wrestle with newfound surety that if forced into a corner, I'd choose Clover over Tempest.

A deep, rumbling growl echoes through the woods. My attention snaps in the same direction.

Clover's terrified cry and Ardyn's yelp send me into a sprint. I clamor through the bushes, uncaring of a silent approach for the first time in a decade.

I break through the foliage, and the creature freezes, ears flat against its skull as it whips around to face me, the new threat.

A massive dog lies in wait for me, hackles raised and lips curled back from sharp teeth. A Rottweiler, black as pitch and nearly the size of a pony. Its eyes gleam with a feral sort of intelligence as he watches, unmoving. He's fixed on the snarling man before it.

"Rio!" Clover shouts. "Be careful—"

The two of us animals circle each other, growls rising in intensity.

The dog lunges, its hot breath grazing past my face. I duck and roll to the side. His snapping jaws barely missed me.

Clover shrieks behind me, seizing Ardyn's arm to pull her away. I spin around enough to ensure she's not hurt because her scream sounds like the dog got her. But then I realize that her cry of agony is her worry for *me*.

The beast turns, drool dripping from its razor teeth. My ragged heart twists—I can't let it get to them.

I surge forward and slam into the dog, pinning it to the ground. He snarls and writhes beneath me, claws scraping against the earth. Up close, his eyes are crazed and bloodshot, foam frothing at its lips. This dog is either rabid or trained to look it.

A metallic glint peeks out from the dog's collar, barely visible in the dim light, but I know what it is. A tracking device.

"Get back!" I shout to them, struggling to keep the dog down. My muscles strain as he bucks and snaps.

Clover pulls Ardyn away, her eyes white with terror. I can't bear to see her afraid—it ignites a fury in me like nothing else could.

The dog wrenches free for a moment, jaws clamping down on my forearm. Pain explodes through me as his teeth sink in, grating against bone. I grunt, adrenaline numbing the agony.

With my other arm, I grab the dog by the scruff of its neck and hurl him away. He yelps as he tumbles across the dirt.

Breathing hard, I climb to my feet. The dog does the same, shaking himself off. But now there's a limp in his gait, and he's favoring his left hind leg.

Good. Now, he can't chase them anymore.

The dog snarls at me, hackles raised, but stays in place as I slink in a half circle in front of it until I'm standing in front of Clover and Ardyn.

"You've lost, Dog," I say under my breath. "Go back to your master."

He and I may both be trained killers, but I don't kill animals if I can help it.

He limps away into the brush, wheezing. His sounds fade into the forest. Only then do I look down at my arm.

Four deep puncture wounds ooze blood. The pain hits me then, hot and insistent. I press a hand over the injury, my lips twisting.

I whirl around to Clover, my anger simmering. She straightens and lifts her chin, refusing to cower.

Brave, foolish girl.

"You should not be out here." I keep my voice low, my tone lethal. "Do you have any idea what could've happened?"

"If no one is going to find Lauren, then I had to do *something* to give Bianchi a reason to let her go." Her eyes flash with defiance. "How could I have known there'd be a feral dog in the woods—"

"Because Bianchi will stop at *nothing* to have you."

My hiss is nearly a shout. It hurts my vocal cords, but by God, it's worth it if it means I can frighten some sense into her.

"I refuse to let another girl take my place!" Clover shouts back.

It's been a very long time since I've feared for anything. Anyone. But lacking the words to explain how she makes me feel, I snarl at her instead.

She huffs out an exhale, then holds out her hand, revealing an iron key. "We found this at the fountain. It looks old, maybe antique. I thought—"

I snatch the key from her palm, my patience fraying. She has no sense of self-preservation, constantly putting herself in danger and me in fear for her.

But at the motion, Clover sucks in a breath.

She touches my arm. "Rio, you're hurt."

I shake my head. "It's nothing."

Protecting her is all that matters. No wound could keep me from that.

Clover gently takes my arm, examining the bite. Her touch is soft, hesitant. "We have to clean and bandage this."

"You will not leave my sight again." I grab her arm with my wounded one, my grip tight. "Do you understand?"

Clover sets her jaw, attempting to wrench from my grasp. I hold fast, staring down at her.

After a tense moment, she nods.

Ardyn wisely remains silent, hugging herself with lowered eyes. She'll get this same treatment from Tempest, I have no doubt, so I'll reserve that for him.

I release Clover's arm and pull her under my wing, guiding her and Ardyn through the woods. The key weighs heavily in my pocket, but after a moment of thought, I take it out and hand it back to her.

Lucky worked hard for it. I'm not one to take the fruits of other people's labors, unless ordered.

"Thank you," she whispers brokenly, her hair covering her lowered eyes.

"Next time you decide to disappear," I warn, "things will not end so pleasantly."

Voices drift ahead, followed by the crunch of leaves. I tense, pulling Clover behind me and stepping in front of Ardyn.

Three silhouettes detach from the trees, resolving into familiar figures as they approach.

Tempest strides forward, Morgan and Xavier on either side of him. They've been patrolling, ensuring the area is secure before we venture in. Rossi stayed at the manor, ensuring no outsiders made their way inside.

"There you are," Tempest growls, scowling at Clover first, then leveling a promise of punishment at Ardyn.

Clover wrenches her lips to the side, clearly unrepentant. "We had to find where the poem led. I can't sit back and wait for you to come back with Lauren or for the Vultures to find the jewels. I am a part of this."

"Sacrificing Lauren is worth keeping you safe." Tempest doesn't pause in his stalk toward her. "If you want to be one of us, dear sister, lose the morals."

Clover meets his eye, but her lashes flutter.

Though he makes a valid point.

"Lauren's a *person*, Tempest," Clover argues. "And whatever they're doing to her..."

"As someone with a moral compass," Tempest smoothly interjects, "you don't want me to explain to you what those things could be."

I watch the exchange, my eyes flicking between the siblings. Tempest's words are harsh, but they're true. Clover needs to understand that she's no longer living in the sheltered world she grew up in.

It's when Clover's shoulders slump with defeat that I look away.

I know she's right, but the thought of her risking her life for someone else's sake fills me with dread. Clover is not a Vulture. To prevent her from becoming one is a goal her brother and I share.

But Clover's bravery is admirable. I can't help but feel a sense of pride in her.

Tempest spins away from her with a grunt of impatience, spearing his fingers through his hair. "Fuck, I'm so goddamn tired."

Clover stares at him, mouth agape.

Actually, so do I. It's a rarity to witness Tempest in a state of stress and uncertainty. Dominating is what we do. Intimidation and triumph is our life.

"Tempest..."

Ardyn goes to him, wrapping her arms around his waist and burying her face in his chest.

He glances down at her like he wants to both bite her head off and fuck her. The warring emotions, a conflict between love and sacrifice, swim in his eyes.

I can relate.

Clover opens her mouth to argue, but I cut in. "We

shouldn't linger. There could be more out here."

Morgan cocks an interested brow.

Xavier asks warily, "Fuck, what now? More what?"

A howl pierces the night, followed by the baying of hounds. My blood turns to ice as the sounds draw closer.

Morgan asks me wryly, "I suppose that didn't come from you, beastie?"

"Bianchi's hounds," I say before Morgan's expression goes slack with disbelief.

And now the dogs have caught our scent.

CHAPTER 16

RIO

I take a deep breath, my fingers tightening around the handle of my knife as the baying grows louder and more frenzied.

"Fuck," Tempest mutters, his grip spasming around Ardyn's arms like he's about to throw her over his shoulders and sprint out of here. "We have to move. Now."

I nod in agreement, my eyes scanning the woods for any signs of movement. The howls grow closer, and I can hear the rustling of leaves as the dogs draw near.

Ardyn is right behind Tempest, her hand on his back as they lead the way.

"We can't outrun them," Xavier points out, his voice tense.

Morgan snorts. "We don't need to outrun them, Sports Balls. Just need to outrun you."

Ignoring their squabbling, I move to place myself between Clover and the rest of the group.

"Stay behind me," I tell her, my tone brooking no argument.

I do it just in time. The first dog bursts through the undergrowth, eyes glowing in the darkness. It's a massive creature with a coat as black as the first.

I don't want to hurt the mutts, but I know they will tear us apart if I don't fight back.

I take a defensive stance, my eyes fixed on the dog's movements. It charges at me, its jaws snapping. I dodge to the side, my knife flashing in the moonlight. The blade slices through the air and sinks into the dog's side. To my displeasure, the beast yelps in pain and falls to the ground.

Their companion's fate does not deter the rest of the pack. They circle us, growling and snarling, ready to pounce. We're surrounded, but we've formed a tight half circle with Clover and Ardyn behind us. Clover backs up against a tree, saucer-white eyes peering between our bodies and glued on the dogs.

I swing my knife in a wide arc, trying to keep them at bay. They're fast, and their teeth are sharp. One of them sinks its teeth into my leg, tearing through my pants and drawing blood.

I grit my teeth and lash out again with my knife. Tempest and Morgan have pulled theirs out. I'd say Xavier has, too, but he flings it around like it's a snake about to bite him.

My blade hits another mark, striking one of the dogs superficially in the neck. It falls at the same time Tempest incapacitates another.

Morgan takes a widened stance, using his arms to appear bigger, and snarls at the remaining three canines, saliva dripping from his teeth as he roars like a wild animal at them.

"Christ, they're not bears." Xavier regards Morgan like he recently broke out of a psychiatric institute. "You can't scare them off just by screaming at them."

"At least I'm not flinging a knife about like a limp dick in the wind—"

But the other dogs are hesitant now, eyeing Xavier and Morgan's quarreling, unsure if they should continue the fight.

I take advantage of their uncertainty and lunge forward, my knife flashing in the moonlight.

I swipe at each of them in turn, threatening them with my blade. Eventually, the dogs howl and retreat into the forest, whimpering.

With the danger subdued, I let out a deep breath and turn to check on the others. Tempest clutches his arm, blood seeping through his fingers. Ardyn huddles next to him, tears streaming down her face. Morgan's face is twisted in pain, and Xavier favors his right side again, panting heavily.

But my attention is immediately drawn to Clover, who is still backed up against the tree. I can see her body trembling. She's in shock.

I make my way over to her, my movements slow and cautious. When I'm close enough, I crouch down in front of her, my hand reaching out to touch her arm. She flinches at my touch, and I withdraw my hand immediately.

"It's okay," I say softly, my voice gentle. "They're gone. We're safe now."

But she just shakes her head, tear tracks glinting on her face.

"He takes innocent girls and animals," she whispers. "Twists them into pawns or monsters. Forcing us to hurt them. It's awful. This is so *perverse*."

I feel a pang of guilt in my chest. It's true that I've been so focused on surviving that I haven't stopped to consider the toll our situation is taking on Clover—only that I want to keep her out of it.

But is that even possible?

"Hey," I say, cupping her face in my hands. "Listen to me.

You're strong, Clover. You've made it this far, and you're going to make it through this. I can't promise it's going to get easier. There will be more fighting and more bloodshed. But I won't let anything happen to you. We will protect you, no matter what."

"Too right," Xavier agrees.

Morgan nods, a manic twist to his lips. "That was over much sooner than I wanted. Not even a bite mark on my delicious, meaty thigh for my troubles."

A crashing sounds to the right, branches breaking under the weight of enraged speed.

I have enough time to see the flash of white fangs and gleam of black, depthless eyes before Clover shifts from beneath me, swiping the knife from its sheath at my hip and lunging for the dog on a broken scream.

The brute howls at the blade's plunge through its coat, then limps off through the brush, whining and wheezing.

Clover's breaths come in short gasps.

All members of the Vultures stare at her.

"See?" Clover asks shakily, spinning to include all of us, bloody knife dripping at her side. "I told you I could be one of you."

CHAPTER 17
CLOVER

We make our way back to the manor in silence, Xavier and Morgan at our rear covering our tracks and scent, now that we're aware Bianchi's set dogs on finding us.

Ardyn walks beside me, but I glance at Rio every few steps. He's sustained multiple injuries from the pack's attack. It's a miracle he's walking so smoothly.

Probably because ... he's endured far worse.

When we arrive, Tempest and Ardyn go to their room to clean up. Xavier and Morgan head into the dining room with plans to debrief Rossi.

I sit Rio down in the kitchen and begin cleaning his wound. The sting of antiseptic makes him grit his teeth, but he keeps still.

I work carefully, gently. I hope my hands are warm against his skin like his always are on mine.

"You should have been more careful," Rio says, breaking the silence.

His anger is a pot just before boiling. It simmers beneath

the surface, as constant as the pain in my heart at what happened in the forest and the animals that were hurt, all because of my rebellion.

"Going out alone, where I can't protect you," Rio continues, talking to himself more than to me. "You're lucky I found you in time."

I pause in my ministrations, waiting until his eyes meet mine again.

"I'm sorry," I say sincerely. "I didn't mean to worry you."

"You always worry me."

Rio clamps his mouth shut the second the words leave his mouth. He looks away, jaw clenching.

Silence falls between us.

I bite my lip. Hesitate.

When I speak again, my voice is tentative.

"Rio, I..." I swallow. "I care for you. A lot."

His pulse pounds against my hand. He won't lie to me, but the truth is more than he can bear to give.

After a long moment, he says, "I know."

I exhale a soft sound.

My fingers brush against his cheek, turning his face toward mine. He lets me.

"Then don't send me away like I know my brother wants to after tonight," I whisper.

He closes his eyes, leaning into my palm.

"Let me stay."

Rio's eyes open, and he stares at me for a long moment. A battle rages within him, the fear of losing me warring with the need to protect.

Finally, he leans forward, his lips meeting mine in a fierce, possessive kiss. I yield to him, my body melting into his as he deepens the kiss.

Our hands roam over each other, tugging at clothes and seeking out skin. I moan into his mouth as his hands cup my breasts, his thumbs brushing over my hardened nipples.

"Bedroom," Rio growls against my lips.

I nod, and he scoops me into his arms, carrying me down the hall to his bedroom. He gently sets me on the bed, his eyes locking onto mine as he strips out of his clothes.

I watch, my breath catching in my throat as he reveals his body to me. He's lean and muscular, his skin tanned and marked with old scars, save for the fresh ones on his arm and thigh. His cock is hard and heavy, jutting out from a nest of tight curls.

"Your turn," he murmurs, his voice husky with desire.

I scramble out of my clothes, my fingers fumbling at my jean's buttons.

Rio watches me as I slide out of my bra and panties. His eyes drink in my body, his lips parting. The air grows heavy between us, suffused with our mutual lust and need.

I crawl onto the bed and lay on my back, spreading my legs wide as I reach my hand down to caress my cleft.

Rio's breath hitches at the sight of me. He watches as I slip a finger inside my pussy, pumping it in and out in a steady rhythm. Each glide of my fingers brings me closer to release, sending shards of pleasure throughout my body.

A sheen of sweat breaks out on my skin. Rio licks his lips. He walks toward the bed, his hands working on his cock.

I moan as my eyes rake down his body, taking in every inch of his muscular frame up close.

He's perfect.

He's beautiful.

His eyes never leave mine as he crawls on top of me, his

hands settling on my hips as he buries his face in my neck. He kisses me there, trailing his lips to my shoulder.

He kisses me everywhere, his mouth trailing over each inch of me. My heart swells, my body hums in anticipation. The craving for him is unbearable, and I writhe with every pass of his lips.

Finally, he settles on my pussy, his tongue flicking over my clit. He groans into me as his tongue laps upward, favoring my clit with slow, deliberate flicks. The pleasure is sharp, so intense it's almost painful.

I moan, my hands reaching up to twist in his hair as he brings me to the edge. My hips buck against him, and he holds me down with his hands, never once breaking the achingly slow rhythm of his tongue.

Heat burns down the length of my spine as I reach the peak of my pleasure. I shatter apart, my moans echoing through the room. Rio pulls away, groaning low in his throat as he watches me come.

Then Rio's mouth is on mine, silencing my cries.

His tongue delves into my mouth. I taste myself on his lips and moan. He presses his body against mine, our skin sliding against each other's so smoothly. He's rock hard against my palm.

I start pumping it in my hand. His hips rock into my touch as he kisses me, his tongue dueling with mine.

He breaks the kiss, panting.

His eyes are wild, animalistic.

His body is tense.

With one hand, Rio steadies himself against the bed. With the other, he reaches down to guide himself to my entrance, to the slick wetness of my pussy, already dripping with desire for him. He eases himself inside me, filling me.

I moan as Rio begins to pump into me. My legs wrap around his waist. My hands glide over his back, up to his shoulders, and back down to his ass, massaging his firm cheeks and urging him deeper into me. My nails dig into his skin, and Rio groans at the fresh pain.

He fucks me faster, harder.

His cock pounds into me, sending me spiraling into pleasure so intense it's all I can do to keep breathing. It's almost too much. I find myself on the brink of coming again.

"Come for me," Rio rasps into my ear. "Now."

I moan, my nails biting into his back. Rio tenses between my thighs. But he lifts his head until his eyes meet mine.

Then I explode, my orgasm washing over me in wave after wave of pleasure. I scream into his mouth, clawing at his back as I break apart.

Rio grunts, and then he's coming, as well.

He spills into me, my pussy tightening around him. He shudders, rocking into me, his body taut.

I bury my face into Rio's neck, breathing in deep until the tension slowly eases from his shoulders. But he stays inside me, his cock hardening again.

I smile into his nape, reveling in the feel of him filling me. The need we have for each other is a constant thing, flowing always.

The thought of not being with him, of not feeling him inside me, is more than I can bear.

It's ridiculous, but I can't imagine my life without him.

Rio rolls off me, and I prop myself up on my elbows, staring at him.

He looks at me, eyes questioning.

I know what he wants.

He wants me to be strong.

He wants me to tell him to let me go now before I get hurt.

But I can't.

Truthfully, I don't want to. I want to stay with Rio. I know what being with him means. I know the Vultures are my destiny, and I accept that.

I lean forward and kiss him. He returns my kiss, his lips molding to mine, his tongue sweeping over my lower lip. His hand trails up my neck to my face, cupping my cheek. His thumb traces my cheekbone.

I smile against his lips, my heart beating hard.

I am his.

I always have been, and I always will be.

I collapse onto Rio's chest, sated and exhausted. With the steady thump of his heartbeat in my ear, I nuzzle against his skin.

I *will* spend the rest of my life with these men, and nothing will tear us apart.

Not even a Mafia empire.

CHAPTER 18
CLOVER

My eyes snap open, heart pounding as Xavier's hand roughly shakes my shoulder.

"Clover, wake up. We need to move."

I sit bolt upright, blinking in confusion. "What's happening?"

The urgency in Xavier's pale green eyes sends a spike of fear through me.

"One of Rossi's informants just called with a solid lead on where that bastard Bianchi is keeping Lauren. We're gathering supplies for a rescue mission. Now."

My breath catches. An icy chill runs down my spine, imagining her terror while being locked away somewhere unknown to her, bare of essentials and filthy.

I blink, surveying my surroundings. I'm still in Rio's bed, the black silk sheets sliding against my skin, but they're as cool as the spot beside me.

Rio's not there.

Xavier doesn't seem surprised by my presence in Rio's bed,

quickly exiting the way he came with a sharp gesture for me to keep close.

I follow Xavier out to the living room where the others are gearing up, faces grim.

Rossi stands at the head of the table, unrolling a blueprint as he barks orders.

"Tempest, you'll access the security system and disable the alarms. Morgan and Rio, take out the exterior guards. Xavier, get the van ready for our escape."

The air crackles with tense energy as they continue strategizing counterattacks and contingencies. Xavier squeezes my hand, a silent promise that he'll keep me safe before he joins in and starts packing black duffel bags.

But my heart aches for the girl I hope we'll save tonight—the girl who reminds me too much of my own captivity.

Ardyn steps to my side, pressing her weight reassuringly against me.

She and I may not have the skills of the Vultures, but we're along for the ride, determined to help in any way we can.

The seven of us filter out of the manor and climb into a black van, none of the men objecting to our presence.

Not even Tempest, which means this is serious.

We race into the night, speeding toward our target, wherever that might be. The Vultures haven't said a word, but I trust them implicitly.

Xavier's grip on the steering wheel is white-knuckled as we drive without headlights. The others sit tense and focused, going over the mission details one last time, a sleek black laptop open on Tempest's lap.

"I'm in," he says, his fingers tapping rapidly on the keyboard, his gaze tense and focused.

"Good. We'll have a ten-minute window before they detect the breach," Rossi says.

Morgan nods, sliding a round into the chamber of his gun but pocketing it.

"Never preferred these things," Morgan says.

Xavier shakes his head. I notice his eye roll in the rearview mirror.

Morgan reads my tense expression. "Wondering why I don't take the easy route in disabling Bianchi's men, little leaf?"

I un-stick my dry, cracked lips. "Actually, I—"

"Do you know how much pressure it takes to pull a trigger?"

Tempest glances up from his monitor at Morgan's question.

I shake my head in answer to Morgan, though I'm sure I'm going to regret it.

"Five pounds." Morgan gives an absentminded shrug. "That's all the pressure it takes to end a life by pulling a trigger. Now, without getting all meta about it, where the fuck is the fun in that?"

"I choose to shoot at a distance," Xavier says.

Morgan chuckles. "I've only taught you knife skills so far, Sports Balls, which you utterly failed at in the forest. You're lucky I've seen your more successful sides, too."

I send a curious look at the back of Xavier's head since he won't meet my eye, through the rearview mirror or otherwise.

Has Xavier killed? Has he applied those five pounds of pressure, or did he cut into his victim excruciatingly slow?

Yet I care for him still. Always.

"You okay?" Ardyn asks quietly beside me.

"As much as I can be," I answer just as softly.

Morgan holds up his favorite knife, the blade well-maintained and probably sharper than anything I can imagine.

"I'll take out the exterior guards first," he says. "Silent kills."

My heart batters my ribs. Everything is happening so fast.

A metallic, oiled smell overtakes the cramped air, weapons being taken out of a duffel by Rio and inspected. He reaches over the seat, handing Tempest a handgun while watching Morgan wryly.

I slip my hand into my pocket, fingers closing around my weapon since I doubt I'll be provided a knife or a gun (not that I think I want one).

The ornate iron key I discovered yesterday settles coldly against my palm, oddly reassuring in this car full of deadly assassins.

This old artifact is our only clue to finding Sarah Anderton's hidden fortune before Bianchi, and it's the only power I have.

"Once we have the girl, we get out fast," Tempest commands. "No stopping for anything."

His tone brooks no argument.

The men murmur in agreement, their expressions as murderous as I've ever seen them.

Then the car goes quiet.

Ten minutes later, the van comes to a hard stop.

CHAPTER 19
XAVIER

I nod to Rio as we slip out of the van, sticking to the shadows as a Morgan emerges, too. We close our doors behind us and start toward the small winter fishing cabin, which is tucked away into the woods. Both of us are tense, on edge. I hear the gentle rush of a stream in the distance and smell the scent of evergreen carried in by the wind.

The windows are dark. There isn't a porch light to guide us, but that's not to say there aren't motion detectors outside. If this is indeed one of Bianchi's strongholds, it will be set up as if by a techie with OCD.

I clench my hands into fists at my sides. The knife Morgan gave me nestles in my pocket next to my thigh. The whole thing makes me fucking nervous.

Then I think of what Lauren is going through and what Clover endured despite my being by her side during her captivity.

Tempest and Morgan have already circled around back to take out the exterior guards and make sure no one can escape the property. They want to leave no witnesses behind; none of us do. Rossi stays with Ardyn and Clover in the car, albeit with great reluctance.

The old professor is as bloodthirsty as the others, but he does care about the safety of the girls since they tend to run headlong into danger without thinking first. If anything happened to them while we weren't there...we would never forgive ourselves for being unable to protect them from harm.

Rio carefully opens the front door, which creaks eerily on its hinges, but they won't budge any further than that. Apparently, some sort of security mechanism prevents intruders from entering uncharted territory without permission.

My breaths come fast but steady, focused. I visualize our route, mentally checking off each phase of the plan.

Slip inside, disable any interior guards, find Lauren's room, and get her out.

Simple, except nothing is ever one-and-done with Bianchi and the Vultures.

It remains unclear who Rossi's informant is, no matter how much Rossi relies on their intel or credibility, but I'm not keen on a nameless, faceless informant putting us in dire situations in the woods.

Ever since Clover twisted all of our insides—including Rossi's—nothing is going the way we'd prefer.

The hounds are the first of many surprises, I'm sure. My hip still smarts from one of them locking onto my belt and yanking me around like beef jerky, though I half wish I'd received wounds like Rio's because then maybe Clover would have administered to me the way she administered to him.

Ah, now there's a new plot twist—Clover sleeping with Rio.

But, as with all things enjoyable, I have to ponder it another time.

We reach the side door. Rio pulls out his lock pick tools, and in seconds, we're inside a dim hallway.

I scan for cameras or traps, but it's clear.

So far, so good.

Floorboards creak upstairs. Morgan's wild eyes gleam in the dark as he appears on the landing, bloody knife in hand. He jerks his head—the coast is clear.

We move swiftly up the stairs. According to Rossi's intel, the third door on the left is Lauren's. Morgan and I stand guard as Rio picks another lock. The tumblers click, and the knob turns.

Inside, a waifish girl cowers on a bare mattress. Her wrists are raw from restraints. I find the whites of her eyes in the darkness.

"Lauren," I whisper. "It's all right. It's me, Xavier. We're getting you out of here."

She releases a hollow, low cry as Rio bends down to cut her bindings. "Thank God. Please—help me."

My blood turns to ice at the sound of her voice. "Rio, don't—"

The girl tackles him to the ground. A syringe glints in her hand, aimed at his neck. Morgan grabs her wrist just in time.

"She's not Lauren!" I say, all too late.

We've been played.

Morgan wrenches the syringe from the girl's grasp and plunges it into her thigh. She squeals through Morgan's hand over her mouth, then crumples into his body, unconscious.

That is the moment I get a good look at her face.

"Christ. That's Minnie Davenport."

"Oh!" Morgan's eyes light up with delighted surprise. He

glances down at her almost lovingly. Definitely creepily. "Hello again, friend."

"Go. Now," Rio says to us, motioning to the door. "They know we're here."

I nod, adrenaline pumping through my veins. We were so *close*.

"Xavier." Rio points at Minnie. "Carry her out."

Rio's ultimate command is this: If I can't carry Minnie despite a bum knee, I'm of no use to the Vultures and will be left behind as bones for Bianchi's men to break.

This is a brotherhood, true, but it must remain a strong one. You prove your worth until you can't anymore.

Gritting my teeth and picturing my dark maiden waiting for me at the end of all this, I bend toward the girl without argument. I scoop her into my arms, and we head down the stairs, Rio's and Morgan's feet a lot more stealthy than mine.

Out front, a black SUV screeches to a stop, blocking our escape route. Doors fly open, and Bianchi's men emerge, guns drawn.

"Back door, now!" Tempest slams into view, appearing in the doorframe with a blood-speckled face, shoving us back inside.

We pivot and crash through the kitchen. Bullets pepper the doorframe behind us. Rio returns fire over his shoulder while I shield the girl with my body.

Not because I owe Minnie any favors. But a hostage is a hostage, and beggars can't be choosers.

We burst into the backyard, and the other three vault over the fence before Morgan wheels around and takes Minnie from me, and I leap over, too, a lot less gracefully. My right knee *twangs* with a warning.

Tires squeal on the dirt road, paralleling us. I draw my head up and hitch my stride.

They've surrounded the house, penning us in.

Tempest dashes close to me, his eyes darting around, seeking options.

"The creek," he decides. "We can follow the current downstream."

Trusting him, I follow and plunge into the frigid water with the same lack of hesitation he does and let it carry us away from the ambush.

The icy water shocks my system, but I stay focused, allowing myself to be carried by an instinct that has served me well these past months.

The sheer cold of it paralyzes my body, and I struggle as my sodden clothes become leaden weights, dragging me deeper.

Up ahead, the creek bends out of sight. If we can make it around that corner unseen, we might slip Bianchi's net.

My lungs burn with effort, my limbs numb.

And then I hear them ... shouts echoing up from the creek's bankside. Their flashlights slice through the murk, piercing through our cover.

Rio floats to my side with such stealth, I nearly curse in surprise when I register the polished shine of his eyes through the darkness.

He places his finger to his lips in warning, then, without further ado, takes a deep breath and submerges, taking hold of me securely and bringing me down with him.

I clamp my mouth shut just in time. The world goes silent and dark.

Blindly, he drags us along the creek bottom, sheltered from view. My chest tightens, but I don't dare surface until Rio does, though apparently, he's a seal now because *he does not fucking surface.*

Finally, when my vision starts to tunnel, Rio pulls me upward—I believe. I've lost all sense of direction.

Once the water breaks over my face, I gasp and gulp air greedily.

Within seconds, I register that the flashlights and shouts have faded into the distance.

"Clover?" I asked between coughing fits, spitting out lingering droplets of creek water still trapped in my lungs.

"Safe, Rossi got them out of there before the reinforcements came," Rio replies calmly as if this kind of life-and-death operation is second nature to him.

I suppose it is.

Morgan grins at me as I climb onto the mud bank, his snake eyes glinting as Minnie dangles in his arms like a neglected rag doll.

"Aw, Sports Balls. You're shivering. Let's get you out of those wet clothes, love."

I snap him a look, but his insufferable attitude is slightly welcome after that insane chase-and-swim.

Because seeing that psychotic arsehole means I'm well enough alive.

CHAPTER 20
CLOVER

The heavy wooden door creaks open, and I step into Blackwood Manor, the others filing in behind me.

I'm one step onto the main staircase when Rossi instructs Morgan to carry her into the basement instead of carrying Minnie upstairs to one of the many available, though cobwebbed, rooms.

"The basement?" I echo, one hand on the banister.

It was terrifying enough that one minute, Rossi stared intently at the log cabin where his Vultures went, and the next, he cranked the van's engine and veered us into the woods, both Ardyn's and my heads knocking back at the sudden force, but now *Minnie* is unconscious and in Morgan's arms, looking like a ghost of her former self.

No, not even that. This is the shell a ghost leaves behind.

When the Vultures swooped into the van after Rossi's curt call to Tempest, all of them wet, furious, and smelling of algae and manure, pulling Minnie in with them, all I could do was gasp and cover my mouth with my hand.

Ardyn knew enough not to launch into questions, but I didn't.

"What the hell? Is that *Minnie*? Where's Lauren? What happened?"

All of my questions remain unanswered despite Xavier's apologetic look in response.

Rossi follows Morgan down the spiral stone staircase into the basement without hesitation, the rest of the men following.

"Ardyn," I say in a low voice as she approaches the staircase. "Go and grab some clothes, bandages, anything you can think of to help her."

Ardyn acknowledges my words by squeezing my upper arm before sprinting up the staircase.

I slip into the corridor leading to the basement with the Vultures.

Even though I trust them and love them, I'm not ready to leave these men with Minnie—a girl who was a nasty bully to me but does not deserve this punishing fate.

By the time I make it downstairs with the rest of them, Minnie's curled in the dusty corner, facing away from us and still unconscious, her filthy white shift barely clinging to her frail body. A row of light bulbs illuminates the vestibule before the arched corridor into the crypt. The air is cool in that way stone-lined basements are, and a chill seizes my body despite my sweater, jacket, and pants.

Minnie's shift is torn open, exposing her bare back.

Except it's *not* bare. Pink, puckered lines deform what I always assumed was flawless skin.

I step closer, inspecting the lines as they form into letters, and then—

Revenge.

That is what's carved down her spine, the letters in reverse.

I recoil even though Morgan confessed to me what he did. And I fucked him for it, let him spread me on his classroom table and enjoy the reward of hurting my enemy.

You were soaked the minute you found out what I did to your enemy, weren't you, little leaf?

"What ... the fuck?" I whisper hoarsely.

Morgan scoffs at Minnie's crumpled form.

"Another dead end. This darling clearly won't have much to give us."

He cracks his knuckles, his eyes growing small as he assesses her.

Rossi's face is stone. "We need to wake her up. Find out what she knows, regardless."

Rio crouches down close to Minnie, studying her intently. "She's been tortured extensively. Burn marks, lash marks ... she may not even be coherent when she wakes."

"I didn't want this." My voice rises as I say it. "I didn't think it would be like this..."

As he pushes to his feet, Rio exchanges a look of silent communication with Morgan.

One I don't enjoy witnessing.

Rio's eyes flash with anger for a moment before he composes himself.

I feel a pang in my chest, looking at Minnie's pitiful form. No one deserves this. Not even her.

Rossi turns to Morgan. "Get the ammonia capsules in my apothecary chest in Clover's room. That should rouse her."

Morgan's lips twist into a cruel smile.

And for the first time since meeting him, I want him to drop his crazed look and just be. Be human. Show the man he is in private with the desolate runes tattooed into his fingers, the scars he's inked over, and the sanity he works so hard to maintain due to his constant abuse as a child.

I take a deep breath, steadying my nerves, telling myself not to intercede when they're the professionals—not me.

Information is our only path forward.

But as Morgan returns and waves the capsule under Minnie's nose, crooning, and her body jolts awake, I vow to myself that I won't let them break her further.

Minnie's cornflower-blue eyes fly open, so bright and out of place on her dirt-coated skin.

Until they turn dark with fear.

She scrambles back against the wall, her whole body quivering.

Morgan grabs her chin, halting her from burying her face in her knees. "What were you doing all trussed up in a haunted cabin, Minnie Mouse?"

She stares at him, unable to even manage a whisper.

In watching the exchange, I notice her nails are ripped off. Who knows what other unspeakable horrors she's endured?

"I asked you a question, sweetheart," Morgan asks with feigned patience, his grip digging into her cheeks. "The least you can do after trying to kill me is answer it."

"I ... I don't know," she stammers, her voice barely audible.

Rossi steps forward, standing tall and broad above her. "You were the bait. We were meant to save Lauren Amos. Start talking."

The power of his words crackles through the air, and despite the heated tension in the room, my stomach spreads with ice.

Minnie shakes her head frantically, her long blond hair caked over and lying across her shoulders in chunks, swaying with her nerves. "Lauren was taken, too? I—oh, my God. She wasn't there. I-I didn't see her."

Rio sighs heavily. "Minnie doesn't know anything."

Morgan whirls on him.

"It was *your* neck she tried to stick a needle into, too. I can loosen her tongue, though..." he growls, reaching for his belt and drawing out a knife.

Minnie recoils violently from the sight of it, trembling uncontrollably and begging him to keep away from her.

I rush forward and push past Morgan. "Stop! Can't you see she's terrified?"

Morgan grins wickedly in response, unfazed by my horror.

To get *that* overexcited vision of him out of Minnie's head, I turn to her, kneeling slowly, and smile softly at her.

"Minnie, it's Clover. I can help you."

Minnie studies my face carefully, suspicion clouding her gaunt features. Her attention travels from my eyes and down my face, the remaining cogs in her head turning as she tries to figure out what I'm doing here.

Her focus halts at my neck.

Minnie's eyes bulge. "Why do you have that? *Why the fuck do you have my necklace?*"

"What?"

My mouth drops open. I glance down at the necklace Rio gave me, dangling close to my cleavage, its heart-shaped diamond glinting even when close to a crypt.

I swivel to Rio. "What is she talking about? This was a gift from you!"

Rio licks his lower lip in thought, saying nothing as his eyes say everything when they remain on mine.

I return to Minnie, picturing what's written on her back.

It wasn't only Morgan who broke into Minnie's dorm and avenged me.

"Somebody get me a bucket of warm water and some bandages." My voice shakes, but I glance up at my men sharply. "Ardyn should have grabbed some by now."

"Clover," Rossi warns in a stern voice next to me. "We don't have time for this."

I ignore him. Someone has to show Minnie kindness, and it's clear none of them have it in them to do so themselves.

After what feels like an eternity, Rio comes silently up to me, handing me bandages without saying a word. He returns to the spot no one knew he left in the first place in the corner of the room.

Minnie doesn't pull away as I slowly start cleaning her wounds with a cloth. Instead, she sobs.

My heart breaks.

I didn't want this. I didn't want this. I didn't...

Silence falls over us like a heavy blanket as the others exchange weighted glances but say nothing as I move from cleaning her arms to her legs and finally to her face, where she winces at every touch.

"We'll be back shortly," Rossi says, jerking his chin to his men to follow him up the stairs.

To talk about me and my incurable ability to disobey them, probably.

I push back the sick twist of guilt in my gut. If I had been stronger, smarter, I could have protected Minnie from this fate.

From the moment I opened Sarah Anderton's lost grimoire, it was my fault Minnie ended up in a run-down manor's basement as a bare semblance of herself.

And now the Vultures expect me to obey them after seeing

her this way. How can I when another innocent victim has been claimed by misery?

Minnie's a bitch, but she's not evil.

Though, I can't be mad at them for acting like who they are.

When Xavier's arms shielded me from Grimmer's gun, when Rossi kneeled by my side and stitched me with tender hands, his voice unexpectedly gentle ... they stirred something in me. A magnetic pull I'm terrified to name.

I brush Minnie's matted hair back, my fingers trembling. She looks so small, not an unforgiving tormenter at all, her wrists ringed in bruises.

There's a creak on the stairs, and I snap to attention.

Rossi descends, his hulking frame casting twisted shadows on the wall.

Rio follows, his face an emotionless mask.

"The perimeter's secure. No sign of Bianchi's men, but Tempest is on patrol to ensure it remains that way," Rossi's gravelly voice seems too loud in the heavy silence.

Xavier stalks in last, his gentle gaze finding mine, but I can sense the power coiled within him.

The power I'm drawn to against my better judgment.

I turn back to Minnie, hating myself. The Vultures are monsters, but now they are my monsters.

I'm terrified of what that makes me.

Minnie tries to speak but only manages a choked whisper.

"Shh, you don't have to talk yet," I soothe, dabbing her cheek with a damp cloth.

Rossi steps forward, his gaze intense. "No, her break's over. What happened to you, Minnie? What did they do?"

She swallows painfully. "They took more girls. Not just Lauren. From the arts building, the quad—" Her breath hitches as she fights back tears. "Girls who don't have many people looking for them if they leave. We were sent to TFU, after all, a college in the middle of nowhere where family could forget us. But the men who grabbed me ... they kept talking about a fortune. Getting rich for exchanging us."

I freeze, then feign ignorance when I ask, "What kind of fortune?"

"They kept mentioning another girl. Sarah." Minnie's voice strengthens with urgency. "She hid jewels. Some old, fat, ugly man named Bianchi's looking for it, and I don't know what the *fuck* that has to do with me. Please, let me go home."

Rossi's coal eyes burn, his jaw tight. "What else did they say?"

Minnie hesitates. Sobs. "They spoke about their boss being obsessed, convinced it will lead him to power beyond imagination."

The air charges with tense energy. Morgan cracks his knuckles, mumbling about how he should've killed his uncle when he had the chance. Rio's hand drifts to the gun at his hip. Xavier studies me intently as if ensuring I'm able to keep it together.

Their gazes prickle my skin. There's more to this fortune than we realize. And if Bianchi gets there first...

I squeeze the cloth I'm using on Minnie, my heart pounding.

I meet Rossi's gaze, recognizing my own turmoil in his dark eyes. But there's something else there too, a haunted specter that crosses his face and disappears before I can grasp its meaning.

Rossi turns away abruptly, tension etched in the stiff set of his shoulders. "We need to find where these kidnapped students are."

I rise, moving to touch Rossi's arm. He stills but doesn't look at me.

"What is it?" I ask softly. "There's something you're not saying."

Finally, he speaks so low I almost don't catch it. "The informant. The one who led us to Minnie." He pauses, then forces out the words. "They're called the Cimmerian Court."

My mind stalls on the name. I haven't heard of such a thing. "The what?"

"Oh, Rossi," Morgan *tsks*, though he wears a twisted smile. "Tell me you didn't."

"Didn't *what*?" Rio asks ominously, glancing among our small group.

"The Cimmerian Court is a collection of brilliant but morally compromised minds," Morgan answers brightly. "Embracing their dark inclinations, they manipulate events behind the scenes, engineer chaos, and control the narrative to serve their own interests. Quite the fun club membership, so I'm told. I would've joined had I not been ... so very welcomed ... into this one."

Cold shock washes over me. Secret societies are only whispered about in campus lore. They make politicians and rich men richer, but they're not violent and involved in death deals with the Mafia. They're not *real* in this world.

Then again, the Vultures shouldn't exist either.

"You've been working with them," I realize aloud.

Rossi's face is unreadable, but he doesn't deny it.

Betrayal pierces through me, sharp and unexpected. After everything we've survived together, this feels like a breach of trust. What else has he kept from us? From me?

I search Rossi's shuttered gaze, willing him to let me in. To explain why he protected this truth. But the wall between us remains.

Morgan's voice cuts through the tension. "We can deal with Rossi's extracurriculars later. Right now, we need to focus on Bianchi and how he knew to trap us."

I nod, pushing down my hurt and confusion. "We should talk about the key."

I pull it from my pocket, the iron cold and heavy in my palm.

Xavier studies it closely. "Rio told us about this. Do you think this could lead us to the hidden fortune?"

"Could be priceless jewels, gold, anything." Morgan grins wolfishly. "I bet that fortune would be very pretty to see. I'd fuck you on top of all that gold, little leaf."

Rossi shakes his head in irritation while my cheeks flame. "It's not about the money. The Court wants what that fortune can unlock—knowledge, power. Bianchi just craves the prestige." Rossi's voice hardens. "We need to keep it from both."

Morgan scoffs. "Don't get high and mighty. We're criminals, same as Bianchi. If we find that fortune, we take it. No mercy."

I suppress a shiver, remembering Morgan's capacity for cruelty. The way he dislocated his own fingers one by one to get out of Tempest's bindings. His cold smile as he described how he mutilated Minnie for me.

"Enough." Rio's rare voice cuts through the argument. "The fortune is leverage. We use it to control Bianchi, end his human trafficking, and avenge Clover." He levels his gaze at Minnie. "And the rest of his victims."

Xavier squeezes my shoulder as if sensing my internal conflict.

"I'm so sorry, Minnie." My throat tightens with emotion. "I never wanted you involved in any of this."

"She'll live," Morgan replies bluntly.

His eyes never leave Minnie's injuries.

My hands tremble. I'm wound tighter than a spring, my thoughts pinging wildly.

I want to help those girls. God, I want to. Memories haunt me—the fear, the desperation, the sickening helplessness as Grimmer shoved his hand between my legs. And that was when I had Xavier with me. These girls have no one.

But the risks are so damn high. If we go in guns blazing, we could all end up dead. Or worse, recaptured. Bianchi's cruelty knows no bounds. He delights in pain. I risk a glance over at Morgan.

He delights in breaking souls.

I absently rub at the scar on my stomach, reminders of how close I came to being destroyed. Can I willingly walk back into it?

Yet how can I not? To know girls just like me are being brutalized and debased while I do nothing ... it eats away at my conscience.

I'm paralyzed, watching the three men I've come to care for tear each other apart over me.

But I see past their bravado and swagger. Underneath, they are each crippled by fear. Fear of losing the tenuous control they have. Fear of being unable to defend those they care about. Fear of being destroyed by the very darkness they thought they could own.

Their fear mirrors my own.

I used to think the world was black and white, good and evil.

But now I see only endless shades of gray.

CHAPTER 21
XAVIER

My eyes snap open to the sound of pounding on my door. I sit up in bed, heart racing, the thin mattress creaking beneath me. I know it's them. The Irish. They've found me again.

I clench my fist, my reattached ring finger remaining straight and stiff. Phantom pains shoot through my mangled knee. Reminders of what they did to me. Of how they took everything.

"Xavier!" The pounding continues as a gruff voice calls my name. "Time to pay the piper, youngblood."

I squeeze my eyes shut, willing them to go away. But I know they won't. They own me now ever since I made the mistake of falling for Meghan O'Malley, the daughter of their mob boss. I was a foolish lad then, an arrogant footballer who thought I could get away with anything. But they taught me differently.

They grabbed me off the streets of Dublin in broad daylight. Took me to a warehouse where they crushed my knee with a sledgehammer. The pain was blinding, unimaginable. I screamed and begged for mercy. But they just laughed.

Then their boss came in, face red with rage. He grabbed my left hand and took out a hunting knife. I struggled against the men holding me down, but it was useless. With one swift motion, he lopped off my ring finger.

"You don't deserve this anymore," he snarled, holding up my severed digit.

I howled in agony, thrashing violently. But the pain only grew worse.

I passed out at some point. When I came to, they told me I now belonged to them. That I would spend the rest of my days paying for what I did to the boss's daughter. They sold me off to Bianchi. And now I do his bidding, no questions asked.

I wake with a groan, rubbing my face.

There were no sounds at my door—just my pounding head.

I stand slowly, my bad knee nearly buckling. I take a deep breath and limp toward the door, understanding that what I just experienced was a nightmare, but my *life* is a nightmare.

It never hurts to double-check that my demons didn't follow me into daylight.

No matter how far I run or where I hide, they will always find me. The Irish branded me. The Mafia owns me. And I will never be free of them.

I step out into the dim hallway, my thoughts churning.

There are missing girls out there, students from TFU under Bianchi's cruelty, just like I was. Just another loose end for Bianchi to tie up, another life to extinguish.

How many more until it's enough? How much blood has to be spilled before I'm finally free of this?

I pass by the library and pause. Inside, Rossi sits alone by the fireplace, a glass of whiskey in his hand. His expression is haunted, shoulders slumped in a rare moment of vulnerability. Of all people, Rossi understands the burdens I carry. The choices I'm forced to make.

I step into the room.

"Rough day?" I ask.

He glances up, mouth tightening. Takes a long swallow from his glass. Doesn't answer.

I sit across from him. Rossi's secrets are his own, but the umber in his eyes is like mine.

"Sometimes I wonder if it's all worth it," I say quietly. "Surviving."

Rossi is silent for a long moment.

He finally says, "Sometimes there are no good choices. Only less bad ones."

Rossi meets my gaze, and I understand. The plan is in motion. Bianchi will fall if Rossi has to die to do it.

I turn, staring into the fire. Its warmth does nothing to thaw the ice in my veins.

"She shouldn't be part of this world. Clover deserves more than fear and violence."

Rossi sets down his glass with a hollow clink. "None of us deserves this life. But it's the hand we've been dealt."

My fingers curl into fists. Since being smuggled into America, I've done everything to prove my loyalty to the Vultures. I've become the ruthless monster they wanted me to be. But Clover makes me question everything. I want to shelter her from the darkness I've been drowning in for so long.

"I can't let anything happen to her," I say through gritted teeth.

Rossi rises from his chair and places a hand on my shoulder. His eyes bore into mine. "Careful, Xavier. Don't let your feelings cloud your judgment."

I know he's right. Emotion is a liability in this world. But when I'm with Clover, the ice inside me thaws. I'd burn cities to ash to keep her safe.

Rossi sighs, his expression softening. "Just don't do anything foolish. We have enough enemies."

He squeezes my shoulder once before turning away and walking out.

The fire continues to crackle, indifferent to the war raging inside me between duty and desire.

The windowless corridor envelops me as I make my way back to my room, the only light coming from the pale faces of aristocrats painted to sternly look down upon pedestrians in their hallway. My footsteps echo down the empty corridor.

I reach her door and pause, listening.

Silence.

I hope Clover's finding some peace tonight. Since we brought her here, she's had trouble sleeping, often waking from vivid nightmares. I wish I could banish the ghosts that haunt her dreams.

As I continue, the familiar scent of vanilla lingers in the air. I imagine her hair splayed across the pillow, her chest rising and falling in a steady rhythm. Even when we're apart, she's with me.

I step into my bedroom and shut the door firmly behind me. In the darkness, I can almost feel her hand on my cheek, her body pressed close to mine.

Clover makes me believe I could be more than what I am—that I'm still worthy.

I move to the window and look out over the shadowy grounds. I stand at the window a moment longer, steeling myself. The full moon casts an eerie glow across the estate. Somewhere, an owl hoots, breaking the stillness.

I move to the mahogany desk and open the top drawer, removing an envelope. Inside are documents I managed to smuggle in. A fake passport, a one-way plane ticket to Australia, my escape.

It was in my mailbox at the boys' dorm at TFU, Camden House. I'd come across the plain manila envelope a few weeks ago, before Clover and I were taken in the woods. I have my suspicions it was orchestrated by Rio, secretly and quietly, as a way to get me out of Bianchi's clutches before I get in too deep the way he is.

The envelope crunches in my clenched hand.

Bianchi and his Vultures threaten everything I hold dear, especially Clover.

But Clover sees the man I want to be, not the monster I've become.

I trace my finger over what would be my new name, a free identity, on the passport.

A reminder of why I have to deny myself this single escape.

With a flick of my wrist, I toss the papers into the fireplace. Flames lick at the edges, slowly turning a fresh start to ash.

But it's a stand I have to take if Clover is ever going to get free of this life. I won't leave her behind, no matter how much it kills me.

With lowered eyes, I glance at the empty desk drawer, the space like an open wound.

CHAPTER 22
CLOVER

"Clover, a word?"

I rise reluctantly, casting one last worried glance at Minnie. I'd spent the night with her in the basement even though she wanted nothing to do with me and would rather hiss and kick than receive any more "kindness" from me while shackled in a basement.

I can't say I blame her.

But Xavier came down a few minutes earlier with coffee for everyone and sits beside her now, murmuring something that makes her lips curve.

"Sure," I say to Rossi as he looms at the bottom of the stairs, his mouth a sharp, downward line. "I'd like to have a word with you, too."

Specifically about moving Minnie to one of the many free guest bedrooms rather than giving her a dank chamber for a hotel.

Rossi leads me up the chilly stone staircase into the manor's opulent foyer, his expression troubled.

"You wanted to speak with me?" I prompt when he continues to lead me around in silence.

"Not here."

He gestures for me to follow him outside into the cold morning air. Rossi guides me to a secluded part of the courtyard, empty of flowers and trees that likely put the courtyard in gorgeous relief during spring and summer.

Now, it's gray and dry, dark and foggy, the oxygen I breathe as bitter as the neglected statues surrounding us.

Once we're alone, Rossi turns to face me, the distant light of the sun casting his rugged features in white and gray.

"I didn't want you to find out this way," he begins quietly. "I'd prefer if you not know at all, but I can't dismiss the number of times you've proved yourself."

I stifle the swell of pride that wants to stretch my mouth into a smile. Rossi isn't one to send—or receive—gratitude very well, so I just nod sagely.

"Now that you've learned their name, I'm confident you'll stop at nothing to discover more about the Court, including putting yourself in more jeopardy. So I will stand here with you now and cut you off at the knees before you can go any further."

Well. There goes my gratitude.

"The Cimmerian Court ... they helped me once, a long time ago. I owed them and always paid my debts. But when I learned they had details on a missing girl on campus, I reached out and called in another favor."

My breath stutters. I figured Rossi was gearing up to tell me to mind my own business and stay safe and sound in the barbican he's created for me. Instead, he's giving me information rather than making me craft and dig relentlessly for a new adventure.

I try to make sense of it all. "Why would you keep this from the Vultures?"

There's a rustling to our right before I can answer. I turn to see Tempest and Ardyn step through the remains of a stone arbor with dead, leafless vines clinging to its sides.

My stomach lurches at their ominous expressions as they approach. What *more* could happen after last night?

Rossi crosses his arms. He speaks once Tempest and Ardyn join our circle.

"Morgan and the others, they can't know the full truth about my past. About what I've done." He meets Tempest's solemn gaze. "What I did to Nico Bianchi."

I suck in a sharp breath.

Ardyn grabs my hand, hers cold, bony, and thin, mine pulsing with the electricity of fraying nerves.

"Do you remember," she starts, "where we were when Mila died?"

"Of course," I answer.

Mila, Ardyn, and I snuck into a black-tie event in the city. Ardyn and I were prone to sneaking out when our parents tried to keep us locked down too tight. Mila was our vibrant, spontaneous, morally gray friend who often tempted us to do what we weren't supposed to. There, we discovered a black market auction in the basement, and the events after that are too unspeakable to remember clearly.

It all led to a brutal car accident where Mila died, Ardyn lost her memory, and I didn't see Ardyn for two years until she showed up at Titan Falls as a freshman.

I'd lost my two best friends that night. I've never recovered from that kind of heartbreak.

"What does that have to do with our situation now?" I ask her.

"That night at the party, when I was separated from you and Mila, I wandered into the wrong section of the auction," Ardyn continues. "And I witnessed—" Her eyes dart to Rossi's, the whitened sun breaking through the clouds and slicing over her eyes, before coming back to me.

"She saw me kill Nico," Rossi finishes for her.

The revelation hits me like a blow. "That was—Nico Bianchi was Morgan's father."

Rossi gives a single, terse nod, his jaw tight.

My heart pounds against my ribs. "And ... he's the one who ordered your wife and daughter to be killed."

We're quiet for a long moment, the weight of Rossi's confession hanging heavily in the air near my mouth.

"The Court assisted in helping me locate where the auction was being held and ensured that Nico would be there," Rossi explains, though he doesn't have to.

Nico Bianchi made him watch his family die, then took him and forced him into doing their dirty deeds rather than die with them. If I had the skills, I'd destroy that son of a bitch, too.

The only hitch in my understanding is Morgan. He doesn't know. Do I owe him the truth with our delicious sex and tightening bond?

"And now you owe the Court again," I say, angling my head to search Rossi's face better. "Because they gave you Minnie's location."

I think about all those moments I pushed and pushed and pushed for Lauren to be found. Getting frustrated with the Vultures' lack of urgency when girls' lives were being ruined.

Except, all this time, Rossi was working on it. Making sacrifices...

"You made another deal with them because of me," I say.

The muscles in Rossi's cheeks work overtime. "I take debts

on rarely. When necessary. The moment my collar is off, and I remove the last Bianchi from this world, I won't be a servant to anyone ever again." Rossi steps closer, his eyes brimming with ferocity. "I can't risk how Morgan would react upon hearing this. You have to trust me, Clover. Do not share this wit"

I glance among Rossi, Tempest, and Ardyn, knowing we've crossed a line from which there's no return.

I ask my best friend, "You've held on to this piece of information this entire time? Didn't tell me?"

Ardyn rubs her lips together, her cheekbones protruding from her pallid skin as she works to explain. "This isn't my confession to make, Clo. We've been through so much together, but I can't speak for Rossi." She glances softly at Tempest. "Nor can I speak for your brother."

"The Court has ties to Sarah Anderton's legacy, too," Rossi adds reluctantly. "If we can gain access to their knowledge, they could lead us closer."

My fingers tighten around the iron key in my pocket, its three teeth biting into my palm.

"That would mean more favors from them," I say.

"There's something else you should know." Rossi hesitates. "My inside contact is someone highly placed in the Court."

Tempest's eyes narrow. "The informant who gave us Minnie's location?"

"You could call him that." A shadow crosses Rossi's face. "We have a complicated history."

I sense there's more he's not saying, but I don't press.

"Can this person be trusted?" Ardyn asks.

Rossi is silent for a long moment. "As much as anyone in the Court can be. But they know things no one else does. With their guidance, we might just pull this off."

I think of the iron key. Its mystery is still unsolved. "Can they tell us about the treasure? And this?" I hold up the key.

Rossi nods. "If anyone knows, it's them. I'll reach out and set up a meeting."

My pulse quickens. Finally, a chance to further unravel the Anderton secrets.

Rossi meets my eyes, grim. "It won't be easy. The Court plays a long game, manipulating things behind the scenes. We'll need to be careful."

I think of the girls still missing and Morgan's thirst for vengeance. We're running out of time. "It's our only move left."

Tempest scowls. "I don't trust them. This is a mistake."

"Noted," Rossi says evenly. "But I've made my decision."

Tempest looks ready to argue before Ardyn steps in. "It's risky," she says gently. "But have faith in us."

Tempest's expression relaxes as he gazes at her. After a moment, he nods.

Rossi turns to me. "For now, keep that key safe." His eyes are grave. "It may unlock more than you're prepared to endure."

CHAPTER 23
ROSSI

The rain drums against the window, each droplet a reminder of the blood I've spilled.

Nico Bianchi being one of many.

I wish his death had relieved me of the turmoil in my heart and the hurricane in my head, but his corpse lying before me did nothing to alleviate the cold storm swirling and trapping my soul inside this husk of a man's body.

I was most upset that his brain and skull matter ruined my shoes.

Nico's death didn't cure anything. My wife didn't come back from the dead, nor did my daughter get to be the twenty-year-old she should be now. Instead, I was gifted with a new burden: the training of Nico's son, Hunter Morgan, to become a Mafia leader, all while having his father's blood on my hands.

The secret weighs heavy, threatening to suffocate as I get to know the man Morgan could be and the trauma his family has scraped across his body, but I must keep up appearances—for the sake of the Vultures.

"Rossi," a voice calls from behind me, snapping me back to the present.

It's Morgan, the man I might just end up regretting killing if he knew the truth. I turn to face him, my expression unreadable.

"Any news?" I ask, my voice steady and low.

"Nothing yet." He grimaces, his impatience palpable. "But this storm, it feels like an omen."

"Let's not be superstitious," I reply.

But as much as I want to believe otherwise, something wicked this way comes, and it's about to walk through our door.

"We're all waiting for you downstairs." Morgan drawls, "As usual."

I flick the rest of my cigar ash in the ashtray balanced on the windowsill and exit my study, our journey to the sitting room silent.

The tension in the room is palpable as I step through and join in awaiting the emissary's arrival. Morgan paces while Rio leans against the wall, coiled tight. Tempest cleans his guns with restless energy.

Only Xavier seems relaxed, lounging on the couch with a casual grace. But his eyes follow me as I move to the window overlooking the front courtyard.

Clover and Ardyn wait upstairs. None of my men argued when I made the point of keeping our women far away from the Court's curious, prying eyes.

A sleek black car pulls up outside. Its passenger appears, clad in a dark-tailored suit that clings to his athletic frame. Even from a distance, he is striking and noble, almost cruel with his carved features.

He approaches the building with languid confidence, raven

hair tousling in the midnight breeze. I steel myself.

"He's here," I say.

A knock sounds at the door. Xavier rises to answer it, muscles rippling defensively beneath his shirt and his gait much smoother. He's kept up with my physical therapy orders.

Xavier ushers the emissary in wordlessly.

Up close, his dark hair is a styled masterpiece, contrasting sharply with his icy stone-gray eyes that never miss a thing. Instantly, the atmosphere seems to charge with a pull you want to resist but somehow can't. Yet even as he smiles, sharpening everyone's defenses in the room, I glimpse his layers. Well hidden from most, but never from me.

He's the kind of man who knows his effect on people and manipulates it to serve his own interests.

And despite the rain outside, not a single droplet mars his pristine appearance.

"Cavanaugh Nightshade," he introduces himself, voice smooth as velvet. "A mouthful, I know. You can call me Cav." He extends a hand, and I grasp it.

"Rossi." My voice comes out rough, betraying my unease.

His lips quirk.

We size each other up. A spider recognizing vultures in its midst.

"Good evening, gentlemen," Cav addresses the rest of the room in his chilling voice. "I'm the consul of the Cimmerian Court, second-in-command to the Sovereign and your liaison into our cloaked, elite world."

"Well, that's fucking obvious," Morgan quips, his hand instinctively reaching for the knife at his hip.

"Please," the consul says, a cruel smile playing on his lips. "There's no need for violence. At least, not yet."

His eyes slither over and lock onto mine.

Cav chuckles, a chilling sound. And here I thought I'd met all the soulless and the damned.

Xavier shifts beside me, inching closer to Tempest with his line of guns on the dining room table. But Rio meets this interloper's gaze, expression closed.

"You have a proposition for us," Rio prompts.

Cav inclines his head. "My brethren believe an alignment could prove ... mutually beneficial."

His voice is pure sin, crafted to tempt and coerce. But beneath the cordiality, there's an edge.

A reminder that he could end us with a snap of his elegant fingers if we step out of line.

"And if we refuse this 'alignment'?" Morgan asks, brow cocked.

Cav's smile widens, like someone behind the scenes was reminded to pull the strings at both corners of his mouth. "Let's not dwell on unpleasant hypotheticals, shall we?"

But Cav's gaze keeps sliding back to me, assessing, calculating.

He can sense I'm the one he needs to convince.

"The Cimmerian Court can provide the information you seek on the iron key you've discovered and, thus, the Anderton fortune's location," he offers. "As well as the whereabouts of the missing girls."

The others stir at this, a renewed appetite flickering in their eyes. We've been chasing those leads for over a month, always one step behind. But the cost...

"And what price would you extract for such generosity?" I ask evenly.

Cav pretends to think this over. "Merely a partnership. We provide the intelligence, and you acquire the assets. A percentage for us, the rest for you."

"Dirty money for dirty hands," Xavier mutters.

Cav's gaze swivels to him.

"Mind yourself, baby bird. I've plucked far more defiant feathers than yours."

Xavier bristles but falls silent at my pointed look.

I turn back to Cav. "You ask us to become your pets. Retrieve on command." My lip curls. "The Vultures aren't shedding a master to find a new one."

"No?" Cav arches a brow. "Even if it means claiming your last revenge against the Bianchi family? Rescuing your lost chicks from the wolves?" His eyes bore into mine, seeing too much. "We all have debts that must be paid, *signore*. What price for your vengeance?"

I tense, claws of anger and longing raking my soul, though my expression betrays nothing. He dangles what I most desire before me, knowing I cannot resist its allure. But if I take this deal, let him lead me further into blindness...

Will I ever find my way back into the light?

"Define partnership," Xavier demands, arching a brow.

"Loyalty. Power," he replies enigmatically. "And in return, you will help us shape the fate of those who dare challenge our reign."

I feel the weight of my men's stares, their uncertainty hanging heavy in the air. This choice could irrevocably bind us to the Court, and we already have so many ties around our wrists.

But it could also give us the power to shatter Bianchi's empire and reclaim what he stole from us so long ago.

"Let's say we agree to your terms," Tempest speaks up, his voice strained but his posture relaxed as he reclines in his chair. "How can we be sure you'll hold up your end of the deal?"

"Trust is a rare commodity in our world," the consul replies. "But I assure you, the Cimmerian Court does not make promises it cannot keep. The question is, do you trust yourselves enough to accept our offer?"

Morgan replies with a smirk, "And what if we don't pay up? You'll smite us with your mighty quill?"

"Worse," Cav responds without a flicker of emotion. "I'll make sure you wish we had."

I meet each of their gazes in turn. Morgan, his psychotic impulses barely restrained, starving for violence. Xavier, his defensive instincts warring with his simmering uncertainty. Rio, silent and watchful, his thoughts unreadable.

And Tempest, my son from another life, smelling of metal, gunpowder, and loyalty.

In their eyes, I recognize the same visceral need that rakes at me, the craving for retribution we have nursed all these years in the dark.

I straighten.

"We accept the terms of the bargain," I say, my voice low. "You and your Court will have our cooperation."

The consul's lips curve into a knowing smile. He inclines his head in acquiescence.

"A wise choice. I will inform my Sovereign that we have an understanding."

He extends a hand toward me. After a breath of hesitation, I step forward and grasp it.

An unspoken pact sealed in flesh and bone.

The contact seems to linger a moment too long, both of us attempting to exert silent dominance through the press of palm against palm. Then we release. I withdraw from the richness of his cologne, a new form of caution in my hooded gaze.

Cav's smile widens, sharp and cunning.

He has us now.

He reaches into his inside suit pocket and takes out a folded piece of paper, which he smooths and lays on the table. The map shows a part of an underground tunnel network marked with an "X."

"The girls are being held here." Cav's voice drips with satisfaction. "A subterranean chamber accessible only through this abandoned mine two hours outside of town."

Beside the map, he places a black-and-white photograph with yellowed edges of an antique vault door and an old architectural drawing full of symbols and coded notations. It's been amended over time, with newer notes overlaying older ones. "This, gentlemen, could be where Sarah Anderton hid her jewels—in a secret vault beneath the estate that became Titan Falls campus. A vault designed by her lover, a renowned architect and craftsman of the time."

Morgan's eyebrows leap. "Sarah Anderton's lover? X marks the spot, indeed."

"Is that Lily Anderton's father?" Xavier asks, pondering with his hands on his hips as he leans over the photo. "Clover would—"

A harsh clunk sounds out of Tempest's boot hitting Xavier's heel under the table.

Cav stares at the exchange with the interest of a snake tracking a gerbil.

Dammit. He can't become curious about Clover. I simply won't allow it.

"And what is your third piece of information?" I ask, redirecting Cav's attention.

Cav leans over the table, his eyes catching the ambient light as he flips the photo and points at the intricate drawing of an oval-shaped gem. "Do you see this magnificent creation right here? It's not just a rock; it's legend incarnate. Some say it's the cursed heart of Sarah Anderton herself, crystallized into the most alluring ruby ever known to mankind. Forget the Estrela de Fura, that 101-carat tinker toy and largest known ruby. If this exists, it would render it a mere footnote in history."

He leans back, folding his arms. "Rumor has it, when Anderton was burned for witchcraft, the flames couldn't consume this gem. They say it contains the sum of her mystical powers, her rage, her undying love—essentially, her immortal soul. The Heart, as it's aptly named, is purportedly 133 carats of unparalleled beauty and menace."

"And you want it," I deduce.

His eyes meet mine. "The Court doesn't just want it; they crave it. As for its power or curse, who's to say what's real? But one thing is certain: anyone who possesses The Heart holds the key to untold influence in this greed-driven world. So, what are we waiting for? Shall we make history, or shall we let history make us?"

I glance at each of my men. We don't have to like it, but we don't have much choice. If the Cimmerian Court hides their own Titan Falls treasures and artifacts, we'll never get to them without their permission. Clover's discoveries have been miracles.

Christ, if the Court decides to show interest in her...

As Cav prepares to leave, he stops under the formal room's archway and looks them over. "Make no mistake, gentlemen. This is a pact sealed in blood. The Court will collect its due."

"Yes, because we are rather *unfamiliar* with death deals and life-altering lessons," Morgan says, waving him off with sarcastic flair. "Off you go, Voldemort."

Our pact hangs heavy in the air as we watch the consul's retreating form. The click of his heels fades down the corridor.

Xavier is the first to break our heavy quiet.

"If it's even bloody possible," he says, "Morgan's met his match."

"Well." Morgan runs a hand through his rumpled blond hair and glances at the empty archway. "I'm kind of turned on by that man."

Rio shifts in the corner, arms crossed over his chest. His face is indecipherable, as always. Xavier leans back, brow furrowed.

"It's a risk," Tempest says finally. "But one worth taking if we can get the girls back." His jaw tightens. "And make Bianchi pay for taking my sister."

I stroke my chin in thought. "We knew this wouldn't be easy."

A round of solemn nods, except for Morgan, who spits on his palm and holds it out. "Then let's do this. Till the bloody end, boys."

One by one, we add our hands to the pact. Flesh pressed to flesh, marked by ink and scars and fresh cuts.

Perhaps we are damned. But as we turn to our tasks, resolve settles like mercury in my bones. If this is the road to ruin, we will blaze forward without hesitation. And take as many of the bastards down with us as we can.

I glance at the cobwebs clinging to the corners of the room and dripping from a once extravagant chandelier above the long table. This place was once our shelter from the storm.

Now, we venture into the heart of it, chasing justice on the wings of demons.

CHAPTER 24
CLOVER

A musty scent fills my nose as I trace my finger along the dusty spines of ancient books. I'm upstairs in the old manor's library, a secret sanctuary I discovered during my aimless wanderings when recovering from my bullet wound.

The Vultures have kept me isolated, cooped up in this crumbling estate for my own protection, but I'm once again restless between the shifts Ardyn and I take in sitting and taking care of Minnie now that we convinced the Vultures to move her to a guest room. My only solace has been these books —artifacts from Titan Falls's shadowed history that shed flickering light onto the town's dark underbelly.

I slide a leather-bound volume from the shelf, its title long faded. The yellowed pages crackle as I flip through. My eyes catch on tales of bootlegging, mob wars, and corrupt officials ruling with an iron fist.

I pause on a sketch of Blackwood Manor in its prime, stately columns and manicured gardens. It's hard to believe it's the same decrepit building I'm standing in now, floorboards rotten, wallpaper peeling. Rossi's lair.

I shudder, the cool air raising goose bumps on my skin.

I slide the key from my pocket, running my thumb over the intricate flowers engraved at the top. Its weight feels heavy with promise in my palm.

The creaking floorboards announce Rossi's arrival before I see him. I slip the key back into my pocket swiftly as he appears in the doorway.

His presence seems to fill the small room, his smothered energy almost palpable as he maintains a leash on it.

"Enjoying the reading material?"

His casual voice has an undercurrent of tension. My skin prickles, the air suddenly alive between us.

"Just passing the time." I keep my tone light.

Rossi draws closer, his dark gaze searching my face.

Being near him is intoxicating and terrifying all at once. He's a man of contradictions. Ruthless yet strangely tender, coldly logical but with a buried streak of passion.

I hesitate, wary of getting burned. While my heart is ready to throw caution aside, my mind knows it's too dangerous to let him in.

Rossi seems equally conflicted between his desire at war and his instincts to remain detached and in control.

"You know why I keep you up here, away from it all." His low voice is almost gentle.

I bristle at his words, that familiar frustration rising up at his ability to read my mind.

"Is that how you see me?" I step closer, meeting his gaze unflinchingly. "A delicate, breakable thing that needs protecting? I'm not nearly as brittle as you think."

Rossi blinks. At this moment, a crack forms in that impenetrable armor he cloaks himself in.

But just as quickly, the shutters come down again.

"Maybe not," he concedes. "But there are some things you're better off being shielded from."

I scoff. "Careful. Your Tempest is showing."

Irritation wars with sympathy when I'm alone with Rossi. I know he's endured terrible things, though the details remain murky. Can I blame him for wanting to protect me from the same pain? Yet I refuse to be cast aside, relegated to the role of helpless bystander.

I reach out, hesitantly touching his arm. Rossi tenses but doesn't pull away.

"You don't have to go through this alone, whatever this is," I say softly. "Let me help you."

For a moment, Rossi looks torn, vulnerability flickering across his face. But then his expression closes down.

"I can't," he says gruffly, retreating from my touch.

I let him keep his distance, refusing to let the hurt show on my face.

"Then tell me about the meeting downstairs. How did it go with the Court?"

Rossi clenches, then unclenches his jaw before answering. "A success, I suppose. I made a necessary deal."

I nod, trying to keep my expression neutral even as annoyance simmers. Rossi's evasiveness about Cavanaugh Nightshade grates, making me wonder what transpired between them.

"A necessary deal," I repeat. "That's rather vague. What could someone like Cav possibly offer you?"

Rossi's jaw tightens, his expression darkening. "How do you know his name? Dammit, Clover, did you eavesdrop?"

I bristle at his parental tone. "It was only when he entered and introduced himself. I stayed near the top of the stairs. He didn't see me."

Rossi sighs, casting his eyes to the ceiling. The gesture reveals a rare, unguarded moment, a crack in his usual impenetrable facade.

"Cav provided us with some leverage. Information we needed. I didn't have much choice but to make a bargain, distasteful as it was."

"What did he want in return?" I ask quietly.

Rossi's gaze clouds over. "Nothing that concerns you."

I flinch at the harsh finality in his tone. Rossi's refusal to confide in me stings, awakening old feelings of being shut out and overlooked. Unbidden, my imagination conjures scenarios of Cav extracting favors from Rossi, each one more disturbing than the last.

Rossi seems to read my thoughts on my face. His expression softens slightly, and he reaches out, brushing his knuckles lightly over my cheek.

"Clover, listen to me. I told you before you can trust me. That hasn't changed." His obsidian eyes examine mine, willing me to believe him.

My faithless heart skips a beat at his touch, my skin tingling. I'm sharply aware of his physical presence, the coiled strength in his powerful frame. Heat blooms inside me despite my misgivings.

He moves nearer still, close enough that I catch his cigar and sandalwood scent. The room suddenly feels small and stifling. I'm finding it hard to breathe normally.

Rossi moves from my cheek to brush a strand of hair from my face with unexpected tenderness. My lips part, and I sway toward him unconsciously.

We're a hair's breadth away, suspended on the brink of something unknown.

His phone rings shrilly, shattering the moment. We spring apart, and the spell breaks. Rossi turns away, jaw clenched as he answers. The call is brief. When he ends it, the walls are back up, the intimacy gone.

"I have to go," he says curtly. "Stay here."

His tone accepts no argument. He strides from the room without another word.

Alone again, I sink down on the moth-eaten sofa. I wish I could believe Rossi and trust he has my best interests at heart. But his caginess over Cav and Rossi's use of him at the moment we're desperate raises too many red flags.

I think back to what little I know about the consul of the Cimmerian Court. Cav's appearance alone is enough to make my blood run cold. Deals with men like him never end well.

I know next to nothing about the stoic leader of the Vultures. Rossi keeps himself locked down as tight as a vault. But in rare, unguarded moments, I've glimpsed flickers of a man haunted by his past and tormented by demons he can't escape.

My thoughts drift back to the tense exchange when Cav arrived. There's history there, a twisted dynamic between them I don't yet grasp.

Restless, I rise and begin to pace the confines of the dust-coated room. Rossi's abrupt departure leaves me unsettled, certain something pivotal just occurred.

I'm roused from my musings by hurried footsteps and muffled voices in the corridor. Pressing my ear to the door, I make out Rossi's clipped tone, followed by Morgan's sarcastic intonation about something called a Heart. Most of their words are indistinct, but the tone sounds urgent.

My pulse kicks up.

I strain to hear more, but the voices fade as they move down the hall. My imagination swirls with possibilities, each more ominous than the last. The abducted girls ... Bianchi's next move ... the Court's fresh involvement.

A thousand scenarios, none of them good.

CHAPTER 25
CLOVER

The amber glow of candlelight flickers across the Vultures' faces, their outlines dancing along the walls of the manor's drawing room. Rossi stands at the head of the long mahogany table, his dark eyes glinting as he addresses his team.

"We have less than twelve hours before Bianchi's men move the girls." His voice is low but cuts through the tension swirling in the room. "Cav called. The bastard kept that detail from us during the meet."

Around the table, jaws tighten, and fingers curl into fists. Morgan snarls a feral, unhinged sound.

"I'll carve the information out of that dark wizard's smug face."

Rio shoots him a warning look.

Hidden on the grand staircase just outside, I hold my breath, straining to catch their entire conversation.

Rossi continues, "We move out at dusk. Standard formation, no deviations."

His eyes flick up toward the foyer, and for a heart-stopping moment, I'm certain he senses my presence. But his focus returns to the team.

Rossi adds, "Clover comes with us. Her skills could prove useful."

Surprise bolts through me. Rossi's trusting me with this mission? Warmth blooms over the shock, only to curdle into apprehension. Why does he want me to come along?

Tempest scoffs, breaking the tension. "No way. If she gets herself into trouble, she'll become a liability. *My* distraction. I'd drop everything to get her out."

Rossi silences him with a look. "As would we, Tempest. But it's highly unlikely the kidnapped girls will move from one group of terrifying men to another. Clover can be that buffer. She has a trusting face and empathy—both of which we lack."

My mouth lifts at his compliment.

"You can't deny your sister's proven herself. Either that, or we use Ardyn. You won't like either choice, so I'm making the decision for you, as is my right as the leader of the Vultures. This time, we do this properly. Ardyn will remain here and prep the manor for any survivors, and Clover comes with me. Failure is not an option."

There's finality in Rossi's tone. Tempest concedes with a jutting chin, but at least he's not listing my flaws and all the reasons to keep me sequestered in this manor.

Progress.

My pulse thrums as I creep back up the stairs to let Ardyn in on all my spying. Soon, I'll be descending into the dark with them.

Be *part* of them.

THE RUMBLE of the van reverberates through my bones as we careen down the winding forest road. Craggy rock faces and towering pines blur past the windows. Xavier drives, one hand on the wheel, the other tapping out a chaotic rhythm on his thigh.

In the back seat, Tempest checks his gun for the dozenth time, while Rio stares stoically ahead. Morgan rides shotgun, fiddling with a wickedly curved dagger.

Unease coils in my gut. We're headed deep into the mountains to a hidden mine shaft far from any signs of life. The coordinates came from the Court, which Rossi assures is solid intel. But dealing with Cav must have meant that one of my Vultures, or all of them, made a deep sacrifice.

And they did all that for girls they don't know and will likely never see again; these men are proud of their lack of morals and set in their violent ways.

There is still humanity in them. Perhaps I'm coaxing it more to the surface. I would love it if that were the case.

Xavier notices my discomfort. "Should we have another chat? What's going on in that mind of yours?"

I twist my lips as I look out the window. "It's just ... why does Cav toy with us like this? Giving information piecemeal, making us dance."

Rossi hears my question. "You're right to be wary. But Cav's games serve a purpose for both sides. The rules of this world are complex, Miss Callahan."

I digest his words. The hierarchies, allegiances, and resentments in this underworld have shaped all the men in this car, and so much more. Rossi and Cav circle each other like two mountain lions, neither fully friend nor foe.

Up ahead, the mine shaft's entrance gapes like a monstrous

mouth. Morgan kills the lights and headlights, enveloping us in darkness. I shiver.

Focus, Clover.

The last thing I want is to make them regret choosing me and not Ardyn. I'm not getting scared *now*.

Our van crawls closer to the mine's entrance. Quietly, we all step out, clad in black leather, denim, and cotton.

As he passes, Morgan shoves a small switchblade into my hand.

"Just in case," he says with a smile, the whites of his teeth flashing before disappearing again.

The men put me in the middle, with Rossi and Tempest leading, Xavier and Morgan at my side, and Rio patrolling the back.

With our flashlights aimed forward, we enter into another abandoned, neglected place, holding more old, forgotten souls than I want to try to count.

Ancient wooden beams, cracked and splintered, barely hold up the crumbling rock walls as we pass under them.

This place is a tomb.

"Well, isn't this cozy," Morgan says, sweeping his light over the narrow tunnel. "Really feeling the whole horror-movie vibe. You know, the one where the pretty girl trips and gets murdered in the first five minutes?"

Xavier scoffs. "Keep talking, and you'll be the pretty girl."

"This, coming from the pretty boy."

Their bickering fades into the background as I strain my senses, listening for any sound out of place. The steady drip of water. The scuffle of boots over loose stones. The soft wheeze of our breathing.

Too soft. The air is dead, untouched. We are utterly alone down here.

Somehow, that's worse.

"Why would Bianchi choose an abandoned mine to hold girls he intends to ... sell?" I ask no one in particular. "Wouldn't he want to take care of them?"

I hate I'm even thinking this way, but I can't help but wonder why gross, horrid men would pay a premium for dirty, abused girls.

After a few seconds, I answer my own question with terrible nightmare scenarios, then croak, "Scratch that. I don't want to know."

Rossi answers anyway, his voice flat. "They abuse and torture them into complacency before dressing them up as gorgeous dolls to be bought by collectors. The use of these mines, it's not random. It's a statement, a challenge even. Bianchi isn't just trafficking; he's playing with us. He's showing us that he can take these girls far away from his own empire, in an isolated place he's likely used before and gotten away with. It's like he's flaunting his reach, daring us to catch him or for him to trap us."

Xavier says, "Here's hoping they don't come for their cargo early."

The flashlight flickers. Morgan curses, smacking it back to life, but the brief flash of darkness steals my breath. There one moment, gone the next.

Just like the girls will be if we don't find them soon.

I square my shoulders and keep walking, one foot in front of the other. The air grows colder and the dark more absolute.

"We'll be ready if anyone tries to surprise us," Morgan assures me.

Tempest pauses at the beginning of a fork in our descent, two separate shafts drifting off into opaque black. "I'll lose signal if I go any farther. Go ahead of me. I want to keep contact with Ardyn. I'll double back and alert you if there's any activity on the surface."

We press deeper into the claustrophobic tunnels. The air grows colder, tinged with the scent of damp earth and roughened, cracked walls. Every ten or so feet, pockets of dust fall on us. Our flashlights cut through the oppressive darkness. Evidence of the mine's past operations is everywhere—old, rusting picks and shovels, decrepit carts that once held precious ore, and even faded, moth-eaten old clothing left behind in the miners' haste to abandon the site. The walls are marked with soot, and after one curious arc of my flashlight, I notice old inscriptions.

"Records of ore veins, or maybe warnings, etched into the stone by miners long gone," Morgan muses beside me after he notices where my attention is.

He says it so close to my earlobe that I shiver from his hot breath rather than the cold mineshaft.

Rossi consults the map. "The holding chamber should be up ahead, around the next bend."

His jaw is clenched, body coiled tight.

As we move deeper inside, water collects in dark pools, the liquid a murky black that reflects none of the meager light we're filtering in. The air is thick and stale, filled with the musty, earthy scents of mold and dampness.

Thankfully, the tunnel opens into a larger alcove, its ceiling lost in shadow. A heavy metal door, streaked with rust, waits at the far end. Its hinges are rusted, but the lock is new.

"This better not be a waste of energy," Xavier whispers, his fingers tightly gripping his handgun.

My heart pounds. The girls have to be behind that door.

Rossi signals us to stop. We fan out, the guys with their weapons ready. Joining, I pull out my small knife.

Rossi nods to Rio. He pulls out his lockpick tools and gets to work, brow furrowed in concentration. The door's modern locking system slowly gives way under his expert hands.

With a resounding click, the lock disengages. Rio steps back, his only show of arrogance a small uptick on one side of his lips. "All yours, boss."

Rossi motions me to stay behind him. With a terse nod to Morgan and Rio, Rossi kicks in the door. It slams open with a scream of rusty hinges. The rest of the Vultures follow a tide of leather and steel.

I hover in the doorway, barely breathing. The light from their flashlights dances over pitted concrete walls, exposed pipes, piles of trash...

Nothing. No girls. No chains.

Just dust and shadows.

My heart sinks even as Rossi curses, slamming a fist against the wall. It's empty. Cav lied to us.

Dust hangs thick in the stagnant air. Spiderwebs shroud the corners in gossamer gray, and a hollow silence fills the atmosphere.

Unease prickles against my skin.

"Dammit," Rio murmurs.

At the same time, Rossi spits, "*No.* They have to be here."

Rossi paces the room, his shoulders tense and his face exhibiting lines of stress.

"Uh, clearly, they are not," Morgan says.

I send him a frown, which he dutifully ignores.

Rossi's eyes meet mine in a flash of golden spotlight before whoever's flashlight it was spans away. Regret shadows his face. He knows how much I needed this win. How much those girls needed us.

He knows what it's like to lose and pay the consequences.

I want to rage and scream and put my fist through the wall like he did. But instead, I force my spine straight and chin high.

"Perhaps," Morgan continues, "Voldemort led us astray."

Rossi freezes in the middle of the room. "He wouldn't. Not for something like this."

"What is it with you two, anyway?" Morgan asks. "Why do you trust him so?"

Rossi's eyelids flicker, but he says nothing.

Feeling safer now that we weren't greeted by a line of fire, I trek deeper into the expansive room, refusing to believe we came all this way for nothing.

Rio's warmth stays close to my side, the electric buzz of his presence spurring me to move forward and be braver.

My short study of Cav gave me more information than I usually get with first appearances.

No, I don't think Cav would lead us to an empty room and be satisfied.

"Search every inch of this place," Rossi growls. "There has to be something we missed."

The Vultures spread out, scouring the room. Morgan runs his hands along the walls with lazy curiosity, looking for hidden switches or panels. Xavier checks behind old wooden crates stacked haphazardly in the corners.

I make my way along the back wall, fingers trailing over cold stone, Rio staying close.

A draft whispers from somewhere, raising goose bumps on my skin.

I pause, blinking in the gloom, and spot a tiny gap in the mortar lines. Crouching down, I peer closer. It's subtle, but there's definitely a crack.

"Over here," I call out.

The others gather around as I push experimentally on the stones. They give slightly under my touch. This section of the wall isn't as solid as it appears.

Rossi steps up beside me. "Stand back, Clover."

I move aside as Rossi slams his boot into the weak spot. Stone crunches and crumbles. He kicks again, knocking loose chunks of rock to reveal a small, dark cavity behind the wall.

Rossi grabs a flashlight, shining it into the hole. A passageway slopes downward, swallowed by darkness. He glances at me, eyebrows raised.

Rossi steps through the gap first, gun drawn. I follow close, uncaring if I took Morgan's or Xavier's spot in our formation, nerves thrumming. The air grows colder as we descend.

Then I hear it. The faintest sound drifting up through the dark. A muffled sob.

We move swiftly but cautiously down the passage, senses on high alert. My heart pounds against my ribs.

The corridor levels out, opening into a small chamber.

I stifle a gasp at the sight.

Four young women huddle against the far wall, chained at the ankles. Their clothes are tattered, their faces bony and haunted. Fresh bruises mottle their skin. One of them meets my gaze, raw terror in her eyes.

My fists clench. These girls have been brutalized and abused. Kept like animals in this cold, lightless hole.

I start toward them, but Rossi's arm blocks my path.

Right. We have to check for traps first.

Morgan and Rio move in, sweeping the room while Xavier keeps watch at the entrance.

After a tense minute, Morgan calls the all clear.

The girls flinch as we approach, some retreating farther into the shadows.

"It's okay," I soothe, crouching down to their level. "These men and I, we're here to help you."

Rio examines their chains, then pulls out his set of lock-picks. The manacles click open one by one.

I rub warmth back into the closest girl's numb hands as she sobs with relief.

"Everything's going to be all right now," I murmur.

And I mean it with every fiber of my being.

Xavier's muffled exclamation draws my head up. "What is it?"

I point my light in his direction, then immediately wish I hadn't.

"Bloody hell." Xavier backs away at a slumped form in the opposite corner, shaking his head as his chest hollows out with a heavy exhale. He turns flinty eyes toward me. "I'm sorry, maiden."

I rise and step toward Lauren's body. Her eyes stare up at the ceiling, milky and vacant. Fresh bruises decorate her throat.

"She ... tried to escape," one of the girls croaks.

Sorrow twists inside me, making me sick. "We were too late for her. We waited too long."

Rossi crouches beside Lauren, pressing two fingers to her neck even though we can all see it's hopeless. After a moment, he shakes his head.

"We can still save the others," I say, urgency sharpening my tone. "But we have to bring Lauren, too."

Rossi's jaw tightens. "Clover—"

"We are not leaving her!" I snap. "Lauren deserves more than to rot down here where no one will ever find her."

Xavier and Rio exchange a long look. Morgan shifts behind them.

"There's no time for this," Rossi rumbles.

I step closer to him, glaring up into his impassive face. "I'm not leaving without her. We do this right, or you lock me down here for Bianchi's men to find instead."

"You don't mean that."

"Try me." My eyes grow hot. Tears threaten to escape. "Lauren wasn't the nicest, but she didn't deserve this torture. This death. We *bring* her with us."

Rossi scrubs a hand down his face.

"Blasted stubborn woman," he mutters.

But he bends and lifts Lauren's limp body in his arms, then glances at his men. "Let's move."

Rossi and I bring up the rear as the group hurries through the twisting tunnels. The girls limp along, clinging to each other as the Vultures guide them. We move as quick as their weakened states allow.

But I pause when my flashlight glides upon something not right on the stone wall. "Wait, what's this?"

Rossi bites out, "We don't have time for—"

"No, look," I say, bending and angling my flashlight to better see. "It says, *'a stone circled in summer.'* That's part of Sarah Anderton's clue."

Xavier sighs. "More of Sarah's cryptic nonsense?"

Intrigued but skeptical, Morgan adds, "You think this mine is connected to the jewels?"

"It's fresh." Rossi examines the writing closely, Lauren's body between him and the wall. I try not to look at her. "This wasn't here for hundreds of years. This was carved recently."

I straighten. "Do you think it's a trap?"

Rossi makes a low noise in his throat before saying, "I wouldn't put it past Cav to carve riddles into walls for fun while girls are suffering below his feet."

"That's..." I gape at him.

"Sick? Twisted? Fucking genius?" Morgan cuts in.

Irritated, Rio checks his watch. "We need to move. Now."

I move along with him but look at the wall one last time. "If Cav went to the trouble of carving this here, maybe we're missing something that could give us an edge. I'll re-read the grimoire."

"Fine," Rossi says. "But right now, we need to get these girls to safety and get the hell out of here."

"Agreed," I say.

Beside me as we walk, Rossi is grimly alert. His jacket sleeve rides up as he balances Lauren's body, revealing the edge of a gruesome vulture wing tattoo on his forearm.

Rossi notices me looking for a moment.

"Was bringing you down here a mistake?" he asks bluntly.

I meet his piercing gaze. "I chose this."

He studies me a moment longer, then nods. We continue through the darkness.

The air grows fresher as the shaft widens. We must be getting close to the surface exit. Relief floods through me.

Then a new sound echoes from up ahead—shouts, boots tramping. The girls whimper.

Rio signals us to stop as he peers ahead into the dim tunnel. The heavy stomp of boots grows louder, accompanied by coarse laughter that sends a chill down my spine.

A figure darts in front of us, the men aiming at the form.

But it's Tempest, hands raised. He whispers harshly, "They're here."

Bianchi's men.

"You don't say?" Morgan replies drolly.

He turns to face us and the girls, pressing a finger to his lips.

Rossi murmurs tersely, "New plan. We split up." He hands Lauren's body to Xavier. "You and Morgan take the girls and go. We'll draw their fire."

Morgan hesitates only a moment before nodding. He won't argue with Rossi's command. Or, more likely, he's not looking forward to coming up against men he might know, men who would immediately report his betrayal to Bianchi. Morgan isn't supposed to support the Vultures. He's meant to infiltrate and keep them in line.

Rossi spins to me, his eyes unreadable. "Clover, go with them."

My jaw tightens. He still doubts me. "I'm staying with you."

Morgan chuckles. "Nice try, little leaf. Come on."

The footfalls are near. Shadowy silhouettes emerge from around the bend. Five men, armed and smirking.

They slow their pace the closer they come to us, glancing around.

"The carcass-eaters have to be here somewhere," one sneers.

Rossi steps out with his gun leveled. "*Ciao, bastardis.*"

The men whirl, cursing in surprise. In a blink, Rio and Tempest emerge, weapons drawn from the shadows around Rossi.

"*Now,*" Morgan hisses to me and Xavier, herding the girls in the opposite direction.

Everything erupts behind us. The tunnel explodes with gunfire as both sides open fire. I shield the girls as much as I can, heart hammering. But I have to believe the Vultures are precise. I have to be confident that one by one, the men I hear crumpling to the ground are only the enemies.

Not the ones I love.

Then silence, save for the girls' muffled sobs.

"Let's go," Morgan reminds me as I hitch my step.

Xavier deftly navigates our path ahead. I have no choice but to follow even though my heart screams to turn back and check on my brother, Rio ... Rossi.

The roughhewn walls and crumbling dirt ceiling make me feel boxed in and claustrophobic. Our footsteps are stifled against the surrounding rock.

But I brace myself for the next wave of fear, used to it by now. I won't leave Morgan and Xavier's side, no matter what.

Just then, a deafening explosion rocks the cavern, dropping loose rocks from the ceiling. A cloud of dust and smoke mushrooms up behind us. Cries of alarm sound from the girls as we're ushered into a small alcove, Morgan and Xavier covering us with their bodies.

Coughing and blinking through the dust, I think *this is the end.*

The very death I wanted Lauren to avoid; I'm going to join her in this godforsaken underground, never to be found. I'll become a dark mystery, just like Sarah.

Through the haze, a familiar voice rings out. "Need some help, little sister?"

Tempest.

Rossi called for backup, after all.

An agonized, relieved cry escapes my throat as I climb over Morgan and Xavier despite their protests to keep my ass down, heading straight for my brother. My heart fills at the sight of Rossi and Rio appearing behind him, too.

I hug Tempest hard, adrenaline still electrocuting my veins and giving me enough strength to make my even hardened brother grunt at the pressure.

Rossi walks over, his face rippling with others' flashlights, holstering his gun.

He appraises me with those intense eyes.

"Not bad for your first tangle with Bianchi, Miss Callahan."

I allow myself a small smile as I separate from Tempest, knowing I've proven myself today.

And that's all I wanted.

CHAPTER 26
CLOVER

The van bumps and jostles us as we speed down the winding mine roads. The three girls we rescued huddle together in the back, hollow-eyed and clinging to each other for comfort. I wish I could tell them they're safe now. But the threat won't end with this one rescue operation.

I glance at Rossi's stern profile as he drives. Bianchi hurt him deeper than I can imagine when he and Nico Bianchi took away Rossi's family. And Rossi has been biding his time, waiting for the perfect moment to strike back and ruin their empire.

The van veers around a tight bend. When I brace myself against the door, Morgan meets my eyes from the back seat, his lips slanting with a secret smile. I lift my chin, refusing to let him sense what's on my mind: that I'm worried Rossi might want Morgan to be part of the Bianchi cleanse.

It doesn't surprise me that my immediate thought is, *I hope not.*

Morgan may be unhinged, but he's my madman, just as Rossi is my center stone.

We weave into the long, untended driveway into Blackwood Manor. Ardyn meets us on the steps, and as she descends, she explains she's set up IVs and cots in the ballroom with Minnie's help.

I don't bother asking where these items are stashed or how Ardyn knows to find them. Despite their servitude to the Bianchi Mafia, the Vultures' reach is further than I thought.

The men assist the girls up the stairs, following Ardyn into the manor, with Tempest holding tightly to her hand. When we'd climbed into the car at the mines, dirt-crusted and bloody, Rossi took the time to gently wrap Lauren in a tarp and place her in the trunk, which is where Rossi rounds to now.

"Don't watch this part," he says to me as he opens the trunk without glancing my way. "Go in and rest. I promise I'll put her somewhere safe before we give her back to her family."

"With a fake story, I assume," I say hoarsely from the top of the stairs.

The sharp angles of his profile shift in the paltry light as he nods. "It has to be this way. You understand that now."

Clearing my throat of emotion, I nod in return, then walk into the manor without a second glance.

It's what a Vulture would have done.

I SIT ALONE at the long dining room table, nursing a rare glass of whiskey to calm my nerves, like I used to do at the hole before I met them. The men who changed my life.

The amber liquid burns my throat, but it's a welcome distraction from the thrumming still dominating my veins.

Blackwood Manor is eerily quiet, the others having already retreated to their favorite spots to decompress after the harrowing rescue mission. But my mind races, thoughts crashing together like the sea during a storm.

I close my eyes, inhaling deeply to ground myself. The faint scent of leather and gunpowder still clings to my clothes, triggering vivid memories of the firefight at the mines. Gunshots echo off stone walls, flashes of muzzle fire piercing the darkness, the coppery tang of blood heavy in the air.

The thought of losing even one of these men.

My fingers tighten around the glass, knuckles whitening. They'd cut it dangerously close today. If the Vultures hadn't reacted as fast as they did...

I shake my head slightly, banishing the chilling thoughts. They'd succeeded, fulfilling their mission flawlessly as always. The girls were safe now, far away from Bianchi's cruel plans.

But they weren't out of the woods yet. Not until we uncovered the secrets in Sarah's grimoire and used the treasure to lure Bianchi out, dismantle his empire, then use the remaining funds to free my men.

I glance up when Rossi enters, his lethal grace belying the exhaustion that surely wracks his body, too. His black-brown eyes meet mine, clouded with that ever-present, inscrutable darkness.

He heads to the bar cart, pouring himself a glass.

Rossi takes a long pull of his drink, then sets his glass down with a soft clink, folding his arms as he leans against the wall beside the cart. His posture is relaxed, but I sense the coiled tension humming beneath the surface.

"The girls are safe," he says after a moment. "I've contacted some old friends. They'll get the girls new identities and set them up somewhere far from here."

"What about their families?"

Rossi shakes his head. "They can't go back. Bianchi will find and take them again."

"And the authorities?"

Rossi scoffs. "The Bianchis have been operating for well over a century without getting caught. What makes you think these lonely girls who were targeted because they have no friends, no caring family, will be the ones to break the case?"

"But you think you can."

Rossi's chest rumbles in agreement. "I know I can."

I nod since there is no use arguing with a man on a mission. I'd hated the thought of simply dumping those poor girls back out on the streets after all they'd suffered, so what Rossi can give them has to be enough.

"What will happen to them?" I ask quietly.

Rossi's expression deepens, thunderclouds gathering in his fiery gaze. "After what Bianchi did, they deserve so much more than simple survival. But survival is all I can give them."

Anger resonates in his voice. And anguish. Always anguish. He must have seen his daughter or his wife down in that chamber.

He's seen too much.

So I push to my feet and go to him.

I reach out, resting a hand lightly on his arm. He tenses under my touch, then exhales slowly, the storm in his eyes fading.

"It's enough," I say gently. "You gave them their lives back. That's everything."

Rossi's lips twist in a bitter smile. "If only it were that simple."

He shakes his head, weariness creeping back into his face. "Get some rest. We have a long day ahead focusing on the

Anderton fortune now that we've found the girls. He'll keep taking more until we do."

I nod, stifling a yawn. The adrenaline crash is hitting me hard.

I turn to go, then pause, looking back.

"For what it's worth ... thank you. For saving them."

Rossi inclines his head silently.

Before he disappears from view, I swear I glimpse a ghost of an emotion far sweeter than his usual volcanic resolve.

But then it's gone, and the moment slips away into the darkness of the corridor.

I DON'T GO to bed.

I take a breath to steady myself, pushing down the swirl of emotions Rossi ignites in me—sadness, compassion, denial. There's nothing more I can do for him right now as I leave him behind.

I head to the living room in the opposite wing, where the others still gather, voices subdued. The heady thrill from earlier has faded, leaving behind bone-deep exhaustion.

Morgan sprawls sideways on the couch, arms crossed behind his head. His face lights up when he sees me.

"There you are, little leaf. I was wondering where you got to so we can get to the real celebrations of our daring rescue."

Despite everything, I can't help a small smile. Morgan may be disturbed, but he's uncomplicated in his desires. A refreshing change from Rossi and his secrets.

I walk over to the couch, perching on the edge beside him. His hand comes to rest on my thigh, thumb idly stroking.

Across from us in a faded armchair, Xavier tenses, green

eyes tracking the movement. I tense, too, worried my interaction with Morgan might repulse Xavier even though I have the same feelings for both. Ever since I learned about Xavier's past, I notice his hypervigilance, as if expecting an attack or betrayal at any moment.

Rio lounges nearby, observing Morgan's strokes, too. His face gives nothing away, but I can feel his attention on me like a physical touch.

Heat prickles under my skin as the atmosphere shifts, tension coiling. I may not share Morgan's manic enthusiasm, but I can't deny the spark of anticipation low in my belly. We're all wired and on edge tonight; this could provide the release we need.

Morgan's hand slides higher, fingers grazing the crease of my thigh. He lifts out of his sprawl until his breath caresses my ear.

"I want to make you come so hard you forget your own name, little leaf."

My lips part to suck in a sharp breath.

Xavier makes a low noise, leaning forward. Not of surprise, exactly, but not quite intrigue, either.

I watch Xavier carefully as Morgan bites my earlobe, and I shudder.

"Do you want that?" he asks me, a rough edge to his cultured voice.

Rio says nothing as he watches, but his gaze burns into me. Waiting to see what I'll do or say.

The choice is mine, I realize. I could laugh this off and defuse the rising heat before it goes further.

But tonight, I need the escape.

To feel rather than think.

To let go.

Turning my head, I meet Morgan's lust-darkened eyes.

"Show them," I whisper.

Morgan's wolfish grin is triumphant right before his mouth claims mine.

CHAPTER 27
RIO

Morgan kisses Clover hungrily, all teeth and tongue. His fingers dig into her hips as he drags her closer until she straddles his lap. My rigid length grows at the thought of her pressed against him and grinds into the air instinctively.

Clover groans into his mouth.

"Fuck, yes. Just like that," Morgan says against her lips.

His hands slide under her shirt, claiming her skin. I shudder, already sensitive despite not touching her.

Yet.

Xavier pushes off the armoire, no doubt ready to flee. I had suspicions that he'd been with Clover but never had proof until Clover glanced over at him when Morgan played with her to see if he cared.

With that look on her face, she wanted him to care.

Morgan slants his eyes over to Xavier at the movement. "You know, Sports Balls, you don't have to stand there like a prison guard. Join us."

I sit back, watching the exchange with an amused but cautious eye.

When Xavier turns to me with a puppy-dog *what do I do?* expression, I say nothing but incline my head and relax my shoulders, communicating a sense of, *it's up to you, acolyte.*

Xavier pauses, then glances back at Morgan and Clover.

There's a brief, tension-filled silence before he speaks. "I've been the new guy on the field before. Timing is everything. Is this ... the right play, Clover?"

Morgan smirks while Clover kisses his neck. He answers, "Timing's overrated when you have talent and chemistry. But let's check with our striker, shall we? Clover, are you calling the plays, or should I continue?"

A blush coats her cheeks before she meets Xavier's eye as Morgan runs a hand over her stomach and plays with the hem of her shirt.

"An invitation doesn't have to be formal to be open," she says to him shyly, her lashes fluttering demurely as Morgan moves down to circle her pussy through her jeans. Her legs fall open at his touch.

I nearly come in my pants.

"Very well," Xavier says in a tight voice.

In a bold move that makes my placid expression slip for just a moment, Xavier moves behind the couch where Morgan and Clover are and bends low to nip at her neck.

"I don't want to be left out of this," he murmurs against her throat. "What we did tonight was something good. In a world of violence, I want to keep that good. I want you to make me feel that again."

Clover reaches back, tangling her fingers in Xavier's short hair, urging him on. His hands join Morgan's, rucking up her shirt to bare her breasts.

I decide to descend, arcing over to them silently until I'm on my knees, my tongue flicking her nipple, making her gasp.

Morgan kisses her harder, stealing the breath in her lungs, while I suck her nipple into my mouth.

"That's it," she whispers in a hoarse voice. "That's it, just like that."

Grabbing my head, Clover tries to keep me latched as Xavier lifts her shirt over her head. My lips free her, but only to seek out the other pink nipple. I lick it, tasting the salt left from my earlier suckling. Her skin is scorched wherever I kiss.

I pull her to me, ignoring Morgan's and Xavier's protests, and kiss her deeply. Making my intentions clear, I unbuckle my belt and the zipper of my jeans as I tongue her mouth. I slip my hand inside, stroking my dick through my boxers.

When she stops kissing me to watch me stroke myself, I know I have her.

Moaning, I lift to my feet, taking a few steps back away from her, and whip my jeans and boxers off. Her eyes never leave mine as she kicks off her boots, then works her jeans off her hips. As does her socks and her bra, until she's lying before us, naked.

Her breasts are perky, with tiny nipples that I want to keep sucking on, but I'm looking forward to fucking them into her chin.

Patience.

I'm very familiar with tortured deprivation, so I wait, seeing what the other men will do to my Lucky.

Morgan is the first one to reach her after he strips, his tattooed dick bobbing painfully, and buries his head between her breasts, then across her belly. Xavier watches me, waiting for permission.

"Go ahead," I say.

Xavier moves in, bending between her legs, and inhales deeply.

"Damn, she smells so fucking good. Like spice and sin."

I want to leap on Clover, too, but I wait it out, watching as she widens her legs for Xavier. She's almost a virgin at this moment, and I'm going to indulge in her innocence and her first taste of group sex.

I think she'll like it.

She arches her back with a pleading cry when Xavier's tongue finds her clit.

"Oh my God," she cries out.

Morgan lifts his head, kissing Clover roughly. She opens her mouth for him, yanking on his hair as she works her hips against Xavier's face. Clover arches, lifting her tits for Morgan to keep pinching as Xavier buries his face in her pussy.

Her hand finds my erection and strokes me. I had no idea I'd inched closer, but I'm glad I did.

I close my eyes and lean in to her touch. She's careful and slow, letting me savor the moment, but then she grips my shaft, stroking me faster. It's like she's holding me back.

I grin with my eyes closed. *My sweet Lucky is* edging *me.*

"Fuck!" she moans.

Her fingers tighten as her body spasms. I drop my head back and groan, my eyes flashing open just in time to see her thighs shake.

I reach down and gently pull her trembling hand away from my erection. Her eyes flicker open, and she realizes what I'm doing.

Xavier slides his fingers into her pussy, and she moans, her eyes squeezing tight.

"Hell, yes. You're so fucking wet, so ready. I want to feel you come on my fingers," Xavier murmurs.

"Come for us, little leaf," Morgan adds. "We want to watch."

Oh, I don't think she'll be able to help it.

Clover's body tenses. Her belly tightens. She's so close, really close. Panting, she lifts her chin, her eyes going wide as Xavier presses his face to her pussy.

Her mouth goes slack, and her eyes squeeze shut.

"Come on me," Xavier taunts, his voice dripping with lust.

Her head falls back against the rug. Her lips part, but nothing comes out. She then shakes her head.

"No," she whispers.

"Yes," Morgan and I command together.

"Not without one of you, or all of you, coming with me."

"Then ride me, Clover," Morgan offers.

She shakes her head. "First, I want Xavier."

"Fair enough," Morgan says, surprisingly unperturbed by Clover's choice.

Perhaps because he's too turned on to argue. Admittedly, I feel the fucking same.

"Xav, come here," she says, reaching out for him.

I watch her fingers curl around his wrist and pull him over her body, directing him to her mouth. She kisses him deeply, even as she raises a leg to hook over Morgan's hip. I can't see if Xavier's fingers are inside her, or Morgan's, or both. All I notice is the hunger on Clover's face.

As I watch, Morgan presses his finger into her asshole, and she groans, rocking her hips into his and Xavier's hands.

"She's fucking tight," Morgan gasps out.

It's then I decide to show them exactly how tight.

I swoop in, not one to take turns when I want the win.

I nip her shoulder as I lift her to her knees, then position myself behind her, and then I rub the head of my cock against her asshole.

"I'm going to fuck your ass now, Clover, but you won't come until I'm buried deep," I say, my voice low and even.

"Yes. Please," she whispers.

"Always the perfect answer," I say.

Only, I don't think she realizes what she just agreed to.

I push into her with one powerful stroke of my hips.

Her eyes go wide. Morgan and Xavier freeze, watching my cock pierce her defiantly and effortlessly.

"Well, fuck, that was efficient," Morgan breathes.

I slide my hand under her ass, and then I rock my hips back and forth.

"Damn." I can't help but groan. The feel of my cock stretching her is to *die* for.

"Yes, yes," she hisses.

"She's so damned hot," Xavier observes, pre-cum dripping off his dick.

I want to savor her, but the feel of her walls wrapping around me is so fucking good I can't help but fuck her.

"Harder," she groans.

I happily oblige, fucking her so hard she lifts off my dick, then I slam her back down.

Then I begin to fuck her hard and fast.

"Oh fuck."

"Holy shit."

"Fuck, yes."

Everyone's voices blend. My grunts seem to match hers as I pump my cock in and out of her mercilessly. I can't seem to stop, can't seem to slow down. Her ass is so hot, so fucking tight, her body so fucking pliable.

The minute her muscles begin to tremble, I go completely

still, and then I wrap her hair around my fist and pull her head back.

She gasps.

"You will wait, Lucky. You'll wait until you're stretched so fucking wide around us that you'll think you're going to split in half," I order.

I know she hears me when she tenses.

"Xavier, fuck her pussy," I command.

He gives a sharp exhale—of relief, excitement, both—before bending to his knees, lining up the tip of his cock to her soaked pussy, and thrusting in.

My lips curve. The boy watches and learns fast.

I can feel my dick sliding against Xavier's, and I can feel her muscles flex around both of them. It's so snug and fucking amazing.

I glance at Morgan, who's watching us with dark rainforest eyes and a look of hunger I don't think I've ever seen before. We're fucking his woman, *our* woman, and he's watching me with a predator's thoughts.

"Do you like that, Lucky?" I ask.

"Yes," she gasps. "I love it."

"How many cocks can you take?" I muse.

Her eyes go wide as her head falls back on my shoulder.

"How many cocks can you take, Clover?" I repeat.

"Two," she grunts.

Her answer makes me smile.

"Two cocks are nothing. You'll take three," I promise.

"Three?" she whispers, the word a question.

"That's right," I answer.

"We'll make you so fucking full," Morgan promises, eyes gleaming.

It's not like him to wait. I wonder how much longer I have before he pounces.

I grab Clover's ass again.

"Yes," she gasps. "Yes, yes."

"Xavier, harder," I command.

I'm back to fucking her, but I don't move as fast anymore. I fuck her slowly, methodically, stretching her out.

"God, I'm going to come," she moans.

"Yes," I agree. "You will."

Her hands are on the back of my head as if she's trying to pull me closer. She presses her forehead against my cheek, her eyes squeezed tight.

"Not without us," I remind her.

Her breath catches, and she clenches down. Xavier's breathing becomes harsh, and mine does the same.

"Fuck," I mutter.

"You're fucking incredible," Xavier exclaims between rapid breaths.

"Morgan," I grit out, "Now."

Morgan's shadow is already falling over us, placing his feet on either side of Clover and me, then leaning forward in front of Xavier so he can nudge his black-ringed cock inside her pussy alongside him.

Morgan pulls her head back. Then he kisses her, and as he kisses her, he thrusts inside her. Xavier barks out an exclamation behind him, his dick firmly wedged with Morgan's inside Clover.

Morgan's kiss is relentless and cruel, and I can see his white teeth digging into her bottom lip.

I can feel the burn in my thighs and hear the burn in my lungs. I know how much control it must be taking for Morgan not to fuck her like an animal.

The feel of the three of us all inside her is like a fucking aphrodisiac.

"Oh my God," she gasps.

There's nothing slow or gentle about Morgan when he breaks off the kiss. His thrusts are hard and fast, and he plows her mercilessly while Xavier lowers himself farther to the floor and keeps still, likely trying to contain himself from exploding while giving Morgan more room.

"Fuck," she groans.

"What's that, Lucky?" I ask. "You need more?"

I drive deep inside her ass, and her walls begin to clench. I can feel Morgan's and Xavier's cocks inside her, her flesh squeezing around all of us, and that is the last straw.

She pants, her orgasm working its way up through her spine, sweat coating our skin. She's going to come around both of us, around all three of us.

"Look at me, Lucky," I say, my voice gruff with lust.

Her raven-black hair tickles my shoulder as she turns her face and curls a hand around my neck. Her light-brown eyes, jeweled with lust, meet mine. I slide my hand over her breasts as I kiss her. Her tongue flicks mine, her lips tasting of us.

She's not playing fair. I can feel her stretch around me, making my dick throb.

My lips curl into a smile as I pull back and watch her.

"Fuck her. Fuck her until you come," I order all of us.

And then we all fuck her.

Clover's hands reach forward to balance on Morgan's shoulders as she bounces. Her head falls back as she thrusts her pussy at him and Xavier, and in the next moment, her pussy clenches around me, and I come.

She moans. I groan.

We all stay inside her until she reaches behind Morgan and pinches Xavier's ass, who then spurts his cum inside her.

Xavier shouts his release while Morgan, his face tight with effort, curses, "*Fuck,*" before exploding inside her, too.

We all collapse in the aftermath, Xavier and Morgan falling back and leaving her warmth.

Me? I'm too busy enjoying the feel of her to pull out quite yet.

"You're fucking wet," I say and slide a finger through the slit of her pussy.

She's still getting off. I can tell by how she's rocking her hips against my hand.

"Meh, it was okay," she whispers with a tired, playful grin.

"Oh?" I ask, my voice laced with warning.

I slide a finger inside her and then pull it back out, letting Morgan's and Xavier's cum drip off my finger and onto her nipple. Clover's eyes follow my hand as it moves between her breasts and trails down her stomach.

Morgan perks up.

"You're dripping all over her," he says, his voice husky.

Xavier watches, leaning his hands back against the floor, his eyelids heavy with satiated pleasure and ever-growing lust.

"I know," I answer Morgan.

My finger traces her little pink nipples, making her shiver. As I do, Xavier comes over and works his hands in circles on her thighs.

The way she's watching me makes me hard all over again.

"I think there's more where that came from," I say.

"Most definitely," Morgan agrees and rolls to his knees as he wipes the cum off his hands.

"So be a good girl. Stay very still," I tell her, and before

Clover can respond, I dip my fingers into the cum on her left nipple and move our mess toward her mouth while keeping my other hand busy with her pussy. "Open."

She lets out a breath and does as she's told, parting her lips.

I hum with approval and slide my finger across her lips, feeding her the cum we've collected.

She closes her mouth around me, slowly licking me clean, and even though I'm spent, my cock throbs in response.

When Clover's hips jerk up, I slide my other finger out and press it against her clit.

"Fuck," she cries out.

"Shh." I soothe her. "We can hear you."

Clover moans, and I know it won't be long.

"Good girl," I murmur. "That's it. Come for us."

"Mm." She squirms against my fingers with my cock still deep inside her ass. "Yes."

I use my free hand to tug on her hair. Her eyes meet mine, and they look feral. She was so good, so fucking obedient, and now I'm going to make her come for her good behavior.

She whimpers. Her muscles clench, her body reaching for me in that delicious moment before her orgasm hits.

I let her hair go, and her chin drops to her chest. She takes a breath and climbs off me, wincing as her overworked ass and pussy are forced to release another thick cock.

Clover rises from the floor and falls onto the couch, her knees too wobbly to carry her anywhere else.

When I move to sit with her, Morgan shakes his head and pushes me away.

"My turn," he says.

He stands over her and pushes her breasts together.

Leaning down, he wraps his lips around her nipples, sucking and lapping at her sensitive skin.

I'm realizing Morgan loves to suck on her.

"We might need to give her a break, gents," Xavier says, gesturing to Clover's half-open eyes and her tired rubbing of Morgan's head as he licks her. "We've done her in."

I agree, then yank at Morgan until he clambers off her.

Morgan's eyes are wild, but he does as asked and backs away, gripping his cock tightly and jerking off.

Sometimes, the beast must be leashed.

I lift Clover into my arms, jerking my chin at the door for someone to open it.

Xavier does, what with Morgan being too busy in the corner, and I carry Clover to her room, both of us ass-crack naked but neither of us caring who sees.

Soon, it'll be known who Clover belongs to, whether or not it is accepted.

She belongs to the Vultures now.

CHAPTER 28
CLOVER

The following morning, we keep the library dim, lit only by a few flickering candles. Their faint glow casts dancing silhouettes across the walls, giving the space an eerie luminescence.

I sit at the worn wooden table with Sarah's ancient grimoire open before me. The yellowed pages are covered in arcane symbols and the loopy handwriting of old-fashioned English, detailing spells, rituals, and healing aromatics.

Morgan sits across from me, his expression pinched as he studies Lily's journal alongside me, his nostrils flaring way less than mine at the distinct, corpse-like smell wafting from the grimoire's pages.

A stone circled in summer. What does it mean?

"Look toward the middle here," he murmurs, sliding the journal so I can read. "This section references Sarah calling upon blood sacrifices and demonic symbols. Dangerous practices, even for a witch of Sarah's caliber."

I squint at Lily's entry, thinking, then go back to the open pages of the grimoire, tracing my fingers over elaborate sigils, the thrum of energy from the book sending static shocks into my fingertips.

"She wrote those at about the time she was accused," I say. "And look at these symbols here—she's calling upon dark magic or attempting to. She was desperate. Trying anything to protect her daughter."

Morgan hums in thought. "Messing with these kinds of forces never ends well, whether or not one believes them to be real."

I chew on my lower lip. "It doesn't matter, anyway. Sarah mentions a stone circled by summer. We're at the end of winter. To decipher this clue, we'll have to wait for the seasons to change, and I don't think we have that kind of time."

Morgan reaches out and squeezes my hand, his touch sending little thrills up my arm. "Don't get discouraged. After all, you already saved a bunch of lives and put a dent in Bianchi's human trafficking operation. Not too shabby for a newbie, little leaf."

I give a small smile at his praise. Though we just shared an intensely passionate encounter with Xavier and Rio, Morgan's playful banter still makes me blush.

"I got lucky," I mumble.

Morgan leans forward, his green eyes shifting into a toxic fire. "No. You were brilliant. I always knew you were destined for more than just chemistry labs. This archaic field suits you."

His faith in me never fails to make my heart swell. Morgan saw my potential long before I recognized it in myself.

"Well, I had a good teacher."

He winks. "You absolutely did."

I roll my eyes but can't help grinning.

"So where do we go from here?" I ask. "Because I'm not finding anything useful in the grimoire."

Morgan taps his lips. "Let's reexamine what we know. *A stone circled by summer*. It could be tied to summer solstice rituals. There must be significance in that."

I nod along, turning over the details in my mind. Somewhere in Sarah's arcane riddles lies the answer...

A cool draft wafts through the room, making the candles sputter. I shiver but keep going.

Sarah's handwriting slants across the page in cramped lines, the ink faded with age. I squint at a section describing a ritual requiring a blood sacrifice under the full moon.

Morgan moves from across the table and slides into the chair beside me, his body heat like a *zing* of high voltage wire as he leans close and scans the page with me. "Perhaps not everything is as it seems. Many ancient rites took place out of season as a form of disguise so people wouldn't be caught by settlers who knew about solstice rituals and targeted those who practiced."

I consider this, turning the possibilities over in my mind. If Sarah wanted to hide something important but maintain the spiritual protection she worked so hard to produce, scheduling a ritual at an unexpected time would be clever, to say the least.

"So you think we should look for an actual stone circle?" I ask.

I flip through more pages, searching for any more reference to a stone circle.

"Precisely." Morgan grins, appraising me.

"Maybe the circle is hidden somewhere in the woods outside town," I muse. Then I remember a place Rio once told me about during one of our moonlit walks.

"The top of the bluff," I blurt out. "Up in the northern woods. Rio talked about a deliberate placement of carved stones earlier, didn't he? Half formed now and broken in pieces."

Morgan's eyes light up. "That would be the perfect spot for ancient Druidic ceremonies. Well done, little leaf," he murmurs appreciatively, tucking a strand of hair behind my ear. "I knew we could figure it out together."

His touch makes me shiver, the flicker of desire never far from the surface between us. I think back to the passionate night we shared with Xavier and Rio and feel myself blushing.

Morgan notices and chuckles. "Missing our boys already?"

I nod, wincing slightly at the ache in my center as I shift in my seat, but it's a stretched-out burn I never want to stop enjoying. "It was ... intense. I've never felt anything like that before."

"They care for you deeply, Clover," Morgan says, his voice more serious than usual. "As do I. Don't ever doubt that."

His words warm me. Morgan may be unpredictable, but it's clear my feelings matter to him.

And his faith in me means everything.

I glance back down at the grimoire, hiding my smile.

As I study the faded text, a tiny symbol catches my eye. A flower, *the* flower I'd seen at the top of the tunnel entrance into Anderton Cottage, as well as on the original Titan Falls map from the 1700s, usually hanging in the cottage as well. Here, it's barely visible in the margin.

How did I miss it before when this exact symbol led me to Lily?

My hand curls around the flower. I consider telling Morgan about my discovery, but some instinct stops me, a quiet voice whispering to keep this a secret for the time being.

Sarah meant this flower to be for my eyes alone ... at least until I unravel its meaning.

Moving, I cover the symbol with my elbow so Morgan doesn't notice it as we continue perusing and offering up ideas.

Wherever you are, Sarah, give me strength.

I'm listening.

CHAPTER 29
ROSSI

I stand alone in the study, eyes tracing the map spread across the desk. Call it antiquated, but I've always appreciated a map on paper rather than digital copies on screens. It is better to assess, to learn, and to catch more detail that would otherwise elude me as a clump of pixels.

The current map I'm reading has the city's districts and alleys reduced to a mess of lines and labels. But I see more than just streets and buildings.

I see an *empire.*

The map's worn edges curl under my fingertips. Bianchi's territories bleed red across its faded surface—a plague staining the city. I trace the boundaries and plot new lines, carving up his kingdom. For ten years, I've fought to free myself from his grip. And for ten years, he has crushed all who defied him.

Or so he believes.

We Vultures have survived under his reign, striking back where we could. A ragtag band of outcasts and outlaws bound by vengeance. Bianchi took everything from us.

Now, I vow to take everything from him.

But even *we* are running out of time. Bianchi's men roam Titan Falls, hunting us relentlessly. City boys by trade, they're having a difficult time finding us in the woods, but how much longer can we evade them?

I slam a fist on the table in frustration.

To kill a man like this requires more than courage.

It requires cunning.

The perfect plan.

My attention drifts to the map again. If we strike here, at the heart of his operations...

No, it's too risky.

But what if...

I've spent years studying Bianchi, learning his strengths and weaknesses. As a result, the seed of an idea takes root in my mind.

It's bold and dangerous, but it just might work.

A ruthless excitement surges through me.

Yes, this could work.

But I'll need the others on board. And I'll need to prepare, make sure every piece falls perfectly into place.

The shadows cling to me, shrouding my plans, but they cannot hide the rage coiled in my muscles.

Until the door creaks open, and I stiffen.

Tempest's entering presence pricks my skin, but I manage to school my face to stillness, clutching the map tight.

"You're up early," I rasp.

"As are you."

His eyes bore into mine, seeking answers. My pulse thrums as I meet his gaze. I cannot lose his trust. Not yet. Not when we are so close.

I force a smile that feels more like a grimace. "I'm going

over the routes for Bianchi's future shipments. He may come out of hiding for some of the larger ones. Possibly a few clandestine auctions, as well. He can never resist a relic of war."

A half truth. Let him wonder at the rest.

Tempest hesitates but nods. My shoulders loosen.

The map crinkles as I roll it up and place it out of sight.

Unwanted vulture's wings stretch across my back as I do so. It's why I barely look at myself in the mirror anymore because I'll always catch it in my reflection, and it makes me want to break my jaw screaming. The tendrils creeping up my neck. The cascade of inked feathers down my upper arms, spearing over my elbows. The tattoo Bianchi forced upon me. The vulture wings that mark me as his property.

Tempest's eyes follow my movements as I shut the map in the top drawer of my desk and lock it. His unease swirls in the air between us.

"Is something on your mind?" I ask, looking up.

He crosses his arms, jaw tight. "You're doing something more than just searching for Bianchi."

Damn his perceptiveness.

I keep my breathing even. "We all want the same thing, Tempest. To take Bianchi down."

It's not a denial of his statement, per se.

"Yeah, but I don't like secrets, especially from you."

Tempest steps closer, his height almost reaching mine. Protectiveness wars with suspicion in his gaze.

I meet his eyes steadily. "Trust that I'm doing what's best for the Vultures."

"Even at the cost of yourself?"

"Oh, son, I lost myself a long time ago."

The scars on my back, under all that ink, burn with remembered pain. What I've endured, what I'll endure again, to free us from Bianchi's chokehold.

"But some costs are worth paying," I add under my breath.

Tempest searches my face.

"Just ... don't take it all on alone." Something shifts in his eyes. A softening as much as we can soften. "We're here for you, Rossi. I'm here."

I clasp his shoulder. "I know."

For them, for her, I will finish this. No matter the sacrifice.

I give Tempest a final nod, and he turns to leave. My mind seems to weigh a thousand pounds. In it are the routes, hideouts, and secrets that will bring Bianchi's empire crumbling down.

My footsteps echo down the empty hallway as I retreat into the manor. Lightless rooms have always brought me comfort, shrouding my movements and plans. But now it feels suffocating. The solitude I've wrapped myself in for years no longer protects me—it isolates me.

I think of Clover's face, garnet eyes that see right through me. Since the day she joined us, I've kept her at a distance even as her light has drawn me closer to her fire. I tell myself it's for her safety. But the truth is more selfish.

I'm not the man she thinks I am. The chimera Bianchi created lives inside me, clawing to introduce itself to her. If she knew the corruption in my soul, she would turn away. And I'm not strong enough as a man to face that rejection. Not from her.

So I move in the darkness, and she remains in light. But I cannot make that sacrifice forever. Either the man consumes the monster, or the monster consumes the man.

For now, the man still fights. And for Clover, I will keep fighting. I will finish this, no matter what I must become. She is my last shred of humanity, my final glimpse of redemption. And I will protect her, even from myself.

I open the door to the crumbling stone stairs into the crypt.

The shadows swallow me as I descend deeper into the dark.

CHAPTER 30
CLOVER

The wrought-iron gate creaks open, a ghastly whine piercing the heavy silence. I wince, pausing on the overgrown path cutting through the decaying garden and scanning the deteriorating walls of Blackwood Manor looming in front of me.

Black moss clings to the weathered bricks, blotting out what remains of the once elegant facade. The stench of decay permeates the air, mingling with the frosted scent of snow and ice. This place reeks of death frozen in time, of lost souls trapped in the past.

A raven's piercing caw makes me jump. Heart skittering, I glance upward, spotting the inky bird perched atop a gargoyle leering down from the rooftop, its stone eyes tracking my every move.

The hairs on my neck prickle as I approach the heavy oak doors. The short morning walk was meant to quiet my mind, but I've only added to my trepidation. I can't shake the feeling of being watched even though the manor has been abandoned for over a century, and I know who resides in it now.

Steeling myself with a deep breath, I push open the door. It creaks inward, revealing a vast foyer blanketed in dust and draped in cobwebs. Shafts of light filter through the grime-coated windows, illuminating the sweeping staircase that groans under my tentative steps.

The air grows heavier with each floor I ascend, pressing down like a physical weight. I pass by room after room, most of them unused, their contents shrouded beneath moth-eaten sheets. The girls we rescued were transferred to another location last night by Rio, including Minnie, their exact whereabouts known only by a few—and one of them isn't me.

I should be glad Minnie is permanently out of my life, but instead, I feel cold.

Without their presence, this house is back to a tomb, every surface etched with memories of the tormented ghosts who once dwelled here.

I quicken my pace, eager to escape the oppressive atmosphere. But as I climb higher, the manor awakens, floorboards creaking, echoes whispering.

Reaching the third floor, I peer cautiously around the corner. A tall figure stands with his back to me, examining the dusty paintings lining the hall. Broad shoulders under a button-down shirt and tousled blondish hair identify him before he even turns.

"Morgan," I breathe, relief washing over me.

He glances over, one corner of his mouth curving. "Quite the dreary day for this Vulture nonsense, don't you think?"

His lips widen into a full grin, feral and reckless.

"If by nonsense you mean boredom," I say. "We have to find that circle."

Morgan fixes me with an intense look. "Easy, now. We'll find it."

He squeezes my shoulder, sending a little thrill through me. "I'm under strict orders to get some food in you first."

Despite myself, I smile slightly. Morgan's fierce protectiveness is a comfort, his quicksilver moods aside.

I nod, allowing Morgan to steer me down the hall toward the kitchens. His hand remains on my shoulder, radiating warmth even through the layers of my coat and shirt.

We descend the grand staircase, passing under portraits of Blackwood ancestors. Their stern faces peer down at us, seeming to follow our progress. An itchy unease creeps down my spine.

I glance at Morgan and find his jaw clenched, eyes darting about the gloomy gallery.

"What's wrong?" I ask.

He shakes his head. "Something is off. Can't you feel it, too?"

I strain my senses. The manor groans and settles around us, winter wind howling outside. But underneath it all, I detect a subtle shift in the air, like a drawn breath.

He releases me, massaging the back of his neck. "This rage inside me, Clover. It's uncontrollable. Insatiable. I almost pounced on you when we were supposed to be finished the other night. When you were too tired and sated to go on."

Morgan spins away, movements jagged.

Then he whirls back around, grasping my shoulders. "You have no idea the depraved thoughts in my head. The vile fantasies I have about you." Morgan's eyes glow with self-loathing and desire. "I try to rein it in, but the urge to maim and kill and pleasure is always there, gnawing away at my sanity."

I force myself to hold his gaze. "I'm not afraid of you, Morgan."

He searches my face, then steps back and continues his descent, shaking his head. "You should be."

We reach the bottom of the stairs and start down the central hall. Midway, Morgan stops abruptly. I nearly crash into him before following his gaze.

At the end of the corridor, a silhouette stands framed in moonlight. Tall, broad-shouldered, one hand resting casually on the ornate newel post. As we stare, the figure detaches from the shadows.

"Good morning, Miss Callahan. Morgan."

Rossi.

My heart leaps at the sight of his handsome, chiseled face with such world-weary eyes.

Rossi prowls closer. Streaks of the sun through the windows silver his dark hair further, and I'm struck again by his raw masculinity.

A tremor of excitement runs through me.

"We need to talk, Miss Callahan," he murmurs, stopping just before me.

This close, his cigar and old-books scent envelops me.

My lips part in surprise. Rossi wants to talk to me privately?

I nod mutely. Rossi's eyes burn into mine a moment before he turns, gesturing for me to follow. I hesitate.

Morgan senses my conflict, sighs, and makes a vague hand gesture in Rossi's direction. "Go. Apologies for ... me. I'll make you some eggs and bacon while he smothers you with his brooding depression."

Rossi leads me through the shadowy manor, our footsteps echoing off the high ceilings. I study his broad shoulders as we walk, noticing again his coiled power. He moves with animal grace, comfortable in his skin, at ease in the gloom.

We enter the grand library. Pale sunlight filters through tall, mullioned windows, casting everything in shades of silver and gray. Rossi goes to stand by one of the armchairs, resting a hand on its back.

When he remains silent, I venture, "Are you all right?"

Rossi stares at me with heavy lids. Sighs. "Life in our world doesn't afford the luxury of a clear mind."

I walk toward him, perching on the armrest of the chair, and peer up. "You can talk to me, you know. I'm not just here for a treasure hunt."

I expect him to respond with a grim tightening of his eyes like he always does. Instead...

He looks into my eyes, his hard facade crumbling. "It's not the treasure that's been haunting me, Clover. It's the ghosts—ghosts that don't rest easy."

"Are you talking about your wife and daughter?" I ask softly.

Rossi's hand drops from the back of the chair. "I couldn't protect them. They paid for my mistakes with their lives. After I refused to carry out a hit for Nico on his enemy's children, his men broke into our home. They tortured and killed my wife—Carina." His lips form around the name like it hurts him to say it. "Made me watch as they slit my daughter's throat." His voice breaks. "Then set fire to my home while they dragged me out of it. I've never forgiven myself for being unable to save them."

I dare to reach up and touch his cheek while my throat aches and bleeds for him. "Rossi..."

I freeze when he catches my hand and holds it against his cheek. "Do you have any idea what it's like? To know you've brought nothing but pain to those you care for? I don't—I *cannot*—allow you to be next."

I whisper while pushing to my feet, "I'm here under my own will. You didn't drag me into this life. Don't you think it's time to forgive yourself? To allow yourself to feel again?"

Rossi takes my hand from his cheek and kisses it softly. "Not a day goes by when I don't feel the pull, the desire. Especially around you. But how can a man like me, a man who's lost everything, deserve something so beautiful, so full of life? It hasn't touched you yet, this poison. And I never want it to. What I have planned could put you—"

I cup his face, leaning in closer. "Life doesn't come with guarantees. We fight, we lose, we hurt, but we also love. And sometimes, that love can be the redemption we never thought we'd find."

Rossi stares at me for a moment, for a decade, for forever, his eyes searching mine, then pulls me to his lips into a kiss filled with years of pain, regret, and unspoken, repressed desire.

I melt into the kiss, my heart pounding through the skin of my lips, knowing I'm treading dangerous waters but not caring. For now, I've given him a sanctuary, a pause in his horrific life.

And I'd do it any time he needed.

Rossi abruptly breaks the kiss, resting his forehead on mine and cupping my face dearly. "You should be careful. Wishing for a falling star will get you burned. And that is exactly what I am."

I whisper in reply, "Then let's burn together."

"I don't deserve you. Everyone I care for ends up dead. Or broken." His eyes bore into mine. "But I'm finding it harder and harder to stay away."

My pulse quickens at the raw need in his voice. But Rossi releases my face and turns.

"This can't happen. I won't let the Bianchis take someone else from me."

He stalks from the room, leaving me shaken and confused. When he slams the door shut, it echoes through the silent library into the very marrow of me.

I stand there stunned, trying to process Rossi's confession. The pain in his eyes when he spoke of his wife and child ... I can't imagine that kind of loss.

But my thoughts are interrupted by a sound behind me, and I whirl.

Rio emerges from the stacks, leaning casually against a bookcase. I didn't even hear him come in.

"Have you been there the whole time?" I gasp.

His lips tilt up. "Perhaps."

Rio prowls closer with his feline grace. Everything about him radiates allure, caution, danger, *need.*

My skin sizzles, hyperaware of his presence.

When he lifts a hand to my cheek, still hot from my encounter with Rossi, my lungs constrict.

"Such loyalty in you, Lucky," he murmurs. "I wonder if it will consume you in the end."

My lips part as I meet his hypnotic gaze. "Or set me free."

Rio smiles, showing a glimpse of his teeth. "We shall see."

I open my mouth to respond, but Rio presses a finger to my lips.

"Shh. There will be time for more later."

He trails his fingers down my neck before he melts back into the shadows, leaving as silently as he came.

I release a shaky breath, my blood simmering.

With Rio and Rossi, *all of them*, I am surely playing with fire.

But I will happily walk into the flames.

CHAPTER 31
CLOVER

I take a deep breath to steady myself after that charged encounter with Rio. Though unsettling, his interest flatters me. It's what I've wanted for years—since I hid under tables and behind couches.

I'm still reeling from the day's events—from Rossi baring his soul in the library to Morgan's vulnerable admission about his inner darkness.

It makes me realize that these men see me as more than just a pawn in their war against Bianchi's syndicate. I've become someone they confide in and trust.

An equal.

I pull my shoulders back as I exit the library.

No longer will I be passive, unsure Clover. I'll help Rossi avenge his family. I will be the anchor that keeps Morgan's demons at bay. For Rio, I'll be his liberation from forced silence. And for Xavier, I will be his happiness when he needs it most.

I can't ignore this blossoming love I have for them.

Is it so wrong to care for them all? Society may judge, but in my heart, I know—I've found where I'm meant to be.

I'm a Vulture.

The candlelight flickers against the dark oak walls, casting shadows that writhe like specters across the halls as I head to the drawing room in preparation for our meeting. I take a seat, curling into an armchair as the others enter.

First comes Xavier, cheering up the second he notices me. The memory of his hands on my skin, along with Rio and Morgan, quickens my pulse.

Then Morgan enters, all wild energy barely contained, sandy hair disheveled. His laughter echoes in my mind, low and dangerous in my ear before he licked me.

Rio enters soundlessly, brown eyes unfathomable. He lingers in the periphery, ever the watcher. And finally, Rossi. He sinks into the leather armchair opposite me, every movement controlled and elegant. Our gazes lock, and I feel the force of his stare like a tangible brushing of his fingers against my cheek.

Tempest and Ardyn are next, her hand weaving with his. Even as they settle into the couch opposite me, they don't let go of each other.

Everyone wears somber expressions. The silence hangs heavy with what to do next.

Clearing my throat, I begin.

"We all know why we're here. The 'stone circled in summer' from Sarah Anderton's grimoire makes me think her hidden fortune is at the solstice circle in the forest."

"And how'd you jump from a stoned circle in summer to a solstice circle in the dead of winter?" Morgan interrupts, eyes twinkling.

I shake my head fondly. "Well, you, our resident occult historian, said solstice rituals can happen out of season, so

Sarah's clue can still hold merit. It doesn't have to be summer for us to go there and find what she hid."

Rio's stare tapers, ever pragmatic. "The woods are dangerous this time of year, as you've no doubt already experienced. And what are the odds Bianchi already knows about it and doesn't have his men or hounds waiting?"

"He doesn't," I answer. "He can't. I burned the page with the written 'stone in summer' clue when Ardyn and I were in the archives at the TFU library. Rossi can confirm." I incline my head at Rio's, noticing the stress around his eyes.

Xavier's on the edge of the sofa beside Tempest, his focus flicking from face to face like he's watching an intense soccer game. "Fortune favors the bold. We'd be fools not to pursue it."

Tempest leans forward. "What'll we find? More clues or the actual treasure?"

Rossi hasn't said anything yet. The others turn to him, awaiting his decree. When he finally speaks, his voice is cold steel.

"How do we know this won't add another complication to an already impossible endeavor?"

His question, blunt and searing, hangs in the air. My heart races as our eyes lock. The room, the tension, all fade away. It's just us, a heavy quiet punctuated by unspoken desires and regrets.

"We don't," I finally reply, scrutinizing him. "And none of Sarah's clues have been impossible. Complicated, yes. She's made this difficult so the right person could find it." *Me.* "But even if it is another clue to decipher, isn't it worth finding out?"

The room quiets, waiting.

Rossi and I are at a stand-off in the middle. The pull

between us is palpable, a magnetic force neither of us acts upon.

Then, as if making an internal decision, he says, "If this leads nowhere tangible, I'm done with treasure hunts. We have more pressing matters to attend to."

His dismissal ignites a shocking anger in me. *I've worked too hard for him to be so dismissive.* But I don't waver under his masked expression, instead meeting it head-on.

"You're wrong," I say to him. "This could change everything for us. It could free you."

The word *free* cracks through the air like a whip.

For a breath, his impassive façade slips, and I glimpse the inferno behind his eyes.

Then the shutter falls again, and he turns away contemptuously. The spell breaks, yet he peels his lips back and hisses through his teeth, "Fine."

I lean back, smothering the loud huff that wants to escape from my chest, and cross my arms. The men talk about what weapons and tools to bring, and I internally resolve to pocket the iron key I found—*my* weapon—before we depart.

Oh, and bear spray. I truly wish I'd had it when the hounds came. Or the men in the mines. Or—always, really.

We agree to leave at dawn, and as everyone disperses, a gust of wind somehow slips through the room.

The breeze sends a scatter of cold, invisible spiders down my spine. Is it a clue or a warning?

I don't know, but this trip to the solstice circle will either unveil a long-hidden treasure or bring to the surface the deeper mysteries—ones I'm realizing, as I study Rossi, that some of us would prefer to remain buried.

THE COLD AIR is unforgiving as we hike deeper into the forest two hours before the break of dawn. It will take about four hours to trek, but the circle is inaccessible by car and closer to the forest at the peak of campus than Blackwood Manor, so we're taking the backwoods onto TFU property.

So as not to leave a trail, Rio takes the lead, and Tempest hangs back, scrubbing our footprints from the dirt. Xavier, Tempest, and Rio carry large backpacks full of what we'll need, with Rossi and Morgan flanking Ardyn and me, the two equipped with guns and knives, respectively.

They've armed themselves to the teeth. Morgan and Rossi wear leather holsters to hold their weapons of choice. Every time their arms sway with their prowl, their leather jackets peel open, showcasing shoulder and belt loop holsters. Rossi has a leg strap as well, and Morgan wears one on his wrist. Not to be outdone, Rio and Tempest do, too.

Xavier is less heavily equipped, preferring a knife sheath at his hip and one shoulder holster for a gun he's still getting used to.

And in typical testosterone-fueled fashion, the Vultures have armed Ardyn and me with flashlights.

Or so they think. She and I stockpiled for ourselves, me with the iron key, bear spray, and a switchblade inside my jacket, and her with a small handgun she snuck from their weapon stash at the manor.

We may be exploring a long-deserted, ancient ritual site, but we've all learned from the dog situation and Bianchi's men cornering us in the mines.

Up ahead, Rio's steps are deliberate and confident. There's

a natural authority to his stride, honed from years of navigating these woods, stalking his marks, and hiding secrets beneath its soil.

At one point, he stops and glances back, catching my eye. His gaze lingers for a moment before he turns away.

Morgan speaks up, his tone laden with sarcasm. "The forest's quieter than usual this morning. Did Tongueless scare off all the birds?"

"Or maybe they've learned to keep secrets as well as he does," I add, smiling at the back of Rio's head.

He shows me his profile, offering a half smile in return.

After hours of climbing, then descending, and some tripping where Morgan rights me with honed reflexes before I fall, we reach what Rio believes to be the solstice circle—a ring of ancient, weathered stones standing tall like silent sentinels at the edge of a deathly, jagged cliff face. I dare to toe the edge, looking down at the drop and the iced-over creek below, then wince as my stomach roils at the depth.

I'm not afraid of heights, but to be this close to open air and the chances of a fall—it's legitimately terrifying.

I happily step over to safer land. Uprooted trees obscure half of the six carved, weathered stones, and two are broken in half, their jagged lumps spearing out of the ground like mossy, faded tombstones.

Rio steps into the circle first, sweeping his gaze around before nodding almost imperceptibly. It's as though he's given the space his tacit safety check.

It would be funny in any other circumstance. But with what we've endured so far, he has every right to ensure there aren't any traps, poisons, or dogs awaiting our arrival.

Morgan chimes in, unable to help himself. "What do you think, Rio? Feeling like some circle time with us kids?"

The corners of Rio's mouth bunches at Morgan's question, but he simply presses a palm against one of the megaliths. His eyes slide shut as he communes silently and with respect for the ancient site.

I hesitate at the boundary, sensing the raw energy contained within. Every hair on my body stands on end.

I say, "The clue we're working on is 'a stone circled in summer.' Let's find it."

Rossi folds his arms. "I'll give you all an hour to find something. Otherwise, we return to the manor and pack for the city."

Acknowledging him with a side-eye, I split from the men, examining the stones.

I wonder how many hands have touched these rocks, how many pagans or witches or curious people have wandered under my feet.

One thing I enjoy most about artifacts is how humbling they are. We are not the center of the universe. We just live and die in it, then leave behind trinkets for future generations to marvel over.

Morgan is the one who finds it—a carving that matches the carved flower that's led me to so many of Sarah Anderton's secrets.

"What's this?" he asks, cocking his head as he drags his finger through the divot.

Rio steps up behind him. "A lily."

I perk up. The flower is a *lily*. The carving makes so much more sense. "It's important."

All men turn to me. Ardyn furrows her brow at the pitch in my voice.

"Sarah must have carved it for her daughter as a mark for her to find." I jog over to the stone, feeling the carving myself and welcoming the butterflies in my belly.

Xavier meanders around the stone. "What do you suppose it means?"

"Well, the last time I saw it—"

"You've seen it before?" Rossi cuts in.

I swallow. "In the tunnel to Anderton Cottage. It was carved above a hidden stone entrance."

"Ah," Morgan agrees. "I remember."

He offers a wink at what he and I *also* did around that tunnel.

I glance away before the ache between my legs can take over.

Xavier says, "What do you say, gents? Should we go underground again?"

Rio plants a crowbar beneath the stone in answer, muscles popping from his neck as he attempts to force it open.

He's a robust and skilled guy but not strong enough to move the stone. I sit back on my haunches when, for the first time since meeting them, the Vultures work together to tip the stone over.

It lands on its side with a small *boom*, with a puff of snow and dirt blowing over my face and clothes.

"Christ," Tempest breathes, staring at the spot the stone vacated. "I should expect this by now, but it never gets less fucked."

Standing, I brush the debris off my legs and peer down with him.

It's not stairs like I predicted, but an abyss, a yawning void of darkness. It's like looking into the earth's belly, and for a second, I question the sanity of descending into it.

"Just because we've found a hole doesn't mean we should go in," Ardyn says, wrapping her arm through mine as she steadies her flashlight into the center of it. "Could be filled with snakes or spiders or worse."

But the hole is so deep that the light disappears into nothing.

Rossi's eyes meet mine, full of skepticism but also an underlying tension I've come to recognize.

"What is this, Miss Callahan? I'm not compromising one of my men, nor am I allowing you to heave yourself inside."

Ignoring his negative attitude, I lean closer and notice Ardyn's light hit a metallic glint deep within the hole before moving away—something out of place in this earthen hollow.

"Hold the flashlight here," I instruct Ardyn.

"Where?" she asks.

Rio takes the torch from Ardyn, complying without a word and casting a focused beam of light on what appears to be an elaborate, rusted metal plate set into the side of the hole.

"Son of a..." Tempest says.

With an adrenaline spike of excitement, I reach into my pocket and pull out the iron key that has weighed heavy in my possession since I found it.

Morgan purrs in approval. "Good thinking, little leaf."

"Hold on," Rio growls softly, wrapping his arm around my waist when he realizes what I'm about to do. He steadies me as I lean farther into the hole.

Trusting him, I line up and insert the key into the almost eroded keyhole.

The moment the key turns, we hear a grating sound, like rusty gears coming back to life after decades—or centuries—of dormancy. The noise resonates in the forest, drowning out the natural sounds until all we hear is the mechanized creaking and clanking.

Suddenly, solid stone steps emerge from the darkness, appearing one at a time to form a descending staircase.

"Well, look at that." Morgan doesn't often sound surprised. "Our dearly departed Mrs. Anderton had access to a seventeenth-century Q from *James Bond*."

Xavier chuckles darkly. "A stairway to hell, knowing our luck."

The staircase stills, now solid and inviting—at least to me.

With a deep, audible sigh and a long look at me, Rossi goes first, gently prying a flashlight from my pack.

One by one, we descend, Ardyn and I taking our familiar places in the middle of the Vultures.

Our group is quiet and wary. The atmosphere becomes increasingly heavy and laden with moisture as our heads disappear underground, the air tinged with the musty smell of damp earth, aged wood, and a faint metallic scent.

I palm the bear spray, just in case.

The low glow of our flashlights reveals subtle shifts in the texture and color of the earth around us—the deeper we go, the darker the soil becomes, transitioning from a light, almost sandy color to a deep, rich brown and finally to an almost black hue as we near the bottom.

The distant drip of water echoes through the narrow passage, punctuating our silence, interrupted by the sporadic creak of leather and the occasional rattle and clink of our weapons.

Our descent is roughly twenty-to-thirty feet before we reach a small pathway, the walls a mix of compressed soil reinforced with age-worn, grayish stone slabs that have been painstakingly fit together. The stone is marked with sporadic etchings that vary from the barely recognizable outlines of animals to more obscure, almost runic symbols.

I turn to Morgan with a raised brow, but he offers a shrug in return, the symbols not recognizable to him, either.

When we tread on old wooden boards set into the ground like a makeshift floor, there's a sound akin to a disconcerting moan from the weight of years that have passed with no human footsteps.

We reach a reinforced wooden door at the end, an exact replica of the photograph Cav provided us.

I figure it out the moment Rossi does—and he releases a loud curse at the sight.

"The wizard is at it again." Morgan folds his arms, shaking his head. "He's already been down here, seen this, photographed it, then gifted it to us. What *is* he about?"

"Does Cav have the jewels? Is this all a fucking merry chase to him?" Xavier grits out through the spaces of his teeth, brushing falling dirt off his shoulders. "If that's the case, I'll have no trouble doing him in."

"But could he get through this door?" I ask before anyone else starts to lose it. "Cav Nightshade didn't have this."

I brandish the key, moving to the front. When I slip it into the lock, the door takes it without argument.

I echo my brother's thought: *I should expect this by now, but holy shit.*

Tempest and Rossi both slip in front of me as the door creaks ajar, continuing to play our version of leapfrog as they move in first, weapons drawn.

"It's safe," Rossi says in a low voice a few moments later. "Come in."

With flashlights as our guide, we enter a vault that takes our collective breath away.

Time-worn crates and locked trunks line the walls.

Muskets, pistols, and bayonets dating back to the 1600s hang above them.

And most shockingly, a desk and chair are placed near the east corner, piled high with yellowed, worn leather books.

Morgan brushes past me, the whites of his eyes on full display. "The treasure. Is it here? Does anybody see it?"

Xavier casts a wary eye to the trunks and crates stacked on one side. "Let me guess. We've moved on from cave spelunking to cataloging inventory."

"A necessary evil," Tempest says but offers me his version of a smile. "This shit is crazy, Clo."

"We should take some time to search," Rossi agrees, his voice laced with strain. "Not too much, but if the jewels are here, we should find them."

Should. Not *need*, like he was so adamant about a month ago.

Even though I'm desperate to scour the room, I take a second to study the Vulture's leader, a man who, up until now, wanted to do whatever it took to free his men from Bianchi's vise.

What's changed? What is Rossi up to?

But he's moved from the center of the room, frowning in thought as he inspects the rusted weapons on the far wall.

Not enjoying the turmoil in my belly while watching Rossi, I move to the desk instead, picking up a book at the top of the pile and carefully flipping through its worn, time-stiffened pages. I read entries about healing spells, herbs, mushroom hallucinogens—things I expected to find. Sarah's grimoire has almost an exact copy of these potent mixes, some of which I accidentally dabbled in.

But then my eyes catch on something different yet familiar: a list made in her handwriting, with names next to descriptions like *Eleanor - Opal Horse Ring, Richard - Duke of Northcut.*

My heartbeat kicks up a notch.

I drag my finger down the page, my vision hungrily eating up the words.

LILIUM - KEEPER of Secrets

Nightshade – The Guardian
Marigold - The Seafarer
Bluebell - The Quill
Rosemary - The Shade
Lavender - The Hearth
Sage - The Stablemaster
Jonquil - The Lexicon
Primrose - The Purse
Foxglove - The Watcher
Sweet William - The Emissary
Hawthorn - The Physic
Cowslip - The Masquerade
Snowdrop - The Frost
Daffodil - The Mason
Thistle - The Engineer

THERE'S a chill in the air, heavy and damp, but that's not why I'm breathing shakily. I turn a few more pages, finding a section devoted to "transfers," listed in the same coded language.

As cold realization dawns on me, Morgan breaks the studious silence.

"Looks like we've stumbled upon more than just treasure.

What do you think this is, boys? It can't all have been Sarah and her daughter. Witches don't deal in *weapons*, for goodness' sake. And where the *fuck* are the jewels? Anyone?"

For a moment, I stand there, absorbing the gravity of my discovery. I look up to find Rossi's gaze locked on me, laden with emotion he won't express. Rio glances between both of us. Then, once he reads something on my face, he moves to the journal, his face unreadable, but his eyes—oh, his eyes say it all.

I return his concerned study, my mouth hanging open as I pull out what was tucked into the pages with all those names. A pressed flower—delicate, fragile.

He sees it, then says two words to me: "*Lilium grayi.*"

I'm too stunned to reply.

This room, Sarah's past, has given us keys to the future, but the weight of that breakthrough holds me in an almost fearful silence.

And within that quiet, Sarah's purposes, our desires, and her and our future endeavors intertwine.

CHAPTER 32
CLOVER

The underground room feels like it contracts, space tightening around me as I realize I'm not holding records of Sarah's stolen jewels.

I'm holding the name of women.

The jewels are women.

Women *saved* by flowers.

"*Lillium grayi*. Or Gray's lily. A rare wildflower," Rio explains with his scarred voice, tenderly extricating the dried, pressed flower from my fingers. "Grows only at high elevations around here, and in early summer."

"Lillium, Sarah's daughter." I point at the first name on the list. "Keeper of Secrets. She was named after a flower. And so were all these people, named in code for Sarah's underground network."

"Her what?" Xavier asks, slowly withdrawing his hands from an open crate.

Rio hums in answer, then angles his head in study. "Is that what has you so pale, Lucky? There is more than one witch involved in the treasure?"

Rather than answering, I lift the open book to my face and read further in a shaky voice. "'*Lily safely escorted our newest jewel to the meeting point. Opal Horse Ring is now secure. As for the Duke, he'll be searching for a ring he'll never find again...*'"

It hits Rio like a bolt of lightning, freezing him more than his usual still posture.

"What's going on?" Rossi demands.

He stalks over, eyes slitted.

Ardyn notices, too, and immediately comes to my side in solidarity and support.

"Sarah wasn't just a witch," I say, my voice tremulous. I'm almost in tears. "She was more than what the town accused her of. She was a savior. These hidden 'jewels' were women, saved from slavery, indentured servitude, sexual exploitation, marriage markets ... the list goes on. Look right here. There are hundreds of these entries—all these books." I gesture to the multiple piles on the desk. "'Opal Horse Ring' wasn't an accessory paid to Sarah for a murder; it was this Eleanor's coded identity, a cloak of protection as she was logged, then transferred out of Titan Falls to somewhere safe."

As I leaf through the first journal, the weight of its contents fills the room. It details Sarah's efforts to save young women from a horrible fate, all written in a delicate, looping script.

The tactics she outlines—coded messages, secret rendezvous points, working agents—all sounding so surprisingly modern.

"We've been chasing a legacy," Xavier says as he draws closer, his voice tinged with respect. "Not just money or jewels but an actual, noble fucking legacy."

I look up, my stare first connecting to Rossi. No words are exchanged between us, and I have no idea if he or the others feel the weight of this revelation, this monumental shift in understanding.

We didn't just find a treasure today; like Xavier said, we've stumbled upon a legacy, a hidden history of women fighting back, resisting in the only ways they could in a world that wanted to crush them.

The tension between Rossi and me feels like a living entity in this confined space, but there's something more potent now. The "jewels" we'd been so intent on finding are no longer gemstones or trinkets. They're lives saved, priceless in their humanity.

But in doing so, they've taken away the Vultures' lives.

"Did you know?" I ask Rossi, my voice growing stronger.

His brows jump, the rest of his face remaining impassive.

"This," I clarify, pointing at the book in my hands. "Is this why you became so unconcerned with finding the jewels? Because you figured out they're not rare and priceless jewelry to make you rich, but were women sold into slavery and sex? Useless in modern value?"

As I talk, Morgan looks at the ceiling and drags his hands down his face, his expression crumpled with disappointment.

"No, Miss Callahan," Rossi answers. "I hadn't a clue this was what the Andertons were really doing."

"All those tunnels, hidden rooms, passageways..." Tempest's voice drifts off. "It all makes sense now, but god-*fucking*-dammit, these jewels were meant to gain our freedom!"

He ends on a broken shout, the rest of the Vultures, my men, my poor men, pacing angrily, arms down at their sides, heads bowed, fingers itching toward their weapons, because that is the only way they know how to solve problems.

What have I done?

The Vultures are in servitude, just like those Sarah fought to free. The skill acquired by these men—my *brother*—their deadly precision, their waking hours spent honing those talents just to keep breathing, all in the face of so little hope. But they had it, even if they couldn't admit it. They thought there was a chance to leave this life.

Sarah's treasure hunt was *fun* for me. Deciphering her clues, growing closer to these jaded men, and becoming part of their group was an addictive revelation, but one I was willing to accept because it was exciting. It made *me* excited, respected, admired.

When the truth is, I had so much more to learn before ever discovering Sarah's secret.

I didn't believe it until now, but I was showing off my cleverness, quick thinking, and calmness under pressure to prove I belonged when, in reality, I don't.

The point of this mission has always been to free the Vultures. Unclip their wings.

Because they're suffering.

They're dying.

I carefully set the journal back, my vision filled with unshed, blurry tears. I move farther into the cavernous room, sweeping my flashlight over the other sealed containers.

In one dusty crate, I spot the unmistakable sheen of metal barrels.

"Over here," I call to Rossi, clearing my throat of emotion. Morgan comes with him.

They stride over as I pry off the lid. Inside sits an arsenal of antique weaponry: muskets, flintlock pistols, and bayonets, all engraved with the lily flower seal. Morgan lets out an impressed whistle.

"Now this," he says, lifting out one of the pistols, "we can definitely use."

He checks the firing mechanism with an expert hand.

Despite their age, the weapons are in excellent condition. Relics from another era, one where rebellions were won with blood and sacrifice.

Rossi steps closer, his body radiating heat in the cool underground vault. He trails his fingers down my arm, leaving goose bumps in their wake.

"I promise you, Miss Callahan, even in light of this discovery, Bianchi has no idea what's coming for him," he murmurs.

I shiver at the promise in his words. Appreciate his assessment of my emotional state, despite his refusal to acknowledge our feelings for each other.

"Dear Uncle won't be pleased the treasure isn't real. We'll need to be ingenious if we're to outmaneuver him," Morgan replies behind us.

"We'll outthink him," I say. "We're already one step ahead. He still thinks there are buried jewels in Titan Falls."

My breath catches at the faith in my voice. Rossi stays close. The space between us is charged now, our bodies mere inches apart. I want to close the distance and feel the solidness of Rossi against me...

"Enough scheming for one day," Xavier says. "We'd best get moving before Bianchi's dogs get curious about our whereabouts. The last thing we want is for him to find this, too."

The musty air of the underground vault envelops me as Rossi's fingers dig into my arm. The connection between us still hums like a live wire.

"Leave us," he orders them. "Go back above ground and make sure we've covered our tracks completely. We'll go a different, indirect route home."

They hesitate, especially Tempest, glancing back and forth between Rossi and me.

"Sir..." Tempest looks ready to argue against me and his boss alone in the underground but catches Rossi's resolute stare and physically fights to keep his mouth shut.

Ultimately, they all follow his command and retreat up the steps.

Once they're gone, Rossi's penetrating gaze returns to mine.

My heart scrapes against my ribs. The vault seems to close in around us, the ancient artifacts and documents—Sarah herself—watching like silent sentinels.

Rossi doesn't hesitate. "Never question my motives in front of my men again."

My mouth works. "I didn't—"

"You think I wanted to lead them down here and watch this revelation suck their black souls out of their bodies? Do you believe I get off on hurting my men the way Bianchi does?"

"Of course not," I hiss. The backs of my eyes heat with humiliation and fury.

"I know how you feel about me," Rossi continues relentlessly. "I've seen it in your eyes, felt it in your touch. And that has caused you to become too familiar with how you speak to me."

My mouth falls open. "Are you seriously giving me a dressing down right now?"

Brutal black eyes lock with mine. His beauty, handsomeness, severity, hotter still.

He steps closer, backing me against the chilled stone wall. All I feel is ice, yet his breath is volcanic on my cheek.

"If you are looking up to me like some mentor, like a man who might save you, honor you, save it for a boy who would trip over himself to impress you, not a man with scars on his back, claw marks in his brain, and complete and utter blindness to love."

My stomach surges as Rossi completely overshadows me with his bulk and pulls out a dagger from his wrist sheath, dragging it across my neck in a cutthroat motion, his eyes so empty.

"I am a killer. *We* are killers. Merciless. We don't offer prayers when our marks die under our hands. We don't try to save them before we mutilate, then destroy, their futures."

Rossi searches my eyes further, my heartbeat drumming along with his voice.

"Now that you've solved your little riddles, you'd best ask yourself if you're still welcome here."

"Stop," I whisper.

"We are not the same, Miss Callahan," Rossi concludes. "Be thankful, be blessed, and stop *fucking* wanting me."

Rossi's words cut through me like the sharp blade he holds to my neck, leaving me raw and exposed. The cold metal of the dagger grazes my skin, a constant reminder of how helpless I am in his hands.

I stare up at him, his face a mask of harsh indifference, and my pulse races with a mix of terror and yearning.

I can't help it. I don't want to help it.

But even as he threatens me, there's a stirring deep inside. The treacherous edge to his words sends a shudder down my back, awakening my primal itch.

"Please..." I gasp, my voice barely above a whisper.

Rossi's eyes temper ever so slightly at my fear, but it's gone in an instant, calcifying over.

"You should be afraid of me," he murmurs, the dagger digging into my delicate skin. "I'll destroy you if you let me."

His words are a warning, a challenge, and a promise all at once.

But I'm not afraid. I want him, all of him. I want his pain, his torment, his anger. I want to be his release, his salvation, his monster's destruction.

"Rossi..." I breathe, my voice a moan.

And then he's on me, his mouth crushing mine in a fierce, punishing kiss. My tastebuds burst with the bitterness of his anger, the pain of his loss, the desperation of his need.

His hands are rough, demanding, pulling me closer until no air is left between us. The dagger is still pressed against my neck, but all I can think about is the ruinous hunger consuming us both.

He tears away from me, his eyes violently fierce with heat and wrath.

"You want this?" he growls, dropping the blade and using his hand, tightening it around my throat. "You want me to dominate you, to damage you, to make you mine?"

"Yes," I gasp, my voice tremulous.

He's frantic, tearing at my clothes, leaving bruises in his wake. I cry out as he slams me against the wall, his body pinning mine, his mouth leaving a trail of scorching kisses down my neck. Rossi's body presses against mine in a way that threatens to consume. And I welcome it, the torment and bliss, eclipse and dawn, all melding into one as we become lost.

His hand wraps around my neck, replacing the blade, but neither frighten me anymore. He's not sleepwalking.

It's a symbol of his power, his control, his dominance. And I submit, craving the rush of every touch, every kiss, every bruise.

I know what we're doing is wrong, unsafe, and even twisted. But at this moment, it's all that matters. His rough hands, his hard body, his fierce love. And I'll take it all, even if it means risking everything.

"Say it," he growls. "Tell me you're mine to command, mine to punish. Mine to fuck and own and break."

"I'm yours," I gasp, jerking against him.

His entire body shudders as he grabs my right arm, holding it tightly behind my back. His lips move closer to my ear.

Voice guttural and full of promise, he whispers, "You will do everything I say."

Rossi lifts and carries me across the room, laying me on Sarah's desk, scattering her ledgers, her hidden truth.

My hands reach for him, greedily seeking out every inch of his body. But he pins them over my head, a slight smirk on his lips.

His movements are hard and urgent, and I whimper with anticipation.

"No touching," he warns. "I'll tell you when you can touch me."

I nod, my mouth an *O* of need as he focuses on tearing my shirt and shoving down my pants with one hand, then removes my underwear and bra. He works in silence, only stopping to take off his own shirt, then unbuckling his belt and unzipping his pants.

"I'm going to fuck you," he says flatly, holding my gaze. "And I'm going to fuck you hard. Tell me I can."

"Yes." I swallow.

A brutal smile spreads across his face. "Beg me for it."

My cheeks flush, the desire and shame making me throb with need.

"Please, Rossi. Miguel. I want it hard. I want you hard. I want to feel you."

"You want to feel me?" he repeats, almost mockingly. "You want to feel my cock?"

"Yes," I reply, my voice quivering.

"Please," he reminds.

"*Please*," I beg.

"I should punish you for that kind of misstep," Rossi scolds. "But I won't. I'll eat your cunt instead and drive you to the brink before pulling back and watching you grieve."

I try to respond, but the words won't come. He drops to his knees, his eyes locked on mine as he squeezes my ass cheeks. Rossi nuzzles my legs, his tongue trailing a path from my inner thigh up to my center. I gasp as his mouth closes over me, sucking on my clit, then biting down painfully, angrily, and drawing blood.

While the pain shoots up my core and makes me cry out, he plunges his tongue inside me. My head falls back as I arch toward him, my hands finding his full, thick hair and clinging to it like a lifeline.

"I said no touching," Rossi warns sharply, pulling away. "Close your eyes."

I obey, squeezing them shut and at the mercy of cold air and lithe movements as he steps back, admiring his work.

I hear Rossi position himself at my entrance, nudging my pussy with the tip of his dick, then thrust inside me. I cry out at the sudden intrusion, the pleasure-pain filling me where I didn't know I was empty. As he jams his dick inside, his mouth ruthlessly assaults my neck, marking me with his teeth.

I'm stunned by the ferocity of our lovemaking and how easily and savagely he's able to navigate my body. Rossi's relentless, coaxing sounds from me I never knew I could make. His hands scrape over my body as we brutally move together, his mouth sucking on my lips, to my breasts, my neck, my nipples, biting, claiming, hurting.

I can't take anymore; I'm on the edge of my release. My hips buck against him, grinding, begging him to give me everything. I can take him deeper. As black and dark as he needs.

Rossi's merciless. His breath quickens as he fucks me, his teeth sinking deeper into my skin, his hand wrapped around my throat, squeezing with vicious precision.

I'm so close, I can feel the tremors already starting in my thighs. And then he flicks and rolls my wounded, still-bleeding clit, and I'm gone, shattering into a million tiny pieces.

The orgasm lasts for what feels like ages, and I'm still coming when he pulls out and releases my neck on a shove.

I open my eyes to catch Rossi's shudder, his chest heaving. He pulled out at the last moment, his cum spurting onto my abdomen and breasts as he erupts; the muscles in his arms and shoulders tense, his body shaking.

Rossi is so destroyed, so plagued, yet so powerful and beautiful.

He exhales on a groan, then leans over the desk, arms braced on the wood on either side of me as he catches his breath.

Rossi's face loses all hardness. His portrait tenderizes in front of me, slashes becoming soft brushstrokes, becoming the man he was.

What he'll never know is, this moment is a glimpse into the man he could be again if he only allowed himself to be loved.

I sit up, wincing as the marks on my skin pull and sting. Rossi straightens, then pulls me to my feet.

"Clean yourself up," he says, glancing at the mess on my chest.

It's a casual order, probably said a thousand times before. But I hear it as a dare.

My bare feet are cold against the ground, but I only put on my underwear and bra before I search for Rossi's shirt before he can grab it and pull it on himself.

He notices with a disapproving scowl but doesn't follow it up, considering he demolished mine. Rossi turns to grab his leather jacket and zip it shut.

But not before I see his back.

"Oh my God," I whisper. "Your..."

He glances over his shoulder, his jaw carved out of his neck like a rocky cliff face. "It's a tattoo. Nothing."

I resist the urge to touch it. Him. "It looks so ... raw."

Rossi busies himself collecting weapons on the other side. He doesn't look at me when he says, "Bianchi had me whipped, then inked vulture's wings over the fresh wounds."

I have nothing to say in reply. I can only express agony at the thought of him being held down, tortured, and branded.

"Rossi..."

"Don't pity me." He shies away as I come close.

"I'm not pitying you. I just want to..." I stall, unsure what I want to do with him. What *can* I do with a man so conflicted?

I lean into him, my lips on his throat, my tongue lapping at the sweat and drops of pre-cum left behind.

Making him forget his memories and remember our present.

I can't move away. I'm addicted to his scent, his taste. I want to devour him. I want to bury myself inside him and never come out.

I'm aching for more when Rossi grabs me by the elbow and yanks me back. His ember eyes sear into mine as he looks at me, cold and pitiless.

"Isn't it horrifying to you?" he challenges. "You wanted me, and you got it. Nasty and heartless. Don't you see? It's the way you look at me. It's the way you smell me like I'm something you'd like to eat. It's the way you talk in that fucking voice. I don't deserve you."

I recoil.

"After everything I've done, all the blood on my hands... how could I possibly deserve someone so pure?"

"You don't get to decide what I deserve," I whisper back, my voice steadier than I feel. "I do."

"I won't pretend to be something I'm not," he says softly. "But don't assume you know me or what I'm capable of feeling."

His hand shifts to gently touching my face, his fingers lightly tracing the contours of my jawline. The juxtaposition of the danger and pain he just represented and the tenderness of his touch make my heart sink in my chest. It's a gesture so uncharacteristically gentle that it takes me by surprise.

It's that vulnerability, that crack in his armor, that compels me to close the distance between us, to press my lips against his in a kiss filled with frustration, yearning, and a touch of pissed off-ness.

Rossi hesitates for a fraction of a second, as if debating with himself, then his arms are around me, pulling me closer to him. The kiss deepens, becoming more insistent and passionate as if we are trying to communicate everything we've been holding back, all the words we haven't said.

As we pull apart, both of us panting for breath, Rossi regards me with a strength that sends tremors into my soul.

"You need to understand. Being with me won't save you from the atrocities of this world. If anything, it might pull you deeper into it."

"I'm not looking to be saved," I reply faintly.

He shakes his head as if in disbelief but doesn't pull away.

"You complicate things," he murmurs, almost to himself.

"Isn't life complicated?" I retort.

"We should go," he says, but neither of us moves, suspended at this moment, realizing that something has shifted, something neither of us can ignore.

Finally, Rossi breaks away.

"After you, Miss Callahan," he says, his voice tinged with an emotion he doesn't name.

Though we're back to formal basics, it seems.

But as we turn to leave Sarah's vault to climb back into a world full of peril and uncertainty, I realize that despite Rossi's warnings and the threats that undoubtedly lie ahead, Miguel Rossi has become another compelling reason to keep fighting.

We're both on the edge of an abyss, teetering on the brink between despair and salvation.

But if we're going to fall, we'll fall together, united in a bloodthirsty twilight that might just give way to dawn.

CHAPTER 33
CLOVER

I suck in air as we emerge from Sarah's vault under the stone circle, the cool morning temperature helping clear my head after the intensity below.

Back above ground, Rossi and I try to steady our breathing and emotions. As the others return, we're back to business mode, and Morgan shoots us a knowing glance at our obvious sex hair but keeps his mouth shut.

The Vultures return to the vault under Rossi's supervision, packing up weapons, books, and any other artifacts worth exploring. None of us plans on returning to the site unless forced because if we did, it would mean we missed something.

And we can't afford to miss anything.

Rossi and Rio lead us through a new hiking path, everyone laden with Sarah's true treasure and new, viscous thoughts.

Three hours later, we arrive at the manor and immediately assemble in the dim light of our makeshift command center, the manor's dining room, with Sarah Anderton's journals and coded documents spread on the large, eighteen-seater formal table in the middle.

The tension and disappointment are palpable, but I'm excited at the prospect of using history to outwit a modern-day monster.

Stop, Clover, I admonish myself. *This isn't supposed to be fun.*

"Listen up," Rossi commands, his eyes scanning the room, pausing momentarily on me. "We're all disappointed the treasure isn't real, but that's not to say we can't use what we've found, both to bait Bianchi since he's yet to discover there are no real jewels and to employ tactics he wouldn't expect. I suppose we knew it all along, but Sarah Anderton was a shrewd woman who escaped notice for decades before being caught. We can all stand to learn from her."

He goes silent as the rest of us take our seats, then Rossi's phone buzzes.

Rossi frowns, then flips his phone's screen so we can all see.

"Ah, Nightshade gifts us with more of his jaunty clues," Morgan says with a vague, dismissive gesture. "Always knew that man could capture a moment."

Morgan's observation is on point. It's a text message from Cav, displaying a photo of Bianchi entering a bungalow in the woods.

But it means nothing to me. I look at the others for clarification.

"Damn," Rio says under his breath. "He's got to one of my cabins."

Rossi murmurs, "Bianchi's getting warm and finding some of our lesser-known safe houses. We've just lost the luxury of time."

"But here's the fun part," Morgan adds, steepling his hands. "My uncle has just come out of hiding and stepped foot on our territory."

"Nightshade." Xavier tests the name on his tongue, his gaze sliding to the side as he thinks. "That was in Sarah's ledger, right?"

I nod, massaging my neck absentmindedly as I connect the dots. "Does that mean the Cimmerian Court was part of Sarah's network?"

Rossi catches my movements, his irises turning black with lust before I drop my hand from my subtly bruised and bitten neck, and he's able to collect himself. "That, I can't confirm, but a Nightshade ancestor listed as a network guardian? I can believe it."

"The plot thickens," Morgan says, running his hand through his hair and sending me a wink. "Just when you thought you solved it all, little leaf."

"Let's get some rest," Rossi orders. "Then, we work."

Tempest and Ardyn rise first and leave the room, the flush to Ardyn's face telling me they may want to unleash some sexual frustration before getting down to business.

I leave them to it, unwilling to ruminate on my brother's sex life too long, the others packing up and murmuring quietly.

But I hesitate at the doorway before exiting. My doubts claw at me, threatening to tear me apart from the inside.

"Clover." Rossi's voice rumbles low. "What troubles you?"

"Other than the obvious," Morgan quips but pauses in leaving, watching me prudently.

"I..." My voice falters. If the time isn't now, then there will never be a time. I could lose any of them to Bianchi tomorrow.

I take a breath, bracing myself.

"I just..." I twist my hands, unable to meet his intense gaze. "Sometimes I feel like I don't belong here. With all of you."

Rio pushes back his chair and stalks toward me. I shrink

back against the doorframe as Rossi gets to me first, bracing his arms on either side, caging me in.

"You think we keep you here against your will?" His words drip with menace. "That we force our affection upon you?"

"No, I—"

"You are ours, Clover," Rio says behind him. "Make no mistake. And we protect what is ours."

My heart pounds wildly. I want to melt into all of them and flee all at once.

"I know," I whisper. "But for how long? This life ... it's dangerous. My love—and I do have so much love for you, all of you—isn't enough to keep any of you safe."

Morgan stands beside Rossi, grasping my chin and forcing me to meet his manic gaze.

"We want to burn the whole fucking world down to protect *you*."

Morgan's words send a quake through me, equal parts alarm and wish. He speaks the truth—these men would raze cities for me without a second thought. Morgan is willing to betray his own family to be with me.

That's not just something—it's everything.

Xavier echoes his agreement by stalking over and completing the protective circle of men around me. *My* men.

Yet as I search Rossi's face, I sense something lurking. A hell in his eyes that speaks of demons I cannot begin to fathom.

"Rossi..."

I lay my hand on his chest. His heart hammers against my palm.

Rossi tenses, his jaw clenching. For a moment, I think he will push me away and retreat behind the walls he's built around himself. But then his shoulders slump ever so slightly.

"Clever girl," he murmurs. "Too clever."

He turns from me and goes to pour himself a drink. The amber liquid glints in the low light as he takes a long swallow. His grip whitens around the glass. "There are debts that must be paid. Blood that must be spilled. That's not on you, Miss Callahan."

I weave around Rio and Morgan and go to him, heart aching. "Whatever you've done, it doesn't change how I feel. We've all got a wrongness inside us."

I lift his hand to my lips, kissing each scarred knuckle.

Rossi cups my face with a tenderness that belies his lethal strength. In his eyes, I see gratitude, craving ... and shame.

"I've told you I don't deserve you," he whispers.

I smile up at him sadly. "Maybe not. But you've got me anyway."

Rossi's gaze burns black as his grip on my face tightens, possessive and full of renewed craving.

"You're the only radiance we have left," he says, his voice low and gravelly. "The unexpected and ethereal that's come out of all the pain and suffering."

My cheeks heat under his penetrating scrutiny.

Despite all the danger and death surrounding us, my heart bursts. I stand on my tiptoes and press my lips to his, tasting the whiskey on his tongue as he deepens the kiss.

Morgan and Rio step closer, their hands trailing over my body, teasing and tantalizing.

I moan into Rossi's mouth as Rio's fingers slip between my thighs, eliciting a gasp from me.

"Would you like us to prove it to you?" Rio murmurs into my ear while I'm still kissing Rossi.

My body shivers with need, desire pooling low in my belly.

I pull back from Rossi's kiss with a gasp, turning to face

Rio. He's so close I can feel his breath on my neck, his scent overwhelming my senses.

"Yes," I whisper, barely able to form the word.

Rio works his fingers under my panties, stroking my clit deftly. I moan, my fingers digging into Rossi's chest as he holds me up against him.

Morgan steps closer, his hands on my breasts, kneading them through my shirt—no, Rossi's shirt. His touch is firm, bordering on painful because of Rossi's previous bites, but it only adds to my intensity, bordering on a bomb going off.

I hear the sound of Xavier's belt being undone. Jackets and shirts are shed. My body tenses with hope.

Xavier steps up behind me, stroking my ass through my jeans. I can feel his hard cock pressing between my cheeks, and I arch my back, pushing against him.

The room fills with our breathing, our moans, and the wet sounds of Rio's fingers sliding in and out of me. I'm lost in the sensation, overwhelmed by the pleasure and the danger of it all.

Rossi kisses my neck, his teeth grazing my skin where his marks were just beginning to heal.

"You belong to the Vultures," he growls. "Even if I can't have you, no one else can, either."

I nod, eyes rolling back, lost in the haze of men.

Rio steps away for a moment, returning with a length of rope. He binds my wrists in front of me, then leads me to the dining room table.

Confused but pliant, I let him guide me first to stepping on a chair, then standing on the table directly below what used to be a grand chandelier but is now coated in gossamers and dust, its sparkling crystals cracked and fogged with age.

Rio pulls my arms above my head and my wrist to the bottom rungs of the chandelier.

I'm so turned on by the move, I'm shaking. The sensation of being bound—tethered for the ones I love—is enough to send me reeling.

Morgan, Rossi, and Xavier climb onto the table with us with swift, sure movements, circling their prey.

I can't help the small squeak of protest that slips from between my lips.

"What's wrong?" Morgan asks as he pushes my shirt up and frees my breasts, his fingers finding my nipples and twisting them. I groan, my pussy throbbing, my clit swollen with need.

"I just want to touch you," I whimper. "I want to taste you."

But they clearly have other ideas.

"Not this time," Morgan says, pinching my nipples hard.

A bolt of pain shoots through me, and my pussy clenches.

Xavier's hands stroke my ass, his fingers slipping under the denim of my jeans to tease me.

"What do you want, Clover?" Rossi asks.

I look up to see him with his blade and using it to cut his shirt off my body.

"I want you," I breathe, tugging on my ropes, my body alive with desire.

My pussy aches for them, my nipples are hard for them, and my mouth waters for a taste of their cocks.

A hand tips my chin, turning my head, and I look up into Morgan's blazing eyes.

"You're giving us trust," he says. "Do you know what that means?"

I nod. "It means you're going to hurt me."

Morgan answers with a cunning smile. "Only in ways I like."

"Rio," I moan as he leans over and unbuttons my pants while I sway under the chandelier. "Please!"

"Tell me you love me," he demands, intent on peeling my jeans and underwear off. "Tell me you're mine."

I arch back against him, desperate for his touch.

"I love you!" I cry out. "I love you, I'm yours!"

I lean into Rossi, his touch so soothing and grounding compared to Xavier's fingers tracing delicate lines up and down my thighs, sending goose bumps scurrying over my flesh.

I'm completely exposed, completely vulnerable.

My body has never felt so alive.

"What do you say?" Xavier whispers in my ear.

I barely hear him. My blood courses through my veins, pounding in my ears.

The four men around me, the ropes binding me, the chandelier's crystals rattling with my quivering, the hands on my body—I'm ready to shatter.

"Please," I gasp.

Rio's firm hand closes around my throat as he pulls me back against him.

"Please," I repeat, gasping for air.

"Please, what?" Xavier's fingers tease the seam between my thighs, and my pussy clenches with need.

"Please," I moan. "Please, more."

I can't believe how easily the words fall from my lips. How little I care for the need to be in control, to be in charge. How much I want these men to use me, to own me.

Rio's grip on my throat tightens.

The sting of tears wells in my eyes, but I fight them, refusing to give in to the crushing of my windpipe.

I hold my breath, waiting and picturing my hand around Rio's throat, squeezing the life from him while I ride his cock.

That would show him.

Just as I'm about to pass out, Rio releases me. Cool air rushes into my lungs, making me dizzy.

My body sways, but his bindings steady me, holding me up for them to continue using.

A small part of me wonders when I became so willing to give up control, but I refuse to dwell on it.

Xavier's hands are on my waist. Rio strokes his hands down my back.

Morgan's on me again, teasing my pussy with his fingers. I'm just about to explode when he pulls his fingers away from me. He lifts his fingers over my shoulder to Rio, who licks them clean.

I close my eyes, fighting the urge to scream.

"Do you want me first?" Rossi's voice is a low growl.

"Yes," I pant.

I'm throbbing, yearning for touch.

I want Xavier's rough hands on me, Morgan's fingers buried in my ass, Rossi's dick inside me, and Rio gripping my breasts so hard that bolts of pain go straight to my clit.

These thoughts, I think vaguely, *are so unlike me. But I fucking love it.*

"We're here, Clover," Rossi says, his hand stroking my cheek, drawing me back. "You get to have all you want. And you're going to give it all to us."

"Yes," I moan, my pussy begging to be filled. "Yes, I give it all to you."

Rio pinches my nipples just like I wanted, and I moan

loudly. He leans around and mouths them. "You're so fucking sexy. So fucking beautiful."

"So fucking ours," Xavier says, his fingers parting my lips as he slides a finger in over my tongue, then a second, a third, before taking them out with a *pop* of suction.

"Yes," I beg. "A million times yes."

To Rossi, I say, "I'm yours."

To Morgan, I say, "I'm yours."

To Xavier, I say, "I'm yours."

"I'm here," I promise, "I'm here."

I'm here, I'm here, I'm here.

Suddenly, their faces are gone. Rio swings me around to face him.

"Look at me," he demands. His eyes are so dark, they're black as ink.

I look back at him, my breathing ragged.

"We're yours, too," he says.

I can't stop the wetness between my legs as I nod.

"Good." He grins. "Now Morgan's going to fuck you from behind. Xavier is going to lick your pussy. You're going to come so fucking hard on his mouth you won't be able to stop."

"Yes," I moan as Morgan pushes into me. He grabs my hips, curving forward so he can push deeper.

The sudden shift makes my breasts sway, and Rossi's eyes are on them. He licks his lips, then reaches out and cups my breasts, flicking his thumbs over my nipples. I gasp and flinch away from him, but the rope keeps me from moving back.

Rossi stares me in the eyes, waiting for me to look at him again before he pulls my mouth to his. He bites my lip, thrusting his tongue into my mouth, then pulls back.

"I'm going to fuck you," he whispers, "while Xavier fucks you with his tongue."

I groan. My pussy is full, throbbing, the pressure building like a maddening itch that's just out of reach.

"Let them," Rio whispers. "And let me watch before I take you, too."

"Yes," I moan, my ass squeezing around Morgan's cock as he nudges it in.

Morgan strokes my ass, his cock teasing my puckered hole. My muscles clench as I think about Xavier licking my pussy.

"Morgan," I whimper.

"Yes, little leaf?"

"I need you..."

"Want me to fill your ass," Morgan corrects.

"Yes!" I cry.

Morgan slams into me, making me grunt. Xavier's hands are on my hips as he bends down, his tongue on my clit, licking furiously.

I moan loudly, my head thrown back.

"Yes, yes, yes!"

"That's it, little leaf," Morgan grits out. "Take it. Take us. Take everything we give you."

I nod because I can't do much else.

I breathe in deep and hold it as Xavier's tongue laps at my clit. His thumb strokes, too, and then presses on it. I feel the pressure in my belly and clench down on Morgan. Morgan groans, his hands on my ass, pulling me even tighter to him.

Xavier's fingers are on my clit, flicking it, teasing it, making me gasp.

"Take it," Rio says, his hand on my throat.

Rossi shoves Xavier aside, lining up his dick to my pussy. When he thrusts in, Xavier bends between me and Rossi and resumes playing with my clit.

My moans fill the room.

The men move in perfect rhythm inside me, and I'm exploding inside, the orgasm so good it's almost painful.

"Fucking hell," Morgan breathes. "I'm going to come."

I want him to.

I want Rio to squeeze my throat tighter.

I want to feel Xavier's tongue on my clit as the men come inside me. I want to feel the pleasure and pain of it. I want the chaos.

I don't want to think about the consequences.

I don't want to think about the future.

I just want to feel.

"Fuck, Clover," Morgan groans, coming so hard that the inside of my ass is drenched with his cum.

There's a wild light in his eyes, a frenzy. I'm sure Rio is the same.

Then Xavier's tongue is back on my clit, stroking it. His teeth close down, and I shudder as he sucks.

"You like that," Rio says, his voice low and rough. "You like making Rossi and Morgan come."

I nod, moaning as Xavier keeps flicking his tongue against me.

"You like Xavier's mouth on you," he says.

"Yes."

I love it, I love Morgan, I love Rio, I love Xavier, and I love Rossi.

I love them so fucking much.

I'm coming, and then Rossi pulls out, and I welcome Rio's cock, and then Xavier is there, his fingers inside me with Rio's dick, stretching me, and then he's coming, too, and then everything is white and black and flashing like fireworks, my orgasm ripping everything out of me.

At the end of it, Rossi's knife flashes, cutting the ropes from the chandelier in a single swipe.

I fall to my knees, spent.

"Open your eyes, Clover."

It's Rossi. His grip on my hair tightens, holding me in place while his huge, thick dick bobs, slick and shiny from being inside me, in front of my face.

"Goddamn perfect," he growls, fist cradling his cock, hand stroking it.

"Yes," I say. "In my mouth."

My lips close around him, and Xavier's fingers slip into my pussy, sliding right in. Rossi's hands are on my hair, his whole body tensing as he rams my throat.

He thrusts hard and deep, fucking my mouth.

Rossi slows and eases back, pulling almost all the way out, then thrusts in again, hard. He does it again, my tongue running along his length.

"Fuck," he says, his hips rocking forward. I swallow, my throat working, trying to take in his cock even though it's too big. I try not to choke.

"Good girl," Rio growls, his fingers back on my throat.

I moan as Rossi's cock slides along my tongue, the salty taste of him making me wet. Xavier's fingers slide in and out of me slowly, so slowly, and then he's adding another. Rio's pressure makes me whimper.

"I'm going to come again," I moan, unsure if I can handle it.

"Yes, come for us," Morgan says from somewhere, jerking off vigorously.

I do, and it's so good, so fucking good.

I almost black out, but I feel arms around me, and I'm safe.

And I have everything I need, just like they promised.

CHAPTER 34
CLOVER

My boots echo through the cavernous dining room as I pace, nerves churning in my stomach. I watch the others making preparations this morning—Rio cleaning guns, Xavier gathering supplies, Morgan poring over Sarah's ciphers, brow furrowed with an empty seat beside him saved for me. Tempest and Ardyn are on the opposite side, glued to his laptop and muttering to each other.

The tension in the air is a palpable force.

Rossi is away, meeting with his contacts to secure vital intel for our showdown with Bianchi. Even though I want to stand strong on my own, I can't help but feel a hollow ache in my chest in his absence.

Then I feel a presence beside me. It's Xavier.

"All right, maiden?" His accented voice breaks through my thoughts. "I have to leave soon, but I wanted to check in."

I force a smile onto my face. "Just ready to get this over with."

He studies me for a moment. "It's okay to be scared. Means you're smart."

My gaze drops to the floor, embarrassment coloring my cheeks.

"No judgment here. We've all been where you are," he reassures, laying a warm hand on my cheek. "Especially me. But you've got this. We'll be right beside you."

Lifting my eyes to meet his, I find a sincerity that anchors me. I might be anxious, but I believe him.

"Thank you, Xavier. I know you've got my back."

He smiles, his beautiful eyes crinkling at the corners. "Always."

Taking a deep breath, I lower my shoulders from my ears.

I can do this. I'm not alone anymore.

Xavier gives me a quick peck on the lips before leaving, Tempest snarling at him slightly as he passes by.

I take that as a positive sign. Tempest may just be coming around to the fact that I'm not going anywhere, and these men are becoming mine.

With this makeshift family behind me, I can be brave.

Rossi returns around noon, the confident sway in his step missing, replaced by a somber intensity that's new to me. He avoids my eyes as he passes me in the hall and heads to his study, isolating himself.

I watch him, my brows knitting together.

Something is definitely off.

I hesitate for a beat before deciding to follow him. When I find him, he's hunched over his desk, head in his hands.

"Rossi?" I ask softly.

He looks up, his eyes bloodshot.

"Yes, Miss Callahan?" His voice is strained.

I move closer, trying to bridge the physical and emotional distance between us. "What's going on? You're upset. Talk to me."

He drags his hand down his face before slamming a fist on the desk. "It's not just Bianchi I'm fighting. It's my own goddamn demons. I want his empire, Clover. I want everything he took from me."

His ferocity takes me aback, and I stiffen slightly. This is a side of him I'm always careful to navigate.

Rossi's shoulders slump, and his voice breaks as he continues. "I am not a good man anymore."

I lay my hand over his. "I know who you are. You're Miguel Rossi. My Rossi. He hasn't taken your name." I lift his chin so he's looking into my eyes. "And when and if you forget, I'll be here to remind you."

For a moment, he searches my face as if looking for some truth he's afraid he won't find. Then he pulls me into his lap, and his body relaxes against mine.

"I've forgotten what it's like to be without you," he murmurs into my hair. "And that's a warning, Clover. Not an endearment."

I cling to him, offering what comfort I can. I sense the depth of his struggle, but I also know our bond is becoming strong enough that I'm sure I can save him.

I have to.

As I tilt my head to kiss him, I glimpse the tips of feathers tattooed at the base of his neck, a permanent reminder of all he's endured. My resolve deepens.

I will see those wings fly free if it's the last thing I do.

We stay wrapped in each other's arms, each of us an anchor for the other in a world constantly shifting beneath our feet. I breathe in the scent of him, this addictively complex man whose soul is a labyrinth I'm still navigating.

The sudden knock on the door fractures our moment of peace.

Rossi detaches from me, his eyes instantly shuttering, the lead Vulture snapping back into place.

"Come in," he growls.

I stand, smoothing my pants and shirt, tucking my hair behind my ears.

The door opens, and I try to hide my surprise at the unexpected visitor. He much prefers tricksy messages over personal appearances.

Cav saunters in, his expression an inscrutable mix of amusement and something darker.

"I thought you'd like to hear the latest whispers on the grapevine from the consul himself," Cav says, his voice silkily deceptive, almost honeyed.

"Out with it," Rossi snaps.

Cav's lips crest in a slow smile. "Bianchi's attending an auction tonight. There's a new, let's say, *live shipment* he's interested in."

"Confirmed?"

Cav nods. "By one of my black market contacts. Bianchi lost his usual merchandise, thanks to you Vultures, and he's out to replenish his stock."

I hitch my breath too audibly. Cav's attention darts to me, then away, much like a horse would do to a donkey. Uninteresting, non-threatening.

But I latch onto the meaning behind his words. Cav's referring to girls. He has to be.

Visions of terrified women in cages, their eyes vacant from drugs and despair, starved and beaten into submission, flash through my mind.

My molars slam together, my fists tightening.

"We have to stop him," I say, my voice edged and jagged.

Cav cocks a brow without looking in my direction. “No one invited you to speak, dearest.”

Rossi fists his hands and rises, his shadow looming over the desk, his eyes aflame. “Speak to her that way again, and I’ll make you part of my flock.”

“Don’t you mean ‘kettle’? Isn’t that what a group of vultures in flight are called? Or no, a ‘committee,’ a group of vultures on the ground.” Cav’s smile is predatory, his teeth almost gleaming in the dim light. “Sounds absolutely *terrifying* either way, doesn’t it?”

With that, he pivots gracefully and leaves, the door closing behind him like the final note of a funeral dirge.

Adrenaline surges through me, electrifying every nerve, every cell. I lock eyes with Rossi and see my own fierce determination mirrored back at me.

“Where’s the auction?” I ask him.

My thoughts drive back to the one time I stupidly, unknowingly attended one, where I lost a friend, and Ardyn’s and my lives changed forever. There wasn’t trafficking there, that I knew. Or maybe there was, and we just didn’t wander deep enough.

Either way, Mila, an innocent, died. Morgan’s father was killed by Rossi’s own hand. Ardyn was driven to involuntary isolation for years.

Who’s to say it won’t happen again? My heart hammers so loudly it nearly drowns out my thoughts.

Rossi rumbles in answer, “He’ll provide me details. Cav always does.”

I glance between Rossi and the door, my forehead tight. “What is your connection to him? How does he hold this much sway over you?”

"He has no influence over me," Rossi bites out. "Cav is simply lucky."

"How?"

"He was friends with my daughter." Rossi clears his throat. "A long time ago. The day she died—he and I lost ourselves to dark paths ever since. We help each other when we can."

I ponder in the direction Cav exited. "Every time he gives us something, it's like he takes more for himself."

"Mm," Rossi acknowledges. "It's how he survives in his world. The same way I survive in mine."

Survival.

Who gets to keep living, and who has to die?

Do our choices decide, or does fate intervene and lengthen or shorten our destinies?

I wrestle with these questions as we all huddle around the dining room table, maps and screens displaying a mix of ancient texts from Sarah Anderton's time and digital feeds of current black market activity.

Rossi is at the head. His gaze flickers, then lands on me for a second before he turns to address the group.

"We have new intel from the Cimmerian Court and can intercept Bianchi at the auction tonight," he says, a tight note of pressure altering his normally steadfast voice.

Morgan strokes his jaw while he reclines in his chair. "The auction is risky, but it's fast."

"Fast and foolish," Tempest retorts, his sharp eyes flicking between Rossi and the digital feed. "But ... I can also procure us new IDs, untraceable and clean. In case we need a quick exit strategy."

After a long, curious look at Tempest, Xavier gives a terse nod.

Rossi looks at each of his men and then at me. "We all know what to do. It's time to sow chaos in Bianchi's ordered world." His voice grows rough. "And then we can walk away."

"But who's to say this isn't a trap set by Cav?" Tempest continues. "You're the only one who trusts him, sir. The rest of us don't."

Rossi clenches his fists but doesn't respond, his silence speaking volumes.

Rossi's daughter died a decade ago. He may have told me how Cav knew her, but the hows and whys are a black void. And despite Rossi having shared so much with me, that realm of his past remains sealed.

Xavier clears his throat, pulling me from my musings. "If it is a trap, I'm the bait. It's a risk I'm willing to take."

I jolt upright from the chair. "What? Xavier, no."

"I'm not good for much, maiden." He gestures to his bad knee under the table. "But I want us out of this as expediently as possible."

"What kind of bait are you thinking, Sports Balls?" Morgan taps his chin. "Oh, I get it now. Pretty boy like you would go for a lot of pennies during the sex auction."

"That's enough," Rossi cuts in, shooting Morgan a warning look.

Rio steps away from the table and approaches me. His fingers softly touch the small of my back, electrifying my senses.

"You good, Lucky?" he whispers, his gravelly voice calming the storm within me.

"I don't know," I admit under my breath so only he can

hear. "I hate the thought of something happening to any of you."

Rio leans in to whisper in my ear, "We're good at what we do."

His words are a balm, but the uncertainty lacing my thoughts adds to my trepidation. This room is a powder keg, with very violent men playing with matches, and I'm struck by how much I care about all of them and how deeply rooted my fears are—not just for the mission but for us.

"I say we go to the auction," Morgan asserts, looking directly at Rossi. "Uncle Marco still believes I'm on his side, so I'll be welcomed in without suspicion. I've been calling the man enough and giving false information, which he's beginning to question. It's best I show my face, anyway. He'll want to show me how to choose the best antiquities and *curios*." His emphasis on the last word insinuates he's talking about the trafficked girls. "Besides, I'll provide a handsome distraction while the rest of you crawl through vents or scale buildings, whatever you need to do to get inside."

"We can use my—*our* family brownstone," Tempest corrects after my raised brow. "My parents are never there, but our wardrobes are always full. Clo, you still have a key, right?"

I nod, not trusting my voice. Father sold Tempest to Bianchi years ago to pay off severe debts, and as such, disowned his son. It's a fact I recently unearthed and am still trying to wrap my head around. Our father gave no indication to me that he did such a horrid, awful thing.

So let's just say, my brother comes by stealth and deception honestly.

"Fine. We're going to the auction," Rossi decides.

A collective exhale fills the room, tension releasing and reforming into a different shape—determination.

Rossi walks over to me, his eyes softening as they always do when it's just us in a crowded room.

When he catches my uncertainty, he says in a low voice, "Trust my judgment, *tesoro mio*."

I've noticed Rossi's Italian—or Spanish, for that matter—doesn't come out unless he's experiencing high emotions. Like now.

With me.

My questions about the risk of Morgan finding out about who truly murdered his father, Rossi's connection with Cav, hovers on the tip of my tongue, but after he calls me that, his precious darling, I can't find the words. He's choked me up.

Instead, I press my lips to his briefly, a fleeting but intense moment of connection.

"I trust you," I whisper back, "but trust works both ways."

He leans down, resting his forehead against mine. "After this is over, no more secrets. I promise."

I nod, knowing that promises are fragile things. But right now, it's enough.

I glance around at the faces of the men I've come to love. Xavier, with his quick intellect and dry wit. Rossi, solid as a rock despite his brooding intensity. Rio, always seeing ten steps ahead. Morgan, whose abuse and barely leashed madness is used as a deadly weapon instead of a flaw.

We have all suffered at the hands of Bianchi and his empire of cruelty.

Giving up is not an option.

I rise, holding Rossi's dark eyes with my own. "This isn't just about taking down Bianchi. It's about what we've built here." I gesture at the makeshift circle around the table. "Trust. Loyalty. Love."

Xavier nods slowly, while Morgan's shoulders lose some of

their tension. Only Rio remains expressionless, but I know he's listening.

For a long moment, no one speaks. Then Rio steps forward, squeezing my shoulder.

"She's right," he says gruffly. "We don't give up on family."

One by one, the others echo him. As their voices blend in affirmation, the knot inside me begins to loosen. We are far from safe, but we are not alone.

Rossi leaves to grab his weaponry from his study, and I'm solitary for a moment, collecting my thoughts and focusing my will.

Ardyn approaches, her arm wrapping around my lower back.

"Ready to kick some ass?" she asks, the levity in her voice a stark contrast to the gravity of the situation. She's been in this longer than I have, faced worse than entering a black market auction surrounded by trained, lethal men.

"Always," I reply, smiling despite the strain.

Xavier leans against the doorway, watching me. He smiles a soft, almost tender smile that says more than words ever could.

Tempest, now resigned to my complicated dynamics with his men, shakes his head. "Well, if I'm going to hell, I might as well go down with my team."

Team.

I grin at my older brother. It's so difficult for him to give me a glimpse into his true self, not out of spite but protection. And here he is now, making me a part of...

"You mean your kettle?" I ask.

His gaze whips to mine, storm brewing. "Fuck, who told you that?"

Ardyn tries to contain her laughter. "Babe, a simple search on the internet will do the trick."

"Well, *we* didn't fucking name us," Tempest grumbles, then shoulders his bag and stomps out.

"Yet another reason my uncle has to die," Morgan says dryly before languidly pushing to his feet and following Tempest out.

Ardyn and I nod at each other and squeeze each other's hands before letting go.

I throw on my jacket and gloves, steel my nerves, and prepare to face the night that could both break us or bind us.

CHAPTER 35
XAVIER

I'm not sure what I expected when Tempest said we'd be stopping by his and Clover's family brownstone to get "dressed up," but I didn't predict this.

We all stand in the grand, high-ceilinged living room. The decor is a blend of modern elegance and vintage charm, and despite its opulence, there's a bleakness that makes it feel oddly abandoned.

Morgan has found himself an antique blade in some display case, unsheathing it with a reverence that would be alarming if it weren't for our situation. Rossi's pacing the room, phone glued to his ear, negotiating last-minute details —with whom, only he knows. Rossi holds everything close to the vest, that one. I have no choice but to trust his knowledge in these matters as I nervously twitch in the corner.

"Okay, I've laid out some options for everyone in the guest rooms," Clover says. "Go pick something you like."

I can't help but chuckle. "Darling, are we going to a bootleg auction or a fashion show?"

She grins with a natural mischief in her eyes. "Why not both? We never get the chance to dress up."

I climb the mahogany stairs and step into a guest room. Designer suits are laid out on the king-sized bed, cuff links shimmering on the bedside table.

Slipping into the fitted black tuxedo, I pad to the full-length mirror. The jacket contours perfectly to my frame, showing off my broad shoulders and narrow waist. I pick up the black silk tie and tie it into a neat half-Windsor knot. It's been ages since I had a reason to get this dressed up, and it's both exhilarating and depressing.

I finish the ensemble with high-gloss black leather shoes, stepping out of the room with a newfound sense of *gravitas*. We're about to sneak into one of the most dangerous gatherings in the city, but damn if we won't look good doing it.

Everyone assembles back in the living room. Tempest is in a dark tailored three-piece suit, his hair neatly styled but with a strand rebelliously falling onto his forehead.

Ardyn opted for a sleek, fitted dress in a dark teal that accents her curves and contrasts against her pale skin and ash-blond hair.

Rio's outfit is the epitome of casual sophistication—a slate-gray suit with the top button undone, no tie. It suits him.

Rossi wears a bespoke black suit that looks like it was woven from the opaque thoughts in his mind. As he buttons his cuffs, there's a certain ruthlessness in his eyes that would send shivers down anyone's spine. I know the man, have slept in the same house as him, even shared a woman with him, but even in his sleep, he's dangerous.

Clover, however, takes my breath away. She's in a floor-length, backless black gown, its bodice adorned with delicate lace. Her thick black hair is down, brushing against her chest like a slow, rippling tide every time she moves.

Her eyes meet mine, and I swear my heart skips a beat.

She's a vision, but the metallic fire in her eyes reminds me that she's a warrior, a goddess, my dark maiden of lore.

But Morgan, of course, steals the show. The man's in a blood-red suit that's as flamboyant as it is alarming. He's like a splash of fresh blood on a monochrome canvas. He had it shipped to the brownstone an hour ago, refusing to wear Tempest's stormy, dour wardrobe.

His words, not mine.

It suits him, oddly enough. His tie slithers into his buttoned-up blazer like a black snake hiding until it's ready to strike. It offers a sharp contrast that almost says, "I may look like fun, but cross me, and I'll eat you as my *amuse bouche*."

It's also a vivid reminder that while we may be predators, we're also prey.

"We ready?" Rossi asks.

"Ready as we'll ever be," Clover replies, her voice as steady as the blade Morgan was previously admiring.

We gather around a table where Rossi spreads out a map of the city's current subway stations. We talk tactics, disguises, and Sarah Anderton's antiques we've stashed in our luxury cars to allow us entry. We discuss how to blend in, how to bypass the heightened security measures, and how to free those innocent souls.

Sounds so very stress-free.

Rossi pushes back from the table. "Let's move."

We exit the brownstone, each step calculated, each movement precise. The weight of the night ahead is a burden we all share, a collective darkness that binds us together. But amid the tension, the danger, the unspoken fears, I look at Clover and find a true sense of peace.

And as we step into our respective cars, the engines purring like caged beasts, I feel a strange sense of completeness.

CHAPTER 36
MORGAN

The night is as black and dashing as the clothes we wear—except for me.

I'd like to see these city streets run red.

Even the city seems to hold its breath, waiting for us to exit our vehicles and enter its gaping black maw so she can chew on us, gristly and heartless as we are.

We're looking for an abandoned subway station, one that the city has forgotten but serves our purpose well.

"Everyone remembers what we're putting up for bid?" I ask, glancing at the carefully packaged artifacts we took from Sarah Anderton's vault.

Rossi holds an ornate dagger, Clover (very reluctantly) holds Sarah's grimoire, and Xavier has an old rifle.

But underneath our clothes and in our disguises are the true weapons we're smuggling in. We're pretending to sell those goodies but keeping them on our persons until we reveal them at bidding time.

Xavier has an eighteenth-century cane sword. It appears as an ordinary walking cane but has a concealed blade inside. He leans on it, pretending his ruined knee is worse than it is, though it's pretty fucking ruined.

Rossi carries two of Sarah's switchblades and one of her palm pistols in his inside pockets for fast deployment. If patted down and caught, he can simply explain he was holding them until they would go on display for buyers.

Rio favored the ancient brass knuckles. They would enhance what I grudgingly accept as his already powerful hand-to-hand-combat skills.

Tempest, that funny Storm Cloud, carries Sarah's (or one of her network's) sleeve daggers attached to spring mechanisms. These allow him quick and surreptitious attacks.

Impressive, I know.

Oh, and me? I'm so glad you asked.

I've chosen an eighteenth-century Balistraria Crossbow hidden in a custom-designed forearm holster.

Say that ten times fast.

This highly accurate mini crossbow fires specialized bolts (which of course I've practiced with, using pretty portraits of my fellow brothers on tree trunks), and with Clover's help and her deep understanding of Sarah Anderton's alchemy, they're tipped with poison or tranquilizers or both.

Now *that's* impressive, but I'm not even done. It's also a tool for psychological warfare, my favorite. The mere sight of the bolt-tip protruding from the wrist holster could serve to intimidate anyone aware of its capabilities.

I can't *wait* to try it out.

I'm not sure what the girls have on them besides a grimoire, but my little leaf is always up to something, and I have full confidence she'll wield it at the exact time she needs to.

After a short walk, we reach a steel door, corroded but

stronger than it looks. Tempest taps a sequence into a keypad he installed earlier; the door creaks open, revealing more darkness, before Tempest tosses the keypad onto active subway tracks—to be run over in the next five minutes.

We descend, using the abandoned ramp to trek farther into the echelons. I'm brushing my fingertips against the filthy wall for guidance, only two of us allowed to use flashlights, and I prefer my knife to a torch always.

The forgotten subway tunnel is neglected but far from empty. Eventually, candles start illuminating the way, each flickering flame an ironic message from Sarah Anderton's time. It's eerie and comforting all at once, reminding me why I'm doing this. For Clover, a girl who finds Sarah so important, a witch who fought against a world who hated her, leaving behind her network and resources as her fortune and not priceless jewels like I would've preferred.

But she did get me thinking. Perhaps *Clover* is my priceless jewel.

Rossi says, "When any of you spot Bianchi, let me know. I will deal with him and I alone."

"Uh, excuse me—"

"Not the time, Morgan," Rossi cuts in. "If you want this done, you leave me in charge. Do you understand?"

I frown, then weigh the pros and cons.

Clover—pro.

Uncle—con.

I grudgingly shrug. "So long as you let me play with him for a while after."

Maybe then I can pull out his fingernails and cut off his toes one by one. Wouldn't that be fun?

"As soon as we get in, we fan out," Tempest instructs. "You got this, Morgan?"

I spare him a glance. "Obviously."

Rio nods resolutely, his lips thin. I suppose that's his way of backing me up.

Ardyn and Clover stick together while the Vultures disperse, and I take the lead.

They slow to a stop at the end of the corridor and before a concealed entrance matching the subway's tiled wall, a mere blemish on the maze of concrete and metal.

I keep my pace smooth, my shoes meeting gravel as I walk up to it and adjust the lapel of my suit.

"Evening, Officer," I offer, mocking civility.

The guard on duty squints as he sees me, a lingering sneer warping his lips. The family in charge of the auction house isn't my *familia,* but they know us well.

He takes note of the tiny pin on my lapel—our family crest of twin serpents facing each other, their tails coiled around a dagger that pierces the bottom of the onyx shield—and his face visibly changes.

"You're late," he snaps, hands tense on his weapon as he stares over my shoulder. "And who are they?"

I lean in, my eyes locking onto his as my voice drops to a threatening purr. "Always fashionably. As for them"—I motion to group behind me—"they're invited guests. Unless, of course, you're suggesting the Bianchis have poor taste in company?"

His eyes narrow. "I don't want trouble."

"Trouble," I muse, letting the word hang in the air like a guillotine's blade. "Trouble is a rather subjective term, don't you think? Especially for those who exist to avoid it. Now, if we don't walk through that door, you'll learn a whole new definition of trouble. One that comes with names and faces you'd rather forget. What's your name?"

The guard blinks. "Ben."

"Yes, Ben, you see, I must get my associates in without exposing their identities. I'm sure you understand the importance of discretion during an event such as this."

His eyes search mine, uncertainty wrestling with authority. "How do I know you're not bluffing?"

"Because bluffing," I reply with icy calm, "is for those who don't have the means to ensure consequences."

I produce a small black device—a scrambler gifted from Tempest—from my pocket. "For the next thirty seconds, the retinal scan will approve any eyes. Turn it on, then forget you ever saw my guests."

Ben's eyes shift between the device and me, sweat dotting his forehead. "And if I refuse?"

"Refuse, and I'll make sure your definition of trouble includes a visit from those in the Bianchi network who specialize in, let's say, 'problem-solving.' This is your chance, Ben, to do the right thing so you don't snag the attention of the wrong people."

The silence that follows is near tangible. Finally, he grabs the scrambler, activating it. A soft chime cuts through the tension, and the retinal scanner flickers off.

"Lovely boy," I say brightly, tapping his cheek, then call over my shoulder, "Come one, come all."

Rossi, Xavier, Tempest, Rio, and Ardyn emerge and line up for the retinal scan. It approves each of them rapidly, one after the other.

Finally, it's Clover's turn. Dressed in her striking, all-black ensemble, she steps up to the scanner. It seems like an eternity, but then the approval beep sounds. She's clear. The guard hastily deactivates the scrambler so the systems come back online.

"If any one asks, you never passed through me," he mutters, a veiled threat in his voice.

I give him my best smile. "That's the spirit, Benjamin. You're learning."

"Fucking psycho..." Ben mutters under his breath. He won't look me in the eye anymore.

As we walk through the entrance, descending into the bowels of the clandestine world below, I can't help but smirk.

It's not about the ease; it's about bending wills to break the rules.

CHAPTER 37
CLOVER

I creep along the grimy tiles after passing the retinal scan, focused on the pinprick of light ahead.

The gloom parts reluctantly, like a curtain in a sordid play, giving way to the garish glow of the secret auction house.

It's as though I've stepped into a world suspended between decadence and despair. Chandeliers, opulent and grotesque, drip with crystals that catch and fracture the light, casting prismatic rainbows on the scarlet walls.

High tables draped in ebony silk showcase a grotesque carnival of riches: jade figurines with eyes that seem almost lifelike, bejeweled daggers with hilts wrapped in ancient scripts, and gold burial masks that leer from their velvet pedestals.

Glass cases secure more perishable assets—rare manuscripts, aged wines, and rumored gold from *El Dorado*—behind reinforced panes.

A smoky aroma of aged whiskey and sweet perfume thickens the air, mingling with the underlying stench of greed.

Around me, men and women draped in black-tie attire move like phantoms, their eyes obscured by Venetian masks, their laughter hushed as if fearful it might shatter the brittle opulence surrounding them.

Blood money, all of it.

Each item a monument to suffering, each bid a nail in someone's coffin. As the auctioneer's gavel falls, confirming yet another transaction of vice, a chill runs down my spine. I'm in the belly of the beast, surrounded by soulless extravagance.

I edge closer to a long, lacquered table near the entrance where we hand over some of our items for sale. The gorgeous, stick-thin woman manning the table gives us each a card to prove we've given over the item. She doesn't argue since we have Hunter Morgan Bianchi's signature of approval on the authenticity of all items. Tempest rattles off an account to send the payment if the items sell, minus the commission of the auction house.

At the next curtain, we move to a long table covered in a dark plum-colored velvet cloth. Atop it lies an elaborate display of Venetian masks, a morbid array designed to anonymize the faces of debauchery. Each of us chooses one.

Rossi reaches for a black mask adorned with intricate gold scrollwork that contours the eye sockets. Morgan eyes a half mask with dark red and black feathers fanning out from the top, resembling an infernal crown.

Xavier picks a sleek silver mask that gives off a glimmer in the auction house's chandelier light, and Rio opts for a mask of dark blue, almost obsidian, unadorned but for a few streaks of silver.

Tempest chooses a black-and-gold full-face mask, stoic and commanding, without a feather or jewel in sight.

Ardyn selects a mask that contrasts with her gown—a

plain white mask, featuring a single golden tear at the corner of one eye.

I select a mask for myself, drawn to one that seems to seethe with subdued fury. It's matte black, covering only the top half of my face, simple yet defined by a series of jagged, angular lines around the eyes, almost like fractures or veins of ore in a rock.

In this chamber of monstrosities, it feels like putting on a piece of armor.

We each don our chosen guises, then spread out.

Tempest stiffens as a man brushes past us before he separates from Ardyn and me, the man's cold eyes raking over me, then Ardyn.

Ardyn's grip on my hand tightens almost painfully. I want to tear off this constricting dress, shed this illusion of belonging among these snakes.

"Let's keep moving," Tempest mutters. "The real event is somewhere below ground. Find it, then get back to me."

And with that, he disappears into the crowd, but Ardyn and I both understand his attention won't leave us for long, if at all.

Men in designer suits mill about, sizing up the goods. I glimpse Xavier through the throngs and Rossi weaving through the crowd nearby.

"Let's separate," Ardyn suggests. "Just this room, then meet at the back wall with any information we've found."

"You mean, we have to talk to these creeps?"

"They're already eyeing us," she murmurs. "It shouldn't be too hard to get them to reveal where the priceless goods are."

"All right. Meet in fifteen."

She tilts her head in acknowledgment and gracefully walks into the middle.

I ready to do the same, but someone grabs my wrist, and I whirl, heart hammering.

Rio's dark eyes bore into mine from behind his blue-black mask, his touch searing my skin.

"Be careful," he says, his quiet desire reaching straight through my ribs.

I manage a single nod before he releases me, his warmth already missed.

I side-step through the predators, hyperaware of each brush of silk and wool against my skin.

A hand clamps over my mouth, and I'm pulled back against a firm chest into a dark corner behind an ancient Roman Gladiator shield.

I smell him in time not to panic, mint and fresh paper, Morgan's breath tickling my ear, his body pressed along the length of mine.

"You look divine," he murmurs, lifting his hand from my lips.

I suppress a shiver at the loss of contact.

"Number one rule, little leaf. Don't go near Bianchi or let him see you. He's well aware what you look like and would love the chance to take you."

Stomach lurching, I nod. "Which one is he?"

"The old, fat one."

I pause. "Which old, fat one?"

Morgan's chest rumbles with amusement behind my head.

He places his inked hands on my shoulders. "Touché. The old, fat one in the navy suit. Over there by the old books."

Now that I know where to look, I have no trouble spotting him. A portly man with reddened, pockmarked skin, a half-bald head (the remaining gray hair severely gelled back) and no mask, probably because he believes himself too godlike to wear one. He twists like a marionette as he watches a man dressed in all black gently place Sarah's grimoire on a display stand.

Bianchi begins talking animatedly to his two companions, large men in suits who also glance toward the grimoire.

"Ding, ding, ding," Morgan says, reaching around me to admire a row of six-figure watches, old and new. "Phase one complete."

I draw a deep breath, feeling the loss of the grimoire like a limb. I didn't want to part with it. There was so much more to read and understand. But it was for the greater good. The girls stuck in the rooms below are my fight, the cause Sarah truly died for. Her grimoire was a mask, a decoy, maybe important to her during the day, but not as important as shipping victims to Titan Falls and finding them new identities and new homes.

I whisper a final goodbye as Bianchi gesticulates wildly to his bodyguards, his eyes never straying from the grimoire.

He'll bid on it. But he won't like what's inside it.

No answers.

None that he'll figure out, anyway. That thought brings a smile to my face.

Voices rise all across the room. The atmosphere shifts to one of excitement and competition. Morgan's eyes glint.

"Time for the show, little leaf."

In a blur, he's gone, leaving the ghost of his touch behind.

I shake off the disorientation and get to work.

Before I can recover, Xavier intercepts me. His eyes are a playful rebellion but hold a warmth that belies his jovial nature.

"Maiden," he greets, a devil's assistant in a well-tailored suit.

His fingers skim along the nape of my neck and down, hooking around the zipper of my dress. A teasing tug, a tempting proposal. For a split second, the world narrows, and the promise of his touch holds me captive. But then he releases me, winks, and retreats, off to play his part for tonight.

After watching him, I spot a group of buyers—men with salt-and-pepper hair, plain white masks, and deep pockets. One of them is the man who leered at Ardyn and me before slithering away.

They see me, and the weight of their gazes is like a wolf's jaw around a fragile bone.

I slip on a sexy smirk that I don't feel and sidle up to them.

"Mind if I join you gentlemen?" I ask.

The tallest among them—with eye sockets devoid of any light—extends a hand toward an empty seat. "Please do. I can never say no to beauty."

Sliding into the seat, I let my attention wander, scanning the crowd and the venue.

"Are you here to bid, darling?" asks the man to my left, his gaze lingering a touch too long on the curve of my neckline.

"I have my eye on a few rarities," I say, matching his gaze without flinching. "What about you? Looking for anything special?"

"We all have our secret desires, don't we?" the first man hints, a shadow of a leer crossing his tone.

"I suppose some secrets are buried deeper than others," I hedge.

My words seem to ripple beneath the man's skin. "Are you looking for something ... specific?"

Leaning forward with ample, corseted bosom on display, I

purr, "I caught whispers about an exclusive, underground auction. One that offers items you can't find unless you're invited downstairs. Have you heard?"

For a moment, their eyes lock, a silent communication passing between them. Finally, the tall man answers, "Special things require special keys."

I glance toward his jacket pocket where a peculiar keychain dangles, catching the dim light. My heart pounds louder, my mind racing through possibilities.

"Perhaps you'd like to be my special key tonight?" I suggest, pushing the double entendre as far as it can go. I have to risk it.

My eyes meet his, unwavering, even as every fiber in my being screams.

He seems to ponder this, contemplating whether my allure is worth the exposure.

"You're a tempting woman," he finally says, reaching for his champagne.

"Aren't those the best kind?" I quip, my eyes tracing his movements behind my mask.

As he raises the glass to his lips, I notice a slight shift in his gaze, a brief flicker downward—toward a nondescript part of the curtains fanning along the far wall. It's fleeting, but it's all I need.

I've found the door.

Grinning like I've won a secret victory, I raise my glass. "To buried secrets and the keys that unlock them."

They toast, unaware that they've just exposed one of their own. But as I take a sip, the liquid courage fortifying my veins, I realize that now comes the daring part—reaching that door without arousing suspicion.

I rise, finding Ardyn's white mask with the golden tear on the other side of the expansive room.

She meets it across the crowd, nodding to me that she's on her way.

"Clover."

The deep resonance of my name makes me turn, and I find Rossi in the shadows. He gestures for me to come closer. I glide between an Imperial Fabergé Egg stand and pedestals containing Renaissance artists' sketchbooks to get to him.

His bottomless eyes shine through his rigid mask. He risks tracing a finger down my collarbone, stopping at the chain holding Rio's locket that I never take off.

Despite Minnie's history behind it, it's a gift from Rio, mysterious and chilling and all him. I can't remove it even though it's stolen and dipped in blood.

I love it. I love him.

"Be safe," Rossi utters behind the porcelain.

I lift to the balls of my feet and kiss his cold mask on the lips, leaving behind a bright red lip print. "I am."

A gruff sound emits from behind it, restraint wrestling against passion. He squeezes my neck gently before departing, his war with Bianchi winning against his need for me.

I follow Rossi with my eyes as he skirts around where Bianchi holds court. I notice a gorgeous redhead has joined Bianchi; her pale, freckled arm crooked around his short, meaty one. Her cheekbones stand out against expertly applied blush. Her lashes are glued on but luscious, and her smile...

That's her. Bianchi's wife.

As if on a string, I move my focus to find Xavier, but I can't pinpoint him anywhere among the sequins, feathers, and silk.

My fingers spasm against my thighs, desperate to cling to him and draw his face to mine.

Before I blow my cover and run around searching for my damaged, now-vulnerable Vulture, Ardyn comes to my side.

"What is it? What have you found out?" she asks.

I blink once. Twice. Snapping out of it, I realize that as much as my men want to keep me safe and I them, the only way to get through this night is to stay on track.

Xavier seems to understand that the moment I do because he turns on his heel and stalks in the opposite direction of Meghan O'Malley before I can talk to him about it.

"There's a special key to get through the doors to the girls' auction," I tell her. "Behind those curtains over there. Two men guard it."

Ardyn folds her arms in thought. "We can do this."

I smile, though it's somber. She's always been my best friend, even while defying direct orders.

The Vultures, bless them, have been all over me tonight, ensuring my safety. I have a brief window before another one comes to check on us.

"We have to go now," I confirm.

Ardyn and I slip past gradually inebriated men and their young, beautiful companions and glide through the artifacts and antiques until we reach the section of curtain acknowledged by one of the leery men I pseudo-seduced.

Swiftly, I pull it open and draw it behind Ardyn and me once we step through. With a *swish,* we disappear from the auction room's view.

And with zero surprise in our expressions, we step right up to two armed men.

My hand slides to the antique dagger hidden in the folds of my dress—one of Sarah's weapons. I slip it to Ardyn.

Before the guards can react, I use Sarah's old trick of sliding powdered sleeping draught onto the lapels of the first guard's jacket, right under his nose.

Just some mug wort, valerian root, and a pinch of belladonna to make him go night-night immediately.

The moment he crumples, Ardyn has the blade pressed to the second one's throat while my hand muffles his cry of alarm.

"Make a sound and you die," I hiss, really getting into character.

His eyes widen, but he stays silent.

"Where's the key?" I ask, keeping my voice flat and husky like Rio's, my stare burning with promised murder like Rossi's.

He gestures with his eyes to the left side of his blazer. With one hand, I slip out the chain with a sleek metal key dangling from it.

"Thank you ever so kindly," I whisper.

I brush the same concoction underneath the second guard's nose.

He crumples noiselessly to the ground seconds later.

Quickly, we cut sashes from the folds of my dress—charcoal silk that I'll never wear again—with Sarah's dagger and bind the guards' hands and feet. Ardyn pats them both down, finding two handguns and giving me one.

I take it while she passes me to fit the key into the metal door's lock and twist.

While she's doing that, I draw another vial from between my breasts and coat the blade of my dagger with an oil also derived from Sarah's grimoire. It's designed to dissolve certain metals on contact just in case the key doesn't fit into any other locked barriers we might run into.

The Vultures have taught me to always be prepared.

We push the door's panel open and step through into a room that shatters my heart.

Large, gilded birdcages under single spotlights line the walls, each holding a young girl. At least a dozen of them.

This is where the real auction is—a secret marketplace for stolen lives. And it hasn't even begun.

Their hollow eyes meet ours, wide with a mixture of sorrow and despair.

"We're here to help you escape," I whisper urgently as we pace through the red-carpeted aisle.

They cling to the bars, terrified and disbelieving.

I gently take the hand of the closest girl.

"We're not here to hurt you," I say softly. "We're here to break you out."

After an endless moment, she nods.

I say to Ardyn, "We're not waiting for the Vultures. They might prioritize Bianchi over these girls. We can't take that risk."

Ardyn moves to the first cage, examining the lock. "Your potion?"

"It helped Sarah break into prison cells. These cages' locks are metal, too. Let me try."

I run the oiled blade along the edge of the lock. It hisses, steam wafting up through the keyhole, then pops open.

We continue, cage by cage, until every girl is free.

Their expressions are almost too much to bear—eyes gleaming with tears yet bright with a spark that was almost extinguished: Hope.

"I'll lead them up the stairs over there. Must be how they were brought in," Ardyn says. "There's an old service exit two levels up that might still be open. I spied it on the blueprints

Rossi studied. You go back to the auction and find where the guys are."

I look at her, then back at the girls. The weight of the decision, leaving her or going with and risk triggering the wrath of the Vultures, anchors me to the spot.

But ... better to ask for forgiveness than permission.

"Get them to safety," I say. "And don't be afraid to use that gun. I'll let the first Vulture I see know we have the girls. He'll meet you at the service exit. Here. Take some of the sleeping powder and the poisoned dagger. Spread the weapons among the girls. In case you run into more guards."

Ardyn nods, her face set. "Be careful, Clover."

"You too," I reply, knowing full well that "careful" has long been forsaken tonight.

I grip the dagger one more time, its bejeweled handle now a talisman of modern lives saved, and give it to her.

Then I turn back to the dark cavern of the auction house, ready to confront whatever—and whoever—awaits.

I SLIP through the curtains back into the main auction room unnoticed, the guards still sleeping soundly, my heart thumping in tandem with the clicking of my heels as I walk into the chandeliered center.

I keep my gaze fixed ahead, chin up, spine rigid, trying to ignore the prickle on my neck that means the buyers are watching me. Judging. Trying to place me.

I reach the Vultures at the far corner of the room as Rossi mutters, "It's time."

His face is hidden behind his stoic mask, but the tendons of his neck pop out, his knuckles white where he grips the back of a velvet chair.

Beside him, Tempest's fingers drift to Sarah's gun while Xavier and Rio exchange an edgy look.

Morgan hums under his breath, watching his uncle through eyelet holes surrounded by scarlet feathers.

I observe them with both a sinking and certain feeling. My instincts were correct. Rossi *isn't* prioritizing the trafficked girls. All he wants is Bianchi.

"Sir, are you sure about this?" Rio asks. "The guests aren't armed, but many of the bodyguards surrounding them are."

Rossi's eyes are white behind his mask. "Has that stopped you before?"

Rio frowns.

Tempest adds, "He's right, sir. All we have are eighteenth-century weapons on us."

"They work," Rossi snaps. "Is that not what Rio was working on this past week?"

Tempest clears his throat, his face reddening with anger. "Yes, but we should draw Bianchi away, out of the crowd—"

"I have *ordered* you." Rossi's voice is close to a shout.

Morgan keeps humming a tune with his hands shoved in his pockets while he watches his uncle.

My shoulders go rigid as I draw closer to Rossi, trying to read this man under the layers of vacant formality he's trussed in. "Ardyn and I secured the girls."

He whirls, essentially goring me between the eyes with his glare. "I've repeatedly warned you *not* to go against my orders."

I open my mouth to defend my actions—

"But you've forced my men's hands, considering they're also choosing to second-guess me. This ends *now.*"

Agony binds its way around my heart as I assess each of my Vultures and the weapons they've managed to smuggle in.

A cane sword, switchblades, brass knuckles, sleeve daggers, and a small crossbow. They couldn't bring any modern weapons in without being caught by security.

Their collection is enough to defend, but is it enough to fight?

What is Rossi thinking, sending his men into a professional firing squad?

But Xavier catches my eye last, and something's off. His focus isn't on Bianchi or any of his thugs. It's on a woman wandering nearer to us—elegant, beautiful, golden eyes like a predator.

There, draped in a green gown that makes her look like a forest queen, is the one person who could unravel him.

"Xav?" I whisper, but he doesn't hear me.

His eyes are locked onto her, and I see a flicker of something raw, something so utterly human that it cuts through his new Vulture exterior.

I notice when Meghan's eyes shift, a fleeting squint as she scans the room, and then lock on Xavier.

There's a moment, just a fragment of a second, where recognition darts across her features.

It's as if time slows, my gut sinking with dread.

"Maggie," Xavier breathes through the small mouth-hole of his mask, his voice tinged with a regret and anger so potent, it chars his throat.

She mutters something to Bianchi. Bianchi's eyes flare up like a hellfire, snapping from her to us.

"Guys—" I start to say, grabbing Rio's sleeve.

He twists to me.

I open my mouth to repeat my warning, but a commotion erupts on the far side of the room.

All heads turn to see Bianchi shouldering his way through the crowd, flanked by armed men.

My heart seizes.

Rossi's hand closes around my wrist.

"Stay here," he orders.

I swallow hard, pressing into the shelter of the Vulture's bodies as the first shots split the air.

CHAPTER 38

CLOVER

The auction house, draped in curtains and flickering chandeliers, plunges into a tumultuous fiery underworld nightmare.

Bianchi has no regard for anyone as he shouts for us to be caught, killed, or both.

Crystal shards scatter as gunfire punctuates the air, drowning out the wails of frantic attendees who scuttle like insects, their black-tie attire now mere camouflage from the guns or protection from the growing flames against the walls.

Rossi grabs me, and we take cover behind an ornate column, its carved lines standing placidly amid the violence.

With a flick of his wrist, he releases a switchblade from his cuff links, throwing it with lethal accuracy into the throat of an approaching gunman.

"Stay down," he hisses at me.

Across the room, Xavier maneuvers gracefully despite his cane, now revealed as a deadly, needle-like sword. He aims for their knees, buckling them, then stabbing them through the throat.

I wince even though I know it's necessary. I've just never seen him like this. So fueled with rage and vengeful, his knee a long-forgotten pain.

The sword slips back into the cane with a satisfying click and a smile.

Morgan is a hailstorm of calculated violence. The mini crossbow strapped to his forearm fires off bolt after bolt, each one hitting its mark—neck, chest, eyes. Men fall, clutching at bolts embedded in flesh, remaining eyes wide with shock and confusion.

Gripping a brass knuckle knife, Rio dances through the fray like a dark wraith. His swings are quick and surgical, slashing tendons and arteries, never missing his mark.

My breath catches as a new wave of armed men part through the thickening smoke and head straight for my column.

Before they can reach me, Tempest breaks through the smoke and flames, drawing out one of his knives. With powerful thrusts, he embeds the weapon into two of the men, incapacitating them instantly. His eyes are aflame, not with the reflection of the auction's fire but with ferocious grit.

My focus skims through the opulent chaos as I cough, removing my mask and bending lower to the ground to get better oxygen, finding Rossi again. He has his eyes locked on Bianchi, who is shielded by a remaining coterie of loyal henchmen. The air between them practically sizzles as years of loathing manifest into a standoff in a room slowly killing us all.

I make a grab for him. "Rossi, don't—"

Heedless, he rips his mask from his face and shakes me off, barreling forward and leaping over a line of fire with his fighting arm raised.

I crawl out from my hiding spot, pressing myself against the wall to avoid the crossfire.

Out of the corner of my eye, I see one of Bianchi's men taking aim at Rossi's unprotected back.

Without thinking, I grab a chunk of debris and hurl it, striking the man's hand just as he pulls the trigger. The bullet goes wide, giving Rossi the split second he needs to dive behind a pillar starting to fracture.

My lungs turn into mines housing too much coal. I cough and hack, bowing forward.

That was too close.

Rossi's too emotional to be doing this. We need to leave here, not be buried here.

Across the room, Xavier eliminates the last of the shooters with a ruthless stab through the kidney. For now, the gunfire has stopped, leaving only the sounds of fists striking flesh, agonized screams, and the terrifying rush of fire.

Morgan finishes his last opponent with a twist of his dart in a man's neck and looks up, finding me through the war zone.

His face is splattered with gore and ash, but he grins, feral and alive. "Nice throwing arm, little leaf."

I open my mouth to respond when a blood-curdling shriek rends the air. Whirling, I come up against a woman on the floor, the top of her blond ringlets covered in dripping blood.

Dripping because...

Rio clutches his shoulder, dark blood spilling over his fingers and onto her.

My shout is a painful, tattered, "*Rio!*"

Tempest is at his side in an instant, pressing down on the wound.

"Flesh wound, brother," Tempest mutters, his fingers painted in red. "Nothing you can't handle."

Rio just nods, jaw gritted against the pain.

Before I can feel relief, a cold voice cuts through the tension.

"You stole my pet, Rossi."

Bianchi emerges from his human protection, his figure a rotund silhouette through the gray and black polluting the air, revolver aimed unwaveringly at Rossi's chest while his basilisk eyes turn me to stone.

His cruel smile taunts. "She's quite fetching. Tell me, does she perform all her tricks well?"

Rossi's expression twists with rage. Smoke piles on the ceiling above us, fire and brimstone raining embers. We don't have much time left.

I glance back and forth between them, heart in my throat.

Rossi's hands flex at his sides, ready to draw his ancient weapons at the first opportunity.

But Bianchi just chuckles.

"I expected more from you, old friend. After everything we've been through. Though I suppose betrayal was inevitable for a buzzard like you."

"If anyone preys on people here, it's you," Rossi rasps. "You're the one who took everything from me. Who made me watch as your brother slaughtered my family."

Bianchi shrugs. "Collateral damage. I did what was necessary to keep you obedient."

He cocks the hammer on his revolver. "Just like I'll do now if you don't surrender. Your little band of misfits is outmatched. Look around you—my men have you surrounded."

I glance around quickly and see he's right. We're penned in on all sides by Bianchi's soldiers, guns trained on us.

If they're wobbling like us in the smoke and flame, they don't show it.

They're skilled fighters who took down a dozen men, but not even the Vultures can take on these impossible odds without their usual weapons.

Rossi's face carves out of the smoke, as if the gray tendrils refuse to obscure such savagery. I was well aware of the roiling rage inside him, the desire for vengeance warring with pragmatism, but I never truly *saw* it until now.

Rossi inclines his head at Bianchi. "Are you a coward, *bastardi*?"

Bianchi's smile turns triumphant. He gestures with the revolver. "I like to think of myself as practical. I'll leave you to it and take my prize. The girl comes with me."

Fear lances through me at his words. I back away, but two sets of hands shoot through the flames with an iron grip behind me.

"No!" Xavier surges forward, only to get slammed down by one of Bianchi's men. Morgan lets out an enraged shout that turns into a ragged cough, struggling violently against the three men holding him back.

"Uncle, *no*!"

"Oh, Nephew," Bianchi tuts, ash blackening his chin. "I expected so much more from you."

I twist and fight, but my captors are immovable. Bianchi approaches, trailing the cold barrel of the gun down my cheek. To my horror, it's grown warm from the encroaching fire. Revulsion rises in my throat.

"Don't worry, I'll take good care of her," he croons. "She'll fetch a high price from the right buyer."

Rossi stares at me, anguish in his eyes.

"Ensure they don't get out," Bianchi orders, keeping his attention on my face as his surviving men descend on my Vultures, and I'm pulled backward away from the fire.

As I'm dragged away, screaming and choking, I meet Rossi's gaze. And though no words are spoken, a promise passes from him to me.

I'll get you back, tesoro mio.

My hands are bound behind me as I'm shoved into the back of an armored truck.

Bianchi climbs in after me, settling onto a bench on the opposite side. His men slam the doors shut, enclosing us in musty darkness.

"Just you and me now," Bianchi sing-songs softly. His eyes rake over me in a way that makes my skin crawl. "We're going to have such fun."

I press into the corner, putting as much distance between us as I can. Bianchi just chuckles.

"Where's your *wife*?" I hiss.

The truck lurches into motion.

My mind races, trying to formulate some kind of escape plan. But my options are limited with my wrists tied and Bianchi's guards in the front seat of the van.

Bianchi slides closer, trailing a finger down my arm. I jerk away, suppressing a shudder. "Why, she's in our Bentley, of course, being driven home to await my cock after I dip it in you."

"Don't touch me," I spit.

His smile widens. "Still so defiant. I'll enjoy breaking that spirit of yours."

Before I can react, he grabs my chin in an iron grip. I try to wrench free, but his other hand encircles my throat, cutting off my air. Panic pierces my chest as black spots dance in my vision.

Just when I'm about to pass out, he releases me.

I double over, gasping irregularly, smoke inhalation warring with strangulation.

Bianchi just watches with an amused glint in his eyes.

"A little bird told me that's what you like before he strayed. We're going to have so much fun, you and me," he croons.

I stare at him with pure hatred, refusing to let the fear show on my face.

Bianchi reaches for the top of my dress, his expression intent on tearing it open, but the truck swerves violently to the right. Tires squeal as we fishtail across the road. Bianchi and I are flung sideways. He slams into the wall with a pained grunt.

The truck careens wildly before skidding to a stop, the engine sputtering and dying. Dazed, I push myself up as much as I can. Bianchi is sprawled on the floor, out cold.

What the hell just happened?

The back doors fly open, and there's my brother, looking fierce and pissed off as he aims his semi-automatic at Bianchi.

"Found our semi-automatics," he says flatly, reaching for me with his free hand.

Behind him, Rossi's slick black car pulls across the road, blocking our path.

"Clover!" Xavier's voice is tight with concern as he throws himself out of the passenger side before the car stops, uncaring of himself and instead taking in the bruises and raw skin at my throat.

His jaw clenches, and his eyes flash with barely contained rage. But he stays focused, gesturing for me to come to him.

I don't hesitate. Scrambling over Bianchi's prone form and with Tempest's assistance jumping down with my hands behind my back, I slip from the truck into Xavier's waiting arms. He crushes me against his chest, just for a moment, before quickly ushering me behind him.

Rossi appears, cold resolve freezing his features into deadly promise.

Without a word, he slices the ties at my wrists in two, hauls Bianchi's unconscious body from the truck, and zip-ties his wrists together.

"We need to move now," Tempest says. "Morgan and Rio are holding off the rest of Bianchi's men, but they're heavily outnumbered."

The distant pop of gunfire echoes through the alleys. Xavier's grip on me tightens.

Rossi seethes, "I'll take care of this piece of garbage. You get Clover out of here."

Xavier doesn't hesitate, but Tempest does.

"Sir..."

"I said *leave* us be," Rossi hisses through his teeth, his numbed expression slipping.

Keeping his gun ready, Tempest and Xavier hurry me toward the sleek black car. I glance back once at Bianchi's prone form, a tiny flare of satisfaction curling through me.

Xavier opens the passenger door, and I slide in. As he rounds the car to the driver's side, something loosens in my chest.

But my eyes, my focus, stay with Rossi.

CHAPTER 39
ROSSI

The dark and damp alley smells of rotting things. My heart is part of this decay.

Bianchi lies at my feet, bound. His expensive suit is torn and stained. The fallen king is now just another piece of refuse in the gutter.

I nudge him with my boot. Still out cold.

Not good. I want him awake for this.

Awake and aware.

Crouching down, I grab a fistful of greasy hair at the back of his scalp and yank his head up.

"Wake up, Marco."

Bianchi's eyes flutter open. It takes a moment for awareness to dawn.

When it does, he starts blinking rapidly. He tries to speak but only manages a strangled groan.

I let his head drop back to the concrete. The dull thud is music to my ears.

Bianchi killed my wife and my child and threatened to take Clover in the same way.

He took everything from me.

Now, I will take all from him.

I dig in the knife and quickly slice a long gash down his neck. Blood spurts, spraying my face, but I avoid the jugular vein.

"You still have much to answer for," I say to him.

This is my time, my moment. His life drips from my hands like blood from a fresh kill.

And it feels *good.*

Bianchi garbles out a scream as I press the knife further into his neck.

He hums in pain, his voice growing hoarse. One more cut and his neck will be open to the bone. I can picture his hot blood sloshing over my hand.

The alley is deathly quiet. No one comes to investigate the commotion. The Vultures are too busy protecting Clover to notice what I'm doing, and I'm glad for both of those things.

Bianchi struggles to talk. I lean close.

"Why?" I whisper near the shell of his ear.

"Why ... what?" he croaks.

"Why did you kill them? They were innocent. Harmless. Deserving of full lives."

I grind the knife against his neck, drawing a fresh flood of crimson.

"*Innocent,*" I repeat, spittle flying. "They were happy. They were good. They were everything. And you stole them from me."

"It was necessary. Your talent was too good to waste. I—"

"My talent? But you never had any intention of using it. I was a tool to you. A disposable weapon."

"You were my favorite stallion in the stables," Bianchi replies, his mouth trying for a sneer but seizing at the edges.

"I never wanted that."

"It doesn't matter. You needed me to find you a place in this world."

"I had a place. A destiny. You took that from me, too."

"That was a matter of business."

"You took my life, and you call that business?"

"If you'd stayed under my orders, you would have been set for the rest of your life."

"You think this servitude is a *blessing*? That I was bound for this?" I dig the blade deeper, indenting the skin on the side of his neck.

"No." Bianchi releases a wet sigh. "You wanted something better before I got to you. Something pure. Something perfect. None of those things exist in this world—mine or yours. You're not meant for perfection, Miguel. You were misshapen long before I came along..."

I don't answer, but his words are like bullets.

"And what about Valentina?" I ask him. My daughter's name reopens the scar tissue in my throat, her ichor bleeding through my tendons, muscles, skin, turning me to flesh-eating acid. "Was she disposable, too?"

"In the end, yes."

Dark, hot flames of rage blind me. The knife trembles in my hand.

I lean in close and whisper in his ear, "I will enjoy leaving you to die. As blind as I am. How does it feel to have your own creation end you?"

I slice the tip of my blade across both sclera of his eyes.

Bianchi tries to scream, tries to fight, but can't.

I look down on him as I would a surgical patient, angling my head this way and that as I watch his vision turn to a white pulp.

"One more thing, *Soldato*, before you go," I say. "No Bianchi heir will assume control of your empire after your imminent death. I will make sure of it. No, it will be taken over by *me*. I am the new Don, Marco. And I will poison your empire from the inside out and swim in all your profit."

"Nuh—*guh*—"

I slam a fist into his mouth, knocking out a few teeth. He screams blood.

I sweep my knife across his neck, tearing it wide open. His blood spews from the wound in a syrupy waterfall.

"I know more about monsters than you ever will," I rasp.

I dig my thumb into his mess of an eye socket. Bianchi howls.

This intimidating barrel of a man is reduced to a writhing mass, shitting and dribbling all over himself, the one remaining taillight of his van providing me with the best view of his demise.

And there's nothing he can do about it.

"Mig—*Rossi*—I can—"

His words break off in a spurt of blood as I jam the blade through his brain.

Then his body goes limp.

I take a moment to gaze at him. His leaking eye sockets stare off into the distance, as empty and as dead as my wife and daughter.

Then I laugh. I laugh at Bianchi's stupid last words.

I stand, wiping my weapon on my pants leg, then lean down and wipe my bloody hands on his face.

Next, I stoop to pick up his clip-on bow tie. I shove it into his mouth, taking a moment to spit on him again.

I lean in closer and whisper, "Enjoy hell, *cretino*."

Then I walk away, letting him rot alone.

And slowly.

CHAPTER 40
CLOVER

Xavier slams the driver's side door and revs the engine. Tires spitting gravel, we peel out onto the city streets, other cars becoming more prevalent the deeper south we go. My heart pounds with exhilaration and lingering fear as skyscrapers, my old home—blow past.

Xavier's jaw is clenched, eyes laser-focused on the road ahead. Tempest grips the upper bar in the passenger seat, the line of his jaw similarly cut.

Visions of Meghan O'Malley's regal beauty, vicious smile, and shrewd eyes swim dangerously close to my heart.

"Xav, are you all right?" I ask quietly from the back, my fingers digging into the leather seat.

"Dandy," Xavier clips out, staring straight ahead.

Tempest's head twists toward him, assessing. Like the good brother he is, he knows exactly what I'm referring to.

"We should have assumed she'd be there," Tempest says, his voice almost as low as the engine.

His version of an apology.

Xavier lifts one shoulder. "We were consumed by Bianchi.

Rightly so. But Maggie ... she's as psychotic as him. To punish someone for not being interested in her by enslaving him to the mafia—she's evil. A vicious fucking woman. And, she is nothing like you."

Xavier's eyes meet mine in the rearview. "I do not hold any love for her, Clover. Know that. Her presence brought back my torture, not my heart. I dumped that she-demon for a reason."

I give a small smile of reassurance in response. It's funny, I never assumed his reaction to her was heartbreak. There was no jealousy in seeing him stumble at the sight of her, only concern and possessiveness.

I know he's mine.

Broken, tortured, traumatized, but *mine*.

Never hers.

Xavier returns me to the present by adding, "Check under the seat beside you, love."

Curious, I reach under until I feel a velvet covering. Pulling it out, I gasp as a streetlight arcs over the prize.

"Sarah's grimoire!" I say.

"Did you really believe I'd allow it to be left behind, knowing how much it meant to you?" Xavier asks.

"You could've been killed trying to get this," I say.

Xavier clenches the wheel, his expression hard. "I wasn't. I won't be."

"Well done." Tempest clasps Xavier's shoulder, rare respect flowing across his features.

"Do you think the others will be okay?" I ask, holding the stinky grimoire close to my chest.

I now believe there are smells that exist worse than it—cloying smoke, gunpowder, blood, and a man's hands snaking over your body to drag you into his van and claim cruel ownership.

"Rossi will make sure Morgan and Rio get out safe," Tempest says. "We just have to focus on putting distance between us and Bianchi's men right now."

I nod, despite witnessing Rossi hang back with a trussed-up Bianchi. I should feel glory at the fact that Bianchi's defeated, but all that runs through my mind is the look on Rossi's face. Not vengeance exactly, but...

Victory.

Glancing at the side mirror, a rush of relief hits me when the city turns into pinpricks of light behind us as we head to the open road.

We drive in apprehensive silence for several miles before Xavier pulls off onto a dirt road nearly invisible between the trees. He kills the headlights and creeps slowly along until we reach a small clearing.

Morgan's sleek black Ferrari is already there, along with Rio's motorcycle. Before we've even stopped, Morgan stalks over and wrenches my door open.

"Took you long enough," he snaps at Xavier, but his eyes are worried as they rake over me.

Xavier is instantly at my side. "Had to make sure we weren't followed. The others?"

"Here," Rio says gruffly, appearing from the trees. "We need to keep moving, get back to Blackwood."

Rio steps close, searching my face.

"Lucky?" he asks softly.

I manage a shaky smile. "I'm fine now."

Tempest claps a hand on Xavier's shoulder. "You did good, getting her out of there."

Xavier nods, jaw muscles ticking.

"Ardyn, she has the girls," I say.

Tempest nods. "I'm well aware and ensured their safe

crossing." He then levels me with a look. "We'll discuss what you two did later."

I feign ignorance, tucking my hair behind my ears and gazing anywhere but at him.

Tempest doesn't buy the charade but moves on. "Ardyn's waiting for me at a safe house in the city. I'm off to get her. Rossi's given me a contact to send the girls to and get them out of the area permanently."

Just hearing that eases some of the panic constricting my chest.

Morgan tosses Tempest a set of keys. "Take mine."

Tempest spins and slips into Morgan's car, the engine purring and our shadows lengthening with the swing of Tempest's headlights before he drives out.

"Rossi?" I ask. "He's still with Bianchi. He could be—"

"Alive and well."

The words are spoken behind the dense tangle of snow and branches. Then comes the crackling sound of footsteps on the forest floor.

Rossi emerges from the trees, but he's not alone.

At least six men in black suits flank him on either side.

I rapidly scan for chains, ties, anything holding Rossi hostage and showing he's with these men against his will.

But nothing is restraining him.

These men—*Bianchi's* men—fan out along the perimeter, stone-faced sentinels with guns trained on us. At the center stands Rossi, his long coat swirling in the breeze.

Though I don't know the full reason yet, my vision blurs with hot tears.

I take one step toward him.

"Rossi?"

Xavier's eyes narrow, the bones of his knuckles popping

through his skin as he grips his pistol. Morgan's stillness radiates an impending rampage unless a satisfying explanation reveals itself right fucking now.

Their unease feeds my own, dread cascading up my spine, over my shoulders, into my breaths.

"Hello, boys." Morgan greets the six men around Rossi first. "May I ask what the fuck is going on here?"

Rossi scans our faces, frigid delight—victory—drenched across his face, both in blood splatter and expression.

"Come now, aren't you going to say hello?" he asks.

Rossi's nonchalance ignites a spark of dismay in my chest.

"Is this a *game* to you?" I ask, visibly shaking. "I thought you were hurt. I was so worried you'd—"

"Cross over into the dark side," Morgan finishes with a curl to his lips, folding his arms. "I should give you first prize, Rossi. We did *not* see this coming."

For a moment, a precious second, Rossi's cold, imperious gaze crumbles, his coal-black eyes warming as they land on mine, his lips twisting as if it hurts him to look at me.

Then his face smooths, and he turns back to ice.

Xavier snaps with a tight, panic-laced tone, "Perhaps Morgan wasn't specific enough. Rossi, why are Bianchi's blokes here?"

Rossi's mouth curves into a sly smile so unlike him that my face spasms in pain.

He answers, "Because I killed the old bastard and took over. His empire is mine now."

Xavier's mouth falls open. Morgan looks ready to erupt, a volcano of madness. Me, I'm reeling, grasping for solid ground as my world tilts on its axis.

I stare at Rossi, heart destroyed.

This man I've fought beside, bled for, and trusted with my

life now stands before me a stranger, eyes glinting with cool triumph.

"You backstabbing bastard," Morgan hisses, vibrating with fury.

Rossi's gaze swings to Morgan. "I'd think carefully before you do anything stupid, boy."

Morgan bristles at being called boy, years of resentment and abuse simmering to the surface.

This isn't the Rossi I know. That man gave me purpose. His protection saved my life, gave me courage. I handed him my heart, and now he's betrayed us.

The realization is a scalpel twisting in my gut.

"Why?"

The word tears from my throat before I can stop it.

Rossi's triumph diminishes a fraction. "It was time. Past time. Did you really think I'd let that bastard live after what he did to my family?" His voice drops, becoming bleak.

"I thought you wanted to be free," I whisper.

Rossi starts toward me. Behind him, Bianchi's men tense, fingers on triggers. He ignores them, spreading his hands beseechingly.

"I can build something better," he says. "With no one to answer to. I did this for us."

I stare at him, heart and mind at war. I want to trust him and believe things will be different now that Marco Bianchi is gone. But doubt roots me in place. Rossi keeps so many secrets, this one being the worst. He never wanted to be free. He wanted to be *king*. How can I know where his true loyalties lie?

Beside me, Xavier's confusion rolls off him in waves. His attention darts between Rossi and the silent ranks of Bianchi's men, brows drawn together in disbelief.

"You meant to be Don all along?" he asks slowly. "Are we

still your Vultures, then? Or is that all over now, like you swore?"

"We were always Vultures," Rossi insists, looking briefly at each of us. "I just turned the tide."

"Into a *fucking* tsunami," Morgan seethes.

To my right, Rio shakes his head, face bloodless.

"Why didn't you tell us?" Rare, heart-breaking grief threads through Rio's voice.

"It was my burden to bear, Rio. But we're free of Bianchi now."

He moves toward Rio and grips his shoulder. Rio braces himself against the pressure, his fists clenching.

"We do this together," Rossi says. "Or on my own. Your choice to leave the Vultures still stands. For all of you."

Rio searches his face, the struggle clear, the desire to cling to the family he's found here warring with uncertain treachery.

The forest clearing is eerily still, even the birds going silent when a predator is nearby. Bianchi's men fan out in a loose semi-circle. Their sharp eyes track our every movement, bodies coiled.

Protecting their new king.

My ribs crack under the *booms* of my heart.

Morgan shifts restlessly on the other side of me, rage simmering beneath his skin.

"You've got to be fucking with me," Morgan growls, the disbelief etched across his face transforming into a snarl. "You've been scheming this all along and didn't say a word?"

Rossi releases Tempest and draws closer to Morgan. "What would you have done? Sabotaged it because you weren't the center of attention?"

Morgan's eyes are flinty, wild even.

"I had a right to know," Morgan hisses. "I am the heir, after all."

Rossi leans in, almost whispering, "I killed your father, Morgan. A year ago. I've been Don for longer than you think."

The forest clearing loses all oxygen. I have trouble breathing.

Morgan reacts as if he's just been slapped. He sounds like he's choking. His face loses all blood, but then it comes back with a force, a surge of red.

"You—you *motherfucker!* I had a right to know!

Rio's voice slices through the two of them. "You claim to be Don, Rossi, but you've just killed your own legacy."

The air seems to restrict. Rossi's eyes meet Rio's, and for a moment, there's a glimpse of vulnerability there, an acknowledgment of the disloyalty and the weight of Rio's words.

"How could you?" I ask Rossi with a hitch in my breath. "How could you just blurt it out to him like that, without any care?"

Rossi's eyes meet mine last, and there's an ache there, a pained love he doesn't hide quick enough. "Clover, this doesn't change—"

Morgan lunges for him.

But two of Rossi's new men grab him first. Morgan struggles violently as they pin his arms behind his back.

"You cocksucking son of a bitch!" he spits at Rossi. "*I* am the rightful heir! You listen to me, not this half-Italian, traitorous *il bacio della morte!!*" Morgan snarls, "You are marked for death, Rossi, on my orders. *Kill* him," Morgan demands of the men.

The men don't move.

Rossi's face is impassive. "I did what I had to do. These men serve me now. I gave them a choice, you know. In a way you wouldn't have. I let them either stay with me or walk away. No bloodshed. Higher wages." He pauses. "They chose to stay."

The two men tighten their grip, pushing Morgan closer until he's feet away from Rossi.

Rossi rasps, "You hated your father and your uncle both, Morgan. Would you have done any differently if you'd known?"

"I would've had a choice!" Morgan snarls, struggling against their grip. "I would've been the one to end them, to take up the mantle or abandon it, on my terms."

Rossi holds Morgan's gaze. "Life rarely offers us the luxury of choices where we want them."

Rossi signals his men to release Morgan, and they push him back just enough to create distance.

I watch it all, feeling like I've been severed in two.

The proof stands right in front of me, blood dripping from Rossi's fingers. He meets my gaze, and I search those dark eyes for some flicker of the man I thought I knew. The man who held me close.

Is he still in there somewhere? Or did I only ever see what I wanted to see?

"Miss Callahan," he begins but stops. Whatever he is about to say dies on his lips.

I shake my head, bile rising in my throat.

He steps toward me, but I back away instinctively.

Hurt flashes across his face.

"Please," he says hoarsely. "I never meant to lie to you. But I couldn't risk everything falling apart too soon."

My laugh comes out strangled. "And what about us falling apart? Did you ever think about that?"

Rossi reaches for me again, but I evade his touch. His hand falls back to his side.

"I was trying to protect you," he says, voice low. "I need you to trust me on this."

"Trust," I scoff.

My trust feels irrevocably shattered. I don't know how to bridge this canyon that's opened up between us. I don't know if I can find a way back to how things were before.

The silence in the clearing is deafening, no one moving, everyone witnessing.

Rossi's eyes search my face, but whatever he wants to see, he won't find it. The girl who looked at him with stars in her eyes is gone. Now, there is only a vast barrenness, like a nightless desert threatening to turn us all to dust.

"Clover," Xavier urges gently, touching my arm. "Get away from him."

Rossi's shoulders fall. He gestures to his new men to let Xavier pull me away.

Xavier guides me with his hands on my shoulders, my legs wooden, each step an effort. Morgan lingers, torn between Rossi and us. His usual manic energy is subdued, shocked into compliance.

But as we retreat into the car, I glance back once.

Rossi stands alone among Bianchi's men, his expression etched with agony.

At that moment, he looks small. Vulnerable.

But then his eyes harden, jaw locking with determination. The Rossi I thought I knew was suffocated under layers of ruthless objective: To successfully avenge his past family, he was willing to lose his present one.

I could've healed him. I could've helped shave the scar tissue off his heart.

Not all of it, never all of it, but he could have lived a good life with me. No, a *wonderful* one.

He could have been unshackled, set free.

Xavier's hand tightens on my arm. "Are you all right?"

I force myself to nod. But inside, I'm screaming.

We drive to Blackwood Manor in silence, with Rio following us on his motorcycle. Ardyn waits at the top of the stairs, concern on her face when we pull in and she sees the state of us as we step out.

"What happened?" she asks, eyes scanning as she counts heads. "Where's Rossi?"

Xavier shakes his head grimly. "Everything's changed now."

Ardyn pales. She pulls me into a fierce hug. I cling to her, desperate for something real in my rapidly dissolving world.

"Tell me," she whispers.

And so I do, the words spilling out in a torrent. The chasm inside me grows deeper and darker with each sentence while Xavier, Rio, and Morgan approach Tempest in the foyer.

When I finish, Ardyn steps back, eyes wide with shock. "God, with the looks on all of your faces, I thought Rossi died. I thought—"

We're jarred into the manor when we hear a cacophony of blows.

Tempest's delayed reaction comes in the form of whirling and punching the wall, pulling a vase off the center table and shattering it. Moving to chairs and slamming them against the wall until they explode.

"In a lot of ways, he did," I murmur to Ardyn beside me.

Ardyn runs to Tempest, pulling him by his arms, pleading with him to look at her. The cries eventually reach him and the fog of wrath in his eyes fades.

Draining, ever so slowly.

Tempest slumps. Ardyn curls into him, and he bows over her, holding on.

We all remain standing, surrounded by destruction as the sun dips below the horizon, bleeding crimson across the darkening sky.

"What do we do now?" Ardyn asks the room quietly, her head against Tempest's heaving chest.

I shake mine in answer. I don't have any solutions, only a bone-deep exhaustion that threatens to drown me.

But Xavier's voice is firm. "We keep going. We look out for each other. We survive."

CHAPTER 41

CLOVER

The flickering candlelight casts dancing shadows across the spines of ancient books. I sit curled in an armchair, idly tracing the faded gilt lettering on the cracked leather binding in my lap.

Across from me, Xavier lounges on the sofa, one leg draped casually over the armrest. His eyes are closed, but I can tell by the crease between his brows that he isn't sleeping.

Tempest and Ardyn retired to their room two days ago and, as far as I know, haven't come out. My brother is devastated since learning that Rossi, the only true father he's ever had, left him. Rossi hasn't said a word to Tempest since revealing his true intentions to us in the clearing.

Morgan paces the library, muttering under his breath. His fists are clenched, knuckles white under his ink.

I glance at Rio leaning silently against the bookshelves. He's deliberately aloof, but there's a wariness in his eyes as he keeps Morgan in his sights.

"I can't believe the bastard," Morgan growls, wheeling around.

Xavier cracks one eye open. "What did you expect? Rossi's despised the Bianchis for years. With Don Bianchi gone, he's seized his chance for control."

Morgan slams a fist against a bookshelf's sidewall, making me jump. "He had no right. The Vultures answer to me now, not him."

"Oh, yeah?" Xavier closes his eyes again and nestles further into his chair with folded arms. "See how that goes."

I bite my lip, fiddling with the frayed edges of my black denim skirt. Morgan has always been volatile, but Rossi's revelation about murdering his father, with the new addition of his uncle, has pushed him over the edge.

I'm about to attempt to say something soothing when the heavy oak door to the library creaks open.

And Rossi strides in.

He's flanked by two hulking bodyguards. Instantly, the room tenses, the air spiking in temperature.

My hand stills on my skirt. I can't seem to react, move, rise, blink, nothing.

But Xavier pushes to his feet.

Morgan whirls, eyes blazing.

"Well, if it isn't the great new Don," Morgan sneers. "Here to claim your crumbling kingdom?"

Rossi regards him coolly. "I don't have to claim anything. My authority's already recognized." His cold gaze sweeps over Xavier and Rio, remaining obscured near the stacks. "Whether you accept it or not."

Morgan takes a threatening step forward. Rossi's guards react, hands going to their guns, but he halts them with a glance.

The sight of his commanding stare at Bianchi's men pisses me off. "If you want to speak to us, leave your men outside."

Rossi's gaze snaps to mine as soon as I say it, my tone flat, my heart run over.

Rossi's jaw works. He doesn't break our stare.

"Very well," he says with a sharp motion of his hand.

The bodyguards reluctantly leave.

"Brave of you, considering how well you've trained the Vultures in our kills," Morgan spits. "Oh, unless those are the ones replacing us?"

Instead of answering, Rossi shoots up a hand, halting Rio's stalking around him in a half circle. His aim was to come at Rossi from behind, but Rossi was too quick to notice.

"I'm well aware of how skilled you all are," Rossi says. "But you won't kill me. You're too eager for answers."

Rio draws himself out into the light, his expression remaining dark. "It's not us you owe answers to. I'll get Tempest."

Rio weaves around him and into the hallway without argument from Rossi, returning a short time later with a fuming, barely restrained Tempest.

"You arrogant bastard," Tempest fumes. "You sincere *son of a bitch.*"

"I know you're angry," Rossi says quietly as Ardyn holds on to Tempest, grounding him before he can vault over us and excavate Rossi's heart. "But I did what I had to do."

"I followed your every order." Purple tendons pop from Tempest's forearms and the backs of his hands. "I've been your infallible second. Every gunshot I took, every wound sliced into my body, every lie I told—it was for you."

Tempest stalks closer, his hands hanging at his sides enough for Ardyn to release him without fear that Tempest will strike. His voice drops, tinged with a bitterness that brings fresh tears to my eyes.

I had no idea how lonely my brother was before Rossi, the Vultures, Ardyn.

"I would have walked through fire for you, Rossi. I've killed for you, trained to become a killer under your hand. All you had to do was tell me the truth. Was I just a pawn? Is that all I ever was? All that loyalty, all that sacrifice, and you reward me with betrayal. You shattered not just my trust, Rossi, but my belief that loyalty means something."

Rossi works to control his features, but he can't control the answering sheen to his eyes. "You're not a pawn. You were never just a pawn to me. But this world, this life we lead—it doesn't give room for faith in a person, never completely. I wanted the empire, and yes, I was protecting myself from it in the only way I knew how."

He studies Tempest, as if trying to reach the young man he had trained, molded, and came to care for.

When all he gets in response is Tempest's murderous, reproachful stare, Rossi turns to Morgan. "Your father and uncle destroyed everything, not just my family, but hundreds of innocent lives. Girls. Sex trafficking. Their greed was going to ruin us."

"So you decided to play judge, jury, and executioner?" Morgan's voice drips contempt.

"I wasn't alone in wanting them gone." Rossi's keeps his level stare. "You hated them as much as I did. Don't pretend otherwise."

Morgan hesitates and it's enough for Rossi to press his advantage.

"The Vultures need decisive leadership now more than ever. I can provide that." He spreads his hands. "Work with me, not against me, and we can bring this family back together. Or —" he continues before any of us can protest, "You may walk away. I meant what I said in the clearing. Anyone who wants to be free can be free. No bloodshed."

Morgan paces the library, his expression a mixture of fury and, surprisingly, relief. Finally, he stops. "You're right; I hated my father. And maybe if I had known, things would be different. But one thing I do know is that you've always acted like you're the only one who has the answers, the only one who can make the hard decisions."

Rossi's jaw muscles form into a rigid line, but he nods. "I never said I was perfect, Morgan. But I've done what I thought was necessary. Can you honestly say you would've done differently?"

"I'll never know, will I?" Morgan throws back, but the anger has bled out of him, replaced by a kind of weary acceptance. "But you're Don. You've made sure of that, haven't you?"

Rossi glances at Rio, then back at Morgan. "Yes. Even if you hate me for it."

Morgan glances at me, then at Xavier and Rio. He sighs. "I never wanted the title, but it irks me to no end that you've just ... taken it. Without even a *please*."

At last, Rio speaks up. "Rossi is Don unless any of us decide to leave."

I feel the weight of his words. This is no longer just about the Vultures or the Bianchis. It's about the seven of us and the future we could have together.

Are we together, or will we split apart, fractured and lost all over again?

"The manor is yours to renovate and use as you see fit," Rossi continues. "I've transferred the deed to Tempest's name."

Tempest grimaces like the words physically hurt him. He folds his arms, refusing to look at his boss, a man I know he loves.

Loved.

"Continue your education at Titan Falls University if you want. For real, this time. I have no need for this house anymore. I'll be moving to the city, restructuring the syndicate, rerouting the profits, changing the dynamic—but I am still a Don. We will specialize in weapons, drug exports. But no girls. No women. I promise you that."

I stare at Rossi, my vision wavering. "You're moving?"

Rossi answers me, his eyes as dormant as I've ever seen them. " I owe you a home, a place to grow ... or to heal."

"What if I want to do all that with you?" I ask, leaning forward in my seat. Getting closer to him, but not too close.

"I want that more than anything," Rossi admits, his midnight eyes shining. "But you have your own path now, and I have mine as the Don. Even if we all stayed, things wouldn't be the same. I won't chain you to a life filled with even more danger and uncertainty than before."

My lips part, but no words can escape through the fissures forming from my heart, into my chest, up my throat and seizing my mind.

Rossi, sensing my heartbreak, adds tenderly, "Sometimes, loving someone means letting them find their own destiny. As much as it tears me apart, I have to let you find yours, without the burdens my new life would impose on you."

"I don't want this," I whisper to the floor, through blurred vision and clamped teeth. "I'm *so* angry with you, but I don't want you to leave."

Rossi releases a shuddering sigh. "May Clover and I have the room?"

Morgan peels his lips back to deny him, but Rio stops him with a look, then nods in my direction. "Whatever Lucky wants to do."

Tempest wars with similar emotions, sniffing hard, glaring harder.

They wait for my answer.

"All right," I say to Rossi, soft as a whisper.

The remnants of the Vultures leave the room, all with reassuring gazes or promises they'll be right outside if I need anything.

I smile gratefully at them before that smile dissolves against my teeth, and I regard Rossi.

"The Bianchis are no longer a threat to you. You've discovered the truth of Sarah Anderton's treasure. You helped save over a dozen girls. You are a wonder, *tesoro mio.*"

His eyes lock onto mine as if grappling for my soul.

I rise from my seat, blinking away tears. "Why does this feel like a goodbye?"

Rossi doesn't answer, which is answer enough.

"You're a part of my happiness," I say. "You've always been."

"No, sweetheart. You're starting something new, something that promises a different kind of blissfulness. With Morgan, with Rio, and Xavier. One I can't give you."

He takes a deep breath. His eyes cloud over, shimmering as if on the brink. "I've been a part of a life that's falling apart based on deceptions and bloody power plays. How can I offer you anything pure when so much darkness shrouds me?"

"You don't get it, Rossi. *Miguel.*" My voice hitches on his first name. "Love isn't about purity; it's about acceptance, scars and all."

A pained smile forms on his lips. "You deserve more than acceptance, Miss Callahan. You deserve men who'll treat you right and give you the world without asking you to wade through their shadows."

"I love your shadows," I confess, my voice cracking, and it feels like my heart splinters into a thousand shards, each one piercing me deeper than the last. "I love every dark, twisted part of you, Rossi. Don't I get a say in what I deserve?"

Rossi closes the gap between us, and I feel his breath against my skin, hot and heavy like a secret. "If I were a better man, your say would be the only thing that mattered. But I can't be that man. Not in this lifetime."

His lips meet my forehead in a lingering kiss—a whisper of a touch that speaks volumes, echoing a love that's too potent to be contained yet too destructive to be set free.

"Goodbye, Clover," he murmurs against my skin as he pulls away.

And then he's gone, leaving nothing but an echoing silence and a heart struggling to piece itself back together.

The finality of it settles over me like a burial garment, and I allow myself to break.

I fall to my knees, covering my face as I sob.

Because saying goodbye to Rossi isn't just the end of us; it's the relinquishing of a dream, a future that could've been but will now never be.

And it's devastating.

CHAPTER 42
CLOVER

I'm adrift in the empty manor.

The ticking of the grandfather clock echoes down the cavernous hallway, a metronome keeping time in a place where time seems to have stopped.

My fingers trail along the wall, catching on gilded frames and ornate sconces. Everything once so familiar is now strange and foreign.

This was our home, our sanctuary, for so long. Now, it's just halls and rooms haunted by memories that linger like phantoms.

In the study, I sink into Rossi's chair, the scent of sandalwood and tobacco still clinging to the worn leather. How many nights had I made an excuse to come in here while he worked, content just to be near him?

The ache of missing him sits like a river rock in my chest.

I should hate him. Rossi lied, deceived, and broke my heart. But part of me still loves him and mourns what we had. I cling to the hope that he'll come back, choose me, choose us.

But life moves forward despite the silence pressing down, and I straighten my shoulders.

And then I see it. A small envelope lies at the edge of the desk, my name etched on it in Rossi's distinctive handwriting.

My fingers tremble as I pick it up, almost afraid to break the seal and read what's inside. But I have to know, even if it cracks me open all over again.

Carefully, I open the envelope and pull out the folded piece of paper. As I read his words, my eyes blur with tears.

Clover,

As I write this, I'm weighing every word, knowing that ink and paper can't capture the complexity of what we've been to each other. If words were sufficient, we'd have figured all this out a long time ago.

I still remember the night we met when I caught you sneaking around the archives, the way your eyes held a kind of desperate courage. They still do. But while courage can fuel a war, it can't always determine its outcome. And, tesoro mio, *we've been at war—against the world, against our pasts, and most of all, against the worst parts of ourselves.*

You deserve more than the man I've become. You deserve the sort of love that elevates you, not the kind that demands a price for every stolen moment. I can give you many things, but I can't give you that. Not without asking you to share in a darkness that could swallow us both.

I've left you something—a dried clover leaf. I hope you'll keep it as a reminder of the different kind of love that's possible. Love that doesn't require you to pay in pieces of your soul.

Please know that my decision to step away isn't a testament to any lack of feeling on my part, but a brutal acknowledgment of the emotions that run too deeply for my own good, or for yours. I love you too much to make you an accessory to the life I've chosen, to the man I've become.

In another life, in another world, I would have fought gods and monsters to keep you by my side. But in this one, the greatest act of love I can offer is to walk away.

Keep the clover leaf. Keep the men who make you whole. And find it in your heart to keep a sliver of me, locked away somewhere safe, where the darkness can't touch it.

Forever yours,

Miguel

THE TEARS SPILL OVER, hot and unforgiving. I fold the letter carefully, tucking it back into the envelope. As much as it hurts, this is his final gift to me—a poignant memory that I can keep, even if I can't keep him.

Before I leave his study, I tuck the letter into a drawer. I'll read it again someday, when his absence is less raw and the open wound has turned into a puckered scar. But for now, I close the door behind me, letting Rossi's study remain what it has always been—a fortress of secrets, a place where love lived and died.

THE MORNING SUN streams through my bedroom's windows, dust motes dancing in the warm light.

I slip out of bed, taking a deep breath, and make my way downstairs.

In the kitchen, Xavier leans against the counter, sipping coffee. His green eyes meet mine, crinkling at the corners.

"Morning, love," he says. "Sleep okay?"

I pour myself a cup, the simple domesticity of it soothing. "Not really. You?"

He shakes his head, his smile fading. None of us have been sleeping well since Rossi left. The ghouls of this house linger.

Xavier sets his mug down and pulls me close. I relax into his embrace, comforted by his familiar scent of spice and citrus. We stay like that for a long moment.

"We'll get through this," he murmurs against my hair. "Together."

The sound of footsteps causes us to pull apart. Morgan strides into the kitchen, usual manic energy subdued. Dark circles ring his eyes.

"Morning," he mumbles.

"There's coffee," Xavier offers neutrally.

Morgan nods, shuffling to the pot. An uneasy silence settles over the room.

I clear my throat. "I was thinking of going into town later, picking up some things for class, catching up on all the stuff I've missed. Ardyn says she's busy, so do either of you want to come?"

It's both a peace offering and a reminder that we're free.

We can *leave* this place.

Morgan's mouth quirks up at the corner. "Yeah, sure. I'd love the chance to spoil you, little leaf. We can take the SUV and you can fill it with all the schoolbooks and stationery you desire."

The flash of his old grin heartens me. Things will never be the same, but maybe they can be better.

I smile in return, rinsing out my cup.

Xavier gives my hand a final squeeze before releasing it. "As riveting as that sounds, you two have fun. I'll hold down the fort here."

We make our way through the sprawling halls of Blackwood Manor, footsteps echoing across marble floors. The emptiness weighs on me, memories etched into every surface.

At the massive front doors, Morgan pauses, consternation between his brows. "Do you think he's really gone for good?"

We haven't spoken Rossi's name since that night, the wound still too raw.

"I don't know," I answer. "But it's out of our hands now."

Morgan presses his lips together and nods tightly. "Was it ever *in* our hands?"

I don't have an answer to that.

We step out into the morning sun, a new warmth dawning over the decay of winter.

The Range Rover rumbles to life after Morgan gets in and I slip into the passenger side.

Morgan rests his hands on the steering wheel, hesitating for the first time I've ever witnessed.

"I can't keep living in the past," I say. "Can you?"

He is silent for a long moment. Then, slowly, he shakes his head.

"No. No more ghosts." Resolve settles on his face.

He guns the engine, gravel spewing behind us as we speed toward the gate. It looms ahead, imposing wrought iron that has contained us for so long.

Morgan comes to a sudden stop before the gate, exhaling slowly.

I lay a hand on his shoulder. "Morgan, we don't have to—"

Without a backward glance, he hits the gas. The Range Rover surges forward, crashing through the gate in a screech of metal.

"Morgan!" I shout as I'm careened into my seat. "The—car!"

An alarm blares but soon fades as we speed down the drive, the manor shrinking behind us.

He answers calmly, as if he didn't just mangle his car, almost kill us, and bust through a gate on impulse. "We've been given a chance to fuck right off. I say we take it."

Morgan's gaze stays fixed on the road ahead, his thoughts clearly turned inward. I know he's still grappling with the revelations about his father's criminal legacy and Rossi's role in concealing his murder all these months.

Learning that the man who accepted you for all your violent quirks in a ruthless underworld is actually more ruthless than you is no small thing to understand. But Morgan has an inner strength that astounds me, a core of light even his father's and uncle's brutality couldn't extinguish.

Once I've collected myself and can speak over my pounding adrenaline, I reach over and squeeze his hand. "Hey. Stay with me in the present, okay?"

He blinks and looks over at me, a faint smile touching his lips. "Sorry, little leaf. Just ... processing."

"You have a hell of a way of doing it," I say with a shaky voice. "One step at a time, though. We've got this."

In the back seat, Rio leans forward, his elbows resting on his knees.

"So where exactly are we going?" he asks quietly.

I cry out in alarm at the same time Morgan veers the SUV, spitting gravel and curses, "What the actual fucking *fuck*?? Announce yourself why don't you, Tongueless?"

Rio grins devilishly, palming both Morgan's and my seats.

Morgan shoots him a withering glare through the rearview

mirror, his hands tightening on the steering wheel. "You could have killed us, you reckless bastard."

"Says the man who happily smashed through a gate he has the passcode to," Rio responds.

Morgan grumbles under his breath, but I can see the amusement glittering in his eyes.

Despite Rio's usual creeping around, we're all feeling a sense of freedom, a release from the shackles of our past.

We're leaving Blackwood Manor behind, leaving Morgan's family legacy behind.

"Let's go to my dorm room first," I suggest. "I haven't been there for a while."

Rio moves his face closer to mine, his eyes brightening with interest.

Morgan voices Rio's thoughts, grin in full effect. "Your place, huh? Are you inviting us over, little leaf?"

"Definitely," I answer, growing warm and relishing the ache between my legs.

Then I bite my lip. "But first, let's go back for Xavier."

CHAPTER 43
CLOVER

TWO MONTHS LATER

The morning light splinters through the gaps in the heavy velvet curtains, forming a lattice of golden rays that crisscross the room. I shift in the cocoon of blankets, treasuring the cozy warmth that wraps around me like a hug.

It's hard to believe that months have passed since Blackwood Manor became our sanctuary, our home. I blink the sleep away and scan the empty spaces on the bed beside me. Xavier is likely lifting weights in the revamped gym we installed. Morgan is probably poring over ancient texts for his advanced occult studies class at TFU. Rio, well, he's undoubtedly in the woods that surround the manor, still ever the watchful protector even though danger hasn't lurked near us for months.

With a smile that feels like home, I throw off the covers. My bare feet pad across the cold marble floor, a luxurious contrast to the plush rug that once adorned my dorm room at TFU. I follow the scent of freshly brewed coffee into the dining room, where a spread of culinary delights awaits us.

"Morning, maiden," Xavier says warmly as I slide into the chair beside him. He presses a kiss to my temple.

Morgan leans back in his chair, his eyes meeting mine as he hands over a steaming cup of coffee. "You look radiant. We didn't keep you up too late, did we?"

I accept the cup, its heat seeping into my palms, and chuckle. "No such thing."

I spear a strawberry from the fruit platter, struck again by how different this all is from my old life.

But with these men, I've found a sense of belonging I never dreamed possible.

Tempest strolls in, laptop under his arm with Ardyn coming up beside him, Hermione grumpily mewling in her arms before she leaps out.

I brighten at the sight of her old, mangy white cat, happy to see her alive and well since she was too old to wander a cavernous, deteriorating mansion—we'd never find her if she did.

Now that Blackwood Manor has been cleaned, freshened up, and brightened with new windows, Hermie's found enough courage to explore, unearthing more rats than treasure.

I'm distracted when Morgan brings out chocolate-dipped strawberries, placing one in my mouth with a suggestive wink.

Rio and Xavier both raise their eyebrows, but it's Tempest who verbalizes first. "You know, some people bring home stray animals, like Hermione over there. My sister brings home a collection of lethal men."

And just like that, the room's temperature seems to rise by ten degrees. I swallow hard, looking at the men who have become my world, each in their unique way.

"Shall we move this to a more private setting, then?" Rio suggests, his voice lower than usual.

Morgan and Xavier nod, a silent agreement passing between them.

I glance at Tempest, who shuts his laptop with a click. "Just keep me out of your triangle or quadrangle or whatever fucking shape you are. I'm out."

"Don't leave me here," Ardyn beseeches him, scrambling to leave as my men eye me hungrily.

I laugh, overwhelmed with love and affection for these incredible guys.

We all rise, leaving the dining room as a unit, a new kind of family, bound not by blood but by choice and by the complex, beautiful love we share.

As we reach my bedroom and I lock the door behind us, I can't help but feel that despite all the battles we've faced, the best is yet to come.

The end of the Vultures is only the beginning for us.

And for the first time in a long time, the future looks nothing short of normal.

CHAPTER 44
ROSSI

HALLOWEEN – 8 Months Later

A sea of masks and costumes dance before me as I step into the grand ballroom of Blackwood Manor. Chandeliers drip with amber light, casting twisted, golden shadows over elegantly dressed bodies. The room is a kaleidoscope of sensuality, laughter, and the haunting notes of a live orchestra.

But none of it touches me. All of it is a void.

Because the moment I enter, my eyes lock onto her.

Clover. She's dressed like a queen of the underworld, clothed in black lace and burgundy silk, a matching mask shrouding her eyes. She looks ethereal, otherworldly, but her eyes ... her eyes brim with hurt.

I'm so absorbed by her that I don't register the hand reaching out to hook onto my arm until my instincts have the man slammed against the corridor's wall, my forearm under his neck.

Cav's gray eyes slice through the shadows. He chuckles under my deathly grip. "Nice to see you, too, Don Rossi."

"You're an idiot," I growl into his face.

"I prefer idiot savant, actually."

Cav reaches up to adjust his lapels under my forearm, unconcerned that I'm less than an inch from crushing his trachea.

"Might you release me now?" he asks dryly.

Reluctantly, I drop my arm and step back. "I'm not here for you."

"That much is obvious. I'm only requesting what I'm owed."

I hiss out an exhale. "Yes, we found the treasure, theoretically. There's no ruby, Cav. The Heart, it turns out, wasn't a gemstone but perhaps the crux of Sarah's mission—to save innocent lives."

Cav smirks, and for a moment, his eyes flicker with something unidentifiable. Disappointment? Amusement? Desperation?

"How poetically fitting," he says after clearing his throat and adjusting his tie. "Sarah Anderton, the accused witch, is now a verified savior, tricking us all from beyond the grave. You have to respect that level of cunning."

I ask, with clear suspicion in my tone, "You're not upset about the non-existence of the Heart?"

Cav's smile grows, a mischievous twinkle lighting up his malevolent stare. "Oh, I'm always up for a good twist in a tale. Besides"—he leans in a little closer, lowering his voice— "who says the gemstone doesn't exist? You simply didn't look hard enough, distracted as you are by power and revenge and..." He waits for me to follow where his attention lands. "Sweet, stunning innocence."

I tear my gaze from Clover and narrow it at him.

Cav straightens, and as he turns to leave, he says, "You should visit the Cimmerian Court sometime, Rossi."

Then he disappears into the crowd.

Shaking off the eeriness that is Cavanaugh Nightshade, I walk toward Clover, each step heavier than the last, dragging the weight of my new life behind me. I am Don Rossi now. A man shackled to duty, obligations, an empire of evil. And Clover ... she's the moon in my black sky.

Heads swivel, eyes drawn to the tall figure framed in the doorway. Murmurs ripple through the crowd as I step inside, an exquisite black-and-gold Venetian mask obscuring my face. But Clover will know the broad set of my shoulders, the prowl of my gait.

When she notices the quieting of the room, she turns, finding me.

Clover remains still, clutching her champagne glass tightly. Waiting.

She senses the inevitable collision of our paths the same way I did all these months I obsessed over her, drawn together like binary stars trapped in each other's orbit.

"Clover." My voice is a low caress once I reach her. "You look ravishing tonight."

"It's you," she whispers, more to herself than anyone. Still, I incline my head in silent acknowledgment.

"May I?" I ask.

After a brief hesitation, she takes my gloved hand and we meld into the music, bodies close but not touching, just like our lives—always in proximity but never really converging. I want to pull her closer, to feel her flesh against mine, but something stops me: The undeniable truth that I am no longer the man she fell in love with.

I am a Don.

A kingpin.

A ruler of the underworld.

The music shifts, a slow melody replacing the lively tune. I seize the moment and pull her closer. Our eyes meet and hold. A hot lump of coal forms in my throat.

As I twirl her, I catch glimpses of Xavier, Rio, and Morgan watching from the crowd. They're in identical masks—Vulture feathers that expose the bottom half of their faces under a curved beak made of black enameled wire.

All except for Morgan, of course.

Their eyes meet mine with unspoken recognition. And unspoken questions.

Xavier's gaze follows Clover, his eyes keen. Rio's jawline remains carefully relaxed, though his fingers drift to the hilt of a hidden dagger I'm confident is hidden in his suit jacket, despite the months of peace I've given them.

But as I've realized, *there is no peace* when it comes to us.

Morgan's lips twist into a savage grin, clearly relishing the chaos of my sudden reappearance. His green eyes glint with madness and anticipation behind his Harlequin mask.

There's a new energy in the room now, an undercurrent of anticipation. The former Vultures have caught my scent, even if they haven't started pecking at my flesh yet.

I release a slow breath. This reunion has been a long time coming, but that doesn't make it any less dangerous. The fragile truce binding us together now feels tenuous and on the verge of splintering.

Clover's study draws me back to her, her eyes searching, always searching, for the truth behind my walls. "Why have you come back?"

My fingers itch to caress her neck, to draw her lips to mine.

But I hold back, sliding a note into her palm instead. Her breath catches, eyes widening.

I don't wait for her response before I disappear into the crowd.

Meet me in the library, it reads in bold slanted script. ***Please. For me.***

I make my way through the darkened halls, the sounds of the ball fading behind me. My footsteps echo on the polished floors, announcing my presence to no one but the long-dead portraits. I pass no other guests. They remain ensconced in the ballroom's sparkle and laughter.

Only Clover will venture to where I await, lured by her insatiable curiosity. She remembers this library as I do—the scene of clandestine meetings and fevered encounters, a refuge where roles and rules fall away.

I slip inside, inhaling the familiar scent of leather, parchment, and wood polish. Memories swirl through the room like the ghosts that constantly follow me. I trail my fingers along the freshly dusted shelves, reading their spines through touch alone, waiting for the one book I most want to open.

The door creaks softly as she enters, a bar of light falling across the floor before she closes it behind her. I turn, drinking in the sight of her silhouetted against the door. Her eyes glint through the dimness, wary yet wanting.

I step forward, out of the cloak of darkness.

"Clover." My voice rushes over my tongue like sand. "You came."

"Because I need answers," she says, her voice a husk of its usual melody. "What are you doing here? Why now, after all this time?"

Slowly, I lift off the mask, letting it fall carelessly to the floor.

"For so long, I was hell-bent on avenging my family. I killed Nico Bianchi exactly how I wanted—and I felt nothing. But after some reflection, I realized maybe it was because I didn't torture him enough, hear his screams like I heard my family's."

Clover keeps her expression placid, her time with us showing in the relaxed planes of her face as I discuss torture and mutilation as an afterthought.

I continue hoarsely, "Thus, I made Marco Bianchi suffer. Cut out his eyes. Bled him out slowly."

Clover doesn't flinch. I don't realize it at this moment, but I will later. I'm testing her. Seeing if she can still love the beast *and* the man.

"He died the way I wanted, and I still felt nothing. Then I took over his empire, and I stayed empty. But the moment I met you, I felt *something*." My tone strains with emotion, the kind I'd swallowed a decade ago. "This new life, Clover ... it's hollow. It lacks the vibrancy, the color, the very soul I found with you and the others." I keep my gaze steady, raw, on hers. "I've missed you all terribly. I made—"

But I can't say it. *A mistake.*

She reads it in my face, anyway. Her breath catches at the vulnerability I'm allowing to break through my usual stoic gaze. The Rossi she knew was like a fortress, impenetrable and remote. Yet here I stand with my defenses cracked open.

Clover frowns, shaking her head. "Why reach out now? We were all just starting to move on and—"

"Have you really? Can you look me in the eye and say you feel nothing for me now?"

"That's not fair."

I move closer and tilt her chin up gently. Our gazes lock. Her lips part slightly.

"I *want* to come back," I rasp. "On terms we negotiate,

terms you're comfortable with. Let me prove myself again. Let me come home."

"With the help of Xavier, Rio, and Morgan, I've moved on, Rossi," she replies, but her voice wavers. "It's like ... you've just become this haunting melody in my head."

One hand trails down to rest lightly on her hip. "A melody you still hear, no? One that plays in both our dreams late at night when we're alone?"

She shudders at the truth of my words. We stand chest to chest now, and she has to tip her head back to keep meeting my eyes.

"Maybe it does still echo," she admits. "But it's a ghost, Rossi. A fond memory."

"I know all about ghosts." My tone shreds with the confession. "The shape of them, the sickly sweet smell, the relentless pounding of their misery inside my head. You, *tesoro mio*, are not my ghost. Nor will you ever be."

My fingers tangle in her hair as I hold her. Clover breathes me in.

"I've been lost without you," I murmur against her hair. "This life, this power—there's no point to it if I can't give you my soul to hold and protect. To keep my humanity from leaving this world."

I pull back just enough to keep addressing her. "Being the Don, ruling Bianchi's empire, it's all cinders compared to what we had."

Clover's eyes search mine. There's pain imprinted in the lines of her mouth, likely never to disappear. Her heart aches for me, as mine does for her.

"I thought I was doing the right thing, taking control to protect the Vultures and take what was rightly owed to me," I continue. "But every day has been meaningless."

I brush my knuckles along her cheek. "You were my truth, Clover. You, Xavier, Rio, Morgan—you helped me continue existing."

Clover blinks back tears.

"I can't give up being Don," I continue. "I've made enough sacrifices. But what I can promise you is that after all these months, leadership has a new meaning for me. Power is not just about control."

"True power contains trust," she whispers. "Care. Collaboration."

"Yes. You've taught me that, even if I refused to acknowledge it at the time."

"I've felt your absence like a lost heart," she confesses softly. "Turns out, I need five now to function."

For a brief moment, time freezes. And at that moment, I understand. I understand that love never truly ends; it merely changes form.

My vision blazes bright. I rip the mask off her face and crush her against me, sealing her lips in a binding kiss. Clover melts into it, the rest of the world shrinking, forming our shape, becoming just us.

No more disguises.

Clover's hands curl into the lapels of my jacket as she returns my kiss with equal fervor. For so long, I've ached for her touch, her taste, the soft strength of her body against mine.

I grip the back of her head, angling her as my tongue delves. She clings to me, a low moan building in her throat.

When we finally break for air, foreheads touching, she whispers, "I've missed you so much, *il mio amore*."

I release a shaky exhale at the endearment. "You've learned Italian while I was gone."

"Only a few phrases—as a way to address you if I ever saw

you again."

"And are they all as sweet as that one?"

Her smile curls through the shadows. "There were some ... unkempt ones."

I back her against the bookshelves, hands roaming urgently over her body. She arches into me with a soft moan, heat pooling in my cock.

"I need you," I say hoarsely, nuzzling her throat. "Need to be inside you again."

Clover trembles in response. "Yes. Please."

She cups my face in her hands, using her body to swing us around and push me against the shelves. Books rattle above our heads dangerously, but I couldn't give a fuck.

I slide my hands up her thighs and hook my fingers under the hem of her dress, and she shivers. I drag the dress up her legs, her thighs, and she raises her arms to allow me to yank it over her head.

She's left in nothing but a delicate black lace thong and matching bra. I stare at her, taking in the sight.

I've missed this. Missed her. *How can I have been gone so long?*

But never forgotten. Not until death greets me, and even then, I'd barter my soul for her happiness.

I wrap my arm around Clover's waist and watch her face as I finger the string of fabric between her ass cheeks.

She's breathless when I trail down and finally slip my hand underneath and inside her.

Clover grinds against my hand, cries out when I slide two fingers inside her, and grasps my face again, tightening her hold. Her hips rock forward, my fingers pumping into her, her walls tightening.

I pull my hand from her underwear only to tear it off her,

flinging it somewhere beside us.

Her eyes are hazy with hunger. "Rossi—"

"I need you, *tesoro mio*."

I yank off my shirt and throw it aside, then reach for the buckle of my belt. Clover doesn't wait for me. She grasps my belt and pulls me to her. Her fingers fumble with the buckle and at the buttons of my pants. Shaking. Trembling.

She slips her hands into my pants and wraps her fingers around my hard length. My cock twitches at her touch.

I shove my pants and underwear down and kick them off. My cock springs free, and she stares at it.

"Clover ... Christ, don't keep me waiting."

"In a second." She licks her lips, staring hungrily at my length. "I've missed it, too."

She reaches down to grab it, but I catch her wrist and pull her hand away.

I've changed my mind. I don't want her to touch me.

I want *her*.

I want everything about her.

I want her to feel loved.

I want her to feel safe.

I want her to feel loved when I take her.

I want her to feel loved when I make her come.

I want her to feel loved when I make her mine again.

This time, I whirl us and push her against the bookshelf.

This time, the books rain down on us.

I lock Clover's hands over her head and kiss her, her moans vibrating through her body. I pull away, then bring my mouth to her neck, sucking and biting. She drops her head back, and her chest rises and falls quickly as I continue to kiss down her neck and across her collarbone.

I kiss her chest, my mouth sliding over her bra, and she

keens at the sensation.

I move my mouth to her nipple, licking it through the lace. She clutches my hair, and I suck it into my mouth.

I move my mouth to the other nipple, my hand moving down her stomach to her bare pussy. I brush my fingers over her clit, and her breath hitches.

I rise, gripping her ass, and pull her hips to me. "You're mine, Clover," I growl.

"I am."

I slide into her, filling her, and her cry of pleasure echoes through the cavernous library. She fists my hair, nails digging into my scalp, and I close my eyes and savor the sensation of her body, the heat of her, the clench of her muscles around me.

She makes love to me, wraps her legs around my waist and her arms around my neck and moves in sync with me. Our bodies move together, our mouths locked in the kind of kiss that doesn't end, that only intensifies with every passing second.

"I love you," I murmur into her mouth.

She moans and presses her face against my neck. "I love you, too."

Every thrust of my cock sends her closer to the edge, and she holds me tighter, gasping for air. Each breathy gasp of her voice, each shudder of her body, makes my heart swell. *She's so close, so close.*

I slide my hand between our bodies and find her clit. She cries out and shudders around me.

I kiss her neck, my mouth moving over the sensitive spot behind her ear. "Come for me."

Clover cries out, and her walls clench around me as her orgasm tears through her. My mouth finds hers, and I kiss her as she comes, her screams of pleasure feeding me.

A moment later, I still above her and let myself go. We cling to each other, trembling and gasping for air while we recover.

When our breathing returns to normal, I lower my mouth to hers and kiss her softly.

"I've missed this," I murmur. "Missed it so much."

"Me too."

"I've missed you."

"I missed you more."

"No." I press my face into her neck. "You're wrong."

She kisses my forehead. "I love you. I love all four of you."

I draw away from her, my heart squeezing. I run my knuckles down her face. "You're everything to me, Clover. I can't lose you again. I won't."

"You won't," she confirms.

"I need you to understand this."

"I do."

I cup her face in my hands. "I want this. I want us."

Clover takes so long to respond, her stare begins to burn. "If you ever do anything like that ever again—"

"I won't." I kiss her, fast and hard. "I was scared."

"I know," she whispers. "I know."

I kiss her again. And again.

And again.

"I love you," I murmur. "I'm never letting you go."

She wraps her arms around my neck, and I bury my face into her neck.

Her touch makes me feel like I've at last come home after ten years of wandering.

I've come home to family.

I've found my home with Clover.

And I feel free.

CHAPTER 45
CLOVER

I'm boneless, weightless with clouds bolstering my footsteps as we return to the grand ballroom, Rossi's hand a steady warmth on my lower back. The melancholy refrain of a violin wafts through the air as we enter, couples twirling gracefully across the dance floor.

As we walk hand in hand, I spot Tempest across the room, standing like an emperor surveying his domain. Tonight, he's in a dark, Venetian-styled mask and a tailored tux that makes him look like a 007 villain—or, as Ardyn said to me from the side of her mouth as we got dressed, a fantasy within a fantasy.

Our eyes meet. Tempest's brows lift above the mask—first in surprise, then in detection. With a jerk of his head, he beckons us over. Rossi and I share a glance and approach.

"Rossi," Tempest says, a hint of bafflement clouding his eyes. "What the hell is this?" Tempest ensures he has my attention when he adds, "I've read *Oedipus*, you know. Never ends well."

Rossi, who carries the weight of his past like a second skin, simply nods. "I understand this might be confusing to you. Almost a betrayal."

"Not almost."

"You know better than anyone that life is full of unexpected turns. Some lead to darker alleys, others to a path you didn't know you needed. I fought against this, Tempest. I fought as hard as I could and lived in a hell of my own making. Clover brought me out of it. She showed me how to stay human. And I couldn't fight it anymore. Not without losing more of myself."

Tempest's focus shifts to me, losing their edge. "I've had a hell of a time accepting my men into becoming yours, Clo, and last I checked, my fatherly figure wasn't on your fucking wish list."

"I didn't expect this, either, Tempest." I squeeze Rossi's hand. "*Any* of it. But I can't reject it, either. It feels right. Every single one of these men feels *right*. And I'm sorry—I am, that I fell in love with Rossi, but—"

"Wait." Tempest holds up his hand. "You're in love? With all of them."

The last sentence is a statement. A realization that his dark little isolated world is expanding further into the sun, whether he tries to stop it or not.

And I don't have to answer him. The truth is at the very core of my being, shining through my eyes.

Tempest's pause hangs heavy in the air. He searches Rossi's face and then mine.

Right when I'm confident he's about to throw a punch, his focus moves to the dance floor, where like a magnet, he finds Ardyn, dancing and laughing with my old study group, dressed in pure white and a mask with gold streamers. She sparkles, and it's not because of the gold.

"Love's a rare currency, especially in our line of work," Tempest says, never tearing his eyes off his soulmate. Then he comes back to us. "Be sure you both can afford its price."

"I'm aware of the cost," Rossi replies, the pain of his years reverberating in his voice.

Tempest sighs, perhaps recognizing our solemn expressions and the seriousness of our intentions. "Then all I can offer is a reluctant blessing." He pauses to glare at Rossi, so piercing and so deep that his mask trembles with the effort. "But don't expect any more 'father-son' bonding activities. You're now Clover's partner, which means I will treat you about as well as the others. Which is to say, I'm happy to kill you if you break her heart. Fuck. Four men." Tempest is about to scrub his face, then remembers his mask. His hands hang in the air, as confused as he is. "If I weren't already a killer, Clo..."

His words, laced with his peculiar blend of brotherly exhaustion, malice, and sincerity, settle me. I move into his arms, hugging him tight.

"I love you, too, Tempie."

"Call me that again, and you're dead to me. I'll mourn your absence, but you'll still be dead."

But he holds on just as snug.

As he shakes his head and steps away, melting back into the crowd with a direct path to Ardyn, Rossi regards me, his eyes reflecting a blend of pain, relief, and perhaps a glimmer of hope. "Was it worth it?"

"Every risk, every revelation, every unexpected twist," I reply firmly.

Through the sea of color and costumes, I spot Xavier, Rio, and Morgan gathered near the balcony, watching the dancers with hooded eyes behind their masks. They turn as one when we stride across the dance floor and approach, silent communications flickering between them.

Rossi gives a barely perceptible nod, and the others relax, a noiseless, familiar understanding passing between them. Things have changed, shifted, but their bond remains unbroken. They understand Rossi's lasting connection to me, because they have it themselves.

We all do.

"Somebody has lots of explaining to do," Morgan singsongs. "We've missed you, oh holy leader. And possibly forgiven you for murdering my psychopathic family, so long as you don't come for me next."

He says it with his usual half-cocked smile, but I register the vehemence behind his stare, hard, opaque, and gritty.

"Your forgiveness, while undeserved, isn't something I take lightly, Morgan," Rossi says. "Your father and uncle took something irreplaceable from me. But understand, I never took pleasure in taking them from you."

Morgan's grin fades, giving way to a more serious expression. "You've carried that burden longer than a decade. That's penance enough. Besides, if you didn't take them out, someone else would've. Revenge is a cruel mistress. She takes and takes and doesn't give back. I lost my family because of what they did to yours. A never-ending cycle. The question is, are we going to continue it?"

Rossi's eyes soften ever so slightly. "I have no intention of perpetuating it any further. Not if it puts her in the line of fire." He turns to me, his gaze lingering.

"And for that reason alone, I'm willing to stop the wheel from turning," Morgan says, following Rossi's stare, then going back to him. "Here we are, both scarred and flawed but still breathing. Still fighting. If you're good enough for Clover, then the past is the past."

Rossi manages a single, quick smile of agreement. "Just know, taking a life—even one that the world might be better without—still leaves a mark on your soul."

Morgan folds his arms and raises his chin. "Then let the past die with the men we were, not the men we've become."

Rossi gives him a look of quiet gratitude before turning back to me. "Would you care to finish our dance?"

I smile, taking his proffered hand. "I'd love nothing more."

As he sweeps me onto the dance floor, Morgan leans in to whisper to me, "Just keep an eye on him, okay? Forgiveness doesn't mean I've forgotten."

I nod, touched by the fragile truce forming among my men. "Don't worry, I've got enough love for all of you, every piece of darkness and light."

Rossi leads with one hand on my waist, the other clasping mine. We move as one, my skirts swirling around us.

For the first time in months, the missing piece of my heart feels mended. Not fully healed, perhaps even whole. The jagged edges are smoothed.

As the final notes fade, Rossi brushes his lips against my knuckles. "Thank you," he says softly. "For this. For us."

The warmth of his breath hits my skin, sustaining me, and I tilt my head back to look into his eyes. There, I see something new. Vulnerable and raw.

I feel a sudden urge to protect him, to keep him safe from the venom that seems to follow him wherever he goes.

I lean in and press my lips to his, and he responds immediately.

My breath hitches against his mouth as he dips me low, his

eyes holding mine behind our masks. There's a final brush of his lips against mine, his kiss gentle and tender.

As he pulls me back up, my other three men watch with varying degrees of amusement and longing.

Rio's eyes are dark and intense, his jaw clenched as if restraining himself from joining us on the dance floor. Xavier's forehead is wrinkled, yet his mouth is relaxed, as if he's remembering something that he's lost and has finally found it again. Morgan's eyes are bright, amused, untamed.

Rossi seems to sense their gazes, and he spins me around with a flourish. I feel his hand slip from my waist, replaced by another's. I glance up to see Rio, his face inscrutable behind his Vulture feathers as he leads me into a slow, sensual dance.

His electric touch sends shivers down my spine. His coffee-colored gaze never leaves mine. His body presses so close, I feel the ridges of muscle under his shirt and jacket. His hand slips lower, to the small of my back, his fingers tracing circles as we move.

I'm lost in the rhythm, in the heat of his touch, when I'm suddenly spun around and come face-to-face with Xavier.

"May I have this dance, my lady?" he asks, his accented voice low and smooth like honey.

I take his hand, allowing him to pull me into his embrace. His touch is different from Rossi's and Rio's. It's lighter, more playful. We twirl around the dance floor, and I can't help but laugh as he spins me faster and faster.

His knee might be sore, but his footwork is flawless. Xavier dips me low, his lips brushing against my ear as he whispers, "I can't believe I'm lucky enough to be able to hold you and never let you go."

As I'm upside down, Morgan grins down at me, his eyes dancing with mischief as Xavier lifts me.

"My turn," he declares, sweeping me off my feet and into a tango.

His movements are wild and unpredictable, his touch sizzling and thrilling. He twirls me around, his fingers tracing their own melody across my arms and down my body until my heart races in my chest.

As the music fades, I find myself back in Rossi's arms, my body humming with desire and my heart full of love. The others surround me, my defensive circle. My possessive Vultures.

In that moment, I know that I belong here, with these men. I know that they will protect me, that they will love me, and they accept me as I love and accept them.

The song ends, but we remain standing still in a room full of movement, holding onto this moment.

"Ladies, gentlemen, persons, it is now time for the unveiling!" the master of ceremonies announces over the speakers.

Rossi reaches behind me, untangling the string of my mask. As it falls away, they see me—really see me—

And I see them as their masks fall away, every one of them standing in the light.

My men.

Tempest and Ardyn come up to us, grinning and passing out flutes of champagne. With a rumble of agreement ranging from Rossi's quiet acknowledgement, Rio's curved smile, Morgan's crow of triumph, and Xavier's wink and biting of his lip as he stares at me, and with all of our faces bare, we raise our glasses high and crash them together until they chip or shatter above our heads.

And from now until forever, I will believe in impossible things.

CHAPTER 46

DID YOU THINK I WAS DONE?

Ah, Halloween.

The veil between worlds thins, and even the air tingles with the electric charge of hidden truths and concealed fears. It's the perfect night for subterfuge, for warning shots across a bow one didn't even know was aimed at them.

The former Vultures and Clover are holding a party for TFU. How sweet.

Here, in the lavishly decorated ballroom of Blackwood Manor, the mood is jovial. Masks and makeup, yes, but also a sort of collective exhale—a moment of reprieve. How little they know.

I straighten my midnight suit, the dark fabric rippling over my frame. A stark contrast to the flamboyant costumes around me. Every step I take is a study in refined chaos. My smile cuts across my face, sharp and calculating, my eyes scanning faces both familiar and forgettable.

They won't see me coming.

I prowl closer, my gaze landing on her. Clover. She stands in the center of the room, a vision in emerald silk. Her lips are painted blood red, her ebony waves cascading over her shoulders. Even in repose, she radiates strength, determination etched into her delicate features.

My, my, what trouble will she stir up next?

I saunter toward her, drinking in the sight of her. She stiffens, sensing my approach, her body coiling tight as a spring.

Our eyes meet, and her lips part, surprise flickering through her emerald irises.

"Cav," she says, my name poised on the tip of her tongue. "Thanks for coming."

I flash her a smile, all charm and razor-sharp edges.

She thinks she knows me. She knows nothing.

"Is it all you hoped it would be?" I inquire, leaning in. My voice is a soft caress, the embodiment of secrets and shadows.

Clover turns to face me. Her eyes narrow for a second as if tuning into a frequency she didn't know existed but should have. "Excuse me?"

"The peace, the love, this gathering—you do know it's but the eye of the storm?"

My words are wrapped in a seductive undertone, a contrast to their dark implication.

Her eyes widen, and for a moment, I see the weight of responsibility settle on her shoulders, heavy and immediate.

"I'll protect them, no matter what's coming," she asserts, her voice tinged with a steely determination.

Ah, the indomitable spirit. How it thrills me.

I glance around; the ballroom is bustling with guests. Faces hidden behind masks, bodies swaying to hauntingly festive melodies.

Above us, ornate chandeliers hold dominion, their light painting a deceptive tapestry of safety.

"You'd do well to remember, Clover, that not all masks in this room are made of fabric," I murmur, my eyes locking onto hers, ensuring she grasps the full extent of my words.

Before she can reply, I retreat, melting into the crowd as if I were a figment of her imagination, leaving her with a sense of unease she can neither place nor ignore.

As I walk away, I feel her eyes on my back, her mind undoubtedly whirring, attempting to decipher the enigma I am and the even larger enigma I herald.

The Cimmerian Court.

A storm is coming. And as much as she wishes to protect her newfound Eden, she'll soon learn that it takes more than love to fight the dark.

Ah, the anticipation—it's almost too delicious.

And as the clock strikes midnight, I can't help but tell you that her story is just the beginning.

My story, you see, is yet to be told.

You survived the Vultures, but are you ready for Cavanaugh Nightshade's seductive traps in Wicked Court? He's but one 4 depraved, alluring men

(though never as perfect as me)

Coming Early 2024

<u>Preorder now</u>

Keep coveting the dangerous, little leafs...

And if you're in the mood for our version of holiday cheer, whether or not you celebrate Christmas, I'm sure you're curious what we do around a Christmas tree....

Get Access to the Loyal Vows Bonus Scene Here.

ALSO BY KETLEY ALLISON

all in kindle unlimited

If you want more bullies and secret societies, read:

Rival

Virtue

Fiend

Reign

The Thorne of Winthorpe:

Thorne

Crush

Liar

Titan Falls:

Cruel Promise

Loyal Vows

also writing as S.K. Allison,

contemporary romance:

If you like your bad boys and bullies as standalones (no series, one book, a happy ending), read:

Rebel

Crave

If you like a grump turned into a protector for his woman, read:

Rock

Lover

If you like your playboys with tormented hearts and scars, read:

Trust

Dare

Play

If you like small-town, angsty vibes:

You Will Want Me